Brutal

Saint and Sinners

Ruby Vincent

Published by Ruby Vincent, 2021.

Chapter One

B *rutal*

"What do we do with her?"

"We can't keep her in there forever."

"Why can't we?" That came from Sinjin.

"She isn't actually your pet," Cash snapped. He shoved off the couch, resuming his pacing on the rug. "She's the lying, deceiving killer who we all happen to be in love with!"

"And they say soulmates don't exist," Mercer replied. He reclined in his usual spot in his usual pose. An excellent attempt to appear unbothered.

"She fucking wormed her way into our lives to get her hands on the ledger."

I heard Cash shout more during this conversation than I had in the years we'd been working together. Adeline Redgrave had certainly wormed her way into him.

Phantom fingers skated over me, trying to tease out a laugh as hers whispered in my ear.

He wasn't the only one.

"Technically, we wormed her into our lives," Mercer reminded. "We forced her to work for us. You and Sin made her go on jobs. If she told us who she really was and what she wanted from the beginning, we would've killed her. She didn't have much of a choice."

Killian's jaw ticced. "Are you her lawyer now, Mercer?"

"Nope, I'm just giving insight into how this interrogation will go. We blow in there spitting mad, and the lovely Adeline will remind us this is our own doing," he said. "And she'll be right."

Leaning back, I spotted a speck of dust on my sleeve. I was up and across the room, riffling through Cash's cabinet. His office was one of the few rooms to be spared Sinjin's rage. As such, other than mine, it was the only room I'd remain in without beating his face in. We'd gone for each other's throats three times in the period she was gone. Tension made me clean and him destroy. With her return and the revelations it brought, it was time for a truce.

I found his lint roller next to a row of identical black ties.

One. Two. Three.

The lint was gone by two. It did not change what I had to do.

Four. Five. Six—

"Anything you want to add, Brutal?" Sinjin spoke up.

Seven. Eight. Nine. Ten.

There was plenty I wanted to add. It had been two days since we walked into the trap at the club. Two days since we discovered the true Kieran. Two days since we found out the love of our lives wasn't who she seemed. Two days since we put her in a cage in the basement and left her there while we argued over what to do. Of course I had something to fucking add.

But I said nothing. Nodding here. Gesturing there. I waited until it was finally time for Adeline.

My count complete, I returned the roller to its place. Straightened a tie. Closed the cabinet.

Turning to Sinjin, I gestured at the door.

"In due time," he said simply.

"—long past the point she should fear us," Killian was saying. "She knew we wouldn't kill her if she told us the truth. She lied anyway."

"We also wouldn't agree to hand over the ledger," Mercer countered. "It always comes back to that. In this city. In our lives. In the lives of every damn person strolling the streets of Cinco. Some way or another, it's all about the ledger."

They fell silent.

Killian returned to his seat, steepling his fingers over his chest. "Redgrave said this all started with her father and a gang called the Lords. Have you heard of them?"

Sinjin, Mercer, and I shook our heads.

"Her father is getting up there in age. We'd have been children when they were running the streets, but I've dug as deep as you can go into the period Kieran was most active—taking jobs as a fixer. I've researched every gang, crime family, and syndicate there was back then. How were the Lords erased?"

"The person with the answer to that is in the basement." Sinjin got to his feet. "It's time."

Killian nodded. "How will you question her, Sin? Like I said, she knows we won't hurt her."

"There are other ways of getting information. Bunny's taught us that if nothing else."

He swept out of the room—the three of us trailing him.

I suspected their minds were a whirl of conflicting thoughts as we traveled down one flight, then another, then another. Battling their feelings for her in the midst of betrayal and distrust. I did not envy them.

The space where I existed did not know such noise. No internal struggle. No push and pull between right and wrong, and me suffering under a shouting conscience. It was a quiet world. A one-way street through a desert path without traffic lights or traffic itself.

As Adeline stood over Lorenzo Bianchi, foot to his throat and smirk hanging off those full lips, I made a decision without pulling over to question. This is the path we're on now.

Me and my Adeline.

We stepped off the stairs, fanning around her.

Adeline sat cross-legged on the bottom of the cage—palms flat on her knees, back straight, and eyes closed. She could almost be meditating.

Our arrival broke the trance. Raising her head, she smiled at us. "Hello, lovers."

"Bunny," Sinjin greeted. He bent and kissed her through the bars.

Adeline turned to us like we'd do the same.

I did. Crouching down, cool metal bit into my flesh as I tasted her, swiping those slightly chapped lips to pay entrance. Our tongues tangled, gifting me the sweetness of her leftover salted caramel cheesecake.

Her imprisonment was different this time around. Mercer brought her meals, and the blanket we gifted her was folded and lying neatly next to the cage. I sensed torture wouldn't work this time around. I sensed it didn't work the first time either. Adeline was always right where she wanted to be.

I traced the curve of her smile. *That hasn't changed.*

I retreated and Mercer took my spot. Linking fingers, he kissed her knuckles, and then reclaimed his place.

Killian didn't move an inch.

Adeline cocked her head. "Have you come to let me out?"

"We've come for the truth," Killian said. "All of it. Right now."

"I've told you the truth. Or did you think I was lying about being a trained killer who's been after the ledger for years?"

"But that's not all of it, is it, love?" Sinjin circled the cage. "I knew there was something different about you. You were never a non-player character. We were written with the same code."

"Yes, we were."

"Sadly." He stopped in front of her. "We've reached the point you must become frightfully *predictable*. You'll tell us everything about you from your weight in ounces the day you were born, to your last thought before we came in this room."

Her smile didn't waver. "And if I don't?"

"Naturally, you'll be punished."

"Punished?" Adeline's brows blew up her head. "What exactly were you thinking because I do so enjoy being spanked."

"Just the opposite," he replied. "No sex."

"No sex?"

"That's right. We're turning off the tap."

Silently, Adeline uncrossed her legs in the tight space, getting to her feet. She pressed herself against the bars. "You'd deny me for the sake of hearing all my dirty little secrets? Good plan, but you forgot one thing."

"What's that?"

Adeline stroked his collar. "It'll be torture for both of us. And I just don't think you can hold out, St. John Bellisario."

"Think so?" She towed him in. "I survived twenty-eight years without that pussy."

"Survived is right. You existed in a steady, unchanging rhythm like a coma patient hooked up to life support. It took finding your soulmate"—she slipped her hand in his shirt—"to get that heart racing again.

"Your soulmate is me, by the way."

Sinjin kept coming, curling his hand over the one holding the bar. "A lying, scheming temptress more deadly than a force of nature." His nose skimmed her cheek. "Sounds about right."

"Sinjin," Killian warned.

"I had to lie to you." Her lips trembled—an act so seemingly genuine, I couldn't be certain it wasn't. "If I told you the truth, you'd have tried to kill me. Not the best way to start a relationship." She trailed down, finding his belt and slipping past its barrier. "But that's all behind us now. I know what you want."

She stroked him in earnest—arm banging against the metal. Grunts ripped out of him.

"Sinjin!" barked Killian.

"And you know what I want," Adeline finished.

"What." Kiss. "Would." Kiss. "That." Kiss. "Be?"

Adeline shot away from him, blowing that mask of pleasure into surprise.

"Aren't I supposed to suffer through celibacy hell first?" she asked. "You wouldn't respect me if I gave it up that easily."

Sinjin roared. Grabbing her, the two smashed into the bars, going at each other like this was the last before celibacy hell. Sinjin's belt flew between me and Mercer, striking three knives off the wall.

I set them right—her moans a backdrop to my straightening.

Turning back, Sinjin's pants pooled around his ankles. He lifted her leg, hooked it around a bar, and disappeared between her middle.

Slap, slap, slap, slap.

"Ah! Saint!" The flesh-on-flesh smacking of the vigorous plundering of her wet pussy competed with her heightening moans.

Adeline threw her head back—lips round in a screaming "o" and smooth, perfect throat long and begging for my mouth.

She truly was the most beautiful creature I'd ever seen. Beautiful like velvety petals all the same shape and size. Beauty like the hidden, intricate world of snowflakes. Of a fresh blanket of untouched snow. Of that quiet space between waking and sleeping when a day is just beginning, and it still has the hope of being good.

Dancing around the kitchen with a spatula and a grin on her face that said I'd be in trouble if I entered her space—and daring me to anyway. That was Adeline's beauty.

Perfection.

Sinjin spun her around. Adeline grabbed the bars, bending to Sin's hunger. He pushed inside and her cry caught in her throat. Sinjin started pumping. Banging his hips against the cage. Ratcheting her moans up tenfold.

Her hair brushed the cushion. Upside down, she clung to her prison, fighting to stay upright as Sinjin did his best to break her in half. They both came, sounding off to push the soundproofing to its limits.

Adeline collapsed on the cushion, chest heaving, satisfaction etched in her face.

"Shit," Sinjin breathed. "New plan."

The glare Killian directed at his brother could've burned down the building.

Adeline laughed. Gathering the blanket around her, she said, "Why don't we skip future attempts at torture, and you just ask me what you want to ask me?"

"Why bother? We'd have no way of knowing if you were telling us the truth," said Killian.

"There's no reason to lie." She pointed to the bra Sinjin tossed at Mercer's feet. He gathered her clothes and handed them back. "I have no secrets left to protect. At some point, you have to trust me."

She dressed while her statements hung in the air. Adeline was right, but it was a conclusion I came to shortly after we trussed her up, put her in the back of the stolen car, and drove away from Richard La Roche's house.

What else could she be hiding bigger than her true self and motives? She wasn't an innocent cook toiling away in the kitchen when four bangers knocked her off track. She was after what every criminal in Cinco City was dying to get their hands on. Now we knew. What happened next depended on us as much as it did her.

"All right. We're listening. Where is the ledger?" asked Killian. "We were right behind you. You didn't have time to kill La Roche, the guards, and break into the vault. What happened to it?"

A frown broke her smile. "I have no idea. Like you said, I didn't have enough time. You guys caught up to me faster than I expected. When I got there, they were already dead and the vault was ransacked. Someone else got there first," she said. "My guess is it's one of the Kings who got away. Three hightailed it when the bullets started flying. If one of them sacked up and came back for their boss, they would've heard Enzo's confession."

I found myself nodding. The logic was sound. More than sound. It likely happened exactly how she laid it out. Three Kings got away from us, and while we stood dumbfounded in the face of the true Adeline, it was possible any one of them heard something they shouldn't.

Killian studied her. I could almost hear his calculating mind weighing her words for truth.

"What? You don't believe me?" she challenged. "You snatched me up coming out of the vault empty-handed. If I don't have it, who does?"

"No," Killian said. "That much I do believe if only because balance of probability only slides one way. We'll put La Roche aside for now. Tell us about the Lords. What did you mean when you said they were the reason all of this started?"

Sighing, Adeline stretched out, dropping her head against the bars. "Might want to grab a seat. It's a long story."

We stayed still—the only sound Sinjin doing up his zipper and belt.

"The first thing you need to know—the one thing everyone has so wrong—is Kieran is not a name. It's a title."

Killian stepped forward. "What does that mean?"

"There was once a Kieran. A long time ago," she said. "He possessed the ledger. He used it to bend the city to its knees. Then, he was discovered, slaughtered in his bed, and the ledger found a new owner who adopted the name to go with it. So it's been over the years. A long, bloody history of the ledger changing hands. Richard La Roche wasn't *the* Kieran. He was a Kieran."

We exchanged looks.

"So while everyone was looking for an old man with twenty years' worth of mileage," said Killian, "the real owner of the ledger moved his chess pieces in the shadows."

She clicked her tongue. "Exactly. It's almost genius. Most were looking for the wrong person, but enough people did find the right one. Like Bianchi unearthed La Roche," she said. "It's hard to say exactly how many Kierans there have been. It almost doesn't matter. Once they had the ledger in their hands, they were tapped into all of the operations the original Kieran started.

"The gunrunning operation through Merriman Circus. A cut of the drug money from the Bowery Boys. Kieran's guiding hand on the mayor. It's all in the ledger. And through the years, it's grown as new Kierans added their own rackets." She blew out a breath. "I can only imagine what's in there now after however many years of Richard La Roche's reign.

"The collection of criminals he brought under his roof for that party was astounding. If he's got means for blackmailing all of them..." She fixed on Killian. "Just look at the power he had over you."

Stiffly, he nodded.

Their understanding wasn't shared by the rest of us.

What is she talking about?

"What's she talking about?" Sinjin demanded, voicing my question.

"I always wondered why Kieran forced me out of forging," Killian said. "He ordered me to stay straight when a crime boss such as him could've made me work for him instead. Flog my art with him receiving the bigger cut. I didn't put together that a year before I received the call that wrecked my life, I met a man in a gallery, boasted that I was better than him, and snubbed his offer to bring me under his wing."

"Seventeenth-century Dutch oil paint," Adeline said.

"Vermeer." Killian shook his head. "The single artist La Roche couldn't forge."

"You even taunted the man with *The Lacemaker* on your second meeting. No wonder he hated you."

"He got his revenge," Killian hissed. "The whole time it was personal. The ledger gave him the pressure he needed to force an arrogant pup out of the business. No chance I'd rise to become truly better than him."

She held out her hands. "Such is the power of the ledger. All the strings the original Kieran connected to dozens of people, dragging down their wives, husbands, daughters, sons, and friends. Growing to hundreds in his pocket who spread the corruption he plants in their soul. With every new

Kieran, it grows. It's not an exaggeration to say that whoever owns the ledger now, owns all of Cinco City."

"And it started with your father," Mercer put in. "How? Why has no one heard of the Lords?"

"That was the way they wanted it," she replied. "The Lords based in Waterford, but like you guys, they didn't fight needless wars over territory. They didn't spray-paint their tags on buildings, or roam the streets with tats announcing their affiliation to everyone who walked by. They worked in a very specific racket, and dragging attention to themselves made as much sense as armored truck drivers posting their routes online."

"And that racket would be?" Sinjin pressed.

"Come on, guys," she said, smiling. "Haven't I set it up by now? The three leaders of the Lords were fixers and kingmakers. Oscar, Soren, and *Kieran*."

"What?" Sinjin sprang forward, grabbing the bars. "Kieran? The first Kieran?!"

She nodded. "The one and same. He wasn't a King like you all assumed. He was a Lord. Stretching as high as the ceiling. Waves of brown curly hair. Hands dwarfing my little body as he picked me up and bounced me on his knee. Kieran Foley and Soren Cross grew up in the same foster home as my dad. They were closer than brothers—"

"You knew him," Saint sliced in. "He was your father's fucking best friend?! My father died in the search for the man who doddered in the rocking chair right next to yours!"

Adeline stood, placing her hands over his whitening knuckles. The teasing smile was gone. "Please, Saint. Let me finish."

"What more is there to fucking say?! Your father could've told me the enemies they made. The one who came after the man confessing his sins to a priest." He rattled the cage. "You could have!"

"There's so much more to say," she cried. "I don't know who sent those men to your father. Neither does my dad. If he did, you can believe my father would've killed them himself. He had a code. The three of them did... until everything went wrong. Let me finish," she said. "Then you'll understand all too well."

Killian gripped his brother's shoulder, drawing him back.

"Go on," Mercer said.

Taking a deep breath, Adeline did so. "They were smart and savvy. A team. Their business started small at first. A few favors for friends who needed a problem taken care of. Then those friends passed their names to their friends. They started charging, and their number kept ringing. Soon, they all had their parts to play.

"Kieran fielded the requests and collected the payments. He answered the call when the phone rang. Soren did the recon. He checked into backgrounds and named the people in play. And my father carried out the jobs—on his own, or with the men who became a part of the Lords. No one could pinpoint a single Kieran because there were actually three. Soren sitting in a dingy bar whispering in the right ear. Oscar slipping into his house to steal the precious painting a scheming ex-wife lost in the divorce settlement.

"That was all it was in the beginning. Fixing problems for the desperate of Waterford. Then the name Kieran made it into Harlow. Then Leighbridge—where the scheming ex-wives were worth millions, and the problems needing fixing could explode a city the way only the wealthy can. My dad said if they were going this deep, they had to draw a line.

"No kids. No hits on the innocent. It was one thing to stage a fake shooting to sway public sympathy for the mayor's reelection. It was another to murder witnesses in a rape trial. You don't want to know how many times they were called up to kill a pregnant mistress that made the mistake of saying 'child support.' Dad refused to be a soulless shithead's cleanup crew. They'd take the money and have them quietly relocated instead.

"They agreed to the rules, and that's when Kieran proposed they keep records in case a client ever thought to protect their secrets by cleaning up the loose ends."

"Thus the ledger is born," Mercer said.

"Yes," she said softly. "Time passed, and they amassed more clients, more money, more entries in their black book, and more respect behind the name Kieran. By the time I came along, they were the true kings of Cinco City, and no one knew."

"If life was so good, why did they turn on their clients?" asked Killian.

"I told you," she said, "I came along. So did Gianna. Oscar and Soren found themselves with two little girls, and they wanted to give them the world. Why keep grudging along as the Cinco elite's bitches when it could be the other way around? They could leave us a throne, and that's what they intended to do."

She shrugged. "It's not like it went against their rules or their conscience. The people in their ledger were far from innocent. Why not get their slice of the pie? Why not take the power and fear the ledger gifted them? *Use me*," she whispered. "*Use me.*

"Can you imagine how the ledger whispered in their ear?"

Yes, we can.

"It was like having the fountain of youth in their backyard," Adeline said. "It was only so long they could resist before finally taking a sip."

"But something went wrong," Killian said. "Soren Cross is dead. Your father is spending his days in a senior home instead of a beach in Malta, and if I'm keeping track, the true Kieran was slaughtered in his bed. What happened?"

Adeline swept over us, meeting our eyes in turn. The odd glint swimming in those brown pools stiffened our backs.

"What?" Saint pressed.

"You four... do you trust each other?"

"Excuse me?" Killian asked.

"You talk of trusting me, but do you trust each other? Well?" she prompted when we didn't answer.

One by one, we nodded.

"Because you're united in the same goal. A shared enemy. Kieran and the ledger. You can trust you won't turn on each other while you need the other to help you get what you're after."

"Does this have a point?" asked Killian.

"I admire that." She went on like he hadn't spoken. "Honestly, it's one of the things I love about you guys. That you actually see a future where the four of you rule Cinco together—sharing the ledger. My father believed in that future too, but he was fucking wrong, and so are you."

Saint's lips peeled back from his teeth. "What's that supposed to mean?"

"It means exactly what every comic book, superhero movie, and nursery story tried to tell us. Absolute power corrupts absolutely. Once they finally gave in to temptation, Kieran started getting ideas in his head. It was his name feared through the streets. It was his idea to keep the ledger. He had no children holding him back or messing with his judgment. Why keep to my father's rules? Why keep to any rules at all?

"At some point, Kieran reclaimed the mantle, and began sinking his hooks deeper into Cinco. Clients weren't about to come to him after the Lords got into the blackmail business, so he found other ways to make people beholden to him. Buying loans off of sharks was just one of the ways. He hit the streets again under a new name and with new partners, taking the jobs they once turned down. By the time my dad and Soren realized what he was doing, it was too late."

Adeline turned to me. "Remember the story I told you? There was an accident at work and my dad lost his job. His best friend was killed. Afterward, new management took over, fired everyone, and hired new people. Well, that was true.

"There was an accident. Soren confronted Kieran with the rumors, and the bastard was far from repentant. He was done being held back by them. He told Soren they could get on board or get the fuck out of his way. The two fought. One of Kieran's new guards overheard and burst in, shooting at the attacker before anyone knew what was happening."

She dropped her eyes. "Kieran said he regretted Soren's death. Swore he never wanted it to happen that way, but..."

"But what?" Saint asked.

"But Soren's death proved what Kieran knew all along. The ledger could not be shared. He was taking it, and if my father didn't let him go in peace, he'd be forced to kill him too," she replied. "My father didn't back down. He faced him believing the Lords were on his side. Some were. Most were not. It was a one-sided, gruesome battle.

"My father woke in a pool of his own blood, surrounded by the bodies of the men who stood with him. Kieran and the ledger were gone."

Adeline folded her arms, leaning against the cage. Anger leeched into her tone, but calm colored her face. The true story of Kieran had lived with her—defined her long before either of us learned his name.

"The upside is the men who betrayed my father didn't crow their victory for long. Kieran took the final step. With the last person tethering him to humanity dead, he slaughtered everyone who knew his true identity and what he possessed. Then, he sunk into the arms of Cinco royalty. The penthouse in the sky. Drivers. Limos. Everything a poor boy bouncing from foster home to foster home dreamed of. He thought he was safe—"

"But your father survived," Mercer finished.

"Dad bided his time. Laid low. Worked all day to provide for me and Gianna. Stayed up all night planning to avenge Soren and take back the ledger. He didn't believe Jocelyn's threats to disappear with me if her long list of needs weren't met. Until she did."

She sighed. "Everything changed after that. Dad let go of his rage and desire for vengeance. He started all of this to give me everything, and now he had nothing. He put everything into finding me. Months into his search, karma visited Kieran. He was found by someone else, and they killed him and took the ledger. By the time I was safe by his side, the trail was cold. He didn't know where to begin, and he didn't put much effort into trying.

"He was a single father to me, and then Gianna when her mother checked herself into treatment for depression. Eventually, she decided to stay in the facility outside of Cinco, and Gianna got emancipated. It was just the three of us. No room for the ledger. But still he raised us to take care of ourselves. He made certain that if anyone tried to hurt us, they'd only do so once."

"He really gave it up?" Skepticism laced Mercer's voice. "Oscar Redgrave. Arguably the one person in this city who has any rights to the ledger. He just washed his hands of it?"

"Daddy decided I was more important. He loved me more than any little black book." She shrugged lightly. "I have that effect on people."

I cracked a smile. *Of that I have no doubt.*

"But you wouldn't let it go," Killian said. "Against your father's wishes, I assume?"

"You assume correctly. The ledger tore him, Soren, and Kieran apart. One brother dead. The other a monster. The Lords forgotten. A daughter severely traumatized. The other without a father. If that wasn't enough of a cautionary tale, Kieran's murder, and the bloody trail of bodies that followed in his wake should do the trick. Dad refused to let the ledger ruin me like it ruined everyone who knew of its existence.

"But the fact remains that ledger was always meant to be mine. I can't give Gianna or my father everything we've lost, but I can reclaim the ledger. I can mold our city into the place he dreamed of, and I'll do it as the little girl he raised to be a queen. He never understood that I'm doing this for him, and that's why I won't fail."

Saint tipped his head, grinning. "And why let a little thing like the men you claim to love get in your way? Savage, Bunny. Again I'm torn between whipping that ass raw or making that pussy beg."

Licking her top lip, she winked. "I'll take both if you're offering."

"Mmm." Sinjin advanced on the cage. He was held back by Killian and Mercer.

"Maybe you want to sit this one out, Sin," Mercer said. "You seem to be distracting each other."

"I should hope I drive you all to distraction," she said. "You feel the same as I do for you. As fucked up and twisted as we all are, that's the single thing the five of us know to be true. I admit, my motives were less than pure in the beginning, but all that has changed. I'd no more hurt you than you'd hurt me."

She cocked a brow. "Saint keeps no less than six knives scattered about his room that would've slit his throat while he slept soundly next to me. Ditto Killian and his love affair with bombs and guns. Brutal, I found a lovely pair of silver knuckles tucked away in your bookshelf. Mercer, you're not shy about eating everything I put in front of you. Not to mention the room we're standing in right now. The point is if I really wanted to get rid of you and clear a path to the ledger, I've had that option many times. Obviously, that's not what I want."

"Of course not." Sinjin shook them off, approaching her. "You want us to be your... what was the word... courtesans."

She straightened. "What I want is for us to be partners. You my husbands and me your bride. If there ever is an Alfred Jr., I will be his mother."

"Is that so?" Killian returned.

"Yes," she snapped. "The four of you are mine. You belong to me, and I'm getting tired of repeating it. If you try leaving me, I will kill every bitch you give a sideways look. Read my lips: Mine."

I ducked my head to hide that smile. It'd only serve to piss her off, which wasn't what I was going for.

The woman's in a freaking cage in our basement, saying that she owns us.

Didn't know if I believe in the concept of soulmates, but I didn't doubt for a second that there was no one else on the planet like Adeline Redgrave.

"Hey, I haven't started questioning my ownership yet." Mercer circled the cage. "Merely why this partnership can't be equal. You're who we've been waiting for, gorgeous. One chat with you, and we find out we had it wrong the entire time. We came this close to getting the ledger once. We can do it again. Together. Rule Cinco City," he said. "Together."

"That sounds nice, Mercer." She moved with him—as if wary of keeping a predator at her back. "It really does. But you heard our story. There was a time Kieran, Soren, and Dad would've died for each other. My father couldn't fathom either of them betraying him. Then came the ledger.

"It *can't* be shared. The Lords tried. I'm sure other former owners of the ledger tried too. Letting their friends, spouses, and right hands in on the secret. It's likely the reason they earned the title *former owner*. Eventually, you'll disagree. One will want more while the other says pull back. Your interests will clash. Your operations will eat into each other. All the while, new players enter the scene who haven't graced the pages of the ledger.

"They'll need to be stalked. Dissected. Brought to heel. Someone has to make sure the book remains a lethal weapon, but once they've got the goods, who's to say they have to share?"

Adeline echoed through the small space—her whispers a siren song she likened to the ledger.

"Why not hold on to the information? Give themselves an edge. Then another. Then another. Until you reach the natural conclusion that it should all be yours. A kingdom only has one king."

She smiled as ours were wiped from our faces. "See? You don't want to admit it, but people like us weren't built to stop at enough. If we want more, we take it and tell the bitch who was in our way to thank us for the pleasure. I can't stand to see the Merchants go the same way as the Lords. I love you," she stated. "The only option that makes sense is for me to claim the ledger, free you from its hold, and disappear."

Sinjin snarled.

"But," Adeline continued. "I anticipate a very long and deadly manhunt if I attempt such a thing, so there's option two. You accept that my birthright is mine absolutely to do with what I choose. In exchange, you'll have my love, body, and cooking till the world burns to ash around us." She beamed. "Isn't that great? There is no downside."

"And you're not worried we'll turn on you?" Killian drawled. "You think we can't trust each other. Why do you trust us?"

"You've chosen me over the ledger before, Killian. Why shouldn't I believe you could do so again. That you will do it now."

He fell silent.

"We'll run different parts of the operation like you intended from the start," she went on. Adeline flicked to Sinjin. "We'll see through what you set out to do. The true Kieran racked up untold enemies behind my father's back. It's a surprise to me that he felt any sense of guilt that he'd confess his sins, but he was raised Irish Catholic, so there is a chance he brought destruction through the doors of your church."

Sinjin looked away, jaw tight.

"My father doesn't know who it was that sent those thugs to torture him, and I swear to you I asked. If it proves I'm on your side, I'll put you guys in contact with him. I wanted you to meet him anyway. He's willing to answer your questions about Kieran. There's not much to hide now that he's dead."

"Where is he?" Saint demanded.

"Let me out and I'll call him."

"Address," Killian said.

"Ah." She pulled a face. "Can't do that, I'm afraid. The incident with Tara Duncan was a wake-up call. Thanks to you guys, I was finally able to afford moving him to a safer location far from baby monitors, Jocelyn, and boyfriends that may get ideas in their heads. My father will never be used against me again."

"There it is." Killian propped an arm on the bars, resting his forehead on it as he gazed down at her. "You want us to trust you. Give up everything for you. But you don't trust us."

She met him unflinchingly. "I'm the one in a cage, sweetheart."

Sinjin clapped Killian on the back. "You've given us a lot to think about, Bunny. We'll need a moment to confer."

Adeline held out her hands. "It's not like I'm going anywhere."

Mercer, Sinjin, and Killian filed out.

"Don't take too long," Adeline called. Warning slipped into her voice. "We've wasted two days on this when we should be going after the ledger's new keeper."

They disappeared up the stairs. I wasn't behind them.

Adeline flicked to me. "Baris."

Baris.

One word. My name.

And we both changed.

The fury drained from her face, and for the barest second, profound tiredness overcame her. Dropping her shoulders. Turning her lips down. Years and years she forged the path of her righteous mission, shedding conscience, and letting nothing stand in her way.

I know a little something about that.

For two days I asked myself if I was angry with her. If I felt betrayed, lied to, or taken advantage of. Did I fall for a fantasy?

For two days I waited for the explanation that would set things right.

Waiting is what I did. Counting the days in unending patience.

Until I made it right.

"Let me out," she whispered.

Adeline reached for me. Fingers chipped and shaking reaching through the bars.

"Brutal."

Suddenly Killian was there—standing between us. "We need to talk," he said simply.

I inclined my head, dropping the hand I barely noticed I raised.

Turning my back to Adeline, I walked out of the cellar.

Killian didn't speak until we were upstairs and the door locked and bolted behind us.

His eyes were hard. "She stays down there until we confirm her story."

Sinjin agreed easier than I expected. "Research Kieran Foley and track down her father. Mercer, find the men who got away from us at the club and question them. One of them must have taken the ledger, but in the time it'll take to track them down, Oscar Redgrave can fill in a few blanks. Those *three* were Kieran when my father was killed. He'll know more than he admitted to his daughter."

"He's got health problems requiring daily monitoring," said Mercer, "but if he's anything like an old gangster, he won't stand for being locked in a facility, spoon-fed applesauce. He'll want another place like Waterford Retirement Home."

Killian agreed. The three moved off, talking back and forth.

"Redgrave could've saved enough to get him an apartment and private nurse," Killian added. "We'll have to look into the agencies."

"Finding the Kings and the ledger is our priority..."

Their voices faded, leaving me in the quiet once again.

They could lobby their decisions back and forth. Mine had already been made.

Years I waited.

I fixed on the basement door.

My wait was over.

Chapter Two

A*deline*

I pressed my feet to the bars, dropping my head on my knees.

I told Gianna we were long past using cages to settle our differences. I clearly convinced myself we reached a level in our relationship that we did not.

Maybe I should take it as a compliment. My men don't underestimate me.

My eyes squeezed shut.

It was a mistake to come back. I had let Killian go. Watched him walk out the door knowing the truth could destroy as easily as the lies. But in the end, I couldn't cheat us. If they were going to find out eventually, I wanted the time in between.

One week. Two months. Five minutes.

It was worth it to fall asleep in their arms. And I did for one night.

That was all fate gave me before putting us in that club and laying my soul bare. Fate didn't end her game there. The final twist of the knife, dangling the ledger within reach and then snatching it out from under me.

Whoever took it has had two days to barricade themselves in the underground bunker that will shelter him and the ledger for all time. Three Kings got away from us. Which one heard what they shouldn't? Who showed up on La Roche's doorstep?

Round and round the same questions went through my head. They distracted me from the deep-rooted fear that the Merchants and I were over.

Even if Saint kept me around to keep the tap going, would they always look at me with that narrowed, stiff-jawed expression, wondering if everything I was saying was bullshit?

Who wouldn't?

I tapped my forehead on my knees. Once. Twice. Five times. Still I couldn't drill deeper regret at going back to them. Those guys were mine. We were meant to be together in the same way the ledger was meant to be in my hands. They were born for me. They came together to one day find me. None of us knew our search was truly to bring us together.

"Agh." A groan ripped out of me. Love had reduced me to a sappy pile of goo. For the life of me, I'll never understand why people sing songs about this. It's bittersweet in the nth degree to slowly lose yourself to a force too powerful to comprehend, and feel so confusingly happy about it.

In my next life, both of my alter egos will swear off men. Even if they can land a knife at a five-yard target while merrily flicking my clit. I will not succumb.

A creak sounded in the basement, drawing my eyes open.

I watched polished shoes come into view. Then pressed gray pants. A muscled torso hardly concealed by a silk shirt. And then my Baris—whole and perfect in his put-together way. Not a strand out of place. Not a fleck of dust on his tie.

"Baris?" I croaked.

He looked down at me—that steady, penetrating gaze burrowing deep where even I feared to go.

Tears welled in my eyes. I couldn't say why.

Baris didn't look accusing or angry—though it was hard for even me to know exactly what he felt. He hid so much behind unyielding layers of stoicism, it continued to amaze me laughter and affection made it through. Other emotions not so much.

Maybe that's why I couldn't help myself.

I cracked my heart open to Baris Alexander. I told him first of my horrible, painful history. I shared the agony of my mother's rejection. The fall from grace that left me struggling for everything and receiving nothing. The apartment with the cracked walls and peeling paint. A little girl's dream to disappear into a world that was just hers.

I found that world in a man who took my secrets and kept them where they'd always be safe. So many nights I lay in bed with him, talking for hours and Baris just listening. Never a flick of judgment lighting his eyes, or the fear of my words leaving his lips.

Baris did not know the creature, but he knew Adeline Redgrave better than anyone else did. If meeting the creature made him question that, it would break me.

I blinked, setting my tears free.

"I never lied to you," I whispered. "Not to you."

Brutal crouched down, piercing deep into my eyes.

"I love you."

He opened the cage.

Reaching in, he helped me up and lifted me into his arms. I dropped my nose on his chest, breathing him in to soothe my tears.

Our ascent to the third floor was quiet. I didn't hear the formal newscaster who gave Cash his daily reports, or the noise of men building an empire at work. When he pushed through the door, I knew why.

It was the middle of the night. Felt like hours had passed since they left me in the cage again. It had.

Baris carried me into his room, setting me on the bed. I held my breath as he began removing my shoes. I honestly couldn't say where this was going. Brutal didn't verbalize his intentions. If he wanted to have sex, he had other ways of making it clear. But so much had happened in the last few days, and in that moment, I needed him to speak to me more than I needed anything in my whole life.

Tell me you love me. Say you forgive me and everything will be okay.

Mercer warned me. He said Brutal only spoke when there was something worth saying, and it turned out the only times Brutal felt there was something worth saying to me, I could count on one hand. And none of those times it was to say that he loved me.

He unzipped my jeans, drawing them over my knees and off my ankles. Carefully, he folded them and placed them on the chair beside his bed. I caught his wrist as he reached for my hem.

"I do trust you." My legs slid around his waist, holding tight. "At first I had no reason to, but things changed. When they did, I didn't keep the truth from you because I feared you. This was the first time in my life that... I loved it. I was happy, Baris." I smiled crookedly. "That's kind of a new thing for me and, turns out, more addictive than any of the shit Jocelyn's on. I couldn't let it go—couldn't tell the truth—even if it destroyed everything. Maybe I'm more like my mother than I thought."

Brutal made a harsh noise in his throat. He broke free of me. Grasping my chin, he made me look at him as he shook his head—hard.

My smile wobbled. "Thank you," I whispered. "You still think so well of me after everything that happened."

He nodded.

"You're not angry that I hid things from you? That I want the ledger even now?"

For reasons I could not comprehend, he shook his head.

"I meant what I said," I probed. "Everyone has their place in the kitchen, but there can only be one head chef. Order. Hierarchy. Respect to those who've earned it. Obedience from those that respect commands. I believe in those things, Baris."

He returned to my shirt, lifting it over my head.

"Just as I believe many cooks can come together to create the perfect plate. We can," I said. "As long as the ledger is mine alone. It's the only way it won't rip us apart like it did the Lords. Do you understand?"

His nod followed my bra dropping on my lap.

"Do you agree with me?"

Baris hooked a finger through my thong. No nod. No headshake.

I didn't repeat the question. He heard it. If he wanted to respond, he would have.

"Do you love me?"

He paused—thong midway down my thighs.

This was the first time I asked, because it was the first time I questioned it.

Our eyes connected in the dim light, tracing the other in search of what—I couldn't tell from Baris.

He leaned in, brushing his lips over mine. A soft sigh escaped as he kissed me. Slow and sweet. Teasing my tongue to play with his. Baris always kissed me like it'd be the last time. No quick or rushed pecks.

I broke away dizzy. My heart racing, and disappointment spreading deep. He didn't answer.

If he wanted to, he would have.

I relaxed into the blankets, watching him undress. Falling in love with him was likely my karma. I had to take what Brutal would give me and no more. Just like Saint, Killian, and Mercer had been forced to accept what I was willing to give until it all came out.

Baris climbed into bed with me, lifting my ankle to his lips. A shiver traveled up my spine, popping goose bumps to the kisses tickling my soft flesh.

"Maybe I have to accept that if an 'I love you' comes, it will in your own time," I mused. "But have you accepted that you're mine, body and soul, until one or both of us drops dead?"

He chuckled.

"As long as you have, I can wait for you to say it."

Brutal captured my lips again—this time I suspected it was to shut me up.

"You only ever communicate on your terms. You don't sign, mime, or write notes. You nod when you want to. Gesture when you want to. Push your thoughts into my mind, and I swear, I can hear them plainer than if you spoke it."

His mouth moved down my leg, licking and nipping a trail.

"But I'm told only what you want to make clear to me," I continued.

He rolled a thumb over my clit. Electricity zinged up my core, pulling a hiss from my lips.

"Like you're currently telling me to be quiet and get with sucking your dick."

A full-blown laugh replied, turning to warm air on my thigh.

"I am receiving that message"—a finger slipped inside me—"loud and clear. But, Baris, there is something you have to find a way to tell me." It was all of my willpower to grasp his pumping hand. "Why you want the ledger."

If I expected a reaction, I did not get one. He gently removed my grip and resumed his fingering, picking up the pace.

"I will solve your puzzle, Baris Alexander. One day, I'll know all of your secrets like you know mine. Do you doubt me?"

Looking me in the eye, slight grin dimpling his cheek, he shook his head.

"Good," I said, and my heart only panged a little. "Kiss me."

He did, soothing the hurt even more.

Brutal deepened the kiss to my moans pouring in his mouth. My legs were spread underneath him, stretching to both sides of the bed. His fingers skimmed my lower lips, collecting their juices. Pulling back, he painted my mouth with the gift, tightening my lower belly.

"Are you going to make a mess of me, Baris?"

"Yes."

Heat exploded in me—curling my hands and toes, lighting my cheeks.

It wasn't that he spoke to me. It was he did so because his intent to take me apart was something I absolutely had to know.

It was hard to describe the thrill ride that was sleeping with Brutal. His particularness carried into the bedroom as well, but surprisingly, not his neatness. I tossed pillows on the floor, grabbed his hair, bit his lip, scratched his back, and licked the sweat off his glistening body to pleased grunts. It only served to drive him crazier—which translated into screaming orgasms for me. But there were some things that had to be in Barisland.

He kissed me once. Twice. Three.

Four times.

I fell back giggling.

My love had a crush on things in even numbers. If I came five times, he'd go for the sixth. Sometimes I faked an extra to keep him going.

Alright, so I wasn't always completely honest with him, but a girl's gotta get it any way she can.

His nose skimmed over my chest, leading a trail down. I was already rising to meet him.

Baris cupped my left breast, blowing hot air on it as if my nipple could be any harder. He trapped my gaze as his pink tongue unfurled, flicking the little nub with abandon.

"Yes," I hissed. "Are we... changing the rules tonight?"

He raised a brow, and I swore it said, *Why would we do that?*

"Thank goodness."

Baris moved to the right nipple—torturing it in equal measure. Left, then right. That was how it had to be. I did not question these things.

"Have I ever told you how much I appreciate your thorough approach to foreplay, my love?" He sucked me between his teeth, lightly scraping. The sweet swirl of pain sped my pulse.

I cupped his chin. "Promise me," I murmured. "You won't put me back in the cage."

He shook his head.

"Never?"

Turning, Brutal pressed a kiss to my palm. *Never.*

"Thank you." Getting my leg between us, I planted my foot on his hip, and kicked.

Baris flew off and I took my chance. Scrambling up, I made a run for the door.

"Argh!"

A hard body slammed into me, flinging us both into the armchair. Screaming, I bucked him off. Brutal was back in an instant. Grabbing the back of my neck, he bent my head back, growling in my ear. His erection dug between my cheeks—as assertive as a gun in the back.

My laughter bounced off the walls.

"I'm just not fast enough—" I twisted, snapping my arm up and breaking his hold. I launched forward, hooked him behind the knee, and dropped him hard on the floor. I fell on Brutal, straddling his waist. "Or am I?"

A wicked grin curled his lips.

Couldn't be sure if this tidbit he meant to give away, but I noticed in a few of our boxing sessions that my Baris was getting turned on. I flipped the tables, wrestling him on the floor and mounting him like a bronco. The man fucked the ever-living shit out of me. I was hoarse for two days.

"I say again you should be taking fighting lessons from me." I licked the tip of his nose. "I think I'm the one who's going to make a mess of you."

Grabbing his arms, I pinned them over his head. His smirking mouth disappeared under my pussy.

It was the most illicit crime I ever committed—sitting on Brutal Alexander's face. I ground mercilessly on his tongue, throwing my head back for him giving as good as he got.

I bounced on the balls of my feet, impaling myself on him. My cries filled the room. Loud enough it was a wonder Killian didn't burst inside and carry me back to my cage.

Sweat slicked my body. I was so close, Killian would meet with a violent reaction if he tried.

"Oh, Baris."

The room blurred.

I choked out a cry that wasn't out before I hit the carpet. He flipped me over, pinning me down.

"Mid-orgasm!" I half screamed. "That's just mean."

His laugh rolled from deep inside his chest.

The next thing I knew, I was hanging upside down in the air. I blinked, working to make sense of how my head ended up swinging between his legs.

"Baris? I'm all for wrestling, but if you perform this move, the odds of me sucking your dick will severely decrease."

I shook with his chuckling.

Brutal didn't drop me on my head. On the contrary, I was hoisted up—my legs wrapped around his neck.

My eyes widened. *Is he going to—?*

Brutal descended on me like a starving man.

"Ah!" I gasped.

Sucking, licking, tongue-fucking—he ate me out to make my pussy his bitch.

"Fuck, Brutal, you win! Holy shit, you win." Grabbing the chair, I clawed my way up, holding on for dear life. Waves of pleasure wracked my body, crashing one after the other. Through my haze, I gripped his length, enjoying the hiss of pleasure as my prize.

My strokes were more hard, jerking tugs. From the response upstairs, Brutal had no problem with that. He came without warning, showering my face and neck. This was all it took to set me off.

"Damn," I breathed. He lowered me to the floor. "That was new. Between you, Killian, and Saint, I didn't think there were any positions left for me to try."

He kissed just under my jaw.

"Got any more to teach me?" I teased.

Another kiss, and I was guided gently, but firmly, facedown.

Brutal slid his arm under my waist, propping me up. He pushed in to the hilt and started pumping, rolling my eyes up in my head. I had a sneaking suspicion Brutal counted his thrusts, seeking a specific *even* number. I lost the ability to do such things almost immediately after he filled my hungry cunt to stuffed. So I couldn't prove it.

Baris set a pace to fit his nickname. Hard, punishing, and brutal. I moaned into the rug, nails ripping fibers free. The doused fuse relit, and my cresting orgasm returned fast.

He angled me up, arching my back, and drove home.

My mouth opened in a silent scream.

Baris drilled that spot with wild, reckless precision. He was barely out before thrusting back in.

My muscles tensed, winding into tight, imaginary corkscrews. He struck again and I came hard, pulling those corkscrews to pieces, melting my conscious mind to puddles.

I shuddered on the floor, flopping and tearing out hanks of the rug. Brutal grunted, and hot ropes of cum filled me.

We collapsed in a heap.

My love folded our arms beneath my head, resting his cheek on mine.

"Thank you," I whispered, "for forgiving me."

Those deep, fathomless pools overtook my vision. We kissed, pouring everything we needed to say in an act that needed no translation.

I sighed happily. I had my Brutal. Now for my psycho, playboy, and stubborn asshole.

"Will you give me five minutes?" I asked.

He shook his head.

"Three?"

No.

"Baris," I cried with a laugh. "Let a girl bask in the afterglow."

He got to his feet, scooping me in his arms. I wasn't even getting three more seconds.

Baris padded across the room, carrying me to the bathroom. Another rule for sleeping with Baris. Once the spell was broken, we showered. Didn't matter if it was four in the morning, or Saint was banging on the door demanding my presence.

I sank in his sudsy arms, eyes falling shut. My complaints had no heat. Brutal was very, *very* thorough in his scrubbing of my body. I'd joke we were having threesomes with his loofah.

He skated over my dips and curves, washing away the last traces of my days in the basement. Afterward, he dried and dressed me in his shirt and boxers.

Together we curled up under the sheets. I murmured softly to him for most of the night, telling him everything and more.

Baris dropped kisses on my nose and cheeks.

"Do you think the guys will ever see things my way?"

He shook his head without pausing his task.

I laughed. "You're right. It'll take a lot more effort for me to bring them to heel. They're looking for the ledger right now, aren't they? Chasing down the three Kings who got away. That's why no one's interrupting our loud love-making session."

He didn't have to nod on that one. I knew I was right.

I placed my hand over his heart. "I won't go chasing after them," I said to his unasked question. "No need. If they find it, they'll bring it back here. I'll deal with what happens next when that time comes."

He nipped my nose.

"Brutal," I whined. "I thought you were on my side."

Another nip.

"Fine. I hoped you'd be on my side after a reminder of all you stand to lose if we break up over this." I held his hand between my breasts. "But then again, maybe you're not on anyone's side but your own. I still don't know what you stand to lose."

He turned me over, pressing my back to his chest. The light winked out and cast us in darkness.

The truth was I knew nothing about the man whose bed I shared. His thoughts, opinions, history, and motives were a mystery to me.

I was the first, and second, most dangerous person in any room, but my Brutal—

I burrowed into his side, eyes falling shut.

—was quickly becoming the third.

CLINK.

I blinked awake.

Stretching beneath the sheets, I flipped over for the full view of a naked Brutal setting a breakfast tray on the nightstand.

"I've had this exact sex dream."

A remark like that usually got a laugh out of him. He was silent sitting on the edge of the bed. He slid something across the sheets to me.

"My phone?" I scrunched up my face. "Want me to unlock it?"

I expected this request sooner. I made that thing unhackable—something Killian probably cursed me for over the last few days.

He tapped the screen and the picture of me and my father. No, he tapped my father.

"Dad," I said. "Do you want me to call him?"

Yes.

"Why? Don't you believe me? I told you everything."

Brutal's lips were soft on my forehead. I wasn't sure what the kiss was meant to communicate, but when he pulled back, he tapped the phone again.

I glanced at the steaming mug and breakfast quesadilla cut into ten slices.

"Can I eat first at least? All I've had for two days is what can fit through metal bars."

This seemed to be okay because he got up and left me to it. Moving around the room, Brutal straightened up the mess we made.

I nibbled on my food as I watched him. It was good. Really good. But it would be considering a man like Baris had the patience and attention it took to recraft a recipe.

He bent over, picking up the pieces of carpet I ripped out, and I traced the curves of that shapely backside. Watching him clean was interesting. Watching him clean naked was Christmas.

Baris started in the same place. His bookshelf. Then he continued on from left to right. He dusted the bookshelf—ten wipes over the tomes. He straightened his already perfect dresser. The chair I moved a centimeter was pushed back. Finally, he arrived at the carpet—to give me the show.

"I've definitely had this dream." That finally got me a chuckle. "Do you want to ask my dad about Kieran?"

Brutal faced me. *No.*

"No?" I repeated. "Is this a meet-the-parents thing? Because we can arrange that when we're all on the same page about this relationship shift."

Again, a headshake.

"I'm afraid you're going to have to give me a hint, my love." I held my hand out, lacing it through his. "What do I say when I tell him why I called?"

Brutal looked away. I opened my mouth to repeat the request, and followed his line of sight. Brutal was gazing at the bookshelf.

Books.

"You want to talk about the ledger." It wasn't a question. His nod answered it anyway.

"The boys are out searching for it now. There's nothing my father can say that'll get them closer."

He gazed at me steadily.

"But that's not why you want him to talk to you," I said. "Okay, fine. I'll call now."

I unlocked my phone.

My father's new residence was a smaller, swankier home in Waterford. It was less of a nursing home and more a complex reserved for seniors. Dad was in the middle of interviewing private nurses to monitor his conditions. He was also in the process of getting a cell phone.

I tapped *recent calls.* His new home number would be recorded in here at least.

Scroll. Scroll. Scroll—

I stopped.

Finger hovering over the screen, I stared at it as my chewing, my humming, my mind came to a halt.

"Baris," I heard myself say. "I have to go."

Making for the door, I opened it and the knob went flying. Brutal slammed it shut, arms on either side as he towered over me.

"Baris." Facing him, I cupped his cheeks, drawing him down for a kiss. "I will be back. I promise. I'm done lying to you guys—for better or worse—it's the truth from here on out. Can you trust me?"

He tapped the phone in my grip.

"I'll let you talk to my father the moment I'm back. Please, Brutal, I think something is wrong," I admitted. "I dropped off the map for days, and Gianna and Dad haven't called me once. She went to La Roche to get me. What if the police picked her up? Or someone worse."

I kissed his chest. "You know I have to go, Baris. Please."

The seconds stretched.

"Please," I whispered.

He straightened, hands falling to his side. I gave him a quick kiss and hurried out the door before he changed his mind. My only stop was in my room for a change of clothes.

I was out the door and racing down the street still doing up my top buttons.

What was wrong with me? Why didn't I pick up my damn phone sooner?

Chapter Three

B*rutal*
One, two. One, two.

I alternated jabs, caving the rubber man's chest in.

The ghost of Adeline's kiss lingered.

Interrogation wasn't my role in the Merchants for obvious reasons—though my skills helped to loosen a stubborn tongue while Sinjin asked his questions.

I wasn't known for getting people to speak, except for Adeline. My mere presence made her talk. She filled my silent world with her hopes, fears, and history, competing to crowd out my own.

I liked her talking. Her smoky, soft voice tamed the last fire burning within me—if only till she stopped. But the night before, she talked for hours, and the flames blazed hotter.

She was not the one I needed to listen to.

And she ran out with the only way to contact the person who was.

For decades I've waited. I was starting to feel something new.

Impatient.

One, two, three, four. One, two, three, four.

The dummy snapped back, crashing on the couch that became an unwitting prop in our sex games.

Sex.

I flicked to the mirror. I carried a new collection of scratches, marks, and bruises. My lips curled at the sight.

Sex was just so... messy.

Covered in sweat, spit, and cum. Tangled sheets. Broken headboards. Overturned lamps. Ripped-up carpets. Noise. Chaos. Disorder.

Or that was how we did it.

A new development for me. I had regulated satisfying my body's urges to twice a month. A standing appointment on the first and third Wednesday with one of Mercer's colleagues. She got on her hands and knees, I unzipped my pants, and I counted the even number of pumps until she reached her orgasm, and then I had my own. I was tucked in and out the door before she put her clothes on.

Simple. Orderly. This suited me.

She did not touch me. She didn't roll her palms down my chest, licking her lips like I was a tasty treat she created in the kitchen. She didn't rip my clothes off. Card her fingers through my hair. Hum as she swallowed every inch of me, smiling into my eyes. She didn't hold my head between her legs while I ate her out like a wild animal.

She didn't fight me.

I glanced at the erection straining in my pants. She didn't untether my self-control at the mere thought of her.

Adeline Redgrave had knocked my life into disarray. She told me on the day we claimed her as our own, that I should make one thing clear to Mercer, Sinjin, and Cash. Bringing her in to cook and clean was not a gift. It wasn't just the things I had to do, it was knowing they were done right.

She had not done a single thing right since she arrived. Not in the kitchen. Not in our relationship. Not in my bed. And it both irritated and relieved me.

Adeline was an imperfection I wasn't compelled to fix. The first I'd encountered in twenty years. There could only be one explanation for this.

I righted the dummy, squaring up to go again.

She isn't an imperfection at all.

Against the odds, I found my match in the deceitful killer who danced around my kitchen with flour on her nose. She was mine now—as assuredly as her repeated claims that we were hers. Somehow, together with our messy sex, fights, and one-sided conversations, we made perfect.

One, two, three, four.

In my silent place, I could admit I'd like to keep her, and I vowed if there came a way after all this was over, I would.

But there were other vows that came first. A righteous duty stalled in my search for the ledger and reawakened with the knowledge the man I truly needed had been sitting in a nursing home within reach.

Who knew how long it would take to find the ledger again. Oscar Redgrave was closer. I will discover what he knows—even if it means discovering new skills in interrogation.

One. Two.

Mid-count, I stopped. My gaze drifted to the bookcase.

I stepped in its direction, paused, returned to the dummy.

Three. Four.

Count completed, I was free to approach the shelves. *Poor Fellow My Country* nestled on the fourth shelf. Its thick, blue spine determined its place, and somehow, it still stuck out—screaming "I do not belong."

The hollowed-out book split open on my palm, revealing the secret only it and I shared.

I stroked the barrel of the gun. Taking it out, I replaced the hollow book, carrying the gun to the mirror.

Dozens of weapons in our home, and no one knew of this one. No one would until the time came that I fulfilled what I was meant to do.

"Brutal? Brutal!"

Thunderous footsteps sounded in the hallway. I acted quick, shoving it behind my back and through my belt.

My door flew open.

"Where the fuck is Redgrave?" Killian barked. He charged to the bathroom. "Is she with you?"

I heard Sinjin and Mercer stomping around outside, tearing the place apart for her.

I shut my eyes. *Always so much noise.*

"Brutal, did you let her out?"

I nodded.

"Why—?" He cut the shout off, taking a breath. "Where is she? Is she still in the house?"

No.

Killian and the others had long ago trained themselves to ask me yes-or-no questions.

"Do you know where she is?"

No.

"Did you break her out to get your dick wet?" he snapped.

I laughed. *No, that was just a bonus. And a surprise I still couldn't see the mess we made any other way but so.*

"I expect this shit from Sinjin—"

"What shit?" Sinjin shoved inside. "Where's Adeline?"

"Brutal let her out. She's gone."

Sinjin leveled hooded, shadowed eyes on me. "Now why would he do that?"

"He'll have his reasons," Mercer broke in. He propped against the door-frame. "What she said about her dad carrying out the jobs and making the rules, I knew you reached the same conclusion."

Eyes still closed, I nodded.

"You released her so the lovely Adeline would share the rest of her story under more favorable conditions," he stated. "I'm impressed, Baris. You're taking a page out of my book. Though, seduction is easy when the target in question already wants to snuggle up for pillow talk."

"The rest?" Killian repeated. "If we're speaking about what I'm certain we're speaking about, there isn't much more Adeline can say. She was a baby when it happened. Her father would have to fill in the blanks."

"Brutal knows." Mercer's smug tone grated. "By now, he's grudgingly come to that conclusion. Brutal has also realized what Adeline doesn't willingly divulge, he'll have to extract from her father. A difficult task without one of us there to speak for him." He tsked. "Vows can be so tricky to navigate."

I opened my eyes, pinning him through. "I can break my vow for this."

The three of them stiffened—their immediate reaction to my voice. Nothing like Adeline who craved every word that fell from my lips.

"Won't be necessary if we find the ledger," Killian said. "A route I suggest you take lest Adeline demonstrates just how easily she can get to our throats."

"A route I was going to suggest we all take," Mercer added. "Brutal was right to let her out. I was on the edge of doing so myself after speaking to her. There's no need for a cage. Adeline will come back to us."

"Because?" Sinjin pushed.

"She loves us. She tried more than once to leave and couldn't. The quickest way to change that is for us to continue pushing her away."

Killian frowned. "We're pushing her away?"

"She's expressing her love the only way us psychos know how. Adeline's laid out what she wants, and to tell you the truth, I don't believe she's lying. We either take it or leave it."

"What she wants is to be our boss," Sinjin drawled. "That will never happen."

"Must I say it again?" A smirk stretched across his face. "Even to the master con man Killian Hunt himself? She's *in love* with us. Adeline thinks keeping us away from the ledger is the only way to prevent that love turning sour. We simply convince her otherwise.

"Every day loving her and worshiping her body. Every night whispering in her ear that she's safe with us. We'd never betray her. So what if she gets to the ledger before us? As long as she's in our grasp, it will be too. Once you have their love, you have them."

"Their love," Sinjin said. "A mark."

"She's not a mark, Mercer, and there's just one problem," Killian said. "We're in love with her too."

"That's why she's been winning." Mercer flashed his phone. "Time to join the game, boys."

Sinjin's face changed. "You put a tracker on her?"

"You know I did. I couldn't break into the damn thing, but I slipped a tracker in her SD slot just fine. She can stash her father away. She can chase down the ledger too. We'll always be a step behind."

"I told Killian we shouldn't kill you." Sinjin snatched the phone. "Let's go."

"Wait," said Killian.

"Wait for what? We're not—"

He grabbed his shoulder. "Sin, listen."

Thud. Thud.

Noise traveled up the floors.

Slam.

"I told you she'd be back," Mercer said.

We tromped downstairs, entering the abandoned sandwich shop. She beamed at our arrival.

Our expression did not mimic the emotion.

"Who the fuck are you?"

ADELINE

Mercy Park was still one of the most beautiful spots in the city. That a section was blocked off and bits of torn money lingered in bushes and piles of leaves here and there, did not change that fact.

I breathed deep, inhaling the crisp, clean morning.

There weren't many people here on a weekday. It left me free to hear the leaves crunching beneath my shoes. The wind whistling their songs through the trees, reminding me of an almost perfect day with my best friend.

The park map laid out in my head, leading me down a winding trail past grassy mounds. Soon, the faint babble of rushing water beckoned me forward. Vintner Bridge loomed ahead. Standing upon it, leaning over the balustrade was a lone figure.

Gianna ran to me. "Addy, are you okay?" She hugged me fiercely. "I've been worried sick."

I hugged her back. "I'm okay."

"I figured there was no point in blowing up your phone or storming your place." She threaded my arm through hers, leading me to her spot on the ivory bridge. "Your *boyfriends* weren't about to let me traipse through the door. Plus, they've threatened me to control you before. I thought I'd make it worse by getting in the middle. Did you work everything out?"

"I don't know," I said honestly.

"Did they lock you up again?"

"Yes."

She shook her head. "You five really need to find better methods of conflict resolution than locking each other up."

"Agreed." I leaned on the rail. Down below, my wavering reflection shimmered in the sunlight. "But I didn't call to discuss the guys, G."

She nudged me. "Another planning session?"

"Hope so."

I placed my phone between us.

"The other day, I made a call outside the club, begging you to come and help us. A call I thought I ended, but that actually went on for almost an hour. You heard everything."

"I did." Our reflections became a pair. "I kept listening to make sure you were okay."

"And then you heard something very interesting. Lorenzo Bianchi confessing La Roche is Kieran."

"Big news."

I smiled at my closest friend in the world. "Where is the ledger, Gianna?"

She beamed back. "Somewhere safe."

"Can we go there?"

Gianna turned to the water. "I don't think that's a good idea. Not yet."

"What are we waiting for?"

"For us to have this conversation, love. I hope you will forgive me for abandoning you at the club and leaving you in the hands of the Merchants. There was little time and I had to get to the ledger quickly."

My smile twitched at the edges. "What kind of conversation are we having?"

"One that's been long overdue." She took my hand almost lovingly. "You've changed, Addy."

"I've changed?"

"Ever since those guys locked you in their fire station, you've become someone else. The plan was to use them. Remember that? Use their men and firepower to get to the ledger. Well, the ledger was in the hands of the guy right in front of your face, and you didn't see that because you were caught up in stupid shit with Killian.

"You were never supposed to get so close, and the Addy I knew would not have. She would've been out the second Angelo Castillo made her, instead of once again getting trapped in relationship drama with Saint."

My fist shook in her grip.

"They've ruined you, love," she said. "Clouded your judgment. Made you blind and reckless. You say they're your soulmates?" Gianna scoffed. "Fucking nonsense. They're hulking masses of possessive jealousy who happen to be good in bed. Many women have confused that with love. I just didn't think you'd be one of them."

"Gianna," I said tightly. "If you're trying to say something, kindly skip the insults and get there."

She put up her hands. "Okay, fair enough. I didn't come to bitch you out. A few days in a cage, I'm sure you counted up the knocks that felled you from grace," she said to my darkening face. "You don't need it from me.

"So here it is: I was on my way to save the asses of guys I barely fucking knew, to back you up because their games had put you in danger again, when I overheard that conversation. Suddenly, I had a vision of the future. You'd claim the ledger and set to work building the shining city in the horizon with me as your right hand.

"Not your partner or your equal because, of course, the ledger can't be shared. The cautionary tale that was my father's death proved that."

"Gianna—"

"You'd take it all since not once in the last twenty-three fucking years did you consider that it is *our* birthright. That I too should inherit what my father died for." Something leaked into her voice. "No, it always has to be you, Addy. With your tragic backstory—the mommy who hated you and the daddy who didn't save you from the bad men in time."

I ripped away from her.

"You *deserve* the ledger for all you've lost because of it, and I'm supposed to be happy with your scraps!"

"It's not like that!"

"It's always been like that!" she shrieked. "'*Gianna, go here. Gianna, do that. Gianna, kill him. Shoot them. Blackmail her!*' I've been mopping up behind you for years! Snapping to attention at your orders. But it was okay because we wanted the same thing, and hey, I admit you're one seriously bad bitch. You weren't one to hesitate in doing what needs to be done. Credit to you, I wouldn't have gotten this far on my own.

"Then you met the Merchants." She spat the name. "And I had that vision, Addy. You wouldn't cut them out. You're still clinging to some fairy-tale bullshit where the five of you live happily ever after. You'd take the ledger right back to them, and under their dickmatism, you'd right their wrongs, carrying out their vendettas. Then, you'd crack it open again when Cash needs the ledger to make a deal. Then again when Mercer needs info and threatens to use his cock to get it. Then again when they kiss you and say pretty please.

"You'd give them exactly what we planned all along to take from them, while I morph from your right hand to... wherever I fit as your called-upon-when-needed sidekick."

"That would never happen," I gritted. "I'm disgusted you don't know me better than that."

"That makes two of us." She squared me down. "I won't play sixth best in my city, bowing and scraping at your throne for what belongs to me. Once I really thought about it, taking the ledger myself was the only thing that made sense. You're not ready for the responsibility. You can't make the sacrifice."

I glared at her, head spinning. *What the hell is she saying?*

Scrolling through my phone, I knew with gut-wrenching certainty what that mistakenly unended call and radio silence amounted to. I knew. But I told myself it was anything... but this.

"G." I gripped her forearms. "We both need to pull back here. We're going down a dangerous road and we don't have to. It's you and me, Gianna. It's always been you and me."

She gazed at me, expressionless.

"If I ever gave you the impression the ledger or my dating the Merchants would change that, I apologize." I drew her closer. "There isn't a vision of the future where we're not ruling together as equals."

"Do you really mean that, Addy?"

"Yes." I threw my arms around her, hugging her tight. "Of course, I do."

"We'll make decisions together? Equal votes in how we move forward?"

"Absolutely."

"You're not just saying that so I'll tell you where the ledger is?"

"Since when can't you tell if I'm lying? If that's a recent development, you should've given me a heads-up. I would've tried to get some shit past you."

She laughed. Gianna's hands came up, squeezing me back. "I'm so relieved to hear you say that. I was expecting a knock-down, drag-out fight the likes of which would've blown the rest of Mercy Park away. Kinda why I wasn't in a rush to call."

"It's the ledger, G. It messes with people. Gets in their heads. It doesn't help that I do talk like it will be mine and mine alone," I said. "But I've always seen us as though someone chopped off my limbs and grew you from the parts. You are me. I am you. Nothing could be mine that isn't yours."

"Oh, babe," she whispered. "Thank you. I would've hated to lose you."

"You're not losing me." Pulling back, our clasped hands hung between us. "Now, enough with the drama. We've waited so long for this. Take me to the ledger."

"We can't yet," she said. "There's one more thing we have to do."

"What's that?"

"Kill the Merchants."

The smile froze on my face.

Gianna grew further away, shrinking in the chasm stretching between our linked hands. Through a dull roar, I fought to understand the words she just uttered. It was impossible over the creek's babbling turned shrieking. The wind's singing turned howling.

"What did you say?" I rasped.

"We have to kill them." She shrugged like we were speaking about stopping off for pizza. "I've been thinking, and the only solution is for us to return to the original plan and get rid of them. You must see that," she implored. "Angelo, the auction, Kaylee, Corbin, and almost dying in that alley. They're dangerous for you, Addy. When you're with them, you forget what we're truly here to do, and it's not to right wrongs for every hot guy who chains us up in a basement.

"If they find out we have the ledger, they'll steal it from us. They will," she added when I opened my mouth. "You know they will, and if you've convinced yourself differently, it just proves what I'm saying. Your judgment is messed up when it comes to them. We can't afford to spend the rest of our lives fending off coups from your boyfriends."

"We won't. I told them the ledger is m— ours," I said. "I explained in detail that they'd have their place in our organization, but they wouldn't be running it, and all they'd get from the ledger is what sent them after it."

Gianna clicked her tongue. "That won't do either. St. John Bellisario and Killian Hunt came up from nothing and created one of the most feared gangs in the city. No one knows who they are, where they are, or when they'll strike.

Not to mention their one hundred percent retrieval rate. Why should we let them off the hook when the ledger gives us total control over them?" she asked. "Do you know what we can do with a gang of masked men who can get us anything we want? Of course you do. It's why you wanted them in the first place."

"Things are different now, Gianna. They don't have to be controlled. They'll work for us because—"

"—they love you," she finished. Her eye roll raised my hackles. "They're not going to sit, stay, beg, and do what they're told without incentive, Addy, and this is exactly why I say we have to kill them. It's a clean slate. Once they're gone, no one will know who we are or what we possess. We go back to the harmless cook and part-time actor."

"Let me make something very clear," I said slowly. "I will *not* kill the Merchants. I would no more kill them for the ledger than I would kill you."

She shook her head. "This is the kind of thing I'm talking about. You've known them for a few months. You and I have been together for years. How could their deaths compare to mine?" Gianna took my face in her hands. "I know it feels like your first kill and orgasm rolled into one, but love isn't real, babe. It's chemicals and an overactive uterus tricking you into thinking it's love. If you must play along with it, find another guy or guys. Ones that don't put trackers in your car, and lock you in cages to extract information. They have to go."

"It's not happening, Gianna," I snapped. "Drop it. Drop *all* of this shit. What is wrong with you? Why are you acting like this?"

"What's wrong with me? I'm not the one who's forgotten who I am or what we do. How many men have you killed for knowing less than they do?"

"Since when did you stop trusting me to handle my business?"

"Since I've been dropping everything over the last several months to handle it for you! Do you really not see what they're doing to you?" She waved her hands at me. "They've made you weak, Addy. For what we'll have to do from here on, we can't afford weakness." Gianna peered in my eyes. "As equal partners, we agree right now to get rid of four threats to our organization, or we agree to split ways."

"You would do that?" I asked in disbelief. "Drop me for refusing to kill my boyfriends. I'm your best friend, Gianna. We grew up together. We lived together. You and I were there for each other when no one else was."

"I don't want to do this," she replied, jaw clenched tight. "You're not leaving me with much of a choice. I can't trust you with the ledger, Adeline, and we've sacrificed too much for me to see you piss it all away for guys who wouldn't do the same for you."

Gianna stepped back, hardening before my eyes. "If they're who you choose, go back to them and thank me for making the choice for you. Now the five of you don't have to fear betraying each other."

"This doesn't have to be a choice. It's not you or them. It's not our plans or theirs. I can have both."

"No," she lofted, "you can't. I don't want them. They're either my chained dogs, or they're names on a hit list. You decide."

"I'm not killing them," I said before she finished the sentence.

"Then, it has to be this way."

Silence stretched between us.

I couldn't move. Not toward her, or away. Both choices meant the end of something, and if I remained still, I wouldn't have to find out what.

"The ledger."

"It's mine now," she said gently. "I will do what we planned. It will just be without you."

"You know I can't let that happen."

Gianna cocked her head. "What are you going to do, Addy? You just said you can't kill me, so any threats you make would be pretty hollow. See how love is a weakness?"

"I'm not going to threaten you! I haven't fucking forgotten what we owe each other."

"Then what? Strip me of my funds? Oh no," she gasped. "I have all the money. Every single cent. Are you going to storm my place? Oops. You can't. I spent the last two days setting myself up in a new apartment. Never did get around to giving you that address.

"So what will you do?"

"I haven't decided yet, but you'll stay with us until we figure it out." I returned her mocking grin. "Don't worry. The cage is more comfortable than it seems."

"I'm not going with you," she said. "Please, turn around and walk away. This doesn't have to be difficult."

"You know that's not going to happen. Love hasn't made me that weak." I squared my stance, fists balling. "The ledger is mine as much as it is yours. Like you said, I've sacrificed too much. Do you want to walk or be carried?"

"Neither." She flicked over my shoulder. "Which would you like?"

I launched at her.

Something flashed across my vision, dropping over my head. It snapped around my throat.

I choked—eyes bulging, fingers straining inches from her face. A hard tug, and I flew off my feet, falling on a soft body. I flailed my arms and struck wildly. My fist hit flesh and a grunt was my reward.

"Gianna!"

Pain exploded in my leg. I crumpled on the stone, my attacker shoving me down. Through a blurred haze, I saw her face.

Oh my goodness...

Gianna towered over me. "I told you not to make this difficult."

"G-Gi—" I clawed at my throat. Dark spots danced in my vision, dotting out the beautiful morning.

"Goodbye, Addy."

BRUTAL

The woman stood in the middle of our shop like she was a fixture. She belonged there with the torn leather stools and old display case.

She smiled at their hands hovering over their weapons, and half of her face responded to it. One cheek dimpled. The corner of her left eye wrinkled.

The mass of scar tissue on her right remained still.

Faint white scars cut across her left, revealing the path of the blade. There was a small slit where her right eye should be, and the other corner of her mouth turned permanently down.

"Who are you?" Sinjin repeated. He snapped the knife free from its holster. "How'd you get in here?"

"Used a key." A light, soft voice emanated from her. "I've come to deliver a message to the Merchants."

Sinjin lurched forward and her hand flashed. She trailed the gun between his eyes.

"Uh-uh," she crooned. "That's the problem with knives, St. John. You can't throw before I pull."

"Don't be so sure, gorgeous."

Fire lit in her eyes, twisting her lips. "Fuck you," she snapped. "If you want your girlfriend back in one piece, listen up."

"Our girlfriend?" Killian drew his gun unheeding of her warning. "What the fuck did you do? Where's Adeline?"

"In recognition of what they owe each other, she gives you all one warning. Do not come after her. Do not try to find her. Do not utter her name. If you break the rules, so will she. You've lost, Merchants. Take your second-place prize and be grateful."

"What the hell are you on about?" Mercer spoke up. "Who is her? Did Adeline send you here?"

The smile returned. "Adeline Redgrave is not in charge anymore. My boss will be running things from here on out. Oh, speaking of Redgrave, you may want to help her. I'm quite the expert at knots and if I've got my time right"—she made a show of checking her watch—"she'll be suffocating right about... now."

My eyes flared.

"Where is she?!" Sinjin roared, voicing what my mind screamed.

She lifted her shoulders. "It's a big place, you better start looking."

Sinjin threw his knife. It sailed through the air, striking her shoulder dead-on.

Screaming, she dropped the gun.

I saw all this in the time it took to spin around and race upstairs. Thumping footfalls chased me.

I skidded on the second landing and crashed into the wall. Mercer tore past me and continued up, shouting her name. Cash and I burst onto their floor.

"Adeline?! Adeline!"

Cash ran to Sinjin's room. I kicked open their bathroom. Porcelain tile. The remains of spilled soap and shredded towels left over from Sinjin's rampage.

No Adeline.

I fell on her bedroom door, scrabbling at the knob. I stumbled inside.

On the bed, was Adeline.

She gasped at the sight of me, trying to force something past her purpling lips. The ropes looped around her ankles, securing her wrists in their bindings, and continuing around her neck. Adeline contorted in an unnatural, bow-bent shape—her toes pointed at the back of her head like an executioner's gun. If she relaxed her legs, the rope pulled tighter. Strangling her.

I pounced on her, seizing the knots. The sisal bit my fingers to taste the blood that would be their only prize.

Adeline wheezed, her eyes fluttering shut.

Hurry!

I took off to the kitchen and snatched a knife from the block. The binding knot connected between her feet. I hacked at it, roaring my shame and frustration.

Adeline said there was something wrong. She ran from me with fear in her eyes and I didn't follow her! Why did I let her go?

I raised the knife high.

The ropes broke with a snapping—flopping her limbs on the bed. She lay still.

Lifting her up, I placed her on the floor and breathed air through her soft lips.

Don't do this. You promised to come back to me.

I started the count for chest compressions.

One. Two. Three. Four. Five—

Her eyes popped open. Adeline sucked in a ragged breath, coughing and sputtering.

"B-Baris..."

I gathered her in my arms, holding her tight to me.

"Baris," she wheezed.

"Shh."

"No." She broke free, gripping my shoulder. "O-out," Adeline forced. "We have to... get out. Now."

I carried her out of the room, stopping just past the threshold. Her warnings bellowed in my ear. Cash thrashing around. Mercer stomping upstairs. Sinjin locked in a deadly battle below.

Noise. Noise. NOISE!

The words swelled, and a bind lashed around my throat, forcing them down. Adeline shook in my hold. I was weak. Losing control. Slipping deeper in the dark.

My throat closed tighter and tighter.

"Baris," she whispered.

One fought through.

"Out!" I bellowed. "Out!"

Cash ran out of the spare room.

"Out!" I repeated, running for the stairs. Cash took over.

"Mercer! Sinjin! Get out! Get out now!"

We hit the staircase to thumping over our heads. Mercer sprinted from the third floor.

Sinjin crashed into us coming out of the shop, slamming the door behind him. Bullets splintered holes in the wood.

"Out the basement," Cash ordered.

Down we went, racing to stay ahead of what, we didn't know.

In the corner of the room, behind my trunk, a door concealed in the wall. I kicked the trunk aside, shouting the only word that came to me, "Out!"

Sinjin shoved on the wall and swung it open. We crouched to get in, handling Adeline carefully. Mercer pushed it shut behind, sending us running down the brick tunnel. A thick layer of wet grime coated the walls and ground, undisturbed by years of disuse.

Metal rungs loomed ahead. Cash reached them first. Climbing up, he pushed on the hatch, face reddening as he struggled to heave it one-handed.

A crash, then the hatch banged open.

Cash, Sinjin, and Mercer climbed up. They reached in to help Adeline, gently easing her through the hole. With her safe, I followed—grimacing at the dirty rungs touching my skin.

Teeth clenched, I bore it, moving as fast as possible. My head broke the surface to face rolling hills and two plump, shiny oranges. *Florida Sunshine Citrus* read stark on the crate's logo.

The guys hooked me under the arms, heaving me into the store's storage room. I dropped on a pile of papers. I snatched them up and roughly wiped my hands.

"What the hell were we running from?" Sinjin huffed. "What happened up there? What's wrong with Adeline?"

"Strangled by the marks on her neck." Cash had her now. He stood, sweeping his gaze over the crates filled with papers, disused coupons, and old decorations. Dusty, cardboard-cutout people followed our slow exit. "She's breathing. Conscious. She'll be okay, but we need to get her out of here."

"Who sent that woman?" Mercer asked. "How did Adeline cross her path?"

"We'll find out the answer to that and more. She can't have gotten far with that shoulder. We'll pick her up."

The four of us, and Adeline, emerged from the storage room, coming out into a long white hallway. We followed it out into the bustling store, and ignored the looks coming our way. The sliding doors broke open. Our home sat directly in front of us—front door ajar.

"Cash, take care of Bunny. Brutal and I will follow the blood trail to our visitor before she hops in a car—"

Boom!

A wall of heat smacked us, blowing us off our feet. I flew into a stack of shopping baskets and hit the floor hard.

Ringing deafened me, plunging the world in a muted quiet so much like my own.

"Ah!" The first scream broke through, and the flood poured in. Screaming, running, car alarms, smashed jars, and a rolling can of peaches stopping short of the debris at my feet.

Across the street, the smoldering wreck of our house buckled into the inferno's maw.

Chapter Four

A*deline*

Gentle, self-assured fingers rubbed my throat. Cash spread the petroleum jelly thin, and then raised my head from Brutal's chest to wrap the bandage.

"Apply for ten minutes at a time." The cold pack pressed to my throat. "You'll be fine, Adeline."

No. I won't.

Cash got off the table and moved to Mercer, tending to the weeping cut over his eye.

I curled tighter into Brutal's side. The pack fell off. He picked it up and held it for me.

The five of us were in Elmshire Woods, tucked away in a cabin in the back of beyond after the only person I trusted beyond all doubt tried to blow me up.

Mercer's car was parked two blocks from the wreckage. It sped us out of the city as our own burned with everything else.

The cabin was how I remembered it.

Bare.

No television. No décor. No care to make it livable, but the only place we had left to go.

There were two couches in the living room. One for a silent Mercer and brooding Sinjin. The other held me and Brutal. No, Brutal held me. Arms warm and secure around me as I bore the weight of a thousand tears that wouldn't come.

Mercer broke his silence. "How did this happen, Adeline?" He ducked Cash's bandage and came to me, taking my cold hand in his. "Who did this to you?"

I gazed at him unseeingly. Mercer—all of them—were hazy shapes flitting in and out of view.

"Tell me."

"Gianna." Mercer leaned in to hear. "Gianna... did this."

"What? Did she say it was Cross?" Saint asked.

"Yes."

"Fucking why!?"

Mercer looked at me as he replied, "Because she has the ledger."

My lips trembled, pursing tight to stem the flood. I wouldn't cry. It hasn't solved a thing in my life and it wouldn't start now.

"She does, doesn't she?"

All I could do was nod.

Mercer cursed under his breath. "Why would she turn on you like this? Almost killing you and the four of us. You grew up together. Your fathers grew up together. Why?"

"Because... she—"

I broke.

Hot, gushing tears soaked my cheeks. Heaving sobs tore my sore throat, ratcheting my pain higher than I knew it could go.

"Mercer," Killian said. "Give her a minute. We're not going anywhere."

A MINUTE TURNED INTO hours.

The sun had long escaped the horizon, plunging our slice of nowhere into darkness. A scant light illuminated Mercer moving around the kitchen.

I sat alone on the couch. The guys had bundled me in blankets like they'd keep me from falling to pieces.

When that happened, blankets wouldn't save me.

But I indulged the gesture, grateful to receive tenderness after days of suspicion.

I was no longer the enemy.

"We keep this place for emergencies," Mercer said at me.

Killian, Saint, and Brutal weren't there. Killian began setting up the rooms while Brutal cleaned. Saint was outside doing who knew what.

"Something serious enough to drive us out of the city. Since Killian gave the Leighbridge place away to La Roche and we lost the fire station. This is the only property we have left. Tight quarters, but we have food to last us a few days. That should give us enough time to plan our next move." He set a plate of rice, corned beef, and mixed vegetables in front of me. "I'm not the cook you are, but it should taste okay."

I mumbled something that might have been a thank-you.

"Some chamomile tea will help," he said. "Are you cool with raw honey?"

"She said you guys have made me weak." Mercer paused in the middle of unraveling me. The smile faded from his handsome face. "Giving me control of the ledger... was giving it to you. She couldn't let that happen."

"Did you know she had it?" he asked, stroking my cheek. "You couldn't have expected this reaction."

My voice was a rasp. "No one could have expected this."

"I'm sorry, Adeline."

"Are you?" I knocked his hand off. "Isn't this the part where you crow 'ha ha, you got what was coming to you, bitch'? I tricked you. Deceived you all to get my hands on the ledger, and I would've cut you out as brutally as she did me."

"All true," Mercer replied. "But you wouldn't have killed us for it."

My eyes swam. "No, and that's what cost me everything."

"What do you mean?"

I blinked and salty tears showered my plate. "Gianna gave me a choice. Kill the Merchants and join her, or we were through."

"Sounds very B-movie villain. I wish I was there to hear the monologue."

Subtle though it was, I noted the reprimand.

"I couldn't let you come with me, and you know why. Besides, I doubt your presence would've put her at ease."

He inclined his head. "Try it," he said, voice gentle. "You haven't eaten all day."

I took the offered fork and dipped it in the food. It didn't go farther.

"You see now, don't you?" I whispered. "What the ledger does to people."

"I'm not sure I see much of anything here, Adeline. If she hated us so much that the options were to stay and kill the Merchants, or go and I kill the five of you, you should have stayed. We can take care of ourselves. We would have found a way to get you back eventually."

I shook my head. "Those were not the options. Plus, she would've seen through me if I pretended to be on her side to shield you. We know each other too well. Just like I knew she'd leave us a message we wouldn't forget. That *woman* brought something with her when she dragged me inside. She left it under my bed.

"Gianna doesn't want to kill us. She wanted *me* to kill *you*. It was a test I failed. The cost of that failure will not be a quick death. We're to live long, miserable lives under her thumb until I resent the men I gave her up for, and you resent me." The metal bit into my tight grip. "Like I said, I know her."

"So, what happens now, love?" he asked. "Do you give her what she wants? Or do we get that ledger back?"

I did not answer right away. Fixing on him, I searched his eyes.

"Gianna's new associate said something while she was tying a rope around my neck. She said the Merchants would be driven underground like the rats they are. If you poked your heads up for any reason other than doing Gianna's bidding, you'd find out just what she can do with the ledger."

Mercer's face did not change. "Ominous."

"You should tell me now, Mercer, if you've got a secret in there that you'll kill to protect."

"Why?" He took the fork from me and brought it to my lips. "Are you implying you won't let us kill the woman who tried to kill us?"

"I'm saying this is between me and Gianna."

I swallowed for lack of anything better to do. My hunger reawakened, prompting me to accept more.

"If you guys try taking things into your own hands, I promise you will underestimate her, and it will cost you more than you'll want to let go."

"I see. Is it possible that you're underestimating us? Or likelier, you can't face this fight. If we get to Gianna or she gets to us, you lose."

"It's a shame people aren't willing to pay you for therapy, Mercer. You'd be good at it." It was a harsh, bitter snap.

Now he'd snap back. Tell me off like I deserved, and stomp off leaving me to wallow in grief.

Go on. Leave me like the rest.

Mercer stood, and got as far as the couch. He put an arm around me, tucking me under his chin.

"Whatever we've done to earn her hatred, she won't get to us," he said. "I promise."

My sobs broke free.

"We'll follow your lead, Adeline. You know her best. Besides, you getting your friend back would work in our favor. We can stop this war before it starts."

Even in my misery, I noticed Mercer did not answer my question.

What would a war cost you, Mercer Santos? Why don't you want me to know what that ledger says about you?

THE NEXT MORNING, I was off the couch—though I didn't make it very far.

Flames danced and crackled in the fireplace, forcing visions of burning sandwich shops.

"—stay here forever," Saint said.

He, Mercer, and Brutal were in the kitchen making the mistake of assuming I wasn't listening.

"We need a new place, weapons, and the guys on the street hunting Cross. She has the ledger. We'll end this in a week."

"Her bomber left another message for us," said Mercer. "The short version is we either work for her, retire, or go to war with her and the ledger. I don't need to tell you what option three will do to us."

"Threatening to protect a priest-killer won't make me go easier on her."

"Would losing your girlfriend?" I felt their eyes on me. "Adeline wants to handle this. I say we let her."

"Love Bunny though I do, I'm not fully convinced she won't take out Cross, steal the ledger, and give us the same three options."

Ouch. The remark struck me through for all that it was deserved. I worked against them and nearly got them blown up. I wasn't proving to be a trustworthy lover.

It's got to count for something that I chose them. In the end, I keep choosing them.

I scoffed, flinging another log on the fireplace. Gianna was right, I had changed.

I wonder what I would've done if Raul turned her into a pathetic, sniveling version of herself, and I was looking at a future where the three of us ruled—Gianna dangling from his puppet strings.

Not this, I thought. Deep down in both jagged pieces of my soul, I knew it was true. For as ruthlessly, horridly mangled as I'd become, I could not do this. Not to her.

But she could to me.

How blind was I? How did I miss her resentment?

"Guys." Cash stepped out of the bedroom. His phone was in his hand, speaking with the deep, professional voice of a newscaster. "You need to see this."

Cash sat on the couch. Saint picked me up and plopped us both next to him. Mercer and Brutal leaned over to watch.

Cash turned the screen to me. I reeled back, jaw slackening.

The woman who strangled me, tied me up, dragged me across town, and put a bomb under my bed, cried into the camera lens.

"It was awful," she sobbed. "I was kept in this filthy room, caged like an animal. There were weapons on the wall that— that they'd use on me!" She had to stop to burst into wails.

The close-up angle wasn't too tight to prevent me seeing she was in a hospital room. Her shoulder was bound and her arm in a sling. Crocodile tears poured from one eye.

"It's alright," the reporter crooned. She was a young woman with short brown hair and a hungry expression she tried, and failed, to hide behind concern. "You're safe now."

"I'm not safe. I won't feel safe until they're found."

"Did they do this to you, Miss Tyler?" She gestured at her face rather than say it aloud.

"Yes," Tyler said clearly. "There were four of them. Mercer Santos—"

I shot up.

"—Baris 'Brutal' Alexander. Killian 'Cash' Hunt, and their leader, St. John 'Sinjin' Bellisario."

The crackling fire mocked us in our shocked silence.

"They each took a turn beating me—*raping me*," she cried, "but Sinjin got off on something else. Blood." Tyler clutched her ruined face. "He laughed while he did this to me."

My shirt crumpled in Saint's fist. I glanced at him and wished I hadn't. The look in his eyes was terrible to behold.

"Oh, dear." True sympathy bled through—as it would to the thousands watching. "Would you like to take a break?"

"No," Tyler replied. "Please. I need to say it. The women of this city have to know."

"You're very brave, Miss Tyler. Tell us if you can, how did you end up in that basement?"

"I— I used to be an escort." Tyler dropped her head like she was oh so ashamed.

I bared my teeth. *Used to be a fucking actress more like.*

"I went to the address I was given, and walked into the basement believing Sinjin was just another client with kinky preferences. I didn't know once I stepped inside, I'd never leave."

"Miss Tyler, were you aware over the last few years, the bodies of young men and women also working as escorts, have been found on the docks with injuries similar to yours. Those who survived refused to name their attacker—presumably out of fear for their lives. Before us all here today, do you believe the man who allegedly held you captive and the notorious serial killer dubbed the Slasher are one and the same?"

"There's nothing alleged about it." Tyler looked at the camera—at me—and said, "Sinjin Bellisario is the Slasher. He bragged about it while telling me how lucky I was he decided to keep me instead of dumping my body on the docks."

Saint shifted me off his lap, stood, and walked out. The slammed door rattled the cabin.

"How did you get away from them?"

"Sinjin released me from the cage for 'playtime.' There was a club hanging on the wall next to me. I didn't think, I just reacted," she said. "I hit him over the head and ran. Sinjin chased me. We struggled, and I got this." She motioned to her shoulder. "I managed to get away and escape outside. Then there was the bombing.

"I can only think Sinjin and his men knew what my escape meant for them. I knew their names, faces, address, and their crimes. The police would be on their doorstep in minutes. So, they blew up the evidence and bolted."

The reporter nodded solemnly at the camera. "That certainly seems the most logical explanation for yesterday's tragedy. The Waterford community mourns the loss of three of their family. Titus Millwater, Mona Banks, and Chloe Grace have been identified as victims in the explosion. The search for remains within the old sandwich shop, turned up none."

"They're not dead," Tyler stated. "They're out there. Sinjin, Cash, Brutal, and Mercer. Murderers. Monsters. Merchants. The police will find you."

"Merchants? Miss Tyler, are you saying—?"

"Yes. Those four are the leaders of the notorious gang plaguing Cinco City for months. This is why I had to share my story. No one is safe—"

Cash shut it off. "She goes on to pin every unsolved crime in the last decade on us," he said, emotionless. "This interview is playing on every news channel. We're burned, guys. The Merchants are burned."

My jaw worked for a full minute. "I can't believe she did this."

"She did. It's done." Cash shoved off the couch, pacing the floor. "The question is what will she do next? How much did you tell her, Redgrave?"

I was back to Redgrave.

Killian swung around. "Does she know about this cabin?"

"No," I said quickly. "I told Gianna you took me out to the woods to practice shooting like we did with Dad. I didn't say where or mention anything about a cabin."

"That's something at least."

I reached for Baris and he was there. Claiming Saint's place and pulling me onto his lap.

"What else does she know?"

"What doesn't she know?" Mercer threw in. "She has the ledger, Cash. Everything else is just details compared to what's in that book."

Jaw ticcing, he turned to the fire. "You're right. But that fact was always true of Kieran. We went after him knowing the risks. The same goes for Cross."

"She knew that." My sore throat eked out a ragged croak. "Gianna knows we'll come after her, and she made the first strike. There'll be a manhunt for the Merchants. Especially Sinjin. They think you maim people, dump their bodies, and hide women in your basement."

"We do," Mercer mumbled.

"Not now, Mercer," Cash said. "I have to think. I have to think," he said mostly to himself. "Thiago Pais." Killian whirled on us. "There are others who survived him. If we got one to come forward, it'll cast doubt on all of her bullshit."

"Wait. Thiago Pais?" I spoke up. "What does he have to do with this?"

"He's the real Slasher."

Thiago Pais? They knew it was him the whole time?

"That's how you want to do this?" Mercer asked. "Say we're innocent and we've never seen that woman before in our lives?"

"We are innocent and we don't know that damn woman. We get three or more people to say so, and the stuff we are guilty of will get filed under false report with the rest."

"Maybe for the cops, but criminals don't give a shit what they think. We have enemies, Cash. The Kings at the top of the list." Mercer pointed at the phone. "And Tyler just told them who we are."

"One thing at a time. Work the problem. Move on to the next," he said. "We'll have cops, Kings, Blood Brothers, Cross, and their freaking mothers on us the moment we step into the city. We have to thin out our enemies."

"Okay, but is this Slasher stuff our first problem? We don't have money. We don't have weapons. We're hiding out in a shit cabin, and Cross with that ledger is a ticking time bomb. The first thing we have to do is get it from her. With it, we can make everyone from the cops to the governor back down."

"You're forgetting something."

"What's that?"

Killian's gaze drifted to me. Mercer followed. I looked up and Baris was sizing me up too.

"What?"

"You're our main problem, Christine."

In this context, I wasn't sure how to take the nickname.

"If we make a move against Cross, how do we know you won't knock us off track? If we get close to the ledger, what's to say you don't jump ahead and get there first?"

I raised my chin, looking steadily at the man I love. "I will say that I'll do both those things."

Eyes flashing, he bared his teeth. "Don't know what to say about this new commitment to honesty. In a way, it's refreshing." The comment clashed with the look in his eyes.

Baris slid out from under me, joining the line Mercer and Killian formed against me.

"All of you can drop those looks and hear me out," I said. "I promise you that right now we want the same things, but I can't trust that we'll go about it the same way. Gianna *doesn't* get hurt. I don't care what DNA says, she's my sister.

"You all know... what Jocelyn has done to me. If I can't kill the woman who stomped out any shred of familial loyalty to her, then the one who's been there for me almost my entire life isn't an option either. Any plan you make that threatens her life, I will absolutely undermine. I'd expect you to say the same thing to me if it was someone you loved."

"If it was kill or be killed with Jocelyn Daniels, you'd defend yourself, Adeline," Cash said. "Cross tried to kill you. Twice!"

I shook my head. "If Gianna wanted me dead, I'd be dead. I willingly went into that park without backup or weapons. It would've been a simple matter of bashing me on the head and dumping my body over the bridge. Those weren't assassination attempts. It was kabuki theater. My best friend is mad at me. She's lashing out." I gave them a mirthless smile. "Unsurprisingly, a pair of ruthless killers take girl fight to the next level.

"This is between me and her," I stated. "I know what she's planning. I know what she wants, and how she'll go about it. I know how to talk her off the ledge. I'm not saying we do nothing. I'm telling you that from here on, I'm in charge. In a fight against Gianna Cross, only I can win. She can't kill me either."

"And the ledger?" Cash came around the table. "You'll be in charge of that too. Putting us back exactly where we are now."

"Ugh!" I jumped up. "Killian, look around you! Look where we are right now—hiding like gophers in some hole in the woods! Driven here by the person I trusted most because she has the ledger and now believes she has to do this to protect it from me. That is what it does. It's poison!

"Its pages drip with blood, taunting you to remember all who thought to be its owner and were slaughtered as the price. But oh no, not you." My tone took on a high pitch. "You'll be smarter. You'll hide it better. Go on the offensive. Keep your enemies so afraid, they can't *think* about striking against you without pissing their pants. But the thing about blackmailers, Killian, is they never know when enough is enough. Sooner or later, they push the wrong person too far, and end up in pieces on the playground.

"Anyone who possesses the ledger should be afraid of that outcome. They're fucking fools otherwise. Looking over their shoulders. Sleeping behind a dozen locks. That's the rest of their lives till the paranoia has them so twisted, they look sideways at everyone they used to love."

I pointed at Baris and Mercer. "You say you trust these guys. The four of you have lived and fought together for years. Now imagine for a second what I'm going through. Picture what it'll do to you when the ledger is yours, and you're all tearing each other apart just to hold it in your hands."

Flames danced in Killian's eyes. "We're not you and Cross."

"No one is... until they are."

We locked in the no-holding-back, two-undying-wills battle that was my relationship with Killian Hunt.

"I don't want the ledger to control you, Killian. It should be mine for the precise reason that I don't want it!"

He stepped back. "Excuse me?"

"I'm not seduced by its power," I said. "I've seen—lived—what people with power and no conscience do. And it's the Kaylees of the world who suffer. If I could go back and set fire to that damn book before it destroyed my father and his friends, I would. But the least I can do is take responsibility for the beast my family unleashed on this city.

"It's because of the ledger the Kings built an empire too big to crumble. The ledger turned a kind couple trying to save their child's life into gunrunners. I may not have done those things, but it ultimately happened in my name and for my father's dream of handing me a legacy. I will not turn my back on it now, hiding away in a kitchen like it's not my problem."

I met their eyes one by one. "Here's how it is, my loves. I will unchain the innocent people held captive by its ink. I'll curb the gangs willing to do things my way, and stamp out the ones who won't. Corrupt politicians. Gone. Bribe-taking judges. Removed. Child-trafficking monsters." I made a fist. "Dead.

"I will use the ledger to clean up this city, and set it on the path I decide is best. If you all can look in my eyes and tell me right here, right now, that you'll back me absolutely. You'll never be tempted for more." I placed my hand on his heart. "The dark seed in all our souls won't give in to the ledger's siren call...

"If you can swear that to me, we'll share whatever the hell you want. If you can't, step aside and let me leave. This is my fight. I intend to win with you on my side or against."

A thick silence filled the room, penetrated by my harsh breaths. Making that entire speech with a bruised throat wasn't ideal, but it had to be said. If I was in for a battle against everyone I loved, better I knew now.

Killian closed over my hand. "It seems we have another misunderstanding."

"What? What does that mean?"

"Sinjin and I never wanted the ledger for reasons other than the ones you laid out. His father was murdered in front of him because of the ledger. Kieran ruined my parents' lives and what they stood for. Our goal wasn't to become worse than he ever was and pass the same fate on to more children of Cinco."

I held still. *He can't be saying what I think he's saying?*

"Killian?"

"We want the same thing, Adeline. To clean up our city. Put things right." Killian nodded at Baris and Mercer. "Their reasons are the same. We said once Cinco City would exist under the Merchants' law. Well, you're a Merchant too. We weren't the first owners of the ledger, but we will be the last. Its reign of terror ends with us."

I studied the curve of his lips to his eyelashes. "Do you mean that? You're not just saying this because you think I'm vulnerable and weak under your dickmatism?"

"What the fuck is that?"

I threw myself in his arms, burying my face in his neck. "I love you."

"Yeah, yeah." Killian cupped the back of my neck the way I loved. "Despite my better judgment, I love you too."

I laughed. "You don't fool me, Erik. You can't live without me."

Killian kissed me slow and deep.

I broke away, nuzzling his cheek. "About Gianna..."

"Tactical advantage goes to the one who knows the enemy best. You know her. You can get close to her. We'll let you lead this one, Adeline." The guys nodded their agreement. "But—"

"Why is there a but?"

"But," he pressed on. "There is an equal disadvantage in emotional involvement. You and Cross scream that loud enough to level the city. With her, you'll hesitate. I won't."

"I understand." *That's why you'll be sitting in the back while this goes down.*

"Call Saint in," I said. "It's time to plan. We're taking back our city."

LATER THAT NIGHT, I slipped out from under Saint's arm.

The cabin's bedrooms were as sparse as the rest of the place. They had nothing to say for themselves other than full beds and two trunks. Saint and I took one bedroom while the guys spread themselves out among the couches and final bed.

Killian and Baris didn't stir as I tiptoed on the wood. Lying on the floor by his head was Baris's phone.

Of course he had one. Just because he didn't reply, doesn't prevent anyone from calling and talking in his ear. Sometimes a necessity if they were on a job and things were going wrong.

Due to my boyfriend's unwillingness to talk or text, his phone was simply a block of tech in his pocket. He wasn't precious about it. It wasn't locked or stashed like Killian's, Saint's, or Mercer's was at all times.

I bent, fixed on his handsome face.

Baris truly was beautiful to an otherworldly degree. If ten people described their idea of beauty and gave ten different answers, they'd still all describe him.

Full, soft lips skimmed my body as I trembled under him. Long tapered fingers tangled in my hair, defying belief that a touch so gentle could snap a man's neck as easily as breathing. And when he laughed...

I said once that he should bottle his laugh and sell it as a military weapon. Everyone stopped what they were doing when they heard Baris laugh.

I brushed his forehead with a barely there kiss. *Gianna was right.*

You've made me weak.

Taking the phone, I slipped barefoot and all out into the night, walking a safe distance away from the cabin.

I dialed the number I memorized by heart, hoping against hope that she hadn't—

"Hello? Who is this?"

"Gianna," I said. "It's me."

"Addy."

Crickets broke the silence for a full minute.

"Whose phone are you calling me from?"

"Does it matter?"

"Not in the slightest," she replied. "Just thought I'd kick off the small talk."

"I'm cool to skip that."

"Oh, good." Gianna was light and breezy. "There isn't much to say about today's weather."

"Nicely done getting *Miss Tyler* to pose as the Merchants' victim with that sob story all over her face. There isn't a person in this city who heard that interview and didn't pledge to get justice for her."

"Thank you. To be honest, I was a bit tired of the masked-avengers thing. Every other player in this city bares their face for the world to see. The Merchants can do the same."

My nails pierced my palm. "Dad will be so disappointed in you, G."

"Don't."

"He raised us better than—"

"I said don't!" The calm and collected persona blew apart. "I love Oscar, but he and my father didn't raise me to do anything other than what I'm doing now. Rule Cinco without mercy or regret. It's not my fault Oscar got soft. I never did."

I bit back a furious retort. I didn't call to piss her off. It wasn't a smart move when I didn't hold the cards.

"I take this to mean you're no longer interested in making the Merchants work for you," I said in a milder tone. "You did just take away their greatest advantage."

"Not at all. What I took away was their little boys' club. Everyone knows who the leaders of the Merchants are now. It's put an end to them slipping in and out like ghosts, and they can't go on like they used to—not together. But on their own, they're still useful. Sinjin, the cardsharp. Killian, the forger. Brutal, the fighter. Mercer, the infiltrator. There's a lot I can do with those guys as long as they're powerless and brought to heel. Speaking of, pass on that I'm hiring and have openings."

I laughed. "I'll be sure to do that."

"Of course, I'll only work with them if they're no longer with you."

"Naturally."

"Is that it, Addy? You aren't going to ask me why?"

"Why would I do that? I know why."

Gianna fell quiet. "I didn't tell Leah to kill you. The bomb was making a point. Nothing more."

"I know. It didn't blow till the five of us were in full view coming out of the grocery store. I don't believe in luck. The triggerman obviously waited until we were clear."

"I won't have you or your boyfriends coming after me, Addy. You had to see that I was serious, and I hope the lesson sunk in. The ledger is mine, and you'll have to kill me to change that fact—which we both know you can't do."

I smiled wryly. "I'm starting to understand why you called love my weakness."

"It's a bitch, isn't it?"

"We're the bitches, babe." We chuckled. "It's a wonder we've stayed friends for as long as we have."

"Doesn't have to be over. If their corpses turn up on the streets of Cinco, I'll know it's you. You and I can go back like nothing happened."

"I'll keep that in mind." I ventured farther into the trees, snapping twigs beneath my unprotected feet. "So, these are the options. You take the men formerly known as Merchants, hire them as faceless thugs, and I disappear. Or I litter the streets with their bodies as a sign the prodigal daughter intends to return home. What if we stay together?"

"If love and domestic bliss are what you choose, then you're out of the life. Permanently. The five of you go straight. You forget the ledger. Forget about me."

"It's a truce, Addy. Neither one of us makes a move against the other, and in exchange, Mr. and Mrs. Hunt never hear the name Kieran again. And Mercer"—she whistled—"his dirty little secret won't see the light of day."

I frowned. "What secret?"

"Ooh, didn't he tell you? I thought you guys were so *in love*," she sang. "Why doesn't he trust you?"

"This is the problem with best friends. They know exactly how to piss you off."

Gianna laughed. "Sorry, that was mean. I'm sure your boy toy will spill the beans one day, and if you guys stay straight and out of the way, I won't do it for him."

These terms sound good except—

"What about Saint and the person who had his father killed?"

"Let's see."

The faint sound of pages flipping traveled through the speakers. I stopped dead in my tracks. Was the ledger there? Sitting in her fucking lap after all this time?

"There is a name here," she said. "The name of someone who could be very useful to me. Both alive and to keep your boyfriend in line. Although, killing an innocent priest in front of his son is a despicable thing to do. If they'd do that to catch one Kieran, who knows what they'd do to catch me. Maybe it is better to throw them to Sinjin.

"Hmm. I'll think about it."

I didn't push it. "What about Brutal?"

"Brutal will have to ask nicely."

It was my turn for the pregnant silence. "Honestly, these are better terms than I thought we'd get. There is still the matter of the manhunt for the Slasher and his band of thieving rapists."

"Won't be an issue if you hop a plane to a nonextradition country."

"I won't leave Cinco!"

"I knew you'd say that," she replied. "Don't worry, it wasn't a real suggestion. A thousand ledgers couldn't pry you out of this city. How's this? Prove you can behave yourselves for at least fifteen months, and Leah will come forward and admit she made the whole thing up under orders from the real Slasher. Deal?"

"I'll pass it on to the guys."

"Excellent. Pretty sure that covers everything. Unless you have something you want to say?" An undercurrent belied the question, urging me to have something else to say.

I touched the bandage around my throat.

But what else can be said.

"Goodbye, G."

I hung up.

BRUTAL

Adeline leaned on the post, looking out over the green. The rising sun peered over the trees and painted her bare legs and feet in reds, yellows, and golds.

She looked almost peaceful wrapped in our plaid blanket—the wind tickling her cheeks with her hair. I'd believe she was if I didn't know a quiet place is anything but.

The wood creaked, turning her attention to me as I stepped onto the porch.

"Baris." A smile lit her face, and I saw that she had been crying. "Do you want the rest of my tea? Mercer keeps making it for me. Weirdly enough, it does help a bit. If I'm drinking, I'm not sobbing."

She handed me the cup. I took her instead. Trading with the post, I held her against me, dropping my chin on her crown. She sighed.

"I keep telling myself I should have seen this coming, but it must be one of those things. The power goes off in the middle of the night and your alarm clock doesn't wake you. Five minutes late leaving the house and you're five minutes late to catch the bus. You walk instead. On the way, a thief snatches your purse. You chase after him and run right into the car that jumps the curb and mows you down. A series of seemingly random events that influence your fate.

"Maybe it never occurred to Gianna that we'd be here either. And if I hadn't wound up in a bathroom and witnessed four men murder Raiden Spencer, we might not have."

I held her tighter.

"I know this isn't my fault," she said. "But Gianna's fear that in a choice between her and the Merchants, I would choose the Merchants. That fear didn't come from nowhere. I compromised a lot of my plans to keep you. She likely believed she'd be next."

Would she have?

"But that couldn't happen," she said to my unvoiced question. "No series of random events could've made me betray Gianna. It can't be too late to make her see that. It just can't be."

I rubbed her arms—supportive and soothing like a boyfriend should be.

The truth was, I didn't give a shit about Gianna Cross or her insecurities. What I did care about, was that she was in my way. I needed Adeline's father and the ledger in her possession. I held the key to both in my hands, and somehow they were getting farther from me.

How do I stroll into a nursing home and question the man when our descriptions were blasting the airwaves on a loop? How do I rip the ledger from Cross if Adeline's attachment held me back?

I gazed over the perfect view, falling into the not-so-quiet place.

"Come here, son."

Father sat behind his desk. He always seemed so big at that desk—in his chair. Commanding the masters of Cinco City to sit in his presence. Quieting them with a raise of his hand, or the slam of his fist.

I set my coloring down and heeded his call. Father swiveled in his chair and caught me. Swooping me up, he put me on his lap and faced us to the wall of windows. Cinco City lay spread at the skyscraper's feet.

"The Alexanders built this city, my boy. From Trapp Tower to Ellington Conservatory, we're weaved into the fabric. One day, that legacy will be yours to build or destroy.

"I know you won't let me down."

I blinked to the present, allowing the memory to fade.

A promise is a promise, Father— No.

A vow is a vow.

Taking out my phone, I held it in front of us, tapping the screen.

She looked at me. "Do you still want my father to speak to you?"

Yes.

A tiny wrinkle creased her brow. "What is this about, Baris? His history with Kieran?"

His history as Kieran, I thought, but a nod was my reply.

"You believe my father can tell you something that I either haven't told you or don't know?"

Yes.

She raised a brow. "Don't you think you should tell me what that something is?"

I didn't move—not to form a word or to nod. Not even Killian or Sinjin knew the full story.

They picked me up in a Rockchapel warehouse. My knuckles were bruised—two broken—from five consecutive fights in a row. Me plowing my opponents down in a mindless haze while jackals hooted and howled for more blood.

Blood is what I gave them, and it stained the hands I washed vigorously with a bottle of water. Then Killian came up behind, handing me another.

Killian and Sinjin likely thought they could use me. A broken, screwed-up loner trolling the streets of Cinco for a fight, and an Alexander on top. I had uses far beyond enforcer.

I sat down to their free meal, entrenched in my silence, and ate while Killian waxed on. I didn't care what they had to say. I planned to kill them both and leave their bodies in the alley for the mere crime of recognizing me. Then Sinjin said one word:

Kieran.

Three words followed that. Then fourteen. And I was listening.

Sinjin told me of his father's cruel end. Killian shared the story of the shackles around his future, tied to the crimes of parents who sacrificed to give him one. After they finished, I did something I hadn't done for three years.

I spoke.

Twenty-two words exactly.

It wasn't enough to share my entire story, but they were all that would come. Despite this, my short speech ended with the two words that changed the course of my life.

"I'm in."

Years later, I hadn't been able to offer much more than twenty words. They were enough for Killian, Sinjin, and Mercer. Would they be enough for Adeline?

Enough for her to make that call.

The first word rose to my lips. "Kieran—"

"Adeline. Baris." Killian appeared behind the screen door. "Come inside. Food's ready."

"One minute, baby. Baris and I are talking."

"Considering Sinjin is done waiting and plans on taking off the minute he puts his fork down, you might want to get a few words in to convince him not to murder your best friend."

She heaved a sigh. "Okay, we're coming."

Adeline gave me a quick kiss. "We'll talk after, I swear. I don't remember Dad's new number anyway. When we return to the city, which is looking to be soon, I'll arrange a meeting for you."

I grasped her arms, staring into her eyes.

"As soon as possible," she promised. "My dad had to meet my boyfriends some time. Why not while they're fugitives on the run?"

ADELINE

We supposedly had slim pickings, but the bowl of bow tie pasta and garlic Alfredo sauce looked pretty appetizing to me. Saint didn't seem to think so. He stabbed the pasta like it offended him, scarfing it down with barely a chew.

"Eat, Bunny," he ordered. "We leave in twenty minutes."

"To go and do what?" I asked. "We talked plans but didn't decide on one. Is our first step clearing your names?" I looked to Mercer. "Do you know any of Pais's victims?"

"They can't hide considering what he does to them," Mercer replied. "I knew a few of them from attending the same parties. No real names though. They went by stage names, then they weren't around at all."

"We'll put out the word that we're looking for them. I know just the guy."

"They've had months to years to come forward and name their attempted murderer," Saint said. "They did not for a reason. Pais would finish the job."

"People are that afraid of him? This doesn't fit with the guy you described, Mercer. Everyone's just been looking the other way all this time?"

"That's what people do when pimps deal with their whores. They chose a filthy job, a filthy end is what they deserve, right?"

I pressed my lips together. It wasn't right, but it was true that many thought otherwise.

"The man is everything I described, gorgeous. Smart, handsome, and a rigid sense of justice. He doesn't go around mutilating his escorts because he can. Only those who betray him, and it's a punishment they know is coming. It also doesn't help that Thiago's a King. If they're found and taken to the hospital in time, what are they going to do? Report their attacker to the cops in his pocket? After they make their file disappear, they'll have the worst gang in Cinco hunting them down."

"Okay, I get the gist," I said. "No one is coming forward unless they have incentive and protection."

"Yes to both," Mercer agreed. "Money, babe. That's what it'll come down to."

"How much money do we have?"

Sinjin tossed two crumpled fifties on the table. "There you go. Want to count it again?"

"That's it?" Disbelief colored my tone. "That's all the money left?"

"Credit to his dramatic effect, but no," Killian said. "Between the four of us, we have more, and it's nowhere enough to break anyone's silence."

I slumped in my seat. "Alright," I said, holding my head. "Let me think."

"What's there to think about? Forget the Slasher," Saint said. "Our priority is and has always been the ledger. Bunny, where is she?"

"I don't know," I said. "She was going to surprise me with the new place after she moved in. I never got the address except that it's in Leighbridge. That's if she doesn't move again to be safe. Gianna doesn't have our problem, guys. She's got money. Lots of it."

"Ballpark," Killian said.

"Three mill. Two point five if I'm being conservative."

They stared at me.

"How did you two get your hands on that kind of money so quickly?" asked Mercer.

"Killian knows."

"They blackmailed the guests of the Castian, and then outed them one by one," he explained. "With each demand, they were able to up their price by saying 'look what happened to the CEO of Verdant Foods when he refused to pay. If you don't want that to be you, do exactly what I say.' They cleaned up."

"Genius," Mercer muttered—wasn't sure if he meant to say it out loud.

"Thank you. That was one of my better ideas."

"You had plans for that money," Saint said. "What did you tell her to do?"

I swallowed around the needles in my throat. My answer wouldn't make him feel better.

"I said we should approach people like the Slasher's victims and get them to work for us. The ones society throws away—like Captain and Tyler—they make the best soldiers. Once she's got the people, she'll move on to property. The Castian and the Imperial Majesty Hotel operate under everyone's nose because the boss owns the buildings and everyone in it.

"I suggested we do the same thing by starting small. A tiny inn nestled in Waterford that only lets select guests book. An exclusive restaurant that only accepts reservations. It takes money to seed an empire, and more to keep it running. These operations would keep us going for years.

"Then, there's our fund for hits. Hard to play the part of innocent chef and actress if we're running out to put down problems. Gianna's got a stash earmarked for bounties and hiring hitmen." I forced myself to say it. "So, you'll have that to look forward to if she finds out we haven't given up on the ledger."

"Wow," said Saint. "Gotta hate when your brilliance is used against you."

My teeth clenched. "It's no picnic." I took a deep breath. "In recognition of the steps we've taken in our relationship, I'm going for full honesty. I spoke to Gianna last night."

"What?" The guys shoved out of their chairs like she was hiding in the closet with the ledger. "What did you say?"

I told them everything. The entire conversation and the options left to us.

"If Brutal asks nicely," Mercer repeated. "I don't like your friend very much, beautiful."

Baris didn't look pleased either.

Couldn't blame them, though I wondered what Mercer thought of the terms for him.

"I had to speak to her," I said, "to know what we were dealing with. You should also know that if you choose option A and go to work for her, I still won't give you up. Hope you feel comfortable carrying on a secret relationship under her nose."

Sinjin flashed me that crooked smile. "That's my Bunny. Enough with the tears and sniffles, and fuck her terms. This is option A, B, C, and D. We retake the ledger and the city, force Leah Tyler to recant or the next fucker who cuts her up will finish the job." He buried his knife in the wood. "I kill the man who murdered my father, we sign the final death warrant on the Kings, and the Merchants live happily ever after. The end."

He swept over the four of us. "Agreed?"

"What about Gianna?"

"If you want a pet, Bunny, that's fine with me. We'll get our hands on a new cage."

Considering Saint was swearing the night before that he'd slit her neck and hang her like a stuck pig, keeping her captive instead was a big improvement.

"Agreed," Mercer said.

Brutal inclined his head.

"Glad everyone is fired up to go," Killian said, "but we're still broke with no weapons, men, and our own death warrants hanging over our heads."

"Why are we without men?" I asked. "Lucky, Diego, and the rest weren't revealed."

"Money again. We pay our guys to do jobs. Pay them very well. It's how they get over their hang-ups about working for faceless bosses."

"All right. Admittedly, you'll probably lose a few guys if you can't pay them, but not all. Lucky and the others showed up at the club without a dime on the line. They're more loyal than you think."

"Adeline has a point." Mercer reclaimed his seat. "It may be time for the Merchants to become more... traditional."

"Traditional comes with risks. As I'm sure Thiago Pais is dealing with as he fights another battle to take control of the Kings. Once the new regime sets in, he'll put a bounty on the newly unmasked Merchants who killed two of their leaders. Lucky was a hero last week. Next week, he could decide half a million spends better than loyalty. If that happens, I'd like to be the highest bidder."

"It comes back to money," I said.

"That's what it's always about."

"Money is easy, brother," Saint said. "We can always get money."

"We can't risk taking a job. If Cross gets wind the Merchants are working again, she will end the truce. We need to be much, much closer when she finds out we're not playing her games."

"I had something more discrete in mind." Saint slid a look to Brutal. "If you're willing."

Brutal dropped his chin. *Yes.*

"Willing?" I repeated. "Willing to do what?"

"To fight."

Chapter Five

Saint slid onto the expressway well under the speed limit. Flicking on the blinker, he checked his mirrors, and drifted through three lanes to the one that would take us to our exit.

And people said miracles didn't exist.

"I didn't know you could drive this well, baby."

"Gotta keep you guessing," he quipped. "Wouldn't want us to grow stale."

I stroked the shell of his ear. "Like that could happen. Where are we going?"

"We're solving one of our problems."

Saint said after we ate, we were packing up and returning to the city. Our food was cold when our planning came to an end. We finished it all the same, and left.

"Adeline," Mercer spoke up from the back. "Tell us about Raul Perez."

My stroking stopped. "Why do you want to know?"

"You know why," Killian answered.

"Don't you have the full profile on him already?"

"Raul Perez. Struggling model. Drug dealer. Boyfriend of Gianna Cross," Killian rattled off. "We were hoping you could fill in the details."

"That about sums him up," I mumbled.

"He'd know where she is, wouldn't he?" Mercer asked.

"Gianna insisted on keeping him around, so yes. I assume he made the move with her. But Gianna knows he'd be my first stop. She'll have warned him to be careful, and you can bet, if it makes it back to her that we interrogated him, the truce is off."

"So, it doesn't make it back to her," Killian said. "Tell us about Perez."

"Fine. He's one of those guys who's had everything come easy in life. Easy looks. Easy money. He even refused to go to college or get a job because he expected his wealthy parents to support him till they dropped dead and his inheritance did the rest.

"He got a nasty surprise when they kicked his ass out and cut him off. He hooked up with Gianna like a month later, moved in with her soon after that, and tried his hand at modeling to bring in money. Didn't take too long for him to figure out the real money was in supplying the models, agents, and photographers."

I saw Mercer nodding along in the back. "Does he use another name?"

"Joaquim."

"I've heard of him. He's not the main party supplier, but Joaquim's reliable if you want to get your hands on something quick."

"He doesn't do the deals in person. He has to have people for that because most of his life is spent on Gianna's couch, smoking his own product. I can't tell you much more and that's the truth," I said. "He knew what we were about, but he wouldn't let Gianna in on the extent of his business. Some sexist garbage about the drug world being too dangerous for her to get involved. Man, I don't like that guy."

"Look on the bright side," said Killian. "He'll be dead soon."

I wasn't talking them out of their conversation with Raul, so I didn't try. They'd have to find him first.

We didn't talk much on the drive, zipping through the streets of Cinco.

I rolled the window down a crack. Inhaling deep, I breathed in the familiar scent of iron, smoke, and cayenne. I hadn't been away from her long and I missed her. It was lucky Gianna didn't put leaving my city in the terms. That was an order I couldn't follow—truce be damned.

I was resting my head on the window, enjoying the sight of her, when the scenery grew familiar.

"Saint, where are we going?"

"Seems like you know where."

Saint slowed down, turning the corner onto the lane lifting us up to the church grounds.

Our Lady of the Sacred Heart Cathedral.

"Don't get me wrong, I love visiting Sister Edith, but this doesn't feel like a good time for a visit."

"Edie isn't here. She's away on a spiritual retreat."

I squeezed his arm. "What if someone witnesses a couple of fugitives going into the church?"

"Who's going to snitch in a neighborhood like this? Or should I say, who is going to snitch on me? St. John Bellisario is loved around here. They'd never believe the lies Tyler is spouting. It's the safest place for us to hide out."

Saint parked in the lot next to the back door. Memories of our first kiss floated through my mind. As did Saint cutting out a man's tongue.

"Are we hiding in the church?"

"No. A motel three blocks that way." He pointed. "I know the owner."

"Then, why are we here?"

"You'll find out." Saint twisted around. "Mercer. Brutal, keep an eye out. Cash, help with the loading."

We climbed out.

Saint unlocked the door with a key and waved us in.

"Do you know what the big mystery is?" I asked Cash.

"Yes. You will too in about thirty seconds."

The church was empty. The kind of empty that put me at ease. Outside of services, churches should be quiet, solemn places where the noise of life cleared away, and you found peace.

"Up here."

Saint led us up to the second floor. We stepped into his father's old office. I went immediately to the mantle, picking up the photo of young Saint and Father Paul.

"Why don't you keep this?" I asked. "Hang it in your room when we get a new place."

"In case I forget what we looked like?" Saint and Cash lifted both sides of the rug. "Don't need photos yet, Bunny. I'm told I'm psycho, not senile."

"That's not the point of photographs and you know it. He's your father. He should be with you."

"Right now they're picking through the wreckage of our digs. It's a good thing that wasn't with me."

"Can't argue with that." I wiped the dust with my sleeve and set the frame in its place of honor. Facing them, I found my boys standing over a hatch the rug had concealed. "What's this?"

"This has been here for over a hundred years. Can't tell you why one of the priests decided to install bolt-holes"—he opened it and reached inside—"but we're lucky he did."

My eyes bugged. "Saint, what the— Where did that come from?!"

The *that* in question was the Remington rifle lying on his palms.

Saint grinned. "In recognition of the steps we've taken in our relationship, here's some honesty. The Lombard job didn't just provide the church with medical supplies. Knowing what we do about you now, I bet you picked up on how odd it was a free clinic was located so far out of the city and hidden behind half a dozen warehouses.

"Joseph Lombard is dirtier than the stuff we get up to every night, Bunny."

Heat warmed my cheeks. Why did Saint have to say these things in a church?

"A fair amount of his clinics are a front for his smuggling business. Mercer got info of a gun shipment that coincided with my need to teach the bitch a lesson for cheating Edie, and the rest was fate. Pick what you want," he said. "We're taking it all."

My brain was still working to catch up. "Let me get this straight. You played Robin Hood for a nun, and on top of loading her up with stolen goods, you stashed smuggled firearms in the floorboards of her church."

"It's my church, Adeline."

Cash lifted out a small crate of hand grenades.

"My father gave his life to this place. He died in this place. What was his, now belongs to me." Closing the space, he put the rifle in my hands. "You talked of legacies and responsibilities. This place is mine. I will look after it, and in return, it looks after me."

"I can't— I don't even— None of what I said applies in this situation," I cried. I glanced down. "I need to make it clear, I disagree with this in the strongest possible sense."

"Noted."

"But if I'm picking, I want the Margo."

THAT NIGHT, SOMETHING woke me.

A creak. A whisper. My wall-mate shifting on his squeaking bed.

I couldn't tell with the end of the noise. What mattered is I was awake, and Killian wasn't next to me.

I padded across the room to where I threw his shirt. I buttoned it over my nakedness and went in search of him.

The Twin Lakes Motel bore a strange name for accommodations in the middle of a city that was miles away from a lake. Let alone two of them. Either way, its name was the least of its problems.

The elevator was busted. My bathroom didn't have hot water. The beds creaked loud enough to pour through the thin walls, and I found a human tooth on the carpet. All of that aside, I was back in my city, and the man who handed over our keys assured us no one would find out we were here.

I entered the living room/dining room/kitchenette. The guys looked up. Steaming mugs and an almost empty pot covered the table.

"Leaving me out of the tea party?"

"Letting you sleep," Killian corrected. "We would've filled you in over breakfast."

"Fill me in now." I curled up on Brutal's lap, draping my arms around his neck. "What are we talking about?"

"Getting Brutal a fight," Sinjin said. "Won't be easy."

"Because the underground fight ring is almost entirely run by the Kings."

"That's not as big an issue as you'd think," Mercer said. "Lots of gangs put their bangers in the ring. There's a rule that beef gets checked at the door. Seriously, they even strip the watchers of their weapons. The only ones allowed to fight are the two in the ring."

"If that's not the problem, what is?" I asked.

"Just because they won't kill you after you get through the door, doesn't mean they'll let you through it in the first place," said Killian. "You can't just show up at these things. You need a sponsor who's willing to pay the door charge. The trick is finding one who'd take on Brutal. He's been out of the underground circuit for years. Might as well be decades to these guys."

I seized on part of his speech. "You need someone to sponsor him? Why didn't you say so before? I know just the woman. We'll talk to her in the morning." I clapped. "That was easy. Come on, lover," I said to Killian. "You're on duty tonight as big spoon."

I got two feet and was towed back by my shirt. Brutal plopped me on his lap. The question on his mind loud and clear.

"Fine. Her name is Josephine Meza. She's the owner of *From Scratch* and an underground fight promoter. Her husband trains the guys for free in their gym, and she covers their losses. Gianna approached her to make a deal and Jo refused to talk to her, saying she'd only do business with me. Let's hope she hasn't swayed to the other side since."

I beamed at them. "See how I fix everything?" I held my arms out to Killian. "Take me back to bed, please."

He complied.

"Out," he ordered the guys.

I was tossed shrieking on the bed. We didn't do anything resembling sleep till five in the morning.

BRUTAL

The sturdy, brown-haired woman sized me up.

"I don't see you for weeks, Addy, and you show up at my restaurant saying you need me to put some guy in a fight."

"Would it help if we ordered something?"

"Couldn't hurt."

Josephine pointed inside the restaurant. "The booth in the back. I'll bring your food."

We stepped through the outdoor seating area into the air-conditioning. The restaurant was empty. Adeline timed our arrival for after lunch when Meza closed *From Scratch* to prep for the dinner rush.

Looking around the little eatery, I saw why Adeline pegged her as making money on the side. The tablecloths were a fine, gray linen. The floors were marble and the candleholders real crystal.

"I spoke to my dad this morning."

I promptly forgot about the décor.

Adeline hooked my arm, leading us to our booth. "He was beside himself. He saw the explosion on the news and the wanted alerts for the Merchants. When I told him about Gianna, he stopped talking."

I kissed her knuckles. *Go on.*

"Dad invited me to stay with him for a while, and I think I will tonight. With everything that's happened, it's better to talk it through face-to-face," she said. "Tomorrow if Dad's up to it, take the car and meet him at Bluebird Café on Seventh Street. Do you want me there?"

No. Though I delivered my rejection with a smile.

"Why won't you tell me what the ledger has that you need?"

Why.

Whys were difficult. It was rare I could summon the single syllable for yes or no. To be granted enough words to answer a why was beyond the scope.

Maybe she saw that in my expression because she apologized.

"Sorry. You don't have to share if you don't want to," Adeline said. "It's just difficult. I'm trying so hard to be honest with you guys, but you're still holding back. I don't mean by not speaking to me. I accept what comes when it does. But even for the strong and silent type, you're withholding. We've been together for months, Baris, and... I still don't know who you are."

I waved a hand over her. *Look who's fucking talking.*

Adeline cracked a grin. "Alright, that's pretty hypocritical from someone who told you who they really were only a week ago."

It was almost disturbing how well she read my mind. And Adeline said she didn't know me.

"I don't want it to be this way between us anymore. That's all I'm saying." She threaded her fingers through mine. "Think about it."

I spend more time with my thoughts than most. You don't want the truth, Adeline. No one wants the whole truth.

"Here we go, guys." Josephine appeared. "Miso soup with a side of crunchy carrot salad."

"Thank you," Adeline said.

Josephine set down a third bowl and slid in next to her.

"Who are you?" she asked bluntly.

"This is my boyfriend, Brutal. He's a fighter. Been out of the underground ring for a few years, but he hasn't lost his edge."

"If he hasn't been going up against opponents, he's lost his edge." She narrowed on me. "More to the point, that face hasn't seen a punch in its lifetime. Not a scar or crooked nose. What underground ring were you in? Virtual?"

Adeline opened her mouth. "Brutal has—"

"Does she do all your talking for you?"

"No," Adeline said, voice chilling. "I don't. But since Brutal doesn't speak, I thought I'd come along to smooth the arrangement out."

"Ah." Josephine had the decency to look sheepish. "I apologize. From barking orders all day in a kitchen to barking them ringside, I don't get enough practice at tact. Let's start over," she said. "Gianna has obviously filled you in on what I do and the deal I offer my fighters. We're friends, Addy, but I only get in business with a sure bet."

"Brutal is a sure bet. Put him in the ring and you'll see. Look." Adeline dropped her spoon, turning to face her. "I'm not going to bother hiding this from you, because once his name gets around, you'll hear it anyway. We're in a gang that is currently under attack by a well-connected and better-funded opponent. We need money fast to have any hope of fighting back. Brutal and I wouldn't be sitting in your booth right now if we didn't know he could get it."

"What gang?" asked Meza.

"The Merchants."

Face paling, Josephine shoved out of the booth. "No. No, no, no!"

"Jo, everything the news is saying are lies."

"Lies?" she cried. "A victim came forward. They carved up that poor girl's face like a Christmas ham! Out! Both of you." She jabbed at the door. "I don't know what you're into, Addy, but I want no part in it."

Adeline put up her hands. "Jo, just listen. You know me. When Miranda was assaulted outside the Cannery, I spent weeks asking everyone in the neighborhood if they knew the man she described. Do you really think I'd be involved with a band of rapists?"

Josephine's hand lowered a fraction. Unsurety crept into her eyes.

"They didn't attack or cage Leah Tyler. She lied under orders from the real Slasher."

"And who would that be?"

"Thiago Pais."

Josephine clearly wasn't expecting a quick and straight answer to that question. "Thiago Pais," she said slowly. "That's a name I've heard before. His escorts like to come to the fights, tempt the winners into after-parties, and get them to spend their cash. You're saying he did what Tyler accused them of? Why would she do that?"

"You can get there on your own, Jo."

Brows scrunched, Josephine looked from Adeline to me eating my soup.

"The Kings," she began. "They're the well-funded opponent. They made Leah Tyler get in front of that camera and lie under orders from her real attacker. Goodness." Jo appeared physically ill. "That's horrible."

Adeline told me of her intent to blame the Kings on the way to the restaurant. Why she wanted to protect Cross I didn't know because I didn't ask. She said charging the Kings would make things simpler. Josephine Meza certainly looked to be buying it, so she was right.

"I can only imagine how afraid she is of Pais. How afraid they all are. Some days, it seems like the Kings are just that. They're above the law."

Meza sat back down. "What do you want from me?"

"Brutal needs a sponsor to get in the real fights. I know you, Jo. I trust you, and you can trust me. Put Brutal in the cage, and if he loses, we'll cover the loss and you can wash your hands of us. If he wins, you get him in with the serious money. Big pots. Leighbridge promoters."

The assessing eye scanned me again. "I won't make promises until I see how he fights. Be at Meza's Boxing Gym Friday morning. Seven a.m. If you're not on time, I'll know you're not serious."

I granted her a nod.

"How will we communicate?" she asked. "Do you sign? My nephew knows how."

"Brutal has a way of making himself understood." Adeline winked at me. "I'll be around, but he doesn't actually need me to speak for him."

"All right." She picked up her untouched bowl. "I have to start prepping soon. Leave those there when you're finished." She walked off. "Seven a.m."

Adeline shot that grin that reminded me why I moved past my issues with messy sex. "See? Easy." Her toes cozied up my leg. "This is why you need me."

I need no one.

I grabbed her foot, guiding it the rest of the way to my thickening cock. *But if that fact changed, I suspect it would for you.*

ADELINE

"Why would she do this?"

Dad picked up a vase. I rescued it from his grip before it went flying.

"I've asked myself that a million times, Dad." I put the vase on the table and led him to the couch. "Looking for a deeper reason than the ones she gave. But I don't think there's more to say. I took advantage of her, and she feared after I got the ledger, it'd be more of the same times three."

Dad grabbed my shoulders, pushing back against my attempt to make him sit.

"Don't do that." He was hard. Firm. "Stop taking the blame for her actions. Stop taking them for mine, and you can add Jocelyn to the list as well. The things we've done were not because of what you did or didn't do."

I looked away.

"If Gianna felt so used and neglected, she could've opened her mouth and said so. She never had trouble speaking her mind a day in her life. Gianna might as well be my own, but I see her for what she is. A good actress."

"What are you saying?" I whispered.

"I'm saying she betrayed you, and then manipulated you into believing it was your fault. Years ago, Kieran did the same to me."

Sighing, I flopped on the couch, turning my head up to the ceiling.

My father's new home was in the only place he wanted to be—Waterford. We just upgraded the digs a little.

Two bedrooms. Two baths. Furnished with black leather couches, stainless steel appliances, and a plush blue rug that I sank my toes in. He had more independence here. The nurse he hired couldn't enter his space unless allowed. Made it a bit harder to plant baby monitors.

"You warned us about this." Dad draped a blanket over me. "You told me what that ledger does to people. How did I fool myself into thinking we were different?"

"I did warn you," he said, "but I spent longer filling your head with no-tions of grandeur. Soren and Gianna as well. That day in Waterford Home, you were right, Addy. I promised you the city would be yours, then one day I ordered you to give up and fold into a life of mediocrity. Disrespecting your father aside, I understand why you ignored me and went behind my back all these years."

I winced. Dad didn't sound angry. Probably because I already felt lower than scum after what happened between me and Gianna. But he should be angry with me. I should've listened.

Too late for all of that now. The past isn't a place I want to live in. I will find the ledger and hopefully a scrap of our friendship left to save.

I dropped my head on his shoulder, burrowing into his side. "Have you spoken to her?"

"I called a few times. I assume she's ignoring unknown numbers for who may be on the other side of them."

"Yeah."

"I think it's time you told me what's been going on, brown eyes. All of it. Now."

I'd say it was about that time too.

I told Dad everything from the night Gianna and I sat in our dorm room and put veiled comments into action—making a plan to find the ledger. My story continued through the gang leaders, politicians, and Leighbridge elite we've researched, and on through the Merchants finding me and how we fi-nally found the new Kieran.

"What will you do now?" he asked. "Accept Gianna's terms to do what I've wanted for you. Go straight and live your life."

"Dad, you know no one is truly free living under someone else's rules."

He stroked his stubbly, graying beard. "That is true."

"If I'm supposed to see my best friend for the actor she is, I'd have to as-sume one day those terms will apply only to me, not her. She'll give in to the power she holds over my guys. Cardsharp, fighter, forger, and assassin. They brought the Merchants from nothing to feared in months. You don't let skills like that disappear into nine-to-fives and carpools. I wouldn't if it was me."

"Do you understand what this means? What it could potentially do to both of you if you go to war over the ledger? Friends don't always survive."

My heart panged thinking of Uncle Soren. He was so handsome in the way Gianna was enviously beautiful. I used to take his cheeks with both hands and kiss his nose while he laughed.

"I understand, Dad. More damage will be done before this is over, but we will have a different ending. The ledger will not destroy us."

"Huh." Dad rubbed my arm. "Kieran, Soren, and I once said the same."

BRUTAL

"Bring her back," Sinjin said as Mercer tossed me the keys. "Bunny gets one night off. Now she's back in the shit with us."

I put my fingers to my head in a mock salute. In the shit was accurate. I could scrub every inch of this motel for a week and not make a dent in the years of accumulated grime. They'd be fucking lucky if I came back at all—let alone with Adeline.

The Bluebird Café wasn't packed on a Wednesday morning. A few people scattered about the restaurant-slash-bookstore, reading on beanbag chairs or tapping away at their laptops with mugs of coffee on the side.

It was a quiet place. The two baristas behind the counter whispered their conversation. Looking at them, I understood why Adeline chose this café.

No noise.

A flash of irritation balled my fists. How was she doing that? Getting inside my head. Figuring out who I was and what I wanted.

Why was I letting her?

A silent, uncommunicative man didn't pick up girlfriends easily. I did not seek them at all. They did not want to see what was at the bottom of my well. There was no way back up.

Stepping up to the counter, I pointed at the pot of bubbling coffee and then a large cup. My five-dollar bill slid across the counter.

"Coming right up, sir."

Smiling, she rang me up, gave me the change, and went to pour my coffee unbothered by my pointing. Quite a few people took offense, demanding to know why I was too good to speak to them. A silent man didn't pick up many girlfriends, but he picked fights all too easily. Unfortunately for the ignorant asses, I was the wrong target.

"Here you are," she said. "Enjoy."

I took my coffee to a table in the left corner of the restaurant, next to the windows. Adeline said noon. I checked my watch.

11:57 a.m.

There were crumbs on the table. Getting up, I grabbed a napkin to brush them away.

One. Two.

I continued the count up to ten, turned my attention to the seat, and began again. A bell shattered the silence, flicking me to my watch.

Noon. Which meant the man who entered was Oscar Redgrave.

I lowered myself in the chair, taking him in. The newcomer was long one way and wide the other. He filled the entrance, his head nearly touching the doorframe. Sprinkles of salt weaved through his coarse black hair, and Adeline's nose and mouth scrunched as he scanned the restaurant for me.

One look, and I saw him. Almost twenty years ago, the hair and beard were straight pepper. The lines on his face gone, and the look in his eyes sharper. Colder.

It was no wonder I didn't reconcile the man I met as a child with the one Adeline spoke about. Between the nursing home, the weekly visits with food, and her devotion to his care, I pictured a frail old man snoring to his death in a rocking chair.

There was nothing frail about Oscar Redgrave.

I guess we all look different in the eyes of our children, I thought.

"This will be yours to build or destroy. Don't let me down, son."

"You Baris?"

I blinked to, clearing on the man standing in front of me.

I nodded.

"My girl told me you don't speak, but the least you can do is stand up and shake a man's hand."

I did so, reaching out to return his firm grip with mine.

I looked for a glint of recognition, and found none.

"That for me?"

I realized he was talking about the coffee. I slid it over to him without a thought.

"Good of you," he said as he pulled out a chair. "The last place I was at didn't allow coffee—regular or decaf. Fair to them I shouldn't be drinking this stuff, but an old man's got to enjoy the few pleasures he has left. You won't rat me out to Adeline, will you?"

I shook my head.

"I might get myself a muffin too. Give the cholesterol a run for its money."

You. It's really you.

Redgrave downed half the cup. "I intend to keep prattling on, talking at you until I get some kind of indication of why you dragged me out here." The warm tone dropped several degrees. "As I'm sure you know, my girls are locked in a crisis over the shit you and your friends dragged them into. They weren't close to finding that ledger until you four. Adeline may have forgiven you for kidnapping and forcing her to work as your servant."

Click.

"But I haven't."

Oscar sipped his coffee, face expressionless as the gun under the table leveled on my gut.

"I hope you're here to give me a reason I should."

Adeline said her father would like me. Once again, I'm reminded parents look different in the eyes of their children.

Holding his gaze steady, I slipped the note from my pocket.

Adeline believed I didn't write notes or pass her messages to further add to my mystery. That wasn't it. The force that kept my words down had no bearing on my hands. I could type. I could text. I could write. All things I would do if they were enough.

It was impossible to say everything someone needed to know in a single letter. To answer every question or calm every fear. They'd inevitably ask for more explanation. More words. More, more, more.

It was kinder not to tempt them. I did not have more to give.

But this time. The letter crinkled in my grip as I handed it over. *I've said all I need to say.*

Oscar looked at it for a minute, deciding whether to take it. Finally, he dropped the cup and snatched it from me.

I watched his face as he read. The shift from scowling, then his brows furrowing, and his widening eyes when he reached the second paragraph.

"You," he rasped. "You were the boy."

Yes.

Oscar studied me like I did him—as if he was hoping his eyes would contradict what my letter and confirmation told him.

He continued to the end, and set the paper down. Both hands folded on top of it—gun-free.

"Adeline told you our history. My history with the Lords."

It wasn't a question. I nodded anyway.

"Have you spent the last eighteen years searching for the ledger thinking it would tell you where she is?"

I leaned in, bobbing my head.

"Well, it won't," he said. "It's a shame I couldn't end your search years ago. Some secrets are too dangerous to be written down. They need to die with the person who knows them. As foolish and arrogant as I was back then, I realized when I walked away that night that this was one of them."

Tell me now. Where is she?

My tongue touched the roof of my mouth, readying to form the first word.

It lodged. Sticking in my throat, it refused to move higher.

Come on.

"T— T—"

Pressure built in my chest, pushing it up as a stronger force pushed down.

Come on!

I slammed my fist on the table. The already quiet café became pin-drop silent. Half a dozen eyes turned on me.

Oscar hadn't flinched. "Calm down," he said. "I'll tell you what I know. If the truth is to be shared with anyone, it's only you with the right to know. In exchange, you'll make me a promise."

I waited for him to go on.

"You wrote at the end asking me not to tell Adeline. You'd like to do so yourself, in your own way. A man's family, and their secrets, is his own business. Well, Adeline is my family. So is Gianna Cross. I made vows of my own the day Soren died and after Jocelyn disappeared with my daughter.

"I swore our mistakes would not be theirs. Our girls would take a different path. I refuse to say that I've failed," he gritted. "You're a fighter, Baris Alexander, and I don't just mean in the ring. There's a moment within every battle when the tide turns. Your enemy is out of options. They have no weapons. No defenses. It's at that moment you either heed the bell announcing your victory and step back.

"Or you forge on and rip away the last things he has to give. His life, and his dignity. To choose the second is to declare to all it wasn't war you wanted. It was the complete and utter annihilation of your enemy.

"Do you know the moment I'm speaking of?"

Slowly, I nodded.

"Have you made that choice?"

I have.

"Then you will recognize when that time comes for Adeline and Gianna. They are grown women now. A 'don't do that, listen to your father' stopped being effective years ago. They will fight this battle, and you, Baris, will stand in their way if one makes the wrong choice."

Adeline's story of three brothers. There was certainly a point when they should have taken the ledger and thrown it in the fire. Refusing to put them on a path they couldn't come back from. Doing what I did. Making my vow. There was no way back for me either.

"My daughter sees something in you that's worth a damn," Oscar said. "Swear on that, you'll do whatever it takes to pull my daughters from the edge. After you hear what I have to say, you'll find it's the least you owe me."

I took a pen out of my coat pocket. Taking the letter, I wrote in bold, uppercase letters.

I SWEAR.

"All right." Oscar folded it and put it in his pocket. As binding as a contract.

It was one.

"Eighteen years ago, Kieran received a call..."

IT WAS THE LONGEST continuous conversation I had with a person who wasn't Adeline or the guys in twelve years. It wasn't me who couldn't share enough to satisfy. It was Oscar.

I resorted to using my phone—typing out my questions, making him repeat things three times if necessary. Oscar shared what happened that night and his part to play in what went on after.

"That was the last I saw of her," he said. "I can't say what happened to your sister afterward. What I did know, did not make it into the ledger."

He said the same in many forms and variations till I put my phone away. The blanks from that night were filled in. Oscar had given me a place to start. But my search was far from over.

"Let's go." He pushed back from the table. "Adeline's waiting."

I followed him out, veering on the way to leave a tip in the jar. The restaurant was quiet and the employees didn't bother us. Couldn't ask for a better dining experience.

Walking out of the Bluebird, the rush of pedestrian traffic tried to claim me. I hung back and turned my collar up to passing glances. Ten feet ahead, I spotted Oscar's black and gray crown bobbing in the crowd.

The man who shattered more lives in this city than the total number of gang casualties combined, and he walks among the rest of us like a shadow. Seen and, to our mistake, thought to be harmless.

Oscar went inside another café and came out with Adeline under his arm.

"—it go, Daddy?" She smiled at me walking up. "Did two of my favorite men work things out?"

Oscar grunted something. Adeline frowned.

"Dad, were you drinking coffee?"

"Course not, brown eyes. What are you saying? You know I can't do caffeine."

Her eyes narrowed to slits and a snort burst out of me. We weren't the only ones who got that look.

Does she have every man in her life wrapped around her finger?

Adeline kissed me uncaring of her dad behind us. She slipped her hand in mine, tracing a finger along my palm lines.

"Missed you," she whispered.

Yes. The answer is yes.

"I bet you have orders to bring me back to my Saint."

I cocked a brow. She didn't even have to ask.

"I'm heading out with Baris," she told him. "I'll drop by again next week."

"Why stay with them? You're safe with me."

"Me and a certain friend of mine started this whole mess. I can't leave them in it while I kick back on your couch." She kissed his cheek. "Please, just... talk to her if you can."

"I will."

They said their goodbyes. Adeline and I headed in the opposite direction for Mercer's car.

"I say I shouldn't leave you in this mess, but you all are far from innocent. It's amusing telling everyone you don't kill people or lock women in cages because, of course, you do."

She smacked my ass and got a smack in return. Giggling, she bumped into me.

"We're still 'all in this together' but would it be cool if we didn't go back to the motel right away? I appreciate Mr. Hall letting us stay, but we found a mouse in our bedroom and I swear that thing squared up, taunting us to make a move."

A mouse? You're lucky if we ever step foot in that place again.

Adeline didn't have to ask twice. I pulled out of the parking lot, turning right instead of left toward the motel.

I knew exactly where to go.

ADELINE

Brutal drove us deeper and deeper into Leighbridge. I talked at him the whole way, telling him about my time with my dad.

Believe it or not, it didn't bother me in the slightest that Brutal rarely spoke. I loved each of my guys equally and in different ways. That Brutal listened to my problems without judgment or trying to fix them, made him the perfect man in everyone's eyes.

Brutal could keep all of his words inside. There were only three words I wanted to hear.

On your knees.

Ha! No— Well, yes, but the other three words too.

Soon, the skyscrapers were in our rearview. We were in a familiar part of Leighbridge where artists set up shop with their galleries, and a certain company ran a health clinic as a front for their smuggling operation.

"You haven't taken me on another surprise job, have you?"

No.

"A date with Baris Alexander," I mused. "What do I have in store? Candles? Music? Fine dining? We are staying ahead of the cops, so maybe a walk down Trapp Trail? A drive-in movie? A picnic in a secluded area of the park?" I clapped. "Ooh, baby. You're so romantic."

Chuckling, Baris turned the corner on State Street and parked the car. I looked at the warehouses taking up both sides of the road.

"Where?"

He pointed to the building beside us.

"Does it say something about our relationships that I again have to ask if you brought me here to murder me?"

Brutal popped a kiss on my lips. Wasn't sure what to read in that answer, but kisses were always welcome.

Rounding the car, Brutal opened my door and helped me out.

A boarded-over sign hung above the warehouse's double doors. I tugged on the padlock.

"Can't get in."

Brutal fished a key from his pocket.

"He's full of surprises."

He drew the sliding door open. A hand on the back prodded me inside.

"Wow," I breathed. Full of surprises indeed.

A fully equipped gym laid out before me. Heavy bags, grappling dummies, free weights, treadmills, rowers, elliptical machines, and the centerpiece of the room, the boxing ring.

I ran a finger on the treadmill. Not a lick of dust.

The entire place was spotless from the cobweb-free lights to the gleaming floors.

"Come here often?"

Brutal shrugged off his coat by way of answering. The tie went too.

I stood there watching the show, so he tugged on my jeans, popping the button. I followed his line of sight to the ring.

"Are we fighting or having sex?" I waggled my brows. "Or both?"

He put his hands out, grinning like he couldn't possibly say.

I tugged my shirt over my head, and he was gone.

"Baris?"

Looking around, I found him by the water fountains, removing gloves, towels, and workout clothes.

"I see what this is," I called. "Now that my alter ego is out in the open, you want to see how she fights when I'm not holding her back. Might want to rethink this move, baby. You need to be in a good frame of mind for your tryout with Jo. Walking in there after a harsh defeat by your girlfriend would be incredibly demoralizing. May affect your performance."

Brutal laughed out loud—head thrown back, shoulders rippling, eyes dancing.

I've seen a Van Gogh on loan at Abbey Gallery. I've snuck into the opera house to hear the Philharmonic play. I've sat on a rooftop and watched the sun set on my city, bathing us in reds and golds. A collection of beautiful sights and sounds, and none compared to Baris laughing.

"Don't get cocky," I warned. Baris tossed me gloves and a change of clothes. "I can more than take you, my love."

He tossed me a wink and I swear I heard, *"I'm not going easy on you this time."*

We warmed up, stretching it out, and loosening our joints. Truth was, a little workout would be fun. I wanted to see Brutal in action—when he wasn't killing someone.

Together we got inside the ring. I adopted my stance, openly admiring my man in red shorts, shoes, gloves, and nothing else. I wanted to run my hands over the bumps and ridges of his hard, muscled chest.

So I did. Brutal was warm and pulsing beneath my palms. A moan slipped out of me. He caught it on his lips, capturing me in a kiss.

Baris skimmed my bottom lip, demanding entrance which he dutifully received. Our tongues tangled. We began the fight for dominance ahead of the bell.

My hands continued their journey, sliding around his neck. Our groans bounced off the walls.

Baris held my waist, drawing me close, and hooked me around the leg.

I landed flat on the surface.

"Wow," I grunted. "Never had a guy drop me on my ass mid-kiss. You want to fight dirty? I can be dirty."

He rumbled deep in his chest, sounding off his hunger for just that. Heat pooled in my lower belly. Why didn't we go with sex out of the "sex or fight" option?

Baris let me up, retreating to his side of the ring. We faced off, grinning.

There was no bell. No ref or trainer to call it for us. Baris gave me a single nod, and I charged him.

My first jab went wide, knocked aside by his block. In came a left uppercut that missed me by a hair. I spun and kicked out, buckling his knee and dropping him to the canvas. I bent his neck back and kissed him.

"Told you it'd get dirty."

Brutal embraced me, and flipped me over his head.

So our match went. It was unclear whether we were trying to earn points, or get each other off, but we were doing well with both.

This wasn't like the sparring sessions in Baris's room. The illegal boxing moves aside, we faced off as real opponents. I understood immediately why the guys boasted of his skills in the ring.

I witnessed his talents as a killer. Strike hard, first, and without hesitation. The opposite was true in the ring. The single way to describe it was patience.

Brutal toyed with me. Fought hard enough to keep me on my toes, pushing me to use everything in my bag of tricks, and ultimately letting him learn my moves and how I fought. Then he turned it against me.

I pivoted, aiming my right cross for his undefended side. Brutal blurred.

The next thing I knew, my punch was sailing through air. Baris grabbed me around the waist and brought me down with the same move that ended our kiss.

Chest heaving, I gazed up at that devilish smirk.

"I got too cocky," I said. "You let me get in a few good shots, so I'd get overconfident and end up on my back. Impressive."

Brutal dropped kisses on my collarbone.

"Rematch?"

He slid his fingers through the lining of my shorts.

"Rematch of a different type?" I offered.

Baris tossed my shorts somewhere over his shoulder. That was a yes.

Our clothes came off in the rush of frantic fingers, refusing to break our kiss.

I toed my sneakers off, snaked my legs around him, and giggled as I was flipped over to straddle him.

"I'm glad we didn't do a drive-in or a picnic," I said. "Every day, in a bunch of little ways, I feel like you're showing me who you are. It's enough for me, Baris."

His hands skated down my arms and ended their journey enfolding mine.

"Everything you are is enough."

His lips were teased in a slight smile as he pushed our hands downward. Our fingers spread my entrance, drawing a soft sigh from me. Baris placed my other hand on my breast, swirling my fingers around my nipple.

I heeded the directions, teasing myself for his pleasure. Brutal hardened beneath.

It was wild that a man who said nothing could be described as bossy in bed, but there it is. Brutal knew how, when, and where he wanted it. It was even wilder that it ended up being exactly what I wanted as well. The guy was in my head like my thoughts were displayed in a floating cloud above me.

His hand traveled around back, spreading my cheeks. My brows blew up my head.

"This is new. Is this going where I think it—?"

Baris licked his fingers.

"I will take that as a yes."

He probed my entrance, quickening my pulse. "I haven't done this before." Warmth spread through my cheeks. "I'm happy I have a first for you. Hint: I have some other firsts left if you want to get creative in the future."

He flashed an intrigued look. A circle was drawn around my lips.

"Haven't done"—I squeaked as I swallowed his finger—"that," I finished.

Brutal held still to let me adjust. The other hand pointed up.

"Never been in an airplane."

He clasped my wrists next.

"Have you met Saint?"

I moved a little bit, encouraging him to go deeper.

Laughing, Brutal performed a complicated hand wave, making fists and pointing in every direction.

"I don't know what that is, but I definitely haven't done it." I kissed him. "We'll just have to work our way through the list one by one," I said against his lips.

He swatted my backside.

I laughed. "There are other ways to give me the hint to get up. I think you just like spanking me, Baris Alexander." That got me another swat.

I crawled to the edge of the ring and held the ropes. My ass wiggled for him, inviting him to follow.

Hands stayed my hips. Brutal nudged my legs apart, ratcheting my heart rate up a little more.

After many, many, many times in, and out, of their beds, I still got that flutter of nerves when we were together. The creature didn't get nervous. She was pure steel and righteous fire. Both powerful entities that couldn't harm the other, and therefore existed peacefully. Order vs. chaos. Strength vs. destruction. In that spinning battle of yin and yang, there was no room for... butterflies.

That was all Adeline—the lovesick chick falling head over heels again and again. Maybe I didn't have to stop being her now that my secrets were out. In the nonstop madness that was my life, it's possible I could be just a young woman in love with a guy.

And another guy. And another. And another.

Baris buried his face between my legs, eating me out with abandon. My clit purred under his calloused thumb—rolling and tweaking to my increasing cries. They went up in volume as he did, his tongue swirling around my opening.

Saint used to crack jokes that Brutal had white-bread, bottled-water, vanilla sex till I came along. He assumed I was faking the screams coming out of Baris's bedroom.

Brutal's tongue probed up and down from ass to slit.

It was the worst lie Saint had ever told me. There was nothing bottled water or vanilla about Baris Alexander. If anything, the things we got up to made me glad the morning after that increased melanin levels made it impossible to tell if I was blushing.

"Yes," I cried. "Do it!"

The fingers were back—entering, scissoring, and spreading me. I shifted at the discomfort.

Brutal kissed me just above my tailbone. *Relax.*

I heeded the unvoiced command. I trusted him.

Brutal pushed inside.

"Fuck it to hell!"

Peals of laughter spread through the gym.

"Don't laugh at me when I'm in pain," I grumbled.

Brutal rubbed my thighs, soothing me. Slowly my clenched muscles relaxed, and the pain ebbed out.

"I'm ready."

Baris took his time, letting me get used to the foreign sensations spreading through my body. I quickly went from uncertain to questioning why we hadn't done this before.

"Yes, Baris, faster." I rested my cheek on the ropes—bouncing and bobbing to his thrusts.

He brought my clit to the party, and the double team of his stroking and pounding turned up the pressure. I was not going to last long.

I wouldn't last another second.

Climbing higher up the ropes, my head dangled—hair sweeping along my arched back. Brutal gripped my shoulder and firmly brought me down, angling a deeper thrust once. Twice. Three—

I seized, clenching around his cock and earning a groan.

I came so hard, I slipped through the ropes and hung off the side, jerking through crashing waves knocking me down every time I caught my breath. Brutal spilling inside me was the final push over the edge.

He brought me in, curling my body under him, and stretching out on top.

I don't know how long we lay there, content in the place we beat the crap out of each other, but I was happy to never leave. Out there, my friend betrayed me. My boyfriends were unmasked and on the run. Everything I worked and lied for over the last several years had been turned on its head.

"You know," I whispered, "there was never a point I didn't think all of this was fun. Hunting the ledger. Hiding in plain sight. Being in control. I saw it all as a game I was rigged to win. I didn't think my own lesson would be taught to me. The ledger cannot be shared." I turned, facing him. "Tell me that won't be us, Baris. Promise me the ledger won't destroy us."

He kissed me soft and sweet. *I promise.*

"Make me one last promise," I heard myself saying. "If I could think of anything else I wanted as much as the ledger and Gianna back, it's you."

My heart fluttered. A small voice said I should stop. Pull back. Remember I was giving away my cards in a situation where I had none. The five of us were a couple of people who distrusted and loved each other. The former constantly made fools of the latter. Especially if they didn't know the latter to be true. They only wished it so.

But I'm done with wishing. With convincing myself of what he feels because I need it to match my own.

"To hear you say I love you."

It was out there. Carried from my mouth to him, and I waited for a sign of impact.

Baris traced my face. For a moment, I swore his lips parted.

He drifted up, looking around the gym, and they closed.

Baris pointed to me. He pointed at himself. Finally, he kissed me.

I wasn't certain what those actions meant put together. But I didn't ask. Brutal didn't do whys, and maybe I had to accept, he didn't do I love yous.

Chapter Six

"The answer is right in front of us," said Mercer. "I throw a party."

Saint's head rested on my lap. I ran my fingers through his blue locks, secretly pleased he opted to wear his knit cap when he went out instead of shaving or dyeing his hair something less iconic.

I didn't think he was sleeping, though his eyes were closed and he hadn't contributed anything to the conversation.

"Why is that the answer?"

"I get a few of my model friends together, casually suggest someone call in the party favors, and your friend, Raul Perez, comes to us," he said. "Cash, bust out your calculator. Success at one hundred percent probability or what?"

I raised a hand. "There are a few things that might lessen the odds."

The five of us were in the motel, gathered in Brutal's room. The cleanest corner of the building.

Sinjin and I stretched out on the couch. Cash sat at the dining table while Mercer and Brutal stood by the window.

"Raul doesn't get off his ass for love or money," I continued. "He'd send one of his guys to deliver the favors."

"Perez strikes me as the kind of man who will get off his ass for a good party. Lots of booze. Even more drugs. Wall-to-wall opportunities to cheat on his lovely girlfriend."

"You're not wrong there," I mumbled. "All right, then the second problem. How can you throw a party? Mercer Santos is public enemy number four. He's not going to show up anywhere you are. Actually, I suspect only the bluest and finest of Cinco will RSVP."

He laughed. "Confession time. All the stuff I said about not needing a nickname wasn't necessarily true."

"His clients and colleagues know him as someone else," Killian confirmed. "They've never heard the name Mercer Santos."

"Even if you've been going by Foot Long—"

"—I am now."

"—Leah Tyler was kind enough to give a description," I finished. "The sketch they have in circulation isn't a bad likeness of you."

"My *friends* have known me for years." Mercer sank in the armchair. "They won't connect the villain plastered on Channel Nine to the former sociology student who dropped out to study the human body instead."

"That's who they think you are? A harmless college dropout living it up in a North Quay loft? Now I have to know what name you've given this persona."

He grinned. "Want to see me in action, beautiful, all you have to do is ask."

A shiver went up my spine, standing my hairs on end. The man could do that with a grin and innuendo. I almost wouldn't be surprised if the cover story was the true story. Mercer left it all behind for his true calling, reducing people to twitching heaps of chain orgasms.

I assume. He and I still haven't moved past the grins and innuendos.

Sinjin roused. "What will you need to throw this party?"

"Rent a loft downtown. Hire food and music. Payment for the drugs. Plus, time to whisper in the right ears. I can't deliver a direct invitation to Perez. If he isn't a complete idiot, he'll see through that. He's got to hear about the party from a friend of a friend who texted last minute asking if he wants to come, and bring the pills."

"Seems risky," I said.

"But he's right," said Cash. "It's the simplest way to draw Perez out. He won't see a trap till it's too late."

"You say simple, brother," Saint chimed in. He slipped his hand between my legs, heading for my middle like a heat-seeking missile. "Alaric parties out us thousands of dollars. The current size of our bank account will get you cheese and crackers in Waterford Organics' parking lot with the deejay doubling as your car radio." Sinjin gave the proverbial bean a flick. "Think Perez will come to that?"

"Our current financial difficulties are not lost on me," Mercer replied. "Goes without saying, this all hinges on Brutal cleaning up in the cage. I could arrange a few dates to bring in money, but Adeline makes that face when I even think it."

I started. I hadn't noticed my eyes had narrowed and lips peeled back in a snarl.

"There's no need for you to go on dates." I spread my legs wider to give Sinjin better access. "I've seen him in action. Brutal will clean up. The question is how much money is in play? Hundreds? Thousands?"

"Depends," said Cash. "There are the unregulated, street fights where a bunch of guys pick an empty warehouse and beat the crap out of each other while a drunk, shouting audience watches. That's entertainment. The most you can get from a fight like that is a few hundred.

"Then there are the fights organized by the Kings, Rolling Ninety-Nines, and Hell's Outlaws. Those are held on their properties with cages, refs, and bleachers. Security keeping the crowd in line. Pro bookies taking bets. Sponsored fighters. That's business, Redgrave, and everyone in it is looking to make money. Brutal would clear thousands in a match. Tens of thousands in some cases."

"Did the Merchants have a presence in the fights?"

Mercer draped his leg over the chair's arm. "Fighters are the opposite of discrete. Their sponsors have to be known and trusted among the promoters. They step in the cage sans mask. We stuck to the betting audience, making a little here and there, but the kids they put in the cage are a risk. Brutal isn't."

"Leah Tyler shouted the name Baris 'Brutal' Alexander to the world," I said. "Any chance a lot of underground fighters go by the handle Brutal? How bad will it be if everyone knows he's a leader of the Merchants?"

"Hard to say," Sinjin admitted. He lazily slid in and out of me. "We've done a fair number of jobs for the people who'll be in that crowd. The only real enemy we have is the Kings—which is like saying the only illness you have is an inoperable brain tumor. The Kings are enemy enough."

"What'll happen if Brutal gets in a cage with a King?"

"Do you have to ask?"

I flicked to Brutal standing still and calm looking out the window.

"No, I don't."

BRUTAL AND I WALKED into Meza's Boxing Gym at seven o'clock on the dot. We slammed into a wall of noise.

The *thud, thud, thud* of fists against heavy bags. Jump ropes smacking the concrete floors. Equipment clanging and people calling back and forth to each other. The early morning wake-up didn't slow them down.

It was the opposite of the quiet haven tucked away in Leighbridge. I wondered how often he practiced in that gym alone. Not that he was truly alone. In the ring, you fight two opponents. One of them your demons.

"Addy." Josephine waved from the other side of the boxing ring. "Over here, guys."

Jo introduced us to the tall stalk of a man casting a shadow over her. "This is Ian. You'll be sparring with him this morning. I want to see how you move. How you think," she said to Brutal. "So, we're going easy for the first match. Were you trained as a boxer?"

Yes.

"That's something at least," she said under her breath. "Warm up, you two."

I hung back with Jo while the guys went through their warm-up routines.

"I asked around about your friend Brutal here."

"Boyfriend," I corrected. I liked saying it as much as I liked hearing it.

"Boyfriend. Apparently, there are whispers of some kid who used to roam the circuit. Wasn't attached to any person or gang. He just showed up at fights and got in the ring. They called him Brutal because he put his opponents in the hospital. Every single one." Jo gave me a hard look. "Is he the legend himself?"

"I don't know. Really, I don't," I said to her frown. "As you can guess, Brutal doesn't speak much about his history."

"I envy you."

"Do you?"

"Mm-hmm. Do you know how often I wished my husband didn't speak? I live in hope one day I'll get through a movie without commentary."

We cracked up.

"There's a fight tomorrow night," she continued. "There's a lot of fights on as they gear up for— Never mind. Doesn't matter. The one I'm looking at is in Waterford. Figure we not push it by going into Harlow."

Good idea.

"It's a decent pot. Fighters get five hundred just for showing up. Odds won't be on the new guy to win, so he has the chance to clean up. If he has what it takes," she added.

"After all this time, Jo. You still doubt me."

She gave me a lopsided smile. "I recently learned there was more to you than fellow food enthusiast. Forgive me if it takes a while to build a new relationship."

"That's fair."

The guys finished their pacing and entered the ring. Ian didn't have much height on Brutal. It was more he was thick and ropey while Brutal appeared slim. Until you squeezed his forearm and broke your fingers on the steel plate running beneath Brutal's skin.

Trouble is Ian looks like he has the same thing going on.

I didn't doubt Brutal for a second. My concern was Jo's point that someone who practiced in an empty ring, naturally lost an edge sharpened by opponents.

Jo rang the bell, setting the guys circling each other.

Ian was first to make a move. He came at Brutal with a jab that was ducked. Five minutes into the match, I covered a laugh at Jo's wide eyes.

She said they were just sparring. I had an inkling Ian was more than that. He was one of her best guys. Her best guy who couldn't land a solid hit.

There was no other phrase for it but Brutal was toying with him. Left hook came at him, was deflected, and Brutal shot a right uppercut to the chest. Ian stumbled away, and came in hot, roaring his frustration.

Brutal laid him out with one hit.

Jo looked at her guy prostrate on the canvas to Brutal chugging his water, barely a sweat on him.

"I'll see you tomorrow night."

BRUTAL

I parked two blocks down the street as Meza directed.

We were in the affluent part of Waterford. Apartment buildings with doormen and valet parking on Restaurant Row. We drove past the line of five-star eateries with Adeline naming the chef and cuisine for each one.

"I used to see myself owning a restaurant on this street," she mused. "Every criminal needs a day job."

I chuckled.

"Do you know what you'd be doing in another life?"

Yes. I know exactly where I'd be.

I peered in the distance to Global Consolidated. I couldn't see the sky-scraper, of course. We were miles away and well into the night. Still, I knew it was there just beyond my sight. No matter where I was at any time, I knew which way pointed home.

Rounding the hood, I opened Adeline's door and gave her my arm. She liked me doing gentlemanly shit like that. She thought it told her something I couldn't say out loud.

"Jo's directions were to turn on Hamilton Terrace. It's number twenty-six."

Hamilton Terrace was a long stretch of commercial road. A good place to hold an illegal fight. Promoters didn't have to worry about residents call-ing the cops on cars clogging up the street or suspicious gang types loitering around.

We rounded a brick wall and arrived at number twenty-six.

"I don't understand," Adeline said. "Is Jo blowing us off?"

Standing before us was Wilmott's Private School for Girls. The main building loomed above the lot, partially concealing the two smaller buildings behind.

"Why'd she bring us out here?"

I motioned toward the shadows.

Beside the hedge, a man lit up in the glow from his cigarette. I tugged Adeline along.

"Name."

"Meza," she replied.

"Round back. Follow the noise."

We didn't hear any noise till we cleared the main school building and wound up on the path curving through the lawn. Someone went into the gymnasium, and sound poured out the open door.

"They're holding the fight in a private school gym? Is that how it's usually done?" Adeline asked.

I nodded.

Why not? The brick wall around the property provided privacy. Anyone that could stumble in on our activities left campus hours ago, and the principal or members of the school board likely had skin in this game. The Kings and a few other crime outfits had put considerable effort into capitalizing on the rogue blood sport sweeping through Rockchapel.

How to get Leighbridge money in the pot? Where to host the events for moneybags to feel safe parking their cars on the street and walking down blind alleys?

"Good evening." A young woman in a bikini stopped us at the threshold. "Step over here, please."

This was the answer.

The bleachers filled up with men in suits and women in their best. An attendant at the bottom handed out cushions while his counterpart wrote in a notebook, collecting bets. The gym's hardwood floors gleamed. A humming heater maintained a comfortable temperature. In the middle of the gym, stood the six-sided platform and the bars that caged it in.

Some fights were held in their homes. Others on properties they or the Kings owned. Either way, the big fishes were hooked.

There was money to be made tonight. A shit ton.

I spread my arms for the pat-down, enduring the thorough search for weapons. The only fighting, bleeding, or trashing allowed was in the cage.

Meza jogged over to us. "I do like a man who's on time. Come with me."

She gripped my shoulder, leading me to a group of men huddled near the unisex locker room. Adeline was right beside us.

They stopped talking as we approached.

"Gentlemen," Jo greeted. "This is my new guy, Brutal. Consider tonight his qualifying match. If he wins, I want him in the rotation."

"Brutal." A man in a long, black coat and steel-toe shoes stepped out of the pack. Small, narrowed eyes set in a face riddled with pockmarks. "Now, why do I know that name?"

I didn't react as he got in my face, thumping our chests.

"Oh, I recall. That's the name of one of those Merchant bitch boys who killed our boss."

"Easy." Jo got between and shoved him back. "You know the rules, Lane. Check your beef at the door."

"I enforce those rules, sweetheart." His smile was nasty. "I'll let myself off with a warning just this once."

"No, you won't," she gritted. "Or me and my fighters are out. Good luck putting on a good show with the drug-addled bums you drag in off the street."

"Better not risk it," Adeline spoke up. "Especially since your information is off. The Merchants didn't kill your boss."

"Three of our guys escaped the massacre at Infinity," snapped Lane. "They told us the whole fucking thing. Get him out of here!"

"Your friends left out a few details. Unsurprisingly since they took off and left your precious boss to die. Or did they leave that part out?"

Lane shoved past Meza. He tried towering over Adeline and found me in his way.

"Got something you want to say?" he asked, though he didn't look away from me. "Spit it out."

"The Infinity was a trap for both the Kings and Merchants. Your boss, Enzo, unwisely chose to blackmail Richard La Roche into taking a smaller cut of the counterfeiting operation. Any of this ringing bells?"

His eyelid twitched. Adeline rang a bell.

"La Roche sent the Kings to kill the Merchants, and the Merchants to kill the Kings. It's after Bianchi shared the truth of what he'd done that your buddies abandoned him to his fate."

"Abandoned him to be killed by you!"

"Killed by one of La Roche's men," she said, "after he dropped that La Roche was Kieran."

"What?"

They were all listening now.

The men converged on her—twitching for their confiscated weapons. "What did you say?"

"Richard La Roche had the ledger. He was Kieran. I say was and had, because on the same day your boss was killed—abandoned by his guards who hit the door the second he said ledger—La Roche was murdered too. His guards were killed and the safe ransacked. Now, you can direct that misplaced anger at Brutal, or you can ask which one of those traitorous bastards got to La Roche first?"

Lane traded looks with two men from the group.

If I wasn't me, I'd stand speechless in the face of her like the rest of them—if for a different reason. A few words, and Adeline had Lane questioning what he knew. Did his brothers leave Bianchi to die to get the ledger for themselves? And did one succeed?

Lane scoffed. "Fucking lies. You've got no reason to tell us this."

"Just like it's a lie La Roche was murdered less than an hour after Bianchi? Did he up and bash himself over the head?"

"For all we know, you and your boyfriend have the ledger. You want us to distrust our own people. Further destabilize the Kings."

Adeline rolled her eyes. "So, we have the ledger. The single most powerful weapon in all of Cinco City. And instead of using it to get all the money we want, crush the Kings with the weight of their secrets, and set ourselves up in a Leighbridge mansion where the only time I have to deal with you is by ransom note...

"Instead of doing all of that, we've come here to fight in a match, and tell you lies you can easily verify yourself. I see why you are where you are and not duking it out with Thiago Pais to rule the Kings. Strategic thinking isn't your strong suit."

Lane launched at her. I shoved him back, sending him crashing into two of his guys and taking all three of them down.

"Hey! That's enough," Meza shouted.

Lane shot to his feet, eyes blazing.

"Looks to me you're missing some details about how your boss died," she went on. "Not a surprise if his guards fucked off and ditched him. I'd look into cleaning house before kicking off a war that ruins both our businesses. Can he fight or not?"

Lane gave me a long, measuring look. "Yeah," he said. "Put him in the cage. I'll enjoy this."

Josephine didn't budge. "If he wins, he's in the rotation."

"He won't win. But should a miracle happen, yes, he's in the rotation." Lane grinned. "More chances for me to watch the great leader of the Merchants get his ass beat for my spare change."

I thought Adeline might launch herself at him next. I led her away. Wouldn't do any good toward getting us out of our current predicament if we were kicked out empty-handed. Besides, Lane was nothing more than noise and hot air. A true threat didn't shout about what they were going to do. They just did it.

"Don't worry about him," said Meza. The three of us grabbed a section of the bottom bleacher. "Desmond Lane took over running the Kings' fights after Jace Parker died. He talks a good game, but this is the only part of their business not suffering after the hits they've taken. He won't do anything to mess this up. Especially if you bring in money."

Drifting past her, I landed on Lane and those six men in their huddle—with one addition.

A well-built guy in jeans and a ripped shirt bowed his neck in Lane's grip. Lane was clearly intense about something. He jabbed his chest, going on while the other guys nodded.

"The locker room's over there," she said. "Get changed while I talk to the bookies."

Standing up, I shrugged off my tie, folded it, and placed it next to Adeline. My jacket went with it.

"Uhh. Did you hear her mention the locker rooms?"

I flashed her a look amid unbuttoning my shirt.

"Oh, let me guess. You're not setting foot in a place dozens upon dozens of sweaty teenagers have tramped through."

I winked. *Got it in one.*

"Yeah, take it off," someone wolf-whistled.

I looked up and shot them a wink too.

"Careful, Brutal. Or we will get kicked out for fighting."

Laughing, I kissed her in apology. My whistles turned to groans.

Stripped down to my pants, I took my gloves out of my pocket and tugged them on. Now I was ready.

I stepped up to the cage. Through the metal, I watched Lane walk my opponent to the other set of stairs and pat his back.

"Ladies and gentlemen, welcome." The speakers ripped through the chatter. "We've got a treat for you tonight. In one corner, we have the undefeated, unstoppable, unforgiving Gaaaagggee!"

Gage ran up the steps. "Yeah!" Hooting and hollering, he circled the cage, pounding on his chest. The crowd ate it up.

Passing me, Gage drew a line across his neck.

"Don't forget to get those bets in. Once I ring the bell, that's it."

I rolled my neck, eyes falling shut.

"Now for that treat. Facing him tonight is none other than the self-named Brutal." The announcer's voice changed. "Maybe you recognize this moniker as one of the names scrolling on the bottom of the news screen. Baris 'Brutal' Alexander is none other than the leader of the Merchants."

So many inaccuracies in a handful of sentences.

I didn't open my eyes even as the cheers turned to boos.

"A few of you will know him personally as the guy slinking in the corner of the bar, hiding his face while he sells his services to the highest bidder. Well today, folks, he's slinking in here, begging for a handout. I say if *Brutal* wants a beating, let's give him one!"

"Yeah!" the crowd roared—stomping their feet on the bleachers. Don't let the diamonds and finery fool you. Everyone in this room merely vacationed in polite society. This was their true, debased selves.

"Kill him!"

"Rip him apart!"

"Gage! Gage! Gage!"

The noise faded.

"You've got a lot of anger in you, boy."

I ran at Jeffery and was promptly knocked on my butt. Pushing up to my knees, I glared at him.

"What?" he taunted. "You're mad. You can't land a single shot and your constant defeat has grown humiliating. What are you going to do about it?"

"Argh!"

I charged him, gloves up, and readied to strike.

The boxing coach sidestepped. I sailed into the ropes, smashing my face, and winding up where I always did. On my back.

"Want to know what everyone gets wrong?" His shoes stopped short of my head. He peered down at me. "They say to let your rage go. It poisons you. Wears you down. You'll be much happier if you just forgive and forget.

"Bullshit."

My eyes went round. That was a don't-ever-say word.

Jeffery helped me up, dusting me off. "You're eight years old. Old enough to hear the truth," he said. "Anger isn't poison. It's fuel. You think people step into this ring singing, 'Kumbaya. Peace and love. Let's all be friends.'

"They're feeling what you do right now." He rested a fist on my chest. "The fire. The rage. The need to prove yourself. These feelings can either cloud your mind and lead to reckless mistakes like a face full of rope. Or you can channel it. Let it drive you to think, plan, and strike without mercy.

"Anger is good, son.

"The angry don't quit."

Opening my eyes, I walked into the ring.

The shouting and boos were buzzing in my ear. The crowd didn't matter. Their animosity was insignificant. The snarl on Gage's face didn't faze me.

There was only me and what I came in here to do.

The bell sounded.

Gage came in hot. His punch snapped my head around, careening me into the bars. He didn't let me recover. Punches rained down on me.

"Kill him!"

I kept my hands up under blows coming at my face, arms, stomach, and—

I jerked away.

—my groin.

"Brutal!" That voice I knew well. "What are you doing?! Crush him!"

Ah. The dulcet tones of the woman pledged to own me till the day I died and beyond.

I skipped back toward the opposite side of the cage, bouncing on the balls of my feet, and keeping Gage in sight.

He spun in a twirl more suited to ballet and connected with my shoulder.

I went down and Gage jumped on me. He straddled me. Pinned to the floor, again I covered my head as I was pummeled. Through my arms, a malicious grin twisted his face.

"Brutal!" Adeline rattled the bars. "Get up. This guy is nothing. No, he one day hopes to be nothing! Destroy him!"

"Your girlfriend's done, baby," he growled at Adeline. "But if you suck my dick nice, I'll let you—"

I caught his flying punch. Twisting his wrist, I bent his arm unnaturally over his shoulder.

"Argh!"

Gage struck me in the throat. My grip loosened, and he climbed off, retreating to size me up. Again, we circled.

"Come on!" someone screamed. "Where's the blood?!"

"Break his arm!"

"Make him your bitch!"

Must have been the encouragement Gage was looking for. He ran, fist raised, and suddenly, fell to his knee. He swept my feet out from under me, dropping me on my backside.

"Finish him," Lane shouted.

Gage stood over me. He raised his foot, readying to stomp my kneecap.

I rolled out of the way, and kept rolling ahead of his chase.

The watchers howled. "What the hell's he doing?"

I hit the metal—nowhere else to run.

"This will teach you to fuck with the Kings."

Pressure caved my gut and ricocheted shockwaves up my torso. I curled into the kick, and captured his leg. Faster than he could blink, I wrenched his leg, spinning him flat on his face.

I rose to my feet. Unharmed. Ready.

And angry.

So that's what Lane told him. Orders to injure me permanently. If I tried walking into another fight, it'd be with a limp.

I seized Gage by the scruff and pants.

Might as well return the favor.

Lifting him overhead, I bellowed for the frenzied crowd, twisting with my prize.

"Yeah! Throw him! Throw him! Throw him!"

How quickly an audience turns.

I heaved and flung one hundred sixty pounds of him at raw, unforgiving steel. Gage crashed into it headfirst. He collapsed on the canvas—dazed.

Good fighter. Terrible instincts. He should've noticed I was literally pulling my punches, observing how he fought.

Flipping him over, I straddled him, grabbed his hair, and punched him one, two, five times in the face. Blood spurted from his nose—covering my gloves.

"Brutal! Brutal!"

Pain exploded in the back of my head.

I tipped off him, hauling away. I hadn't expected a back kick to the head. The kid may not make a shit embarrassing spectacle of himself after all. He'd still lose, but at least he could say he went down with dignity.

"That's it." Gage reached in his back pocket. "I'm fucking up that pretty face."

He slid his fingers through the brass knuckles.

I showed no outward reaction. There wasn't much of an inner one either. Lane made the rules. He'd break them for his fighter with the approval of all watching. Anything goes in the cage.

I waved my hands.

Come at me.

He didn't. Gage stepped to the side, moving me in turn.

He's learning.

Gage jabbed, forcing me to duck the brass. He jabbed again.

"Baby, you've got this," Adeline cried. "Holy shit, the insanely freaky things I'm going to do to you when you win."

My cock twitched, tripping me up. I quickly recovered in time to lurch back and let the hit glance off my shoulder.

I once believed there was nothing and no one who could distract me in a fight. But then, I hadn't met five foot three inches of raw sexual energy and homicidal tendencies.

Gage slung a right cross. I ducked, clamped his elbow, and drove the momentum the rest of the way. He grunted, hitting his own shoulder.

His elbow locked in my hold, I gripped his wrist and twisted. The pop and bugged eyes went with the dislocation.

"Ahhh—!"

I punched his fractured nose and broke it, dropping him where he stood. Gage didn't get up.

"Brutal! Brutal!"

Fists high, I rounded the cage, showing off the bloody remains of my victory.

This wasn't vanity. It was business. Hated enemy turned champion. The members would demand me back if only to see how many men the Kings threw at me before I was taken down. We'd have the money to throw the party in two weekends. Four to outfit the men we had left for an assault against Gianna Cross. Eight when I could command a higher price—raking in all the money the Merchants needed to rebuild.

And then I would leave.

I halted in front of Adeline. She jumped and clapped, graphically detailing my prizes.

I couldn't leave them—the woman who loved me and the men who became my partners—in a shitty hotel, scrounging their way back on top. My vow recognized what I owed to the people who'd gotten me this far. When Adeline was happy, I would move on.

"Anger is good, son. The angry don't quit."

"Son?"

I tore away.

Father strode into the gym. "Who do you think you are, calling my boy son? He's an Alexander. Grandson of Rudolph Alexander. Heir to this city. While your mother cleans my toilets! If the likes of you is to address him as anything, it's young master or sir."

"Mr. Alexander, I meant no—"

"You meant to act familiar with my son. Pretend as though you are his peer or equal while not even age could grant you either. You're fired."

"But, Dad," I cried. "He didn't—"

"Silence!" Blackening eyes flashed. "How dare you interrupt. You're to stand there and be quiet, boy."

I stood there, and was quiet.

The memory shook me loose, allowing me to climb out of the cage.

"Fantastic," Josephine said. "You and I are going to do very well together, Brutal. I promise you that. Wait here while I collect our winnings."

She released me into Adeline's hug.

"You had me going there," she said. "I know toying with people is your thing, but give a girl fewer heart attacks, sweetass."

Sweetass?

Sinjin she called by his name. To Cash's dismay, he'd been dubbed "toy boy." Sweetass would not be mine. I'd have to stomp this at the knees.

I nipped her nose.

"Ow," she yelped. "There has to be a better way for you to tell me you don't like something."

Her right cheek received a smack.

"That's better," she said, giggling. "But I love it when you do it, so there could be some mixed signals."

We stumbled onto the bleachers, lips locked. I finally broke away to let her dress and clean me up.

Adeline cradled my hand in her lap, dabbing my bruised knuckles with swabs she found in the girls' room first-aid kit.

"I saw him pull the brass on you," she said softly. "I bet all the money we made that Lane told him to mess you up good. It'll be more of that if we get near the Kings and their fights. The Rolling Ninety-Nines and Hell's Outlaws run fights too. Can we stick with them?"

Their guys fight in the Kings' arena. The Kings fight in theirs. I can't be in the rotation and avoid the players who dominate the field.

I gave Adeline a simple no.

"Then I'm coming to all of your fights. Don't try to stop me. You need someone in your corner, warning you if the Kings try something."

As helpful as that would be, her sexy pep talks were bound to get me in trouble.

Josephine returned with a bottle of water and my winnings. Five thousand dollars to show the Kings up in their own domain.

I passed it all to Adeline.

What did I need of money? Like Sinjin said, money is easy. I could always get money. I used to have more in my bank account than ten of the richest families in Cinco combined.

Money was never what I was after.

Adeline brushed her lips over my cheek. "When we get back, I'll give you the rest of your winnings."

I smiled down at her.

Ruling Cinco City alongside a beautiful woman wasn't what I started this for either.

Bellona.

I will find her. I would see through what I started twelve years ago. Then I would leave.

A lock of Adeline's hair wrapped around my finger—gently tugged to bring her lips to me.

We didn't get into this to find each other, for all that she tempted me to forget. I wanted there to be a way that I might keep her when this was over, but it was impossible. Adeline made a vow for her family, and I made one for mine.

If there was any part of her speech in the basement that I understood completely, it was that. I would not hold her vows against her. Nor would I let her stand in the way of mine.

ADELINE

Mercer counted Baris's winnings into neat, glorious piles.

"How much more do we need?" I asked.

He tugged me onto his lap, cradling me between his arms. It was just the two of us today. Killian, Saint, and Baris went out to round up the remaining members of the gang. It was time for the Merchants to go traditional.

I snuggled into his warmth, pressing my forehead against his jaw. It was then I noticed how rare this was. Me and Mercer. Alone together. I wish I could say I didn't know why.

"Another five grand should do it." He moved against me. "A thousand for the deejay. Two thousand for food and booze. The final three will cover renting the place from Zayn, and a snack on the way back."

"Two thousand dollars to serve food for one night? I've been undercharging."

"Don't let Killian hear you say that."

We laughed.

I rubbed the light stubble along his cheek. "So..."

"So?" he prompted.

"Who is this Alaric persona you've constructed? What's he like? What's he into?"

"I've told you the important bits. He dropped out of Cinco University to pursue the pleasures of the flesh. Started working in a strip club where he picked up clients and contacts. The rest was history. Now, Alaric is one of the most sought-after escorts in the city. Potential clients pay just to get his number."

"How much of his story is yours?"

"Ah. Another attempt to lead me into the conversation?" He twisted to let me see his grin. "I told you, gorgeous. You want to know something, all you have to do is ask."

I studied him.

Mercer said that. He may even mean it. But since the beginning, there had been something between us.

A wall.

He deflected my kisses. Didn't touch me the few times I slipped into his bed at night, hoping we'd do more than sleep. I tried to see it as him respecting my feelings. We couldn't be together while Alaric was in business.

I told myself that was the reason over and over. It only worked some of the time. The other times, I'd remember Gianna laughing over Mercer concealing his secret from the woman he loved. It'd be the first thought, with the second being he never told me he loved me. I said it for him. I filled in a lot of blanks in Mercer's place. It seemed easier than asking him.

If Mercer was like me. The shadow. The infiltrator. I'd never truly know the real him. By now, he could be buried under too many layers to find.

"What's that look?" he asked.

"This is my 'should I bother asking when he has no reason to tell the truth' look."

He whistled. "Ouch. I've done a lot of things, Adeline. Lied to almost everyone I know with the remorse of a sociopath. But as much as you may have no reason to believe this, I've never lied to you."

"Never? I seem to remember a certain gentleman telling me he doesn't do nicknames."

"Don't get nitpicky."

Snorting, I giggled. "All right, fair enough. It's a small fib in the grand scheme of things. I suspect you're trying to keep me as separate as possible from Alaric's life." I rested my hand on his. "Thank you."

"It brings me no pleasure seeing that look on your face."

I winced. "I'll work on that. Didn't even know I do it."

"You should see the face you make when Killian deliberately pushes your buttons, and Saint announces his intent to keep you for the rest of his life."

"You really have people all figured out."

"No, love. People are easy. It'll take me a lifetime of study to understand Adeline Redgrave."

"I'm not doing anything for the next seventy or eighty years." I licked my lips, flicking his gaze to my mouth. "I'm happy to be your subject."

Mercer rubbed his nose on mine, trapping my breath in my lungs. "Ask," he whispered.

"Would you ever give up your life as Alaric... for me?"

"Yes."

I don't know who moved first—him or me. Our lips collided in a shower of sparks lighting one nerve ending on fire and setting off a chain reaction that ignited the rest.

My fingers curled in his inky strands, pulling him closer still. If Mercer tried to duck away, tossing me some flirty joke, and saying shit about it not being our time yet. I would kill him.

Flat-out strangle him and toss the body out the window. I was beyond tired of having the man I love within reach, and somehow still too far to touch.

A ragged groan of a dying man ripped from Mercer's throat. "Adeline."

He shot up, upending the table. It crashed to the floor in a shower of bills. Mercer slipped on one carrying me to the couch.

We fell on the cushions, cracking up. My toes curled at the sound.

A real laugh. Not a winking smirk or a measured chuckle. Mercer Santos happy, relaxed, and unrestrained. It was what I wanted this Christmas and all the Christmases to come.

He wrapped my leg around his waist, digging his erection in my middle. Moaning, my head fell back, exposing my throat to his soft, nipping kisses, leaving marks shouting to the world my final love had claimed me.

"Come back here."

I heeded the growl—capturing his lips happily.

There was nothing on this earth like kissing Mercer. All of my guys showed their personality in their kisses. Saint was a wild, out-of-control roller coaster that went off track. Cash was slow-burning passion that left you dazed and hungry for more. Baris was dominance and control—taking without asking and giving more in return.

Mercer was like me. Years of hiding who we were and making ourselves small to fit into the mold others wanted us to be. Gracious, willing lover. Sweet, obliging cook. Freed from those roles, we didn't hold back.

We flipped, rolled, and tore at each other. Our tongues battled in a war of give-and-take—his stroking mine to make me wet. Me biting his to hear that ragged groan once more. It was the sound of Mercer Santos losing control.

He slipped under my shirt. I squeaked as my bra was popped open and slid down my arms. He had that thing off in four seconds flat. That had to be some kind of record.

Mercer cupped my breast, swirling his thumb around the hardened pebble, and dipping in and out to give it a teasing flick.

"Yes," I hissed. *I've waited so long for this.*

I squeezed my thighs, grinding harder on his cock.

"I love you."

Mercer tensed. Rocking back, his mossy green eyes were huge.

"Geez, Mercer. Was it that much of a surprise?"

"Adeline, I— Fuck!" He gripped the arm of his chair, closing his eyes as a shudder went through his body.

My mouth fell open. "Did you just...?"

"I swear that's never happened before. Shit, you just— You drive me insane!"

I had no idea what to say. Mercer/Alaric, Cinco's top escort, shot his rocket before the finish line. I don't think I could've been paid a higher compliment if People Magazine's sexiest men alive for the past decade all dropped on their knees and asked me to be their queen.

I bit my lip to pen a giggle. "It's okay, baby. I told you I have this effect on people."

"We never speak of this again."

Now I did giggle. "Stays between you and me. But you know what this means, don't you?"

He sat us up, pulling me onto his lap. "What?"

"Your fella's got something to prove now. He'll have to spend the next several nights showing me he lives up to his reputation."

Mercer shook his head, slight grin on his lips. "You're dangerous, Redgrave. Oh so very dangerous."

"Are you just figuring that out?"

EVENTUALLY, WE STOPPED making out on the couch like teenagers and collected the money. The two of us packed up in his car, and drove around making the deposits, booking the caterer, arranging the deejay, and handing over three thousand for one night in a Leighbridge loft.

I spun on the carpet, trying to take everything in at once.

When Mercer said loft in Leighbridge, I pictured the one owned by the Merchants. All windows. One bedroom. Exposed brick and no wasted space.

This space ticked off all the boxes, and was still nothing like ours.

A free-standing staircase led up to the bedroom loft. A king-size bed and soft black carpet took up most of the space. Next to it was the bathroom and shower encased in glass. Yes, glass. Anyone getting in there was visible to the entire room.

On the bottom floor, it was sparse of furniture—which suited for a party. The furniture that was there were high-backed leather chairs, more soft rugs, and a long table perfect for food and booze.

I wandered into the kitchen, checking out the goodies the wealthy could afford to outfit themselves with. Believe me, when I had the money, people would pay to take tours of my kitchen. It'd be that impressive.

"I'm guessing I can't come to this party."

"Can't risk Perez seeing you," he replied.

"I know," I sighed. "Still, I've always wondered what it's like to be a guest of a party like this, and not the one holding the tray."

"Don't say that to me." Arms encircled my waist. "Now, I have to drop another ten grand to make that dream reality."

I smiled, so happy to be near him I could bust.

"One day," I said. "When I have something to celebrate again."

I couldn't forget why we were here. Laying a trap for my best friend's boyfriend, so we would have the final showdown that would decide the path the rest of our lives would take.

"You will." He kissed my temple. "Things can get in the way—distract with something that seems better, shinier, or more tempting. At our cores, we know who we are and what we want. At the center of you and Gianna are two young girls who suffered loss and found each other.

"You held the other together. She was strong when you couldn't be, and you for her. She'll realize that friendship means more than any ledger. Especially when suspicion and obsession force her to drive away everyone that cares about her. The ledger is no substitute for you."

Tears prickled my eyes. There Mercer went again—saying exactly what I needed to hear.

"Thank you," I whispered.

"Tell me when you need to hear it again. I'll remind you everything will be okay as often as it takes."

"I might need to hear it a lot," I confessed. "I just wish I could talk to her. Gianna isn't picking up unknown numbers anymore. Dad can't get through to her either."

"This is a conversation that needs to happen face-to-face anyway."

I nodded. *Face-to-face, and alone. After Raul tells us where she's staying, how do I convince them to let me go in there by myself? Won't be an easy conversation considering the last time I wound up hogtied over a bomb.*

"Come on," Mercer said. "We're done for today. The rest of the money is for more alcohol, spreading the word, and paying for a sizable amount of drugs."

I spun under his arm, hugging him as we walked out. "You promised me a snack."

"Farmhouse is on the next street over."

"Farmhouse? That's an all-organic five-star restaurant. Hardly a snack."

He winked. "Time to see what it's like on the other side. You're done holding the tray."

BRUTAL

Adeline drove that night.

It had been a week since my win in a girls' school gym. A few days after, I got the call from Meza that she had another fight for me. I was officially in the rotation.

"The Outlaws are running this one. You fight one of their guys and then the winner goes on to face Zhang, one of the Kings' men. I'm sorry, but there is no avoiding Lane and his beaters. Not in this city. The Kings are the backbone of the circuit," she told me. "At least we'll be on Outlaw territory. As much as I can, I'll get you fights on their or the Ninety-Nines' turf. Less of the bullshit Gage tried to pull with the brass."

I admired her optimism, but we could be on the White House lawn surrounded by Secret Service guys ready to put us down with prejudice, and the Kings would find a way to get their revenge. They didn't care whose turf they were on.

The most feared gang in the city suffered the loss of reputation by the exposure of the Castian, loss of revenue with the outing of their richest and vilest clients, a hit to their business following the death of La Roche and the crumbling of his empire, and the humiliation of one of the men responsible getting in their cage, and tossing their best fighter around like a stuffed doll.

They would do whatever necessary to take those stripes out of my ass. Tonight, I'd be on my guard.

"Nervous?" Adeline rubbed my thigh. "Do you get nervous?"

No.

"Good. Such an unattractive trait in a man."

I barked a laugh. She was good at getting me to do that. So good, she probably thought I laughed this freely with everyone. That was so far from the truth, they were on different continents. Before Adeline, I counted on one hand how many times I cracked a smile in an entire year. After Adeline, it was almost a daily occurrence.

This was how I measured my life. Before Adeline. After Adeline.

"I'm kidding," she said. "It's okay to be nervous. So okay I'll be nervous for the both of us. I didn't like the look Lane gave us when we left the other night. It wasn't a look that said letting go and moving on."

She was right about that.

"I've got your back," she said. "If he tries anything, I'll kill Lane, you kill the fighter, we'll jump the bookies for all the money they've got, and hightail it out of there. Deal?"

We bumped fists. *Deal.*

Never mind doing so would put us on the kill-on-sight list for the Kings, Outlaws, and whoever else felt like taking a piece. What else was new? Riding wanted lists was our pastime.

Meza's directions took us through Waterford and into North Quay. I recognized the address as one of the dock warehouses. Not too far from where Thiago Pais dropped his rejected escorts.

Adeline parked the car well away from number fifty-eight, tucked in the alley between two warehouses.

"It's spooky out here." We broke free of the buildings and headed down the route GPS told us to go. "If this is a trap, this is the place to do it."

I looked at her questioningly.

"No, I trust Josephine. I don't doubt the Kings would pay her a handsome amount to lead us to our deaths, but that woman I mentioned, Miranda. She's Jo's half sister. A guy assaulted her outside a bar. Beat her pretty badly.

"Rockchapel looks like a rough neighborhood from the outside, and I won't lie, we beat the other boroughs in theft, burglaries, and drug offenses, but that was the first violent rape in a while. I papered the streets with the guy's description and tracked him down in a shithole above a laundromat. Jo was just the owner of a restaurant I liked back then. After I dragged that piece of garbage into the police station, we became friends.

"I know it's hard to trust my judgment these days, but there are a few things I can say without doubt. Jo would not do the bidding of a man who did what was done to Leah Tyler. Especially since it's all but certain Thiago Pais is taking over the Kings."

I did not have trouble trusting her judgment. Adeline's instincts about people were spot-on. She picked Desmond Lane as a threat the same time I did. She was allowed to have a blind spot for people she loved.

I wanted to say that to her. I opened my mouth to do so.

My chest tightened—pressure building around my throat, and I let it go.

Instead, I clasped the back of her neck and stroked just under her ear.

She hummed. "I love you too."

Looking in her eyes, I pointed to her, then me, made a fist, and tapped my mouth.

Her brows furrowed. Adeline's mind-reading abilities stopped short of these gestures. She had no clue what I meant.

That was okay. Knowing wouldn't make her feel better. It was just something I had to tell her. I would leave the four of them with a lot left unsaid. But not this.

The last time, we were told to follow the noise. Same advice held true.

We passed Warehouse 54. Our shoes crunched on the wet, gravelly path. Rounding the corner, faint cheering reached us. The crowd was whipped up.

Two guys in leather vests and tattoos covering their visible skin, put us through the routine of asking for my sponsor and patting us down.

"Good luck."

Music thumping, people shouting, naked girls dancing in the cage to whistles and hollers, and none of it was enough to cover their sniggering as we passed through.

Adeline glanced at them over her shoulder. "Jo can't be bought by the Kings, but is there a chance the Outlaws can?"

Even if I could say for sure, I wouldn't. A fighter doesn't worry about what could be. They take the hits as they come.

Tiered seating had been set up in the warehouse as well, allowing everyone their money's worth in seeing inside a cage twice the size of the gym match.

The warehouse better resembled an airplane hangar. It was wide-open empty space.

Jo signaled us from the other side of the cage. We followed her into a back room, getting away from the noise. A small storage area, it didn't have much to say for itself other than an uneven table, some chairs, a back door, and boxes covering the wall. I started stripping down.

"I've made my position clear," Meza said. "If the Outlaws or Kings try something, I'm out. My husband and I have some money saved up. I'm not opposed to early retirement."

"Thanks, Jo." Adeline clasped her friend's shoulder. "But anything goes in the ring, right?"

"'Fraid so. These people pay for blood. The more the better." She jerked a chin at me. "He knows that, and he's ready. We're looking at six grand tonight. Brutal's taking it home."

We smashed fists.

Adeline was right about this one. She was growing on me too.

The grinding music cut off. "Ladies and gentlemen—"

"That's our cue."

"—are you ready to live like outlaws?!"

I jogged out to deafening screams.

"Tonight, we've got one of our own going up against a Merchant himself, Brutal."

The boos were right on cue.

"You probably didn't recognize this bitch without a mask on, but it's fine, you'll get a good look at his face when it's smashed against the bars."

I sought the speaker through the crowd, finding him standing by the bleachers on my right. It'd have to be well after the fight and far from here, but this mouthy shit was next.

"Hatchet's going to teach this fool a lesson, then he's going on to fight Zhang himself."

The roars rattled the cage.

I didn't know Zhang personally. Never fought the man. But you couldn't know the fight scene in this city and miss his name. He was one of the Kings' best.

"Let's hear it for Hatchet!"

A guy in shorts rocking a buzz cut and twice the tattoos of the doormen combined, strolled out of a room next to mine. A brief glimpse revealed a television, food, and entourage.

Hatchet took one look, curled his lip, and dismissed me without another glance.

A kiss landed on my shoulder. "You could take him in your sleep with both hands tied behind your back and an anvil on your chest."

Descriptive.

"Finish him quick, babe. Make it hurt."

I smirked. *Yes, ma'am.*

"Coming in right on time to get his ass beat, Brutal!"

Flexing my gloved fists, I jogged inside the cage. Hatchet rolled his neck and worked out his shoulders. The sneer hadn't improved. On the contrary, it was a full-blown snarl. Far as I knew, the Merchants hadn't crossed paths with the Outlaws. Though it's possible he hated anyone who dared to face him.

Ding!

Hatchet charged me, tossing a punch that I knocked aside and countered with my own. He twisted and the hit sailed past his nose.

Pain exploded under my rib. I grunted—the stroke resounding through my liver.

Hatchet was fast. Very fucking fast. The only person I knew with reflexes that quick was St. John himself.

Meza was stressed that years out of the ring had dulled me. Far from it, grappling with a professional knife-thrower, psychopath, and king of the un-repentant assholes had kept me plenty sharp.

Sharp enough to recognize five seconds in that this guy isn't to be underesti-mated.

Facing him, I grinned. *Good.*

Hatchet's eyes narrowed. His lip curled to contort his whole face. I expected some trash talk would be forthcoming, but he didn't say a word.

Also good. I couldn't stand fighters who couldn't shut their mouth. I inevitably punched their teeth in to shut it for them.

I was starting to like this guy.

Hatchet came in hot again. I spun around and made a run for it.

The announcer cackled. "Giving up so soon, boy? No one leaves Outlaw country!"

"Outlaw! Hatchet!"

I reached the bars, spun, and heaved myself up. Both feet kicked in Hatchet's chest, sending him flying over his feet and landing flat on his back. The man wanted to give a real fight, the least I could do was return the courtesy.

"Agh!" Hatchet wheezed, coughing and hacking, trying to draw in breath.

I circled him—ignoring the obvious chance to finish him for good.

"Brutal!" Adeline shouted. "Don't play with your food."

I laughed. *So my lady demands.*

Clamping his throat, I lifted Hatchet overhead. He wasn't sneering now.

Eyes bugged, he smashed his fist on my elbow, fighting to break my hold.

Grabbing my arm with both hands, he rocked up and hooked his legs around my neck—wrenching his whole body.

We both dropped. The sting of canvas bit my bare back.

Hatchet didn't waste the advantage. He smashed his foot in my jaw, breaking my hold on his neck.

"Brutal!"

Hatchet got to his feet, taking my arm with him, and grinding his heel in my gut. In this position, my arm would break with one jerk.

"Brutal, get up," Adeline cried.

Blue eyes burning, Hatchet dropped one hand and reached for his waistband. He tugged his shorts down in one move, and gripped his shaft. My eyes bugged.

I kicked his thigh.

"Argh!"

Breaking free, I rolled out of the way as the first splash of piss hit the canvas.

"What the fuck is wrong with you?!" Adeline screamed.

Hatchet whizzed a semicircle around me, his contempt rolling over me and silencing the audience. He finished with a rough shake, snapped his pants up, and glared as if asking what the fuck would I do now?

Slowly, I straightened—looking down at the yellow puddle leeching toward me.

Something snapped.

Taking a running leap, I bounded over the puddle, missing the punch he threw at my head. I snapped around, took hold of his arm, and broke it over my leg.

"Ahh!" The scream broke the silence, kicking the bloodthirsty howling to unknown decibels.

Sharp, burning, all-consuming rage swept through my soul and funneled into what became the single purpose of my life.

Destroy this man.

Clamping his neck, I ran Hatchet at the bars—ramming his face into the metal.

One. Two. Three. Four. Five.

"Brutal! Brutal!"

Six. Seven.

Hatchet stopped flailing at four. Limp in my hold, his face was an unrecognizable mass of blood and tissue. I could have stopped.

But there was no number more perfect than ten.

Eight. Nine. Ten.

Roaring, I heaved the unconscious man and threw him. Hatchet slid through his piss and crashed into the metal opposite.

I hunched over, chest heaving, fists shaking.

"Stay close," Father ordered. "Behave in a manner befitting an Alexander."

"Yes, Dad."

"Yes, Daddy," said Bellona.

My sister and I stood with our backs to the car, standing before the entrance to Cinco Fairgrounds. The sun beat on the crowd roaming through Merriman Circus.

Sweat dripped down my neck, collecting in a ring around my starched collar. Bellona had been allowed to wear a yellow sundress with sandals and lace gloves. On my bed, Nanny placed a black three-piece suit to go with the polished leather shoes. Apology etched in her face as she said I wasn't allowed to choose different clothes.

"Stop fidgeting this instant, Baris."

I snapped my hand to my side. "Sorry, Dad."

"I don't need apologies, I need obedience." His shadow cast over us, making me wish for the blazing sun. "The mayor insisted on this ridiculous photo op to prove to the people of Cinco that he is fun and approachable. He invited you both to accompany his children. By God, you will not embarrass me. Is that understood?"

"Yes, sir."

"Let's go."

The three of us—and two bodyguards—set off for the fairgrounds. I fell in step on my father's left while Bellona walked on his right.

That was how it must be in photos, at the dining table, as we strode from the front entrance to the penthouse elevator. My place was the left.

We found Mayor Katz by the big tent, making a show pointing at this and that while the photographers snapped their photos of him, his wife, and their three children.

"Ah, Marshall, there you are, you old so-and-so."

Father's laugh boomed. "Easy on the old."

The two men embraced like old friends. You'd have had no idea just the day before, my father called Nicolas Katz a jumped-up, trailer-trash nobody who did the world a disservice by not dying in that drive-by.

"Why don't we let the kids go off and have some fun?" Katz suggested. "It's another half an hour before the big show starts."

"It's quite a thick crowd, Nicolas."

"They'll be safe. I'll send Toby and Liselle with them." He snapped fingers at his guards. "This'll give us a chance to catch up."

"Fine." Father looked directly at me. "Behave."

Our group split in two directions.

"Where is Bernice?"

"My wife couldn't make it," I heard Father reply. "She isn't feeling..."

Bellona and the mayor's kids pulled ahead. I didn't bother trying to catch up. The oldest, Trevor, was fifteen years old like Bellona and therefore spent all his time flirting with her. The second oldest was Gregory. Closer to my age, but at twelve, he was too good to play with nine-year-old babies. Then was the youngest, Chelsea, who at four years old, was a baby.

The group stopped to see the knife-throwing exhibition—Bellona and Trevor pretending to watch while making eyes at each other.

"Get the sugar cane, Killian. Elsie has earned a treat."

Roaming a small enclosure, an eight-hundred-pound elephant stood still and patient as an older, blond man patted her trunk, looking at her like she was the most beautiful creature.

A kid about my age rescued two long green stalks from a basket and delivered them to his father.

"Would you like to feed her?"

I blinked. "What? Me?"

"Yes, you," the man said. "You don't have to be afraid. Elsie is gentler than a feather blowing in the breeze."

I moved toward the gate, then stopped, seeing the puddle of mud on the other side. The entire enclosure was dirt, leaves, and mud. Even Elsie's gray was hidden beneath a fine layer of brown.

"I can't."

"Why not?" Killian asked.

"My clothes. I'll get them dirty."

"Whatchu wearing a suit for anyway? It's a billion degrees. You look dumb."

"Away with you, boy," his father said with a laugh. "Go help your mother."

Killian took off. His father patted Elsie and came over, a kind smile on his face. "Nice shoes indeed. The best thing about leather is it laughs in the face of a little mud. Just washes right off."

"That's true," I said, perking up.

"Come on. I'll hose you down afterward and no one will know."

"Okay, thanks."

I went to step inside, and tripped.

I fell face-first in the mud, coating my jacket, shirt, and pants. I was soaked through in seconds.

"Ah! Ahhhh!"

I gazed at my mud-caked hands, screams climbing higher.

"Whoa, there, it's okay," said the man. "We'll get you cleaned up."

It wasn't okay. It was so very far from okay.

He lifted me out of the puddle, carrying me to the hose. A trail of mud and urine dotted the path behind.

The memory shook me free after what felt like an eternity, but was actually the blink of an eye. I fixed on Hatchet lying in a bloody heap, and advanced.

Ding! Ding! Ding!

"Brutal wins! Brutal wins!" Panic laced the cry. "Give it up, everyone."

Neither the cheers nor the victory slowed me down.

"Baris."

Adeline appeared in front of me. She cupped my cheeks, bringing me down to her soft kiss. "You were amazing, baby," she whispered. "Take a break now. Rest before the second fight."

I let her bring me out of the cage. Hatchet's gang buddies rushed in to help him. Adeline closed the door on all of that, shielding us in our storage room.

"I can't believe he did that." She sat on my lap, pulling my hands on hers. Carefully, she peeled my gloves off. "Such a disgusting, unnecessary thing to do. They're trying to provoke you, baby. Into doing what, I don't know, because Hatchet getting the shit beat out of him couldn't be the reaction they were looking for."

Adeline held my chin between two fingers. "The next guy is a King. Be careful."

No need. If he pulls something remotely resembling what happened in the last match. He's dead.

I was done playing with my food.

Josephine stuck her head in. She tossed Adeline a water bottle. "We all set in here? Skinner's about to call the second match."

"Did they clean the ring?" Adeline asked.

"They're doing it now. I'll make them wipe it down twice. Ugh. Nasty," she spat. "But then, Hatchet was always a piece of work."

"It's all good. From now on, he won't be whipping his dick out to so much as aim at a toilet. Hope he wasn't planning to have kids."

Jo chuckled. "Get our boy in fighting shape. One more to go."

"Give us ten minutes."

Adeline didn't speak for those ten. She held me tight, head resting on my chest.

She needn't have tried to comfort me. My anger leeched away soon after he was out of sight. I used it and taught him a permanent lesson. Time to move on to the next fight.

A knock sounded at the door.

"You're up," Meza said. "Zhang's a cocky bastard, and he's looking more smug than usual. Fists up. Keep moving. Stay out of the corner. Finish him quick."

I put Adeline on her feet and stretched, rolling my neck and shoulders.

"Adeline and I will be close by."

"Yes, we will." She hopped up to plant one on me. "Standard prizes apply when you win."

I raised one brow, turning the corner of my lip down.

"If you lost, I'd have to shower you with everything in my bag of tricks to cheer you up." She winked. "But you won't lose, so I get to catch those few hours of sleep tonight."

Don't bet on it.

The three of us went out together, forming a line cutting through a group of men gathered by the cage.

Desmond Lane.

Lane bent over a young man dressed in shorts and a ripped sleeveless tee. I assumed this was Zhang by the hopping from foot to foot and him working out his shoulders. Lane looked just as intense.

"—to win," he said.

Lane glanced up, saw us coming, and drew Zhang further to the side. The guy went, but not without shooting me a smirk.

"Anything Brutal needs to know about him?" Adeline asked.

"He enjoys this too much. The blood, breaking bones, and screams," Jo said. "Some nights, the bell doesn't stop him. He keeps whaling until five guys come and pull him off. The guy is a sadist by every definition of the word.

"As for fighting style, he's quick, intuitive and favors his right side. He'll try to force you into a corner."

I closed my eyes absorbing the information.

"Make sure he's truly out before turning your back to him. I've seen him win two fights that way. While his opponent is crowing for the audience, he gets them from the back, puts him in a headlock, and chokes them until they pass out."

"Good evening, my sons and bitches, are you ready for round two?"

"Yeah!"

Jo thumped my arm. "Good luck."

"Brutal made a lucky escape in the first round, but we all know his luck ends here. Who's ready for Zhang to put this pup in his place?"

Dozens of hands went up. Most of them actually, but not all.

"Then let's hear it for Zhhaannng!"

Zhang entered the cage, strutting the length with his arms out and chest puffed.

"And Brutal," the announcer said, flat as a board.

"Frowzy bitch," Adeline muttered. "They should put that announcer in the ring. I'll take his ass."

The comment cracked my concentration, tugging the corners of my mouth up. There was hot, sweaty, bouncing car sex with this beautiful, violent woman to look forward to. Zhang was in the way.

I stepped in the cage, hearing the clang of it shut and chained behind me. I observed Zhang—Meza's warnings in my ear.

"You stepped in the wrong cage, pretty boy."

Zhang was not pretty.

His nose had seen a break—or three. His mouth was too big for his face, and his brow ridges protruded too far over eyes sporting unkempt brows.

Zhang pointed at me, turned his palm, and crooked his finger.

Come and get me.

I flicked down, scanning the canvas for a trace of wetness. A faint scent of bleach hit my nose.

Good. To beat a man in another's piss was a level I hadn't reached. Zhang would be humiliated enough by his loss.

We circled—reminiscent of my fight with Gage.

Zhang stayed low. He crouched, arms up, stepping to the side.

"We looked you up, Baris Alexander," Zhang said. "Looked up you and all your friends. St. John Bellisario, Killian Hunt, and—"

He lunged for my knees. I spun and kicked him across the jaw.

Zhang bounced off the canvas, flipped, and slid across on his heels. He cracked his jaw.

"Not bad. As I was saying, we looked up all your friends but couldn't find much on anyone... except for you."

I ran at him and Zhang raced to meet me. We traded blows.

He struck my temple. I landed a hit to his ribs.

Zhang charged me—head-butting and throwing his weight into the punches. He was trying to shove me back in the corner. I ducked his swing, shot froward, and buried my elbow in his back.

He stumbled into the bars.

It wasn't looking good for him. If this was the best the Kings had to offer, we should end the charade now and I collect my future winnings for the next two months.

"Alexander," he hissed. "*The* Baris Alexander, son of Marshall Alexander."

I bared my teeth, growling. *Shut up. Shut up!*

"No wonder you've been skulking around with a mask and stupid-ass nickname."

I lunged—exactly what Zhang wanted me to do.

He dropped, caught me around the middle, and lifted me off my feet. Zhang slammed me against the bars, bouncing my skull off the metal.

"Get out of the corner, baby." Adeline burrowed through the pain. "You've got this. Don't let him get in your head."

Zhang rained blows on my chest and stomach. Gritting my teeth, I weathered the strikes, breathing in and out.

Unfocused rage is useless. Channel it. Pound the name Alexander from his mind.

I cut my arm across my face and swung, knocking his head to the side. It was the distraction I needed to break free of the corner.

Zhang's eyes glittered. Blood wept from a cut on his forehead. "What happened to Daddy's little rich boy?" he hissed. "The Alexanders owned this city. Your towers filled the skies. Now, no one knows your fucking name—"

"Argh!" I socked him in the mouth. His teeth cut on my gloves, tearing a split.

Zhang bounced off the bars and into another punch. Dazed, he had no defense when I looped around his neck, confining him in a headlock.

Gasping, he elbowed wildly, pummeling my ribs. I gritted my teeth and squeezed tighter.

"Ack—" Zhang abandoned trying to hit me. He clawed at my arm, raking deep, bleeding grooves. Slowly he dropped to his knees. His limbs grew weak. Zhang's arms fell to his sides.

"Ring the bell," Lane bellowed. "Ring it, dammit!"

I let go.

Zhang struck the mat, sucking in deep lungfuls of air. He shakily pushed up, lifting his head to look at me. I stomped his face.

Zhang dropped for the final time—out cold.

Ding! Ding!

"Brutal wins!"

I walked away, my rage steaming under the surface. That wasn't enough. Not nearly.

Zhang and I would fight again, and only one would leave the ring.

Adeline's hug was gentle. "Let's get you home, baby."

I changed in the back room, easing my clothes on. The pain in my ribs said bruised at the very least.

Adeline draped my arm over her shoulder. Together we stepped out, thoughts of a hot bath and warm bed on both our minds.

Two of Zhang's cronies helped him out of the cage. A bruise had begun to form on his jaw and around his eye.

"Hey. Hey!"

We ignored him.

"Bet you think this is over!" A grunt, then footfalls came up fast behind me. "I'm not fucking done with you, Alexander."

"Go away," Adeline said. "Put some ice on those bruises."

"I'm talking to you, pretty boy. You know, I looked up the photos of Marshall Alexander, and you don't look a damn thing like him."

My grip tightened on Adeline's shoulder. She must've sensed something, because she picked up the pace.

"Is that why Mommy and Daddy's brains were blown out on the living room carpet? The dirty slut was getting it on the side and your real dad decided if he couldn't have her, no one could. Naughty, naughty Mommy," he sang. "Just can't trust bitches these—"

I whirled on him.

"Brutal!"

Seizing his chin, I grabbed the back of his head and twisted. Zhang fell to the floor—dead.

"Brutal," Jo cried. "What did you do?!"

I took hold of Adeline, running for the door.

A flash came up out of the corner of my eyes. The announcer sprinted past the exiting crowd, slamming the door shut in their faces, and mine.

We skidded to a halt.

"Not so fast, Alexander." Something hard dug in my back. "You broke rule number one."

Another gun jabbed my side, then the announcer pulled his.

The guests screamed. They pushed and shoved each other getting away. The Kings and Outlaws moved in their place, unearthing guns, knives, chains, and brass—just for me.

"You rich boys don't think they apply to you." The barrel moved up my spine. Sliding it along my temple, Lane faced me. "No fighting out of the cage."

"Lane, stop!" Josephine pushed against the line surrounding us.

"Out of my hands, Jo," he replied.

"What are you so smug-shitting happy about?" Adeline snapped. "Your boy's soul is flying its way down to hell. But let me guess, you wanted this to happen."

"What I wanted doesn't matter. I didn't tell Baris to kill Zhang and violate the rules of the circuit."

"Rules of the circuit?" No less than five guns were pointed in her face. She paid them no mind. "Rules also state no weapons. We're all messing up tonight. Let's walk away and call it even."

Lane howled. "I gave trusted members permission to carry weapons because I was afraid this exact thing may happen. The Merchants have never played by the rules. You attacked the Kings unprovoked—killing two of our leaders. Why should we believe you were here to play nice?" He tapped the barrel on my forehead. "Well? Nothing to say for yourself?"

"Let us go, Lane," said Adeline. "We get the hint. You don't want us here. Let us out and we won't come back."

Lane heaved an audible sigh, shaking his head. "You don't understand what's happening here. You two aren't going anywhere. That's my best fighter dead on the fucking floor. Zhang alone brings in half my crowd every other weekend. Someone's gonna pay for that loss in revenue, and it's not going to be me."

"Lane, don't!" Meza shouted.

Smug-shitting didn't come close to the malice dripping from his grin. "Gentlemen, say hello to the newest contestant in the tournament."

"Yeah!" They whooped, crowing over my jaw cracking.

No, they can't do this.

"Lane." Josephine broke through. "I warned you. My guys go nowhere near your barbaric games. Let us out of here right now, or my fighters are out of the circuit for good."

"Shut her up," Lane barked.

The announcer cracked a pistol over her skull. Josephine dropped at my feet.

"Jo!" Adeline tried to get to her and was thrown back.

"Does this pretty little thing fight too?" Lane touched her mouth.

Adeline chomped down, clamping on his finger.

"Argh!" he cried out, wrenching from her hold as half a dozen guns cocked. "Bitch!"

She spat his blood at his feet. "I don't appreciate being called a bitch by whatever the hell you are."

"Lock them in the back!"

Hands grabbed me. I fought. I punched, kicked, and killed another man. Three men jumped me and were thrown off, flung at the gawkers.

"Get off!" Four guys carried a thrashing Adeline by the arms and feet. They tossed her inside the storage room and aimed to fire.

"Stop or she dies!" Lane ordered.

I stopped.

Back straight, I walked into the storage room, catching Adeline when she ran in my arms. Josephine was tossed in next.

"Thank you for being so obliging, Mr. Brutal. It's going to be a great tournament."

ADELINE

I eased Jo up, propping her on a box.

"Here. Drink this." I pressed the water bottle to her mouth. Some made it in. Most dribbled down her chin. "That was a nasty hit."

Her eyelids fluttered. Josephine was sluggish, struggling to focus on me. That blow matted her hair with blood.

"You'll be okay," I said. "I promise I'll get you out of here."

"I'm... sorry."

"Don't apologize, Jo. It wasn't your fault. I smelled a rat halfway down the street and I still let us walk in here."

"Ben," she whispered.

I squeezed her hand. "I'll get you back to him."

She shut her eyes.

All I could do was let the poor woman sleep. I cleaned and bandaged her wound, thinking of her kind husband, Ben, and if he prepared himself for a night his wife did not come back.

It's a dangerous life we've chosen. I drifted to Brutal—unmoving and facing the wall. *Love makes it complicated. But then, from what I've learned of it, I doubt love is simple for anyone.*

I rested Jo's head on my jacket. Moving to Brutal, I slid on his lap, resting on his chest. He didn't react to my presence. What was I supposed to say? I heard the insults Zhang flung at his back. Digs about his mother and that she was murdered.

I looked into Baris's background. I had Gianna dig into all the guys. She came up with loads of Alexanders, but had trouble connecting a Baris to one family. Baris was too unique a name to get lost among the rest. The only conclusion was he put considerable effort and money into erasing himself. And if the Kings' not-so-subtle remarks were anything to go by, he once had that money.

Which means he can only belong to one.

Marshall and Bernice Alexander were among the Cinco elite. The Alexanders were an old family who built a conglomerate that sunk their hooks into everything—housing, medicine, food, and banking. Over a decade ago, their bodyguards went into the penthouse to begin their early morning shifts, and found Mr. and Mrs. Alexander dead, killed in an armed burglary.

One of the staff later confessed. Marshall Alexander was a cruel man, and he'd endured years of abuse and belittling by his boss. One day, he asked for a loan to help cover the costs of his ill wife's rising medical bills. Marshall fired him on the spot, he lost his insurance, and his wife stopped getting treatment. He walked into the penthouse with a gun three days after her funeral.

There was mention way down in the final paragraph that the couple had two children who both ran away. It cited further proof that Marshall Alexander's nice-guy routine in front of the cameras was a fake.

Two children. If one of them was Baris, does that mean he has a brother or sister out there?

I wanted to ask. It was on the tip of my tongue.

I held it back. Marshall's Jekyll and Hyde nature could've extended to his children. What if Baris was abused so badly he ran away? Then, he picks up a newspaper one day and finds out his parents were murdered. What did he feel? Grief? Relief? Guilt at the latter?

I've wondered how I'd feel if I got the call my mother's addiction had claimed her. Those feelings weren't something I could talk about, and until recently, my history with her wasn't either.

I kissed Brutal's stiff jaw. *I understand, baby. We can do this when you're ready.*

I don't know how long we were trapped in that dark little room, sharing the single bottle of water. Half a day passed at the very least by the time Jo stirred.

"Addy?"

"Jo." I rushed to help her to her feet. "How are you feeling?"

"Not great," she rasped. "What happened?"

"The Outlaws and Kings came together in a giant leap forward for inter-gang cooperation. They pushed Zhang into provoking Baris into breaking a rule."

"He's... dead."

I guided her into a chair, passing over the remains of the water.

"Tournament," she said. "They put Brutal in the tournament."

"That's right, but I don't know what that is, or why it freaked you out so much. What's going on here, Jo?"

She fixed on the back door. "Is it locked?" Jo's eyes were clearing. The confusion leaked away, to be flooded by something else. "We have to get out of here right now. Ben! Oh, Ben must be worried sick."

"I rammed that door till I got this." I showed her the bruise on my shoulder. "Brutal did too. It won't budge. But I need you to focus, Jo. Tell me what the tournament is."

Jo let out a cry that was half sob. "The tournament is a twisted, barbaric event the Kings hold every year. I've had nothing to do with it and I warned Lane, and Parker before him, if they tried getting me or my guys involved, they'd regret it."

"Twisted and barbaric," I repeated. My stomach flipped. This lady trained people to beat the shit out of each other in a cage for the enjoyment of howling jackals. How bad was this that even she had to draw the line?

"You have no idea," she whispered. "They're fights to the death, Addy. They're going to put Brutal and his opponent in a cage, and they won't unlock the chains until one of them is dead."

I THOUGHT I WAS DONE being surprised by the depths of depravity the Kings could reach. When would I learn who I was dealing with?

I paced the length of the room—stopping once in a while to kiss Brutal or stroke his cheek. He accepted the affection easily. It was getting a line on what he was thinking that proved difficult.

"I don't understand. How can this have been going on for years? This isn't like the Castian," I said. "The people taking part in that horrible operation would guard the secret and their reputations to their grave. But a bunch of drunk fools cheering two bangers fighting to the death, and then stumbling home to invite their twisted friends to the next match? Wouldn't that get around?"

"It has," Jo said. "There has been talk of fighters dying in the circuit for years. Most assume it's the consequence of a fight gone too far or one hit too many. No one leaps to it being on purpose. A habit that has served Lane and his predecessor well."

"Why?" I threw out my hands. "Why are they doing this? Why hasn't anyone stopped them? Why do the fighters go along?"

She sighed. "Sadly, those are easy questions to answer. They do it for money, Addy. The door price to watch a tournament match is insane. You'll lose all faith in mankind when you hear just how many people are eager to watch two poor souls try to kill each other. They hand over however much money Lane demands.

"Why hasn't anyone stopped them? I believe our current predicament answers why. The Kings are too powerful to be stopped. And why do the fighters go along? For a few, it's for the money. The Kings, Outlaws, and the rest don't force their guys to participate unless they commit a grave offense. Something that would've earned a bullet in their heads, but they can get a chance at forgiveness by entering and surviving to the end. The chance of winning the tournament beats a guaranteed swim in the docks.

"To get other bodies in the ring, they tempt homeless people. The winner of the tournament walks away with half a million dollars. Again, that looks a lot better than a lifetime on the streets. If that doesn't work"—she gazed at Brutal—"they kidnap enemies of their gangs and force them into the ring."

Jo dropped her head in her hands. "This is the first they've pulled this at a match. Neutral turf. No weapons, no beef. They've always followed their own rules, Addy, and I swear I believed this time would be no different. This is all my fault."

"It's not your fault." Crouching beside her, I rubbed her back. "The Kings hate the Merchants. We were naïve to think they'd put their hatred aside. People like us don't do that."

"What will you do?"

"Kill whoever comes through that door and make a break for it. Brutal is not fighting in any tournament. The Kings can go fuck themselves."

She laughed softly. "Nothing scares you, does it?"

"Plenty of things scare me, but they're not outside that door. They're in here." I tapped my forehead. "The Kings are little boys with toy guns and a need for a nap compared to my demons."

"I—"

The doorknob rattled. Brutal and I shot to our feet.

"Whatever escape plan you've cooked up in the last fourteen hours, give it up. Put the chairs down. Step away from the door," Lane called. "I've got twelve armed guys out here praying you'll give them a reason. Understood?"

We didn't speak.

"Understood?!"

"Yes," I said. "We're sitting easy and breezy. No need to be frightened of us."

I heard a grunt, then the knob rattled again. Lane's gun came in first, fixing on Brutal through the crack. Inch by inch, his arm followed, then a shoulder, then his head.

I'm almost flattered. They pulled out all the stops to capture us, and even now, Desmond Lane isn't underestimating us.

He shut and locked the door behind him. Putting his back to it, he trained his gun on Brutal.

"Thought it was past time we had a chat about how things are going to go."

"Good idea," I said. "I've been hearing all about your little tournament, and Brutal won't be participating. That said, no use sticking around here anymore. Let us out. Now, please."

He laughed so loud his men banged on the door.

"Boss, what's going on in there?"

"We're fine. Stay outside," he said, wiping his eyes. "I don't know who you are or where you fit in a gang of masked men, but I like you... Adeline, was it?" Dropping his hand, Lane waved the gun and tucked it into his pants. "I like you so much, I'm going to let you in on a secret. You Merchants did us a favor killing Enzo— and don't try telling me La Roche's men or one of our guys did it for the ledger," he said when I opened my mouth.

"They were thoroughly interrogated and Thiago's satisfied your story is complete bullshit. You did have us going for a minute though." He grinned like I performed a cute trick. "Truth is, Bianchi was a greedy, tight-fisted bastard who wanted to bleed the Kings dry. I suspect he had a tropical island picked out for his early retirement in a few years.

"He didn't only slash Pais's cut. He came for every operation in the business. Eighty percent of the fights' take to start. Before he died, he was talking about claiming the full door price. My salary would've gone from one hundred and twenty thousand a year to forty." He tapped his skull. "Forty grand, Adeline. Let that sink in. I might as well take up my old high school job working at Cinco City Fried. I would've killed him myself, but I didn't, you did."

Lane turned on Brutal. "Hated the guy though I did, we can't let it get around that a banger can kill one of us, our boss, and then stroll into our fights and walk away with my money. You understand this," he said. "If you were in my position, you'd do the same."

To my surprise, Brutal inclined his head. *Yes, I would.*

"So, here's how it's going to go. You fight in the tournament and bring in more of those filthy rich bags chanting your name. They love you, man. Tossing a man through his own piss? I've gotten five demands to bring you back in the last two hours alone—a huge part of the reason we decided not to gut you, and your girlfriend, and hang your bodies off a pole in Harlow.

"If you die in the process of making me millions." He clapped. "Well, that's a win-win for everybody. However, if you survive the final match, you can take your winnings and walk out the door. The Merchants and Kings call a truce."

A lot of those going around.

"Those are your options, Alexander. Take it, or die in this dirty warehouse waiting for a worker to stumble on your bloated corpses."

"Baris." I went to him and Lane didn't try to stop me. "You do not have to do this. It's crazy. This fool is padded-room and safety-scissors insane and we can't trust a thing he says." I burned a hole in Lane's head. "He's broken his rules to force you into this. Why wouldn't he do it again? I don't believe for a second he'll let you walk away when it's over."

Lane held my gaze steadily. "What choice do you have? Surely the slim chance I'm telling the truth is better than certain death in the next five minutes."

"No, it's not," Jo said. "Addy's right. You'll kill us anyway."

Lane bobbed his head, lips pushed out. "Okay, how about this? Brutal fights in the tournament or I track down Benjamin Meza and give him the punishment we were saving for the Merchants."

The blood drained from Jo's face.

"After I'm through with him, I'll pay sweet little Miranda a visit. Naturally, your mom will follow, and then your gym will mysteriously burn down in a fire." He gestured at me and Brutal. "As for you two, we'll use you as bait to lure the other rats out of hiding and—"

"Stop."

My head snapped up.

Brutal stood, advancing on Lane who quickly drew his weapon.

"I'll do it."

"Brutal, no," I cried.

"I'll do it," he repeated. "The money." Brutal was tensing. Fists balled, the veins popped stark in his neck. "Pay us what we're owed."

"Fair enough." Lane lowered his gun. "In the tournament, the fighter left standing gets a cut of the door price for every match—incentive to keep going. You'll get what you're owed. If you turn on us, try to disrupt the tournament, run away, or if I even see some fucker with a cold wearing a mask, this self-righteous bitch pays the price."

"Fuck you, Lane," Jo spat.

"I might've liked you better if you had. As it is, I couldn't stand the way you strut in our territory, banging on about meeting your terms or you'll take your fighters out. Who fucking needs them? This guy is going to make me more money than I can count."

"That's because you can't count that high, dumbass! You start stumbling over yourself at ten. The circuit makes more in the long-term than the once a year you savages force innocents into the cage, and if you think you're not fucked without me, you've got a surprise coming."

"Hmm. Well, how about this—"

Bang!

Jo tipped off the chair, screaming. She collapsed clutching her thigh.

"Jo!" I fell to her side.

"Don't worry about her," Lane breezed. "She's not your sponsor anymore. The Kings are." He tossed a phone at Brutal. "Pick up every time it rings. Go to the locations I send you. If you miss one text or call, the next bullet goes between her eyes." Lane swept open the door. "See you in two weeks."

We didn't waste a breath arguing with him. Picking up Jo, Brutal and I carried her out, racing to the car. The Kings let us pass, laughing in our bloody wake.

They had us. They knew it, and we did too.

Chapter Seven

"Argh!"

The chair legs impaled the plaster, stuck for a beat, and crashed to the floor.

"How the fuck did this happen?!" Saint bellowed.

"They planned it." I was curled up on the threadbare couch in the same spot since the night before. Spots of blood stained my shirt. I couldn't summon the energy to crawl in the shower. "They wanted Brutal to give them an excuse."

How had this happened? My boyfriend forced to fight to the death. One of the few friends I have left lying in a hospital bed. The other hiding out with the ledger.

"Do not become another casualty in this war. By the time you realize it's not worth it, it'll be too late."

Is there a worse crime your parent could commit than being right when you swore to prove them wrong? Well, I'm fucking admitting it. It's not worth it. Brutal killed or seriously injured to get money to track down Raul, to get the ledger back and save a city that clearly didn't want to be saved. Why was I sacrificing everyone I loved for this place? What had Cinco given me but a hard life?

"What now?" Mercer asked. He knelt next to me, stroking my hair. "I've been to a tournament match. While I don't doubt Brutal's skills, it's another level in there."

Killian rose. "You've been to a match? I've heard talk about it over the years, but the Kings lock the dates and locations down so deep, it's harder to find than their casinos."

"I went once. On a date. The client didn't tell me where we were going beforehand," he said. "They attach weapons to the bars. Pipes, knives, bats, and bottles. The bloodier the fight, the better. If the Kings won't let you go till you wipe out everyone who faces you," he said to Brutal, "the chances of you making it to the end unscathed go severely down."

I threw my arm over my eyes, wishing I could block out Mercer as easily as Brutal's stony expression. Why didn't we climb back in the car and put that warehouse in our rearview?

"This Meza woman and her family," Saint began, "how attached are you to them, Bunny?"

I lurched up. "Saint!"

"That got you up." Saint got between me and the pillow. "We won't let anything happen to her, Adeline. She stood up for you both and took a bullet in reward. Loyalty is respected. But we're not standing by and letting this shit happen. The real question is how attached are Meza and her people to Cinco? They may need to be moved."

I nodded. "I bet she's thinking the same thing right now. Lane was quick to threaten Ben, Miranda, their mom, and the gym. Even quicker to shoot her. He'll pull that again the next time she stands in the way of something he wants—if he lets there be a next time. He stepped over Zhang's body cackling and twirling his mustache over outsmarting us. He didn't give a shit that one of his own died.

"I'll talk to Jo about moving and offer to help pay for the cost. There are other cities with underground rings. The people who run them can't possibly be as dickish as ours."

"Costs a lot of money to relocate a family," Killian put in. "We spent all we had on the party."

"And that's if she agrees to go," Saint added.

JO WOULD NOT AGREE to go.

"No. Absolutely not."

"You're not safe in Cinco." I sat by her hospital bed, thankful Leah Tyler didn't splash my name and description about.

Left me free to sit here and argue with her.

"You're not safe either," Jo said. "Are you packing up and running?"

"Trust me, I'm thinking about it."

I slumped in the chair, bone-tired and feeling every inch of it. Josephine's hurt leg was bandaged and resting atop the covers. She looked better than she did the day before. I put it down to Ben's attentive care. He transformed the room into a florist shop.

"I can't leave, Adeline. My life is here. My family. My businesses. Then there are my guys. They joined the circuit to bring in real money for their family. I joined to protect them from being taken advantage of. You've seen how much Lane cares about these guys. If I leave, there's no one standing between them. To you, this may not seem like an important hill to die on, but it is to me. These kids will fight whether I'm there or not. I make sure they come home."

I curled over her hand. "It is important, Jo. Who knows how many you've saved from the tournament. After I stamp out the Kings and their Outlaw buddies too, you and Brutal will run the ring together. I don't think he'll object. He likes you."

She smiled softly. "I'm getting fond of him too. I hope we both live to see the day we work together, Addy. I truly do."

BRUTAL

The gun lay on my bed, next to a stack of hundreds.

Lane's cell went off two hours ago. The text directed me to a pizza place in Harlow. I left with no one the wiser. Walking inside, Lane clapped.

"Punctual. I'm almost disappointed. I was looking forward to slitting Meza's throat. Oh well, there are plenty of chances for that."

I sat opposite in his booth, ten feet away from a young family and their children. For all his bluster, Desmond was afraid of me. He wouldn't have picked a public place otherwise.

"Just a few things," he said as he wiped the grease from his fingers. "I'm gonna tell you how this will work."

He didn't have much to say that I hadn't heard already. The true purpose wasn't to tell me I'd be pit against five fighters, or that my cut of the door fee equaled ten grand. It was to prove I could be summoned and ordered to sit and stay. Like everyone else in this city, the Kings had the Merchants on their leash.

"Here." Lane tossed an envelope at me. "Your winnings from the last fight."

I made no move to touch it.

"No tricks," Lane said. "I'm not a complete bastard. The next fight may very well be your last. Use it to take the tasty Adeline out for one last night of fun. Fancy restaurant. Hotel room. Spa." His smile revealed rows of stained brown teeth. "I handpicked the best to face you, Brutal. Forget drug-addled bums. These are the top fighters of Cinco, and they have no intention of dying."

He shoved his plate of half-eaten pizza at me. "Have the rest. I'll see you the next time that phone rings."

Back in the motel, I glanced away from the money, eyes moving to the gun as they inevitably did when we were in the same room. Tucked away on a bookshelf. Hidden behind a dresser. I did not need to see it to know it was there, or feel the weight of it on my palm as I did then.

I smoothed a finger down the barrel. Memories bombarded my quiet place one after the other.

"Stupid, useless boy! You made a fool of me today!"

The belt lashed—whipping raised, angry welts.

"Stop," I screamed. "Stop!"

"I was cursed with you. A clumsy, sniveling, whiny brat who can't stand, eat, or walk properly! You're not fit to bear the name Alexander."

Smack! Smack!

"But heaven help me, I will whip you into shape if it's the last thing I do."

"Stop it!"

"Silence!" Father roared. "One more sound and it's my fist through your teeth, boy! Do not speak!"

I clamped my hands over my mouth—face slick with tears. I pushed my cries. My tears. My pleas. Everything down, down, down.

My vision cleared on the gun.

Mercer, Killian, Saint, and Adeline stayed up the entire night working out a plan to spring me from the Kings' grip. Adeline was at the hospital at that moment trying to convince Meza to leave. I barely knew the woman and

I was certain her answer would be no. We were fighters. By our very nature, we didn't back down from one.

I returned the gun to its place.

Years ago, when my family imploded and I was left with nothing, I made a vow that I would find Bellona, or what happened to her. I was ten years old when she was carried bound and crying out the door. Sixteen when I discovered she was a problem Kieran fixed. Twenty-eight when Oscar told me she was alive and still out there somewhere.

He ended my search for the ledger, but not for her. Oscar gave me a place to start and now I had to go there and pick up an eighteen-year-old trail. *There* was very far from here.

I said that my vow recognized the people who'd gotten me this far.

It's almost certain I wouldn't be alive had Killian and St. John not stepped in the path of my downward, destructive spiral. I wouldn't have learned the truth of that night and what became of Bellona if not for the impish seductress who spun me in her web and made me thank her for the pleasure.

And I wouldn't be within reach of half a million dollars if not for Josephine Meza clearing a path to the Kings' fighting ring.

A half mill was more than enough to outfit a new place and see the Merchants on top again. It was enough for me to take a cut, fly to my destination, and sustain me while I searched for Bellona. It would also cover a generous sponsor bonus for Josephine.

Adeline and the guys would not get me out of the tournament. We for fuck sure wouldn't risk Meza's life attempting it. I was exactly where I needed to be.

I was Cinco's top fighter. The intentions of those who stepped in the cage with me were insignificant. I would be the one who left alive.

ADELINE

I trudged into Killian's hotel room, found him standing before a wall covered with paper, strings, and pictures, and pushed him on the couch. I hopped on top of him and snuggled on his chest.

"Hello to you too," he said.

I chuckled. Amazing I could still do that. "Just got back from the hospital."

"Let me guess, she said no."

"Yep."

"Figured she would. Ninety-nine point nine percent probability."

"Wouldn't it be quicker if you filled me in on all you've divined for the future?"

"It's math, common sense, and a little bit of instinct. Not divination." Killian ran his fingers down my spine, popping goose bumps where he touched. "Josephine Meza single-handedly runs a small business in a struggling neighborhood, and trains underground fighters. Tucking her tail between her legs and running away isn't her style."

"I guess I knew that too," I murmured. "But I had to try. It's Baris."

"We'll get him out of this. Baris isn't dying for the Kings' entertainment."

"You always have a plan." I propped my chin on folded hands, gazing at him. "Can I ask you something?"

"No."

I swatted his thigh.

A grin played at his lips. "If you're going to resort to violence, go ahead."

"What's the Merchants' plan for the city and the ledger? It feels like we've come to a silent truce of our own, but if we're pursuing Gianna together, and claiming the book together. We should have this talk."

"Yes, we should." Killian tilted his head back, resting on his arm. "The Kings' operation. The way they've structured their business into parts that both run separately and together. We have the same idea."

"Money, sex, and pain," I said.

"The Kings have taken over Harlow and spread into Leighbridge. Beyond that, their influence isn't as strong, though no one is stupid enough to mess with them. We're not stopping at the borough boundaries. We're taking all of Cinco—"

"—and the ledger gives you the power to do it." I raised my brows. "Will our interests clash?"

"Depends." Killian's tone was light. "You want to clean up the city. Admirable. But our kind of work gets dirty."

"I'm no saint—as you well know. Even so, look at what we've dealt with in just the last few months. Child sex rings, slashers, fake charities, and rich bags cheering as desperate or trapped people fight to the death. Is that the empire you want to run? Tell me, Killian. Are we going to get that dirty?"

"Of course not," he gritted.

"See? You agree, love. Saint once said men like Lombard are the reason men like him exist. When they go too far, someone has to put them down. Hard.

"Cinco took a wrong turn somewhere and the ledger helped guide the wheel. I don't want to bring the fun to a stop. Merely nudge the city back on track. Putting people like Jo and Baris on the fights. Men like Mercer running the escorts who'll let them freaking leave if they want out, and not by way of a sliced face and trip to the docks."

I rose and fell with Killian's breaths. "I can't say you're wrong. I see what you've seen. I've run the numbers. After you told us Kieran became a title, I readjusted the timeline, looking into crime stats, sudden changes in wealth, sharp reversals in policy, and mortality rates.

"Crime's been on a steady climb for the last two decades, and I've picked out three instances of some nobody blowing onto the Leighbridge scene with bags of 'gambling winnings' and buying out Trapp Tower. We've definitely upset the natural order of things. I've nothing against putting it right in the name of bringing the city under our law." He stroked my neck. "As long as we're equal partners. There's no man alive who dare be my boss, and as tempting as you are"—he traced my lips—"I don't see myself bowing before a woman either."

"Hmm." Rising up, I pinned Killian between my knees. "You won't bow before me? Not even if I do this..."

I drew my shirt over my head, dropping it on his chest.

"Nope," he said, golden eyes darkening.

"What about this?" My bra strap eased off my shoulder. "Will you get on your knees for that?"

"Can't do it." Killian gripped my hips, rocking me back on his hardening ridge.

My bra popped off and decorated the floor. "If you really feel that way, tell the girls directly." I pushed my breasts together, feeling no small amount of pleasure at his throat bobbing under hard swallows. "Tell them they hold no power over you."

"There's no reason to bring them into this."

I giggled. "They want to hear it from you." I buried his face in my chest, muffling his groan. "Killian Hunt bows before no one."

"All right, Redgrave. I admit this method will be highly effective." His tongue flicked my nipple. "But you can't keep me under your spell indefinitely. Eventually, I wake up and free my balls from your vise."

"Then, I have to explore methods to keep you under longer, don't I?" I glided to the bedroom. "Should we start now?"

Killian tossed me shrieking over his shoulder. We fell into bed tearing at each other.

Hours later, we tangled in the mess of sheets. Killian's breaths were steady in sleep. I ran a finger through the fine hairs on his arm, drifting between sleeping and waking.

I told the guys we'd be equals. Partners. My hunt for the ledger wasn't mania for power, it was a mission to set things right. I meant it when I said we could share the responsibility together.

I meant it when I told Gianna the same. It didn't stop her from turning her back on me and fulfilling every warning my father gave us. The Merchants and I could be partners.

Shifting, I kissed my sleeping love.

But what do I do if it's not enough?

Someone pounded on the hallway door. It was all the warning we got before it opened and they let themselves in.

"Saint? Mercer?"

No response.

"Baris?" I called. "Baris, if that's you, don't say anything."

His laugh slipped under the door and spread through the room.

Most of my clothes were in the living room. I pulled on my pants and went out to claim the rest.

Brutal propped on the head of the chair. He caught me reaching for my bra and pulled me to him, locking an arm around me.

I smiled. "What do you think of Steelbuns?"

Rough headshake.

"Pillowlips?"

His look said it all.

"Mr. Lovin' 'n' Glovin'?"

Brutal tossed his head back, shoulders shaking. A fraction of my tension leaked out. How could life be anything but perfect when Baris is laughing?

"I'll keep working on it," I said.

He kissed me. *Good.*

"You know we'll find a way out of this, don't you?" I whispered. "You're not dying or killing for the Kings."

Fishing something out of his pocket, Brutal spread my fingers and placed a roll of hundreds on my palm.

"What— Is this the match money?"

Yes.

"Lane gave it to you just like that?" Saying it out loud didn't help it make sense. Neither did Brutal's confirmation. "What do you want to do with it? Jo refuses to move."

Baris closed my hand over the money.

"Me? No, not me. Gianna." Looking in his eyes, I was right. "The plan doesn't change. Throw the party, get to Raul, find Gianna and the ledger." I broke away, pulling on the rest of my clothes. "What about the tournament? Maybe we should be using this money to get *you* out of the city. We can get a few guys to stick close to Jo and her family. Protect them if Lane comes after them. He'll have to get someone else for his cruel games— Why are you shaking your head?"

Brutal held my wrist, holding the money between us.

"The ledger isn't important right now!"

"Yes, it is." His soft, perfect voice was calm. "It's the only way to stop this."

"You—" I halted. "Stop this. As in the tournament? What if Desmond Lane hasn't claimed his own page?"

He lifted his shoulders. *What if he has?*

"It's risky, but it's true we'll be in a ten-times-better position to protect Jo and punish Lane with the ledger in our hands." I nodded to myself. "Okay, okay. Mercer can throw the party as soon as he has the money for the drugs. We do it this weekend, and I'll be face-to-face with Gianna before that phone goes off again." I brought his face down to mine. "I will get you out of this. Do you believe me?"

Closing the distance, Baris drowned me in a soul-searing kiss.

It wasn't until he left that I realized he didn't answer my question.

A WEEK LATER, MERCER threw the party.

I was told it was the blowout of the century. The booze was flowing, the caterer delivered, the deejay peeled everyone off the wall, and the highlight, multiple people took advantage of the glass shower and danced their naked, sudsy, wet bodies for everyone to see. It was the coolest party I wasn't invited to, and Raul didn't show.

Mercer downed his scotch and banged the glass on the table.

It was the two of us in his room. I stayed up late waiting for him to come back bearing good news.

"The fucker is smarter than I gave him credit for," he said. "He, or whoever he sent, didn't come within fifteen feet of the place. I got a text an hour into the party that my package was delivered and to pick it up behind the pet store a block down. I found a backpack full of coke and E, but no sign of the guy who dropped them off."

I laughed mirthlessly. "That's Gianna written all over it. No contact with targets. No prior details that could be used to spring a trap. Guess he finally let the girlfriend in on his business."

"Think he knows something's up?"

I shook my head. "They're taking precautions. Smart ones. If Gianna knew I was breaking the truce, I'd be hearing about it."

Mercer sunk in the chair. His shirt was unbuttoned to the waist, and his pressed pants creased. He had that sexy, rumpled quality enhanced by the tousled locks and five o'clock shadow. In that instant, I understood what kept the johns and janes calling his number.

Mercer Santos was the faultless kind of beauty that wasn't intimidating. There were gorgeous people that made you want to put a sack over your head and flee the room. Your unworthy eyes couldn't behold their beauty. But that wasn't Mercer.

He was warm smiles, sharp-toothed grins, and laughs that melted your bones. He made you feel safe drawing closer, breathing his air, daring to touch him. Then the trap is sprung, your panties are on the floor, and you're willing to part with everything you own just to keep him.

I sat on his lap, stroking his smooth chest. *But only I get to keep him, so back the fuck off.*

"What now?" I asked. "Do we throw another party?"

"No. There's nothing to stop him pulling the same dead-drop crap. I left too much to chance hoping a friend could convince him to come. No," he repeated. "I have another idea, but it requires a bribe, new clothes, restocking the tools I lost in the explosion, and you."

"Okay, then, let's do it." I got up, tugging his hand. "We can go now."

Mercer towed me back. "It won't be cheap, lovely, and it won't be soon. I'll have to steal the stuff I need and spread out the thefts, so the cops don't figure out what they add up to."

"Ominous," I said. "Define not cheap and not soon. Brutal's first fight is in a week."

"Adeline..."

"What?" I prompted. "Mercer, what is it?"

"It will not take less than a week. Not to set it up or get the money."

"No."

"Ten grand from the tournament—"

"No."

"—would grease the right palm."

"No! Baris isn't risking his life to lure trash like Raul out of hiding. I'll stand in Clark Square trumpeting Gianna's name before I let that happen!"

"Addy, you know I agree with you." My hand disappeared in his. "But we can't stop this. We're down to fifteen guys. If we stormed the location, it'd be a massacre. We can't buy him out of this. We can't trade for something the Kings want more than our end. We can't stop this fight, but after he wins—and he *will* win—we'll be closer to getting us out of this."

He glanced around the cramped, modest space. "I've failed to get the info we need on more than one occasion. Cash has made calculations that turned out wrong. Sinjin hired who he believed was just an innocent cook.

But Brutal. He has never lost a fight. If you're going to put your faith in any Merchant, it's him."

"Stop doing that," I rasped.

"Doing what?"

"Saying what I need to hear."

"Can't help it. The countdown to the end of the world starts when you stop smiling."

I chuckled softly, letting myself be drawn into his arms.

"You won't do it alone," he said, kissing my crown. "We'll be there. All of us."

SATURDAY NIGHT, BARIS and I fled the motel.

The call would come any second. The last place he should receive it was in the humble place that was our rock bottom.

Clifton Grand Public Library was the biggest in Cinco. Five floors and a basement overrun with dusty tomes, flickering lamplight, and hidden corners.

I reclined in an armchair and footrest, Baris lying on top of me. Stacks of books covered the tables on either side. They concealed us in our own little world.

Not that we needed to worry about the outside crashing in. The library closed hours ago.

"I told you it was as simple as hiding out in the bathroom."

He tilted his chin up, peering at me upside down.

"The basement side entrance has a busted lock that hasn't been replaced in four years. That's our way out. What can you do? Budget cuts."

Brutal pointed to the third book in the fourth stack.

"Live there," I said. "Narnia sounds amazing. Equally beautiful and dangerous. Plus, too much Disney got me into the talking animal thing."

Chuckling, he pointed out another book.

"Nope. I'm serious," I said to his surprised look. "I would not want to be transported to the wizarding world. I'm the only eleven-year-old who breathed a sigh of relief when my letter didn't come. Discrimination, prejudice, genocidal maniacs, and hate groups. The real world has enough of those and they're bad enough without magic thrown in the mix. Plus, owls freak me out. What about you?"

Thumbs-up.

Why were we playing a silly game about which fantasy worlds we would live in? For the exact reason it was a silly, fun game. The best thing I knew to do for the man who was risking his life to protect one friend and get me closer to the other, was to spend those last few hours relaxed, happy, and together.

"What about Neverland?" I asked. "I like the idea of a world where we never grow old."

Thumbs-down.

"But you don't." I laughed. "You are pretty inconsistent with these answers. Yes to Asgard, but no to the Enchanted Forest. Yes to Hogwarts, but Middle Earth can take a hike. Will I ever figure you out?"

He looked me straight in the eyes, expression solemn, and shook his head.

"Baris!"

He fell against the chair arm cracking up.

"You're lucky I love you anyway." I brought him back, snuggling his head between my breasts, and resting my chin on his forehead. "I used to come here all the time when I was little. I love how libraries make you feel like you're a part of something. Pages and pages of worlds created by men and women all over the world, stretching throughout time."

I stroked the leather. "I used to fall asleep in this chair. Feeling safer than I ever did at home... with Jocelyn."

Baris dropped kisses on my knuckles—imparting everything he needed to say.

"Bonus," I said. "I haven't had sex in here before. Ready for another first?"

Baris knocked a stack off the table flipping over. It crashed to my squealing.

Buzz. Buzz.

We froze, hands on our buttons.

Buzz.

"It's not too late to run."

The back of his fingers brushed my cheek. He pointed at both of us, curled his hand in a fist, and pressed it to his chest.

"I'm not sure what that means, baby." My eyes swam. "It doesn't feel like a yes."

Brutal answered the phone.

A voice came through the speakers too low for me to make out. The short conversation was over as soon as it started. Ending the call, Brutal passed me the phone.

Lane texted the address. The fight started in an hour.

He tossed in an extra invitation for Brutal's "tasty friend."

"When this is all over," I said, "kill Desmond Lane first."

Brutal raised his hand.

Thumbs-up.

THE TAXI DROPPED US ten minutes away from Holmes Street. We were just outside of Harlow city center where two-story family homes and big chain supercenters took over. A few more miles and we began bleeding into the woods.

Baris and I walked along a dirt path, bypassing an auto shop.

"What's out here?" I asked. "I hope we're not out in some dark field with a hundred people pushing and shoving to see. That'll quickly become chaos if I rip the cage open and bust you out. Which I will if I don't like the way this fight is going." My hold in his grip tightened.

"Mercer says you never lose. Don't you dare change that fact tonight."

He pressed his lips to the back of my hand in response.

In the distance, a fuzzy, black shape began coming into focus. A group of people stood at the edge of the road—waiting for us.

"Bunny." Saint gripped me by the waist, planting me in front of him. "Meet Diego, Colt, Titan, Pistol, Cain, Ted, Frankie, and I believe you know Lucky."

My plaid-wearing former nurse tipped an imaginary hat to me. "Ma'am."

"Hello, boys."

A person could be anyone you imagined them to be behind a mask. The computer-hacking Diego claimed the role of squinty dude with coke-bottle glasses and too-tight pants. Colt fancied himself a modern-day cowboy. Ted was just happy to be here.

Casting a glance over the muscled, steel-eyed, rugged bunch before me, I got a clear picture of why Cash insisted on the masks. My imaginings were just that. These were not faces witnesses would forget. Killer was written in bloodred ink all over them.

"I hope you're prepared to fuck shit up if things aren't going my way."

"Yes, ma'am," they replied.

"Excellent," I said. "Let's go."

"Why the hell do they call you ma'am?" Saint asked under his breath. "All I put you in charge of was my breakfast and my dick."

I swatted his arm. "I take my own initiative."

"Take this too." Saint pushed something in my hand. "Put it through your belt loop and then your belt on top. They won't find it."

I held the long string of coiled wire. "A garrote. Good thinking, baby. Now I just have to get behind Desmond Lane." The name tasted bad on my tongue. "Where's Mercer?"

"Can't risk one of his clients seeing him with us."

I nodded. "Let's get this over with."

We were a silent gang walking the rest of the way to Holmes Street. We passed a closed grocery store and my memory triggered. I knew where we were going.

"The old racetrack."

Brutal nodded. My silent fighter pulled ahead within sight of the doors. I picked up the pace to catch up. He wasn't doing any of this without me. His *sponsor* was hardly going to sit him down and tell him the weaknesses of the men he picked out to kill him. The tasty friend would be in his corner.

Two guards stopped us short at the door. "What's the word?"

"William II," I said, quoting the password in the text.

"That password is for two people. It's in the name, honey." He pushed back his coat, gripping the gun handle. "The rest of you, passwords or fuck—"

Saint pistol-whipped him.

"Hey!"

Cash dropped the second.

"Shall we?" Saint asked, stepping over their unconscious forms. "Cain. Pistol, stash them behind that dumpster."

That was once my fate. Oh, how far we've come.

Danton Racetrack was a mini-course on the fringe of Harlow that used to host birthday parties and weekend adrenaline binges. Now it was an empty patch of overgrown grass and cracked asphalt that hosted secret parties for those kids all grown up and looking to score their highs another way. I had firsthand experience coming to a party out here with Gianna.

Gianna.

That night we drank green glow drinks that made us feel like butterflies lived under our skin. We danced till we passed out in an old race car and woke up to a naked man asleep on the windshield. That was the week Jocelyn tracked me down at our university. Gianna made it her mission that week to distract me and put a smile on my face. For those few hours, it worked.

My friend is still in there somewhere. She'll have to pull the damn trigger before I'll accept the ledger has taken her too.

The memory of that night faded as the new Danton unfolded. Gone were the jungle patches of grass and crushed Solo cups. They were mowed down to make way for the cage illuminated in the middle of the course.

I can't say what I was expecting. The turnout and revenue had to be enough to make life sentences worthwhile. Even so, standing room only did not cross my mind.

"I can't believe this," I breathed. "The stands are packed."

"Good," said Saint. "Witnesses to the lesson Brutal's about to teach. I hope they fucking take notes."

"Gentlemen." Lane broke away from his pack, meeting us on the asphalt. That there were more than two of us didn't seem to faze him. "The Merchants, I presume." He raked Saint up and down. "You must be St. John Bellisario."

Saint clasped the outstretched hand. "You must be Thiago's bitch boy." His smile was blinding. "Is the man himself here tonight? I'd love to go three for three at killing your bosses."

Lane's eye twitched. He tried mimicking Saint's cool along with his smile. "Done denying it, are you? Brutal's girl has been trying to convince us Richard La Roche paid off Enzo's blackmailing with a bullet to the head."

"He did," Saint replied. He made a show of looking around. "But the Kings are obviously determined to hold us responsible, so why fight it? Letting everyone believe us lowly Merchants brought the Kings to their knees only raises our esteem."

Lane's smile melted away.

"Point us to the best seats in the house, friend. Front row. My associate's about to slaughter another King on their own turf. Can't miss a second of that."

"You've got a big fucking mouth," Lane hissed, eating the distance between them. "Didn't anyone tell you it's going to get you in trouble?"

"No." Saint grinned into his snarl. "Has anyone ever told you disembowelment is a slow death? Hours of excruciating agony before you finally die from blood loss." A silver glint hit my eyes. Saint pressed the knife tip just above Lane's belt. "Ask me how I know."

Brutal clapped Sinjin's shoulder. A silent communication passed between them—one I tried to decipher.

Brutal had been odd since he gave me the money. It was hard to read him on a good day. Still, I sensed when something was wrong and I needed to remind him he wasn't alone in his silent world. I did not get that sense now.

Baris attacks Saint and throws my food in the trash without a lick of remorse or fear of consequences. He was not a man to resign himself to fate. Brutal had not met a challenge that backed him down.

Brutal led Saint away.

So why isn't he fighting this?

I gazed at the back of his head, wishing not for the first time that I could read his mind.

There were front-row seats. Surrounding the cage, chairs were put out, granting an HD view of the blood and gore. Bile rose in my throat.

Weapons attached to the bars like Mercer warned. Knives. Steel bats. There was even a chainsaw.

I stepped to his side, both of us taking in the sight. "What's going on, Baris?" My voice barely carried among the shouting and booing. Nonetheless, he heard me. "Why do you want to be here?"

Baris curled through my fingers, kissing my knuckles with his sweet reverence.

"Ku'uipo," he said. "Call me that."

I stood there long after he left—the ghost of his lips lingering on my skin.

"Bunny." Saint was seated in the row claimed by the Merchants. He nodded to the empty chair next to him. "Cash and I are packing," he said. "If the fight turns, we'll shoot the guy through the head and declare the winner."

I peered over my shoulder at the group advancing on us. "They may have something to say about it."

Lane fanned out with his entire crew in tow. "We have a problem," he said. "Seems you guys have missed the security checks. Both Charlie and Al went on a break." He narrowed on Sinjin. "How unlike them. I'm leaning toward jumping to conclusions and reacting on impulse. I'll change my mind if you hand over your weapons. Now."

"No can do," Saint said. "We'll sit and watch without interference for the continued good health of Josephine Meza, but if you try what you and your boys are thinking, it won't end well."

"You're outnumbered," Lane gritted.

"That won't matter for you. You'll be dead."

Lane lurched forward.

"Whoa." I stepped between them. "Let's take it down. Lane, after what you pulled the last time, you can't possibly think I'd go anywhere near you without backup or weapons. Brutal's here. He's fighting. Stop flexing your testosterone and see that you've won."

He chuckled. "Not yet. My win comes at the end of the first round." Lane swept out a hand. "Our seats are this way."

"I'm not—"

Lane snapped his fingers. His men drew their weapons as fast as mine. They stood off—set to unleash a hail of bullets, and me in the crossfire.

"As I said, our seats are this way."

Stiffly, I turned to the guys. "Stay here. Look after Brutal. I'll be fine."

To my surprise, Saint nodded. "We're behind him, Bunny." He flicked to my belt. "Don't worry."

I blew them kisses and then trailed Lane to the other side of the cage. If the man insisted on being within strangling distance, who was I to fight him?

His guys stayed behind—fixed on the Merchants.

Lane patted me down before we sat. He brushed over the wire under my belt like Sinjin knew he would.

"How does this work?" I asked. Brutal stood at the foot of the stairs, bare-chested and waiting to begin. He went through his warm-up routine like the threats and insults coming his way were his workout playlist.

"I'm glad you asked." Lane reclined in his seat. Resting his ankle on his knee, he snapped his fingers again and a nearby woman got up and ran off. "There are three twenty-minute rounds. Five-minute breaks between."

"What if they both get through the rounds?"

"'Sudden death' match. Another twenty minutes. The weapons are removed and they're both given swords. The audience loves that gladiator shit," he said. "After that, if they're both still alive, they've earned themselves a stay of execution. They advance to the next round to face another champ, or each other for the last time."

I absorbed the info. "You're a filthy, worthless, piece-of-shit monster," I replied, voice flat. "You, Jace Parker, and everyone who cosigned this. If ever for a second you think that it's just business, or they can refuse, or at least you're not as evil as 'insert person here.' Push those thoughts away and hold on to this: you're trash in every sense of the word."

"Keep saying stuff like that to me, Adeline, and I'm gonna fall in love with you."

A ripple of disgust went up my spine. I couldn't stand the way he said my name. Drawing out the syllables like a moan.

The woman returned and handed Lane a beer. "Where are my manners? Would you like one?"

I flipped him off, grinding my teeth over his laughter.

Speaker feedback cut through the noise. "Ladies and gentlemen."

I sat up straight. It was time, so soon.

"Welcome to an event like none other."

Why am I just sitting here?! My finger twitched toward my belt. Killing Lane may not put an end to this, but it would definitely hold up the proceedings. *Except...*

Brutal.

I looked at him standing relaxed and ready. Why can't I shake the thought he doesn't want that?

Brutal has plans of his own. I'll stay my hand long enough to find out what they are. I released my belt buckle. *But only that long.*

"—rat's slithered out of his hole to face the nastiest. Fiercest. Bloodthirsty savage in all of Cinco!"

The crowd's roar was deafening—heralding the arrival of Brutal's opposer.

The man emerged from the entrance we came through, surrounded by his entourage. My jaw dropped.

An outfit of white cloth, straps, buckles, and chains bound his arms to his sides. Two women in thongs and sparkly bras led his chains, leading the straightjacketed man down the rows. Burning, green eyes darted above the iron mask, meeting mine as he passed.

"The Headhunter!"

Unease turned my stomach. *Please tell me they call him that because he works in recruitment.*

"Headhunter's won three tournaments." Lane's voice slid in my ear. "As promised, only the best to face Brutal."

"Trash, Lane," I replied. "Internalize it."

He chuckled.

His assistants brought Headhunter to the stairs, putting on the show of unlocking his chains, releasing the buckles, shrugging off his straightjacket, and removing the mask. He raised his fists high, pumping and flexing for the crowd. A surprisingly handsome face hid beneath that mask.

"Kill him!"

"Destroy him!" they shouted. And Brutal stood there alone.

I shot off my feet, racing to him.

"Hey!"

Brutal turned to catch me running into his arms.

"I love you," I said between peppering his face with kisses. "Don't you dare die before saying it. If you do, I'll bring you back and strangle you!"

Catching my face, he crashed his lips on mine. We went at each other like hungry animals—tongues battling, teeth clashing, and the familiar ache in my middle when Baris even crossed my mind.

The boos turned into catcalls.

"Aww, isn't that sweet," the announcer mocked. "Last one before you go."

"That's enough."

Lane's men came for me. I gave Baris one more kiss, let him put me on my feet, and pushed through the grabbing hands. I claimed the seat next to Lane—stiff-backed and head high.

Ding!

The bell rang and the men ran into the ring.

Brutal went straight for him. Headhunter spun, twisting out of the way, and continued running to the opposite end of the cage. He grabbed hold of the chainsaw and ripped it down.

"Yeah! Off with his head! Off with his head!" The chant rolled over the crowd.

"I forgot to mention," Lane began. "Headhunter got his name from decapitating ten out of the fifteen men he's faced. I've got money on Brutal being number eleven."

I ignored him. Nothing was more important than focusing on Brutal.

Headhunter revved the saw, howling in competition with the noise. He charged him.

"Brutal!"

Baris threw himself back, the tearing chains sailing through the spot his chest had been.

"I hope you enjoyed your goodbye," Lane hissed, "and that your friends got in theirs too. This is the end of the great Alexander line."

Headhunter ran at Brutal, the chainsaw a lance pointed and willing to run him through.

"The end of the Merchants. Want to know why I didn't mow them down the minute they stepped inside?"

Brutal spun out of the way, bounding to the other side. Weapons hung within reach, but he made no move to take them.

"Because why should your deaths come for free? One by one, you'll die in my cage. Starting with that big-mouthed, blue shit stain. And the Kings will be paid handsomely for the service." He stroked my cheek. "But not you, Adeline. You, I'll keep."

Howling, Headhunter charged him again, saw swinging through the air.

Brutal whirled, kicked his leg up, and brought it down on his back. Headhunter pitched forward—dropping flat on the canvas and chainsaw sliding into the bars.

Brutal jumped on his back. With both hands, he grabbed him under the chin and pulled, stretching him like a bowstring.

Face reddening, Headhunter smacked the canvas, cries gurgling from his lips.

"Do it," I screamed.

Brutal wrenched.

Headhunter flopped on the mat, unseeing eyes peering into mine for the last time. Baris climbed off him and picked up the chainsaw.

I turned my head as the shower of blood sprayed us, splattering my shirt and Lane's jacket.

"Argh!" Brutal roared to boos and cheers alike.

Hopping off my seat, I snatched the keys from the King standing by the cage and let myself in. Covered in blood and holding a head, I devoured Brutal to more whistles and filthy calls.

"I am going to fuck the shit out of you tonight," I said. "But first—"

I grabbed the head, marched out of the cage, and tossed it on Lane's lap.

He yelped, jumping out of his seat and smacking it away.

I laughed. "You were saying?"

Lane lunged at me.

"Stop."

A hard wall of flesh appeared in our path.

"That's enough, Lane."

"But, boss!"

Boss?

"Take a walk. Cool off." A soft, lyrical sound flowed from his lips. It took a second to connect that it was speech. "Then clean up this mess."

"Yes, sir," he growled.

Lane stomped off, and it was just us.

Thiago Pais turned to me. My breath caught.

The tight, blueish-black suit clung to his frame, revealing the mounds and dips of his muscles, and negating the purpose of wearing clothes. Jewel-toned eyes held me in their reflection, capturing the surprised look on my face.

Thiago Pais was beautiful.

Not handsome, or attractive, or gorgeous. But assuredly the most beautiful man I'd ever seen. A tidy beard and mustache framed full, reddish lips. His long, Roman nose bore a dusting of light brown spots on the arch that spread across his cheeks. Pais smiled and one corner of his mouth rose higher than the other, as if something affected the nerves on the other side. The slight imperfect perfection punched me in the gut.

With that one smile, he descended from the sky and became as mortal as me. Suddenly, he could be touched, spoken to, and had for all the money he demanded.

"Thiago Pais," I whispered.

The smile widened. "Hello. I'm pleased my reputation precedes me."

"I'd say." The fog began to dissipate. "I saw your handiwork with Leah Tyler."

"Who?"

"One of your former employees who you cut up and left for dead."

The dancing light in his eyes didn't dim. "An unfortunate business. I took no pleasure in it. Sadly, there are times when"—he looked pointedly at the severed head—"examples must be made. I'm sure you can appreciate that, Adeline."

"Apparently, my reputation has preceded me as well."

"Of course." He leaned back, sweeping out his hands. "Adeline Redgrave, graduate of Cinco University, hospitality major. Sous chef to one of the best and most temperamental cooks in the city. Leader of the Merchants."

The final statement loosened my tongue. "I'm not a leader of the Merchants."

"Come now." His grin grew knowing. "It's not a meek banger's girl who throws a man's head at someone as dangerous as Desmond Lane. I wouldn't do you the insult of not learning everything there is to know about you.

You're hardworking, dedicated, and at twenty-three you rose to the top in a male-dominated field to become on par with the best. None of that suggests a woman who is willing to be anything but in charge."

I folded my arms. "Wow. I hope you don't take it as an insult that all I know about you is you carve people like Thanksgiving turkeys."

His laugh rolled from his chest—as devastatingly beautiful as the rest of him.

"How do you know so much about me?" I asked.

"The Castian."

My brows snapped together. "What?"

"I spoke to a few of the victims in the hospital. Most weren't ready to speak about their experience in that hotel." He stroked my hair. "But all could not stop talking about the beautiful, copper-haired angel who saved them. When the men who survived the club reported one such angel on the scene and said she was called Adeline, the rest was easy."

I nodded, accepting this. "You're welcome, by the way."

Thiago was still playing with my hair. "For?"

"For killing Lorenzo Bianchi. The man disrespected you, slashed your cut, and tried to strangle your business." I made the same sweeping gesture. "But look at you now. A king of Kings."

"So it was you who killed him," he said, appreciation leaking into his voice. "And you say you're not a leader."

A hand gripped Pais's wrist, removing it from my hair. Sinjin slid between us.

"I would appreciate it if you did not touch my Bunny."

I sensed a presence at my back. Brutal towered behind me. The blood on his chest and face were cleaned with his usual thoroughness. If not for the traces on his pants, you wouldn't have known he decapitated a man less than ten minutes ago.

Then Cash, who made a silent guard on my other side.

Thiago gazed at the hand around his wrist like he couldn't understand how it had gotten there.

"I'm afraid I am just a banger's girlfriend." I gently took Sinjin's hand and laced our fingers. "Well, more than one banger, but I digress. I do appreciate you recognizing my skills as I'm sure you appreciate my getting the Kings out of the child sex-trafficking business, clearing the way for you to take over, and showing up that pile of human waste called Lane. Admit it, you don't like his ass either."

Smiling, he lifted his shoulders.

"I will take my thanks in exchange for a real truce between the Kings and Merchants. One that doesn't require *this*." I pointed over my shoulder at the cage.

"Ah. Unfortunately, that's impossible. Look around you, Adeline." He gestured at the emptying stands. "This is the biggest turnout we've had in six years' worth of tournaments. I stand to make more in the coming weeks than Angelo Castillo saw in a year. If you want that truce, your boyfriend will have to fight for it," he said. "But I will give you this."

Thiago plucked something from his coat pocket and held it out. I took the card.

"What is this?"

"My number," he said, striding away. "You may find you need it one day." The four of us watched him leave.

"You make friends everywhere you go, don't you, Bunny?"

Chapter Eight

I twirled the card on my fingertip, watching the colors shift from gray to black, gray to black.

"I'd hang on to that."

I jumped, sending the card fluttering to the floor.

"What?"

"The card." Mercer checked himself out in the mirror, twisting to ogle a rather shapely butt. "Keep your enemies close. Isn't that what they say?"

"Thiago Pais." That uneven smile floated through my mind.

"Yes," said Mercer. "He has that effect on everyone."

My cheeks warmed. "Enough about him. Pais is just another problem in my way. Today we're talking about the first one. How does salmon pants get us closer to Raul?"

"Patience. It'll all make sense soon."

Mercer and I had spent the entire afternoon following the match, flitting from department store to department store. He got his hands on Brutal's winnings and set to work.

I think. I watched him comparing blue and white polo shirts. *Is this work?*

"Gorgeous, try on that dress."

"What dress—"

"Here you are, madam." An attendant appeared holding a white sundress with sunflowers along the hem. "Let me know if you need another size."

When had Mercer ordered me more clothes? He left me in my little corner of the store for five minutes while he got those pants.

I heaved a sigh. "Alright. But I warn you," I told Mercer. "This is the last one."

Stepping into the dressing room, I shed my standard jeans and food-punny T-shirt, and slipped the dress over my head. It fell around my hips, swaying as I moved.

It was cute. Cute like the fifty other dresses I tried on that afternoon—all rejected by Mercer as "not quite right." I understood his role in the gang was infiltrator. He used his skills, resources, and charm to go where the others couldn't go, and retrieve the information they couldn't get on their own. This was arguably the most important job and Mercer won't leave a thing to chance.

But for the life of me, I couldn't see where the perfect freaking sundress fit in.

"Mercer," I called. "Can you help me with this?"

He stuck his head in the dressing room. "What's wrong?"

"The zipper." I turned my bare back to him. "Will you do it up for me?"

"I dare say I can."

Warm hands encircled my waist, tugging the fabric together. And tugging. And tugging.

I bumped against his half-hard cock—excitement heightening at the mere thought I could get him this worked up just by standing partially exposed before him.

Mercer traced a finger up the bumpy ridges of my back, agonizingly slow, and brushed my hair over my shoulder.

Wetness pooled in my middle. He wasn't the only one raring to go at the slightest provocation. I had all of my men in every way except for him. I was so tired of waiting I could scream.

Mercer blew on my neck.

"Eep." I bit my lip to pen in another embarrassing sound, hoping he hadn't heard the first.

I caught his reflection's grin. He had.

"I see what you're doing, gorgeous." His hands slipped inside the dress, traveling over my stomach.

I lifted my nose. "I'm sure I don't know what you mean."

"I do believe it was a certain sandy-eyed cook who said I wasn't getting any till I hung an out-of-business sign over my cock." Mercer cupped my breasts. "It's not fair to tease a man using every ounce of his self-control to hold back."

"Oh." Mercer captured my nipples between his thumbs and forefingers, tugging on them till they were hard as rocks.

My head fell back on his shoulder. "Got a timeline for when that sign goes up?"

"It's been up for weeks, Adeline. I haven't touched another woman or man"—he kissed the small hollow of my throat—"since you."

My tongue stuck, jaw working as surprise and happiness bubbled through my veins. "You did?" I whispered. "Why didn't you tell me?"

"Because I didn't know how long it could last." One hand broke away, moving south. "What if there was another mark and I had to choose between you or finding out information that could protect you? It's an impossible choice, Adeline, and it'd hurt us both to make it."

Turning, I buried my nose in his sweet, peppery scent. "I promise you, those aren't our choices. There's another way, Mercer. One that may require more creativity and definitely won't be as easy as marks that welcome you through the door, but you can have both."

Mercer pushed past my folds.

"You can be a Merchant and be with me."

"I'm certainly motivated to try."

He teased my clit, dipping in and out of my pussy and collecting wetness on his fingers. Trapping my gaze, he inserted each into his mouth one by one, licking down to the knuckles.

My knees almost gave out.

"Madam?"

I froze with my lips against his skin. "Yes?"

"How's the dress? Is the size okay?"

"It's good." Mercer picked up the pace. "It's really, *really* good."

"Shall I go ahead and charge it for you?"

"Put it on my account, Juliana," Mercer said. "I'll take the white pants, blue Christiane polo, and khaki cardigan too."

"Of course, sir." She didn't sound in the least bit bothered by our dressing room sharing, or the suspicious *slap, slap, slap* of skin on skin. "Right away."

Grabbing his chin, I crushed our mouths together and screamed my orgasm—jerking and bucking against him, and Mercer swallowing it all.

"Damn," I breathed. "Shall I return the favor?"

"Not here. That was Juliana's 'I'm going to innocently walk away and get the manager' voice."

"Are you serious?"

He was serious.

Ten minutes later, Juliana returned with a stern-looking woman in tow. Mercer and I were miles apart. Him comparing ties, and me flipping through a magazine on the couch.

She studied us through narrowed eyes. "Everything okay, sir? Madam? Can I help you with anything?"

"Nope," I said. "Once we have our purchases, we'll be on our way."

We grabbed our clothes and headed out.

"That was the easy part," said Mercer. He molded me to his side. We walked out with me under his arm and feeling plenty happy about it. "Now comes the fun stuff."

A WEEK PASSED. THEN two. And the fun stuff had yet to arrive.

"How much longer is this going to take?" Sinjin asked.

The four of us were waiting outside Baris's room. There was another match tonight and only we were going. For the last few days, Mercer sent the men out to restock his *tools*.

"I should have everything I need by tonight. I'll stay back and get it ready."

I straightened. "Tonight? So that means—"

"We do it tomorrow."

"Does it have to be tomorrow? Why can't we do it tonight? Get Brutal out of this."

"Has to be tomorrow because one of the things I need is the wad of cash Brutal's about to get his hands on," he replied. "I worked out a deal with the manager and he wouldn't be undersold. He wants another five grand when we step through the door."

I didn't know the manager or door he was talking about. Mercer refused to tell me exactly what we were doing, and I low-key felt it was because he thought I'd stop him. Overall, the guys had avoided going too deep into the topic of Gianna.

We talked about getting to Raul, but not what they'd do when they had him. They said no truce was worth losing me or letting Gianna control their lives, but they wouldn't say how far they'd go to get the ledger.

The five of us made a commitment to honesty. It wouldn't be broken as long as we didn't ask questions we didn't want to know the answers to.

"Why won't you tell me what this foolproof plan is?"

I was never good at that.

"Are you planning to do something to Raul that you think I won't approve of?"

"I'm planning to torture him, sweetheart. Mercilessly and without losing a wink of sleep after." Mercer plopped next to me on the couch and pecked my lips. "If you've got even an ounce of fondness for the man, I'd rather you not have ample time to think of a way to stop me."

I hooked a finger through his tie, bringing him closer. "I only need seconds to stop you doing something I don't want you to do."

He growled low in his throat.

"But you've got nothing to worry about from me. You won't find an ounce of fondness here." I released him, smoothing down his shirt. "That doesn't apply to Gianna," I said. "You let me handle her. That's what we agreed."

"We will," Sinjin said. "You're plan A."

"What's plan B?"

He shrugged, grinning. "I'll improvise."

Sinjin couldn't have reassured me less if he said he'd set an atomic bomb and decimate Cinco so no one could have the ledger.

"No," I said. "Hell no. If killing her minions and leaving her without options doesn't do it, *I* will come up with plan B. Recently I discovered there are some things I'm not willing to lose for that damn book. Gianna is one of them."

His eyes were shadowed. "What about what I'm willing to lose?"

I sobered. "We will find out who had your father killed, Saint. I promise, I want nothing else but to make things right for you. All of you," I said, looking between him, Cash, and Mercer. "That's what it's always been about. Making things right."

Brutal's door opened, bringing our conversation to an end.

The four of us piled into Mercer's car, taking off into enemy territory.

Harlow.

The Merchants burned down most of their properties, warehouses, and underground clubs in the war with Angelo. Since, it appeared they'd been working to rectify that.

We parked down the road from an old Powers Brothers warehouse. A wholesaler based in another state that went bankrupt and left an empty building behind.

I wonder if they know their failure made way for other opportunities.

Stands had been set up on either side of the cavernous warehouse. Filling the space around the cage were rows of chairs for the up-front action. It couldn't be possible, but there was almost twice the amount of people in attendance.

Brutal and his opponent sold out the show.

I snaked my arms around his waist. "Ku'uipo," I said. "Beautiful word. Means sweetheart in Hawaiian. Are you Hawaiian?"

He held up two fingers, then one.

"Half," I translated easily. "Your mother's side?"

Yes.

"Ku'uipo it is. I'll still throw in sweetass every now and then."

That got me the smack I knew it would, making us both laugh.

Glancing past him, my smile dimmed.

One of Lane's guys beckoned us over. Lane himself was too busy drilling holes in our skulls.

I patted the little secret beneath my belt. *Let him try something. It'll be his head I toss around.*

Lane's guy directed us to a back room for Brutal to change.

"Wait until you're announced," he said. "We're doing things properly from here on."

"What does that mean?"

"It means you out. No weapons, tips, or advantages other than the ones in the cage. Can't have you slipping your boyfriend an edge."

"Fine."

I kissed him—unhurried by our audience. "I'll be right in the front row, baby. Go out there, and kill."

He saluted.

Outside, Cash and Saint were seated with an empty chair between them. I sat with my guys, hooking my arms through theirs.

"That guy said they're doing things properly from here," I told them, tracking the man's return to Lane. "I wish we knew more about the tournament other than the single match Mercer went to. Headhunter won three tournaments and he was only round one. Who will they pit Brutal against tonight?"

"Whoever it is," Cash said, "they won't underestimate him."

"Math, common sense, and instinct, Cash. What are they saying about Brutal's chances?"

"I can't apply probability to these fights when the opposers are unknown. I'm sure that's the point. I can't research them, their fighting styles, or previous kills. Going in blind puts Brutal at a disadvantage."

"Did you recognize Headhunter? Was he a King?"

"Never seen him before. The Kings are the largest gang in the city. I don't know all the men, or women, in play. If I had to guess, I'd say they're choosing from a special pool of Kings. The ones that get their hands dirty."

"Contract killers."

"Contract psychos," Saint said. "No conscience, no feelings, no fear. Not even of losing their lives. They're the ones who slaughter the sweet couple on Eleventh Street who refuse to pay protection money, and then sit in their restaurant sipping tea while they bleed out."

"Still, I feel like we would've heard about an assassin who favors beheading."

"We're surrounded by woods, Redgrave," Cash said. "Miles and miles of dense woods."

I quieted. In all my years and in the deepest, most depraved part of my soul. I never saw Elmshire Woods for its darkest potential. A graveyard.

"Maybe it's like Jo said. There's been talk of fighters killed in the circuit and people dismissed it. You pick a filthy job, you'll meet a filthy end. The news report broadcasts a gruesome murder every other day. Few stop to take notice of it except for, well, you." I bumped Cash's shoulder. "We've become so desensitized to what Cinco City has become, it's no wonder something like this can go on for years unchecked."

"It's the Kings who've gone unchecked," Saint said. "Who connects the shit we've been dealing with the last several months? The child auctions, counterfeiting, and now this. If Kieran is a title, it's one that a King has held before. Our original theory still applies. The ledger helped the Kings get too big to stop."

I couldn't fault his reasoning. Everything he said was likely true.

"Angelo Castillo knew my father." Their gaze snapped to me. "When the Lords were a young gang, before they created the ledger, a nobody hidden in the ranks of a Harlow outfit approached them asking for a favor. The leader of the Kings at that time was no fool. He didn't go to the bathroom without ten guards protecting his ass. He wasn't an easy target three hundred and sixty-four days out of the year. But then, there were three hundred and sixty-five.

"Every Thanksgiving, Jonas Finnegan visited his parents out of state. They didn't know their son was more than a *businessman,* so the armed guard was reduced from ten to two. It was the best chance to take him out—assuming Angelo could get his hands on the address, location, and time they left. He couldn't, so the Lords did."

"Adeline, are you trying to tell me your father and his friends made Angelo leader of the Kings?" Cash asked.

"Kingmakers, baby. It's what they did," I replied. "Soren got the info and Dad carried out the plan. Fake roadblocks on the street. Plus, him and a handful of Lords in fake orange vests actually tearing up the road. Daddy didn't do things by halves.

"Finnegan asked Dad for an alternate route and he told him exactly where to go. Angelo was waiting."

Cash cocked a brow. "Is this the part where you finally tell me what happened in our basement?"

"Killed him," I said, shrugging. "Stuck a knife in his throat for recognizing me, and then the disgusting things he did following. He busted in that fire station to kill you, and take me. Proving he never gave up on his theories concerning my dad."

The looks on their faces asked for more.

"Angelo saw Dad that day on the road. Dad had to tell him where to wait for Jonas, and he followed the dirt road down to the fork, glimpsing the men putting out the roadblocks and the one leading them. Years down the line, when Kieran took over the city and the ledger came into play, Angelo made another list of suspects and put my father on it."

"Makes sense," Saint said. "Everyone was looking for a fixer."

"He pulled the same shit he did on us. Broke into my dad's place with a bunch of bangers and tried to torture the ledger out of him. Dad slaughtered them and sent Angelo running into the night. The man left a coward-size hole in the wall." I laughed. "He for fuck sure never tried going after my dad again. But I guess he didn't cross Oscar Redgrave off the list either.

"Over a decade later, a certain boyfriend brings me to a sit-down with a crime boss, and the family resemblance came through. Angelo pegged me as the daughter in the apartment's photographs. I assume he thought he finally had leverage to discover if my dad was Kieran after all."

"This explains so much," said Saint.

I gave him a look. "My father hasn't forgiven you yet, by the way. He blames you for dragging his sweet little girl into this Kieran war once again."

"That tracks. I've never done well with parents," he mused. "I had to sneak around with every girlfriend I had in high school. For some reason, their folks kept forbidding them from seeing me."

I observed my blue-haired murderous love packing no less than five weapons on his person.

"Wonder where that came from," he said.

I giggled. "Daddy may rough you up a little, but eventually you'll grow on him."

"Least I have that to look forward to," Saint muttered. "Any chance you're more trouble than you're worth?"

"Nope."

Saint nibbled my bottom lip, winning entrance to entwine our tongues in a panty-melting kiss.

"Huh." He leaned back, taking me with him. "Yeah, I'd say you're worth it."

BRUTAL

"We promised you the biggest, deadliest, most ruthless tournament this city has ever seen."

I filled the door entrance, standing in plain view. Couldn't answer why I was separated from Adeline and directed to another closet, but whatever they had planned, they'd do it while I watched.

"Did we deliver?!"

"Yeah!" belted the crowd.

The announcer was front and center that night. He walked the length of the cage, whipping up the audience. Leather vest. Flame tattoo on his neck. "HO" painted loud and proud on his back. The guy was an Outlaw.

Adeline's lack of knowledge about the tournament was not shared. This was my world. The Zhangs and Headhunters my people.

I've known about the tournament since I was a kid sleeping in a gym and roaming the street with gloves covering my busted knuckles. After a few too many wins, a couple of Kings approached me asking if I wanted to make some real money. They brought me to the matches to witness the bases of human vice.

I blew it off and left—the hard way. I could still hear those guys screaming as they faced the consequences of trying to stop me.

My attention flicked to Lane and his men. *Consequences I could've imparted to him—which Adeline knows.*

How was a mystery. She could sense I gave in too easily. Her ability to peer into my mind was as astounding as it was unsettling. The day would come when she would see what she wasn't meant to. Hopefully too late for her to stop me.

"You all remember our boy, Hatchet."

I stiffened. They couldn't be serious putting that man back in a cage with me.

"Got a face full of piss and three missing teeth." Laughter rolled over the audience. "But did you know Hatchet has a brother?"

"Oooh," the crowd taunted.

"And what's his name?!"

"Axe! Axe! Axe!"

"That's right," he bayed. "For the honor of Hatchet and the Outlaws, Axe is going to..." He pointed to the audience.

"Kill! Kill! Kill!"

The announcer let them go on, jumping and running around the cage—spotting me and wagging his tongue as he drew a line across his neck.

"Ladies and gentlemen, Axe!"

A hulking mass of muscle and ink emerged from the depths of the warehouse. Sans entourage, chains, or straightjacket, Axe bore down on the cage, silencing people as he passed.

Axe was the opposite of Hatchet—a fact which shortchanged him when they handed out nicknames. Axe towered a foot over me and doubled my size. His hair longer, fists thicker, and smirk nastier.

It wasn't fear that unbound my shoulders and propped me against the frame.

It was boredom.

Did they think a giant with a grudge was enough to take me out? Like that wasn't every fucking guy I've beaten from here to Lancaster Street? The big guys, the brothers, the enforcers, and bangers. They were all the same. They always made it personal. Got pissed. Letting anger cloud their judgment or showing off pushed them into picking up a chainsaw and upsetting their balance. One good hit and the heavy tool brought Headhunter down.

This was how I differed. I was always angry, but my rage wasn't for them. They were just the faceless bodies that stood in its path. Every time I pounded them wondering if this would be the battle to sate me—if I could finally stop. They never were, and I moved on to the next.

"—explain the rules for guests," said the announcer. "Three rounds of twenty minutes each. If our warriors are still standing, they go into the 'sudden death' round. We don't have any rules around here... except for one."

He turned and looked at me dead-on. "Warriors risk their lives for the tournament and are honored. Mutilation of the body after death isn't allowed, boy," he jeered. "One rule, and you fucking broke it. You know what this means?

"You face your opponent weaponless. Axe picks one of his choosing, and then all are removed."

"What?" Adeline cried. "You pulled that out of your ass!" She flew at the cage, and he was lucky to be locked inside it. "Like hell that's a rule. What more do you cheating bastards want from him?!"

Guards swarmed her, trying to pull her off the cage. She socked one in the nose.

"You want a mutilated corpse?! Come outta that fucking cage!"

I snorted, and covered my mouth to hide it. Adeline Redgrave was anger. She was rage and fire and beauty in a package that couldn't contain her. She was all I wanted to be, couldn't say, and wished to feel. Never in my highest or lowest point did I believe in the idea of an Adeline.

Cash and Saint joined the scuffle, tossing a few guys into the chairs and scattering screaming people.

Adeline climbed the bars, kicked in the face of a guard that tried pulling her down, and continued screaming abuse at the announcer. He advanced on her, microphone up and threatening. Adeline snatched a crowbar off the metal and—

I winced.

The guy's head snapped all the way around. He dropped to the mat out cold.

Ku'uipo.

My mother used to speak of soulmates. Of two halves finding their whole and there being no question that when you've found them, it's right.

Adeline believed I was still questioning if I loved her, but there's been nothing to question since the third time we met.

"It's not just the things you have to do. It's the knowledge they're being done correctly. And the only person you can trust to get it right is you."

Loving her was inevitable. Keeping her is impossible.

There is something that I have to do, and I must get it right. I had to leave. If I told her I loved her, she wouldn't understand why.

Saint, Cash, and Adeline were thrown out. Four men fought to slide the doors closed and lock them.

I let it happen.

Adeline's passionate defense of me was as endearing as it was cock-swelling, but the Outlaws had not put me at a disadvantage. I was trained as a boxer, then a street fighter. I didn't use or need weapons. Such a thing would not change tonight.

The announcer was carried out of the cage and a new guy took his place.

"Let's begin," he said. "Axe, choose your weapon."

"Axe! Axe!"

Whether they were chanting his name or encouraging his choice wasn't clear. Either way, he lifted the long-handled axe off the bars, howling as he brandished it overhead.

The rest were carted away—walked past me by smirking Kings searching for a reaction and finding none.

"Axe versus Brutal!"

I entered the cage, hearing the chains clink behind me.

"I'm going home with your head, boy," Axe hissed. "You'll spend the rest of your afterlife with Hatch pissing down your neck."

That was an unwise thing to say.

Axe leveled the blunt instrument at my chest like a battering ram.

Ding!

"Argh!" Axe came for me, heaving it high, and I stood rooted to the spot.

He brought the axe down and—

My hand flashed, sinking my fist in his neck.

Axe stumbled. Eyes bugging, the axe slipped through his hands—striking the canvas centimeters from me. He clutched his damaged throat.

I kicked out and buckled his knee. Axe dropped flat on his back.

Picking up the axe, I hefted it in the air.

"Kill! Kill!"

"Axe, get up!"

His Outlaw buddies should save the shouts for their last words.

I tossed the axe away. It clanged against the bars, fell and slipped through.

Axe struggled to get up as I returned for him.

I believe you said something about pissing down my neck.

"Kill!"

Falling on him, I fisted his hair, and struck—breaking his nose on the first hit. The fifth punch cracked an eye socket. The seventh knocked him unconscious.

The cheers reached deafening, covering the roars of the Outlaws and the fury etched in Lane's face.

I did not stop until I sent Axe to a much tidier place.

Stepping away from the bloody mass who used to be a man, my anger wasn't gone, but his was. In a way, he was free. So who really won?

"I'M SORRY I GOT US kicked out." Adeline stretched out naked on top of me, tracing messages on my skin. "I'm supposed to be there watching your back," she said. "Not hitting over the head mini-tyrants compensating for their small dicks."

I chuckled. Adeline cut it off with her kiss.

"There are three more matches after this, but you won't be in them. Mercer says he has everything he needs. He swears we'll have Raul by tomorrow. If I know Gianna—and I do—she'll have the ledger within reach at all times. Finding out where she's hiding is finding the ledger. Once we have it, we'll bring an end to this."

I traced the curve of her lips, wondering if like unending fights, each kiss would forever leave me wanting more.

"You're right," she said. "For one night, let's allow tomorrow to worry about itself."

There she goes again. Reading my mind.

Adeline kissed my fingertips. "I looked up other sweet pet names in Hawaiian," she said. "Like kea aloha and mea aloha."

My fingers stilled.

"Mea aloha." Mom chopped the peppers for the salad, laughing at my wrinkled nose. "Don't make that face, Kainalu. It's good for you."

Kainalu.

Baris meant peace. Mom said she made my second name *Kainalu*, the billowing ocean, to balance me out. Peaceful seas and crashing waves. You cannot have one and not the other.

"*Ku'uipo*," she said.

"Means mushy stuff like sweetheart or girlfriend."

"Very good. What does *ohana* mean?"

I kicked my feet under the island. I hadn't seen Mom in two weeks. I was excited to be with her even if she did put peppers in my salad.

My mom was the most beautiful woman in the world. She had the prettiest laugh. The softest hair, and arms that hugged me so tight, she lifted me off my feet. I buried my face in her neck, breathing in her rose perfume, and wondering when she'd keep her promise to take me to Hawaii.

And never come back.

"*Ohana* is an easy one."

She flicked my nose. "If it's so easy, tell me what it means."

"*Ohana* means—"

"What is this?"

I shot up so fast I tipped in the chair. I crashed to the floor, pain zinging through my skull.

"Baris!" Mom cried, running to me.

Father hauled her back. "I told you about teaching him that stuff."

That stuff.

"The boy can't get through a sentence without stumbling and stuttering like a simpleton. No wonder when you're filling his head with this nonsense—confusing him."

My lips trembled. I could speak perfect English and Hawaiian. To everyone else.

"That's not true—"

"Silence!" he snapped. "See how he talks back? Defies his own father and who is to blame? You were told not to teach him and you disobeyed me."

"He's my son too—"

Father backhanded her. Mom flew against the fridge.

I bit my lip, scream leaking out.

"He's not your son. He's an Alexander. He's to inherit a hundred-year legacy, but how will he do that when you coddle him?" Father ripped off his belt. *"Teach him disrespect."*

Lash.

"Permit his whining and sniveling!"

Lash.

"He's near enough to worthless! Your damaging influence will not be allowed to pervert my son!"

My nails pierced my forehead, hands covering my eyes. I tried to push it down. The pressure built—choking the air from me. I couldn't speak, but he had to stop. Stop or Mom would go away again.

"F-Father—"

"Quiet, Baris," Mom cried. "Please, just be quiet."

"Baris?"

I blinked.

"Are you okay?" Adeline asked. "I lost you for a second."

Brushing back her hair, I drew her in, flipping us over to the sweet sound of her laugh.

You haven't lost me. Not yet.

Chapter Nine

A*deline*

"Eminent Penthouse Apartments." I tipped my head back, following the skyscraper up till it disappeared in the sun's glare. "Does it have a dress code?"

Mercer parked on the side street and climbed out in his preppy white pants, polo, and cardigan. I wore my dress too—feeling slightly like a little girl playing dress-up. After all, it was when I played fairy princess or slipped on a costume designed to get me closer to my target that I wore a dress. I assumed we were doing the latter that day.

"You look amazing." Mercer put a hand around my waist. Together we crossed the street. "Your role is simple. Today, you play my lovely assistant."

"Assisting in?" I pressed.

"Deception, infiltration, incapacitation, baiting, capturing, and information retrieval."

I nodded. "Got it. See how easy that was?"

He was laughing as the doorman stepped in front of us.

"Good morning. How can I help you?"

"We're here to see Mr. Johnson."

"Is he expecting you?"

Mercer motioned over his shoulder. "I believe that's him coming now."

A tidy, balding man in a brown suit rushed out of the building. "Mr. Clark, please. Show them in. The Millers are here to tour their perspective home."

The Millers?

Clark let us through. We followed Mr. Johnson past large antique vases and dancing palm fronds.

The Eminent lived up to its name and location in Leighbridge. We weren't far from Prescott Avenue and the former home of Richard La Roche.

Johnson brought us into a small office made smaller by the desk, hutch, chairs, bar, and bookshelves he crammed inside. All flaunting wealth, if not giving us space to move around.

Johnson skipped the preamble. "Five grand."

Mercer tossed him the money without a fight. "Two days. That was the deal."

His eyes narrowed. "What do you plan to do in there?"

"I've explained this to you." Mercer kissed my palm. "My soon-to-be bride comes from a wealthy family. Her father will cut us off if she marries someone without money—like me. We have to put on this charade to get Dad's blessing. It's the only way." Mercer gripped his shoulder. "This is a win for love."

"Uh-huh." Johnson counted his bills. "You can use the apartment for forty-eight hours and not a second more. You and your guests are to remain there. Do not use the facilities. Do not disturb the residents." He tossed Mercer a pair of keys. "Go."

"Thank you so much," Mercer gushed. "For love!"

He shooed us out, still counting his money. I held it in till the door closed, then burst out laughing.

"Dare I ask?"

Mercer winked. "Only gets more interesting from here," he said, giving me the keys. "Go up to apartment 816. I'll be right behind you."

"Okay."

We kissed and parted ways by the elevator. I took it up to the eighth floor, stepping out in a wide hallway with four doors. I went inside 816 and went straight to the chaise by the window, stretching out next to my city. Mercer arrived ten minutes later bearing two suitcases.

"I could get used to this," I said.

"One day you will."

Our borrowed apartment was furnished on the minimal side. My chaise matched the two couches in the living room that faced an empty spot above the fireplace mantle. The bookshelves were bare. The dining table boasted a bowl of fake fruit.

I wandered into the bedrooms while Mercer went through his cases. The master had little to show for itself, but the king-size bed and downy sheets would do the job just fine.

"So, what's the plan?" I called. "Another big drug order?"

"Didn't work the first time," he replied. "I never pull a failed con twice."

"We have the place for two days?" I flung myself on the bed. "Will we be staying the night?"

"If Perez plays coy, yes. Hopefully, he doesn't for longer than that. Johnson will be looking to throw us out by then."

I climbed off, venturing out to join him.

Mercer closed the case, granting me a glimpse of steel before it shut. He came to me holding a bottle of wine and a tote bag decorated with sunflowers.

"No time like the present," he said. "Shall we?"

My hand closed over the offered bag. I had no idea what was going on. All I knew was whatever Mercer had planned would bring us closer to Gianna. I trusted at the very least that we both wanted her.

"Why are you doing this?" I asked. "Gianna taunted me. Laughing when she said she'd keep your secret and I admitted I didn't know what it was. I understand if you need more time to tell me when you're ready, but you haven't asked for it. We don't talk about it at all. Why is that?"

Mercer closed the distance, threading my arm through the handles, and gently resting the bag on my shoulder. "Some secrets weren't meant to be spoken, Adeline."

"Can you say that in a relationship?"

"It's most important in a relationship." His handsome grin hung on his lips, though I did not sense he was amused. I couldn't tell what he felt. "The biggest lie we spread is that we want to know everything. Does a man want to know his current girlfriend cheated in every past relationship? Even if she's fully committed to him, isn't that information bound to poison them with suspicion and paranoia?

"There are times when that's exactly what the truth is: poison. It erodes people's faith in you. It stops them seeing who you've become because they can't see past who you were." His kiss was soft, sweet, and over as quickly as it started. "I won't tell you what's in that ledger and I'll burn it before you find out. Because I love you."

The confession pierced my heart. How could he confess the most wonderful thing he ever said to me, on the heels of the worst?

I swallowed hard, fighting to maintain an even voice. "What does that mean for Gianna, Mercer? She knows your secret. What's to stop her from telling me?"

His expression didn't change. "I mean your friend no harm, Adeline. Hurting her would hardly get me you."

"You haven't answered my question."

"Haven't I?" Mercer turned away from me.

"What are you going to do to stop her telling me?" I asked louder.

Mercer reached the door, meeting my eyes as he gestured for me to leave. "I'll remind her that she loves you as much as and longer than I have. Deep down, she doesn't want to see you hurt."

I stood stuck to the spot—mind whirling and me unable to voice a thought. The example he gave was good. Such a truth would poison the trust in a relationship. Even so, that truth was not his. His secret could be something I absolutely needed to know.

Shouldn't ignorance be my choice?

You chose the moment you revealed your secrets, a voice reminded. *Doesn't Mercer have the same right?*

Hitching the bag higher up my shoulder, I walked out.

Mercer fell in step with me, resting a hand on the small of my back. I let it stay.

If Mercer believed honesty would cause him to lose me, it was my job to reassure him such a thing couldn't happen.

We waited before the elevators in an odd silence. The wine bottle and his pressing the *up* button were my clues to what happened next. Plus, the heavy bag.

I worked my arm. *What's in this thing?* Peeking inside, I saw a laptop.

Mercer pinched my backside.

"Hey," I cried.

"No peeking."

A couple came out of their apartment pushing a chubby baby in a stroller. I pinched him back in full view.

"Oooh," he moaned. "Baby, please. We're in public."

Giggling, we ducked into the elevator. I rested my head on his arm and pushed away the last traces of hurt.

You'll tell me everything one day, Mercer Santos. In the end, I always get what I want.

We dinged on the eleventh floor. Mercer dropped a kiss on my nose.

"We're a newlywed couple that just moved in," he said. "If you feel the need to get handsy while playing your part, go where instinct moves you."

"What? Like this." I skittered my fingers up his sides.

Mercer shot away, running from me. "I take it back!"

I chased him laughing. How could I not love him? I felt light and happy when I was with Mercer. When have I ever been able to say that in my life?

Mercer stopped before 1102. One of two doors in the hallway. He held out his hand for me.

Playtime was over.

I fixed a bright, just-married smile on my face. *Who is on the other side of the door, and how will they get us closer to Raul?*

Mercer rang the bell.

"Just a moment," a voice called.

The door flew open.

A middle-aged woman with long brown hair streaked with gray blinked at us from over the threshold. She wore an outfit slightly similar to mine. White pants and top, paired with a black blazer covered in daffodils.

I squinted imperceptibly. Something about her was familiar.

"Hello, can I help you?"

"Hi," Mercer said. "I hope we're not disturbing you. My name is Kent Miller and this is my wife, Susanna. We just moved in downstairs."

"Nice to meet you both."

We shook hands.

"We're new to Cinco," Mercer continued. "Relocated for my job and don't know a soul here. So I thought, why not introduce ourselves to a few of the neighbors?"

"Oh," she said, smiling. "Well, you're very welcome. My name is—"

"Minnie?" Footsteps followed the call. "Who's at the door?"

"New residents to the building. Come say hi, sweetie."

A tall man with a full head of silver hair and a strong jaw slipped his arm around her. I took one look at him and knew.

Holy hell. How did Mercer find them?

"I'm Minerva Perez and this is my husband, Julio. Sweetie, this is Kent and Susanna Miller."

"If you've got time," Mercer said, "we'd love to chat and get to know each other." He lifted the bottle. "I come bearing gifts."

Julio's brows reached his hairline. "Prieur Montrachet. That is an excellent vintage, son."

Excellent? Prieur Montrachet went for a thousand dollars a pop. No wonder Mercer drained the coffers on this project.

"Please, come in."

What is this project? I thought as we stepped inside. *What is Mercer planning to do to this sweet couple to force their son out of hiding?*

"Can't have wine like this without a companion," Minerva said. "Sit. I'll get the cheese and glasses."

Julio led us through their sprawling home. Twice the size of ours, it beat us in décor as well. The entire space had a light, airy atmosphere captured in the fluffy white rugs, soft gray couches, white piano, and painted steel butterflies traveling up the wall.

Julio brought us into the living room. Taking up ten times as much wall space as the butterflies, were photos of their only son, Raul.

"Just moved here, did you?"

"A week ago," Mercer replied. "Climbed out of the car into Cinco City."

"Where are you from originally?"

"Florida. This is quite a change of pace for us."

Mercer knew the fake backstory. I let him fill it in while I studied pictures of Raul.

He was an adorable child that grew into a handsome man. The collection of photos took me through the progression of his life—from a smiling, missing-tooth baby to teenager in graduation robes. The photos also showed the progress from innocent to man with a cruel grin and mocking light in his eyes.

What did I say? The only time it was worth knowing a person was when they were a child. I'm sure I would've liked this happy baby more than the cheating, sponging dealer he became.

"That's our son. Raul." Minerva came in carrying a tray loaded with cheese, grapes, and four glasses.

"Handsome man," I said simply.

"He's a model."

"Only because you passed down your looks."

Her laugh was a light, tinkling sound. "I like you already."

I sat down next to Mercer on the loveseat and took advantage of the permission to get handsy. I teased the little curls at the nape of his neck, relaxing as he pulled me closer.

"None for my wife," Mercer said. "She's six weeks in with our first."

I am?

"Congratulations," Minerva gushed. "How exciting. New city, new marriage, new baby."

"Thank you," I said. I tried not to pout at the expensive, rare, delicious wine being served to everyone but me. "We couldn't be happier."

"That's why it's so important to me that Susie makes friends," Mercer said. "She's transitioning to stay-at-home mom while we get ready for the baby, and with me working all day, I can't stand the thought of her home alone in a new place without anyone to talk to."

Minerva waved that away. "Problem solved. You can stop by any time, Susanna."

"Especially if you bring more of this wine," Julio agreed, taking a hearty sip.

"Is your mother back in Florida?" Minerva asked me.

"She is."

"Then, yes, please, come by any time if you have questions or need recommendations. I'm a retired midwife."

"What do you do, Julio?" Mercer asked.

"Inherit money," Minerva said.

"And I'm very good at it," her husband stage-whispered.

We cracked up. Hard to believe this charming couple spat out the likes of Raul Perez.

"I used to be a hedge fund manager," Julio said. "Then I transitioned into real estate, made some smart investments, and here we are. I'm retired now and spending every day with my beautiful wife."

Mercer lifted his glass. "I'll drink to that." They clinked. "How did you two meet?"

Julio stroked his wife's cheek. "Brown University. Minnie was a young, beautiful freshman. I was a junior. We met on the first day of Intro to Art and the rest was history."

"So sweet," I said. I popped a slice of Havarti on my tongue.

"Susie and I are former fragrance chemists," Mercer said. "We met on the job."

"A fragrance chemist?" Minerva asked between sips.

"We develop and test scents for women's and men's perfumes."

She picked up a grape, dropped it, and nearly toppled off the couch reaching for it.

"Whoa, there." Julio sloshed wine out of the glass moving to help her.

"We also do soaps, lotions, and things like that. I can tell you more about the process. What we do is..."

Mercer launched into an explanation of fragrance chemistry and the position he got working for La Fleuve perfume company in Cinco while they paid for him to complete his master's.

The Perezes' eyes drooped during his speech.

Minerva reached for another grape, and tipped onto her husband's lap. Julio slumped on top of her. The glass slipped from her fingers, spilling the remains on the rug.

"—excited to be here," Mercer finished. "About time."

He set his untouched glass on the coffee table. "I laced that bottle with enough to knock out a horse. The polite sips seriously slow things down."

I gaped at the unconscious couple. "What did you give them?"

"Tranquilizers. Sedatives." Mercer claimed my bag. "It's a special cocktail I mix up myself. They'll be out for a while."

I could do nothing but sit there as he set out a laptop, recording equipment, gloves, and a small black pouch.

"It's so much easier with you along, darling. It's socially acceptable for women to walk about with these big bags, and even better, it's rude to look inside them."

"Feel free to use me and my big bags anytime," I said. "Want to tell me how drugging his parents gets us to Raul?"

Mercer slapped on the pair of gloves. He handed the other to me. "No prints," he said simply.

Picking up his glass, he made for the kitchen, leaving me to trail him.

"Your father is Oscar Redgrave. I'm sure your education is extensive. What did he teach you about infiltration?" Mercer tossed me a grin. "Not that you didn't do an expert job on us."

"I'd like to once again point out that you four kidnapped me. I told you all to go fuck yourselves multiple times."

He laughed.

"And not much," I admitted. "Dad did his best not to let their targets see his face."

"Here's a tip: when you're sharing from a spiked bottle, don't stop talking. No one expects you to drink when talking, and while you're running your mouth, the marks will naturally drink to give themselves something to do. They'll down the entire bottle without noticing you didn't take a sip."

Mercer washed, dried, and returned his glass to the shelf.

"Good tip."

"Second." He was on the move again, leading me out into the living room. "You can learn to mimic with some accuracy." Julio Perez's voice poured from his lips. "But don't put it to chance when attempting to fool spouses or children. They've had decades to learn the nuances of their speech. You can't hope to come close."

I just stared at him. "Who are you?"

He winked. "That's where technology comes in, gorgeous. You were kind enough to record our chat."

Joining him on the couch, I watched fascinated as he plugged the recording into the laptop and booted up a program. Loading the audio files, separating voices, calibrating the program. He did it all while rattling off explanations. I flicked from him to the computer, and back to him.

I've always known Mercer was more than an escort and professional flirt. Still, the depth of his skill surprised me. The boys named him invaluable. I could see why.

"So, Mr. and Mrs. Perez are calling their estranged son home."

Mercer matched my grin. "A reconciliation is long overdue."

"I can't believe you took my comments outlining what a douche he is and turned it into this. Was this always plan B?"

"Yep. You should hear what I had planned for C."

Mercer leaned over and plucked Julio's phone from his pocket. "He made most of the sounds. We're missing a few, but it'll be enough."

"What are you going to say?"

He jerked his chin at the screen. Mercer typed out the speech for the program to recite. Its spot-on portrayal of Julio Perez induced a shudder.

"You don't have recordings of all our voices, do you?"

"Oh, good. If you're asking, you didn't notice the Adeline file with photos, recordings, and maps of your movements."

I fell against him laughing. Mercer tucked me under his arm as he pulled up Raul's number.

It rang and rang and—

"Hey, it's Raul. You missed me. Leave a message and I'll hit you back when I can."

Beep.

Mercer hit play.

"Hello, son. It's been a while. Your mother and I have been thinking... This has gone on long enough. You're our only son and we want to make things right. Come by for dinner tonight. Seven. Let's talk."

Mercer ended the voicemail.

"Do you think he'll show?" I asked.

"You know him better than me."

I glanced around the luxurious apartment. "With even the chance all this becomes his when they drop off the twig, Raul will be here an hour early in his best suit and a twice-as-expensive bottle of kiss-up wine."

"Then we better get ready."

HOURS LATER, MERCER'S suitcases were brought up to the eleventh floor and emptied. I watched him lay out the collection of knives, picks, pliers, and hammers like a caterer prepared a table.

The Perezes had long since been moved to their bedroom to sleep in peace.

"Little known fact." Mercer opened the small black pouch, removing a bottle of liquid and a syringe. "The torture dungeon," he said, "was my idea."

My attention drifted to the torture room he created in the Perezes' home. "My gosh," I breathed. "You're the most dangerous of all of us, aren't you?"

"Aw." Mercer popped a kiss on my lips. "Thank you for noticing, lovely."

I shivered—equal parts frightened and turned on. With disturbing clarity, I pictured a scenario where I received a message supposedly from my father, rushed to wherever he asked me to meet him, and fell headlong into this trap. Every way I looked at it, Mercer would've gotten me. There was something incredibly sexy about a man that deadly, and knowing he uses his dark powers for you.

Someone knocked on the door.

I checked my watch. *6:59 p.m.*

Raul called back three times. We didn't answer not wanting to risk the program in an actual conversation. I assumed he would show up anyway.

"I'm always right," I said, moving into the kitchen. I had a good view of the front door. It would swing my way and prevent him from seeing me till it was too late.

Mercer came up on the other side and twisted the lock.

"Mom?" The hinges creaked. "Dad, I'm here. What did you want to talk—?" Raul landed on me. "Addy?"

Mercer moved from behind the door. He secured his head and stuck the needle in his neck in one smooth move.

"What... the...?" Raul sank to his knees. Mercer guided him the rest of the way.

"Shall we?"

Mercer and I set to work.

I expected to feel some twinge of remorse or regret as we bound Raul, set him on the stool, and prepared the tools. Certainly the creature recognized this wasn't Raul's war. He was just unlucky enough to be in the middle of it.

This ends on his word. The sooner he tells us where to find Gianna, the sooner he goes home to her.

Mercer threw a cup of water in his face. He shot awake, sputtering.

"What's going on? Addy? Where the fuck are my parents?!"

"They're safe." I perched on the arm of the chair, crossing my legs. "For now."

Raul twisted. Wrenching his arms, he struggled to get free of the zip ties. The flailing tightened the rope around his throat. He was sitting on a stool, hands tied. The rope hanging from the beam looped around his neck. Beneath the stool was a sheet of plastic. Squirming wasn't his best idea.

"This is about Gianna," he said. "I told her I wanted out of this bullshit! Whatever your fucking problem is, take it up with her."

"Gladly. Tell me where she is."

Raul flicked to the torture instruments lined up on the table. He barked a laugh. "What do you think you're going to do to me?"

"Nothing." My reply was calm. "If you tell me where she is."

He dismissed me. "Mercer, isn't it? Gianna described who to look out for. She also told me your services are *for sale*. I'll give you fifty grand to slap that bitch, get me out of these ties, and put them on her."

Mercer crossed the distance. He kicked the stool out from under him.

Shouting, Raul scrambled to catch himself. "What the fuck?! Fine. We'll make it one hundred."

My love slugged him on the jaw.

Raul swayed. The rope twisted in hungry anticipation.

"Gorgeous, would you mind?"

I righted the stool as Mercer heaved Raul up. He made him stand while I untied the knot around the piano. I pulled the rope taut, giving him barely any slack.

Raul balanced on the balls of his feet—cocky-ass expression gone.

"Why are you doing this?!" he cried. "Addy, we're friends."

"You fuck Gianna and eat my food. How does that make us friends?"

"I've kept your secret. I could've sold that info for a lot of fucking money, believe me." Raul was red under the harsh light. A niggle of irritation pricked for him still looking handsome. "I didn't. I even carried out jobs for you two. What does that make us if not friends?"

I shrugged. "Maybe you're right, but you won't get far tugging that cord. I lied to and deceived my boyfriends. Broke a promise to my dad. And violated a truce with my best friend. All people I like way more than you and that didn't stop me."

"Ad—"

I held up a hand. "Let's avoid any further attempts to appeal to my good side. She's not here right now."

His lips peeled back from his teeth. "Stupid cunt! Demented bitch on a power trip! Do you know who I am? I know five guys who'd slit your throat for a dime bag. I—"

I yanked on the rope.

Choking, he knocked off-balance, wobbling on the stool.

"No, he-help! Addy, stop!"

"You know how I feel about being called a bitch," I said, clicking my tongue. "Pissing me off isn't your best move."

"I'm sorry." He straightened—chest heaving and sweat soaking his brow. "Get me down. We can talk about this."

I passed the rope to Mercer. Eating the distance, I said, "This is how it's going to work. I will ask you where Gianna is. If you tell me, I'll untie those ropes and we'll take a field trip to visit her. If you do not tell me, my boyfriend will teach you the uses of the items on that table. Understand?"

His tongue darted out, licking chapped lips. "You won't do it."

"Didn't I just say? I'm not doing it. Mercer is."

"You won't let him. It would kill Gianna if anything happened to me. You may not give a shit about my life, but she loves me. And you love her. You won't do this."

I waited for him to finish. "Haven't you heard, Raul? Gianna doesn't believe in love." I clapped. "Okay, second try. Where is Gianna?"

"There's no point in me telling you. I don't know how you got into my parents' place, but I can promise you getting to Gianna won't be nearly as easy." His glare pinned me through. "She's ready for you, Addy."

Mercer tied the rope off.

"She was always the smartest of you two. Look at how easily she beat you."

His fingertips ran over the hilts. Mercer settled on a thin blade. Tossing it in the air, we followed it up and dropped our heads as it hit his palm.

"Where is Gianna, Raul?"

"You don't know who she's got behind her. The ledger is everything," he hissed, eyes glinting. "It's changed the game in ways you can't begin to comprehend. You don't see it, Addy, but you've already lost."

"¿Dónde está Gianna?"

He laughed. "When she's through with you, it'll make what Mommy and her boyfriends did look like—"

Mercer flashed.

"Agh!"

Raul's pants split open. A thin line of red appeared on his leg. Blood gushed out—soaking the pant hem in seconds. Mercer sliced the other one.

"Each refusal to answer will result in a cut," Mercer said, matter of fact. "A refusal that is paired with disrespect for the lovely and beautiful Adeline, will earn you two cuts. I'll keep cutting until those legs are too weak to hold you up, Perez.

"So, I guess the question isn't if Adeline loves Gianna, or if Gianna loves you. It's do you love her so much you'll die in this room to be discovered hung and mutilated by your parents." Mercer tsked. "I would hate for that to happen."

Raul's screams leaked through his teeth.

"Minerva and Julio seem like a sweet couple."

I held a deep breath and let it go. I was glad Mercer took over and distracted him. Seeing the flash of shock at discovering Gianna shared my history with him was satisfaction that fucker would not get tonight.

I swallowed. "Where is Gianna?"

"Screw you!" Spittle showered the carpet. "You're dead! You, this whore, the mute, the corpse, and the blue bitch. You're all dead!"

Mercer slashed, cutting open his thigh. Tears leaked from Raul's eyes.

"Does that make Cash the corpse?" Mercer asked. "Where did that—? Ah, I get it. 'Cause he comes off as cold. Very clever. Could do better than whore and blue bitch, though. Dig deep, Raul. We've got all night."

It felt like it took all night.

Raul's legs were in ruins. Blood soaked the stool, making it almost impossible to stand upright on weakening limbs. Tears and snot covered his face. He gave up insulting me three cuts ago and resorted to pleading.

"Addy, p-please."

It was just us. Mercer had gone into the bedroom to give Raul's parents another dose.

"If I tell you, it's over," he croaked. "She's fixed everything. Gianna hobbled my main competitors. She got me a new contract with the agency. A new car, new apartment, and three times the runners. If I betray her, it all goes away. Please."

And then I understood.

This isn't a plea for Gianna. It's a plea for the ledger.

"Shh," I crooned. "It's okay, Raul."

I untied the rope and helped him down—nearly slipping in the blood as his weight bore on me. Gently, I eased him on the plastic.

"You don't need it, Raul. You never did. The ledger can't fix what's wrong in your life, but you have two people who could." I turned his face to the wall of Raul. "This is not a couple who forgot about their son. You are in a place of honor in every room in this house. When your mother speaks about you, she does so with pride."

He choked on a sob.

"Do what you came here to do. Fix things with them. They want to, Raul." I stroked his forehead. "Ten minutes with them and I saw. They love you."

"Gianna will kill me," he whispered.

I kissed his forehead. "Gianna's gonna have bigger things to worry about. Trust me."

Raul was quiet for a long time. I didn't rush him.

Mercer came in and I held a hand up over my shoulder, keeping him back.

"411 Dunston St., Leighbridge. Penthouse apartment. Top floor."

"Thank you," I said. "Everything's going to be okay. We'll get you cleaned up."

"HE'LL BE FINE."

Cash emerged from my bedroom. He peeled off his bloody gloves and tossed them.

"Mercer knows what he's doing. The cuts were shallow. Nothing important was nicked. I bandaged him up and cuffed him to the bed. He'll stay there until he heals."

"What do we do with him after?" Mercer asked. He reclined on the couch, feet up, like it was just another day. "Send him home to Mommy like Adeline promised?"

"Fuck him," Saint said. "Drop him in the sea chained to a cannonball for all I care. Bunny, come look at this."

I heeded my love's summoning, sliding onto his lap. Brutal and Cash moved to peer over our shoulders. The address for 411 Dunston St. displayed on the screen.

Cash whistled. "Fairfield Palace. Perez was right. We're not breaking into that."

"What?" I twisted to him. "Why?"

"That's one of the most secure buildings in Cinco City, Adeline. Second only to Cinco National Bank." He swore. "You know we have a one hundred percent retrieval rate."

"Yes."

"That's because we don't take jobs we can't do," Saint said. "We've rejected everyone that's asked us to break into Fairfield. It can't be done."

I threw up my hands. "Can everyone stop saying can't and tell me why? Yes, I've heard about the Fairfield. Yes, people have said it's impenetrable. I didn't believe it then, and I don't believe it now. There's always an employee that can be bought. A computer system that can be hacked, or an electrical grid to shut down."

"Not this time," Mercer spoke up. "Fairfield has backup generators for their backups. To get past the lobby, you must scan in on the fingerprint reader while facial recognition matches your face. The security system uses a rolling fifty-six-digit encryption that changes the passwords every twenty-four hours.

"Security buttons to bring them down on you in seconds. There are cameras on each floor. In the elevators, bathrooms, roof, and air ducts. Speaking of the elevators, they do not stop at a resident's floor unless they hit the button to give you access. You could push five all day and it won't move."

"Staircase," I offered.

"You need a key, matching fingerprint, and code to enter a floor. Gianna Cross chose the best apartment in the city. She clearly intends to be the last owner of the ledger."

"Do you have friends that live there?" I asked.

"Two," Mercer replied. "They can get me past most of the security measures, and then the elevator stops us cold. No one can get off on Cross's floor unless she allows it."

I didn't bother to suggest bribing. We spent our last cent to get this far. Forking over more to some shady employee would mean more waiting and another tournament match. I wanted Brutal out of that cage. He was not risking his life in an insane, rigged fight for a third time.

I grabbed Brutal's hand, squeezing tight.

"Fine," I whispered. "I get it. There's no plan on this one. No cons, no tricks, no games. Time for the direct approach. We're going to see Gianna, and knocking on the front door."

Chapter Ten

Fairfield Palace had little resemblance to the inside of a computer that I imagined.

I clocked the cameras, scanners, and guards stationed near the exits as well as the mosaic tiles, tinkling chandeliers, diamond studs, and gold watches on the employees. This residence paid well because it charged well.

The guys and I stood by the revolving door. Mostly because the guards wouldn't let us further.

"Stay here."

"No."

"Gianna's not going to let the five of us up there to ambush her," I told Saint. "You know that. Stay here."

"Nope."

I heaved a sigh. "Is this you worrying about me or not trusting me? Do you think I'm going to run off with the ledger?"

"You wouldn't get far if you tried. So it's not a real concern."

"Then it's worrying about me. Gianna isn't going to hurt me. Saint, we didn't go through this for her to have these guards throw us out the door." I rose on tiptoe and kissed him. Cash, Mercer, and Brutal received the same. "I love you. I'll be right back."

Facing the bulky women, I strode up to them. "I'm a visitor," I said. "Here to see Miss Cross."

"Go through."

I surrendered my bag and stepped through the metal detector. After clearing me, one of the guards escorted me to reception.

They are not messing around in here. Gianna must've wiped out the majority of our stash affording this place.

"Hello. I'm here to see Gianna Cross. Top floor. Penthouse."

"Just a moment." He typed something in his computer. "Is Miss Cross expecting you? I don't have an alert to issue a guest pass."

"She isn't expecting me. My visit is a surprise. Call her," I pushed when he made no move to touch the phone. "She can't wait to see me."

He finally took it off the cradle. "What's your name?"

"Adeline Redgrave."

Stewart, according to his name tag, dialed her number. I memorized it upside down, filing it away.

"Hello, Miss Cross. Sorry to bother you. I have an Adeline Redgrave here who— Yes, ma'am, I— She's standing in front of me. Of course. Yes." Stewart held out the phone. "She would like to speak to you."

"Hello, G."

"Addy. This is a surprise." She was making an effort to sound normal. She failed.

"How did you find me?"

"A friend of mine gave me your address."

"Raul."

"Doesn't matter who, does it? Buzz me in. I can't wait to see you." My beaming smile blinded Stewart.

"Now's not a good time actually. I wish you'd called. I just got out of the shower. The place is a mess, and I've a million things to do today. Maybe another time."

"G." I gave him my back, glancing up to the ceiling. "Let me in or I announce the new owner of the ledger to Cinco underworld. Your address will go in the PS."

A thick silence rang in my ear.

"You wouldn't do that, Addy. You'd be signing the billion-dollar bounty on my head. All of Cinco will hunt me down and try to kill me."

"Good thing you're tucked away in that sky bunker. I hope you're prepared to shut yourself inside for the next seventy years. You'll truly be the last owner of the ledger."

"I'm tempted to call your bluff."

"You've known me almost my whole life, Gianna. I don't bluff."

She cursed under her breath. "Are they with you?"

"The guys are here, but I'm coming up alone."

"Why?" she asked. "If they want to do this, let's do it. Give the phone to Stewart. I'm issuing guest passes for five."

My eyes narrowed. "What are you trying to prove, Gianna?"

"Give him the phone."

I searched for a trap and couldn't find it. Gianna threatened them too. She knew the name of Saint's father's killer. They had something to say to her, and this way they'd do it without weapons.

I called the guys over. Together, the five of us were carried to the top floor.

"Are you sure the ledger is here?" Saint asked. He was tight. So wound, I counted the veins popping in his neck.

"She wouldn't let it out of her sight."

"Are you going to stop me from doing what I need to do, Bunny?"

I tensed. "If hurting Gianna is one of the things you need to do—yes."

"I believe we're about to have our first fight."

"Hardly our first."

The elevator dinged. I moved in his path as it slid open.

"Do you love me?"

His eyes flashed. "Don't."

"Do you?"

"I said don't!"

"Do you trust me?"

"When it comes to this? Not a fucking chance."

I pressed my palms to my temple, frustration mounting. "Saint, I don't know what I have to do to prove I'm on your side, but if you make me try, I will fucking kill you!" The shout exploded out of me.

I shoved him. "We've been through too much together to hit replay on this shit. When I ask if you love me? The answer is yes!" Shove. "When I ask if you trust me? You say yes." Shove. "Am I making myself clear?"

Saint caught my arms. I was yanked off my feet and slammed against the wall. The force expelled the air from my lungs, and Saint claimed it, crashing his lips on mine.

It wasn't sweet, or gentle, or loving. It was two wild animals who couldn't decide if they were rutting or fighting.

"You get my cock going like nothing else when you get stern with me, Bunny."

I dropped my head on the wall. I had no understanding of how this man switched moods so effortlessly.

"I'll let you handle this as long as one thing is clear." His tone hardened. "I will not leave without that name."

"Understood."

"Sinjin. Adeline." Cash's voice brought us out of the elevator.

At the end of the hall, standing in the open doorway, was Gianna.

Her hair was still wet from the shower. She wore a pretty pink wrap-around dress and a spot of shaving cream on her leg that was missed. She was so Gianna in every single way, I ached to run and hug her. Whip up something to eat while she called me babe and told me every detail about her day.

Of course I expected these last few weeks to change her. They had changed me.

"G."

"Come in." She went inside, leaving the door open.

Gianna must've described her dream apartment a thousand times. I could've drawn the layout before I stepped in the room.

A gold and blue paradise with cheeky pops of purple. Blue couch, golden brown coffee table, and purple throw pillows. A blue television stand and prints of Cinco above outlined in purple frames. A purple high-backed velvet chair placed on the raised platform opening up to the balcony. There were three doors leading into this room, and a long hallway to more penthouse. The place was five times the size of her old one.

Gianna finally has everything we wanted.

She sat in the purple chair and began fussing with her hair—parting sections for a braid.

"Well?" she prompted. "I'm sure you went through a lot of trouble to get here. Say what you have to say."

Saint stepped forward. I put a hand on his arm, shaking my head.

"We've decided not to accept your truce." I took a seat on the couch. "When you think about it, torture, forging, conning, fighting, and killing aren't employable skills. I'm the only one who'd make it in the real world and it's impossible for five people to get by on a sous chef's salary."

Amusement curled her lips.

"I won't live by anyone else's rules but my own, Gianna," I said. "But you knew that. It doesn't surprise you that I'm here. This was coming either way, so owing to the fact that you were expecting me, I hope you gave some thought to what you anticipated I was going to say."

"What? The six of us and the ledger. One big happy family." Gianna slid past me. "Oh, no. Your boyfriends don't like that very much. They want nothing to do with me."

"They want to be free of the ledger."

"What about what I want? When does that start to matter to my best friend?"

A scoff sounded behind us. "Fuck this."

"St. John," Gianna said. "You have something to add?"

"You're good, Cross. Very good. Those acting lessons weren't wasted on you—"

"Saint," I said.

"—but unlike Adeline who has a habit of finding the good in people where there is none. I see you for what you are."

Gianna raised a brow. "What is that?"

"Jealous."

Her eye twitched. "Excuse me?"

"You're jealous, Cross. Daddy up and died on you, then Mom decided she wasn't interested in a daughter. You had to stand by and watch Oscar sacrifice for his kid. He showered his princess with everything he had, and raised her to be stronger, smarter, deadlier, and, oh shit, she's prettier than you too."

Bright splotches stained Gianna's cheeks. "That's enough."

"She even found the ledger before you. All your ass did was sneak around and listen in on phone calls." Saint advanced on her, moving me to the side as I got in his way. "It fucking burns you up, doesn't it?"

"I said that's enough!"

"Your supposed victory is due to Adeline. The ledger Adeline found, the plan Adeline made, the money Adeline earned. Adeline, Adeline, Adeline. You were nothing without her and you're nothing now. Still feeding off the better sister. Because that's what this is." Saint's blazing eyes pinned me to the spot. "Cain and Abel. Sibling rivalry. The same damn story told a million times. You had everything she wanted, and she had you. Then you met us and didn't need her anymore."

Saint spread out his hands, laughing. "This tantrum isn't about the Merchants, or money, or even ruling Cinco. It's the ugly stepsister finally beating Cinderella."

"Sounds about right," Mercer drawled.

"One hundred percent probability," Cash said.

Then Brutal, whose few words hit harder than an entire speech. "Pathetic."

Gianna's balled fists shook. Red-faced, her mouth disappeared in a thin line.

"Gianna, that's not true," I said. "Tell me that's not true. All this can't be about punishing me. My dad loves both of us. We've always been a team and I could never replace you. Tell me you know that."

She fixed on Saint.

"Gianna? Say something!"

She turned to me. Opening her fists, Gianna smiled. "No, Addy. It's not true. As amusing as it is to be analyzed by a psychotic psychotherapist, I'm not riddled with envy or low self-esteem. The fact is I wanted the ledger, so I took it. The end.

"I gave you the chance to be here beside me and you refused. Then I ended the fight and offered to let you have your happily ever after, and you didn't take that either. Those are hardly the actions of someone who wants to punish you and leave you with nothing."

Her smile took on a hard edge. "So, it begs the question, why are you here? The love of your Merchants just wasn't enough, and now you've come to take everything away from me. I'm not the one who needs to have it all, Addy. It's you."

"What have I taken from you, Gianna? What the fuck have I done?!" I threw up my hands. "Have I strung you up? Blown up your place, or hunted your new friends? You're determined to make me the villain, but look around you. One of us is sitting on a throne in our tower, laughing about what she got away with, and it's not me."

Her smile widened. "No, babe, you're not the villain," she replied. "But I'll show you who is.

"You say all your boyfriends want is freedom from the ledger? What will they do to me to get it?"

Saint reclined in her chair, spreading his arms out. "Do to you? Nothing. What will I do to Raul Perez on the other hand?" He whistled. "The method of torture I invent for him will be named after me. You get your boyfriend back when I get the ledger. He won't come with all his parts, but there'll be fewer the longer you make me wait."

"Oh, please." Gianna flapped a hand. "Keep him. Raul and I broke up."

"Since when?" I asked.

"As of him telling you five where to find me," she said. "I should've listened to you, Addy. I can't trust that guy."

She clapped. "Well, with Raul out of the way, what does that leave you? You going to hurt me, St. John?" Her grin was wicked. "What will they call the method of torture you invent for me?"

Growling, Saint shoved off. I gently eased him back down, murmuring to him.

There was an odd note in Gianna's voice. Whatever she was setting up for, I wasn't letting her complete the play.

"No one is going to torture you, Gianna. We know the ledger is here somewhere. All we have to do is find it."

Holding up a finger, Gianna went to her blue television stand and opened a drawer. "You mean this ledger." A thick, leather-bound book the size of a legal pad rested in her hand.

It can't be.

The guys came alive, converging on us.

"Go ahead." She offered it to me. "Take it."

I took a step. Then two. My hand closed over the spine.

"Although, I should mention this isn't the original ledger."

I froze.

"I threw that in a fire weeks ago. This is the copy I made in a code that only I know." She was grinning so hard she stifled a laugh. "The book might as well be written in gibberish. I can't believe there have been so many owners and none thought to do this. Just goes to show it was meant for me. Those idiots couldn't handle it." Gianna nudged my arm. "Check if you don't believe me."

Saint snatched it out of my hand when I didn't move. He pawed the pages—tearing a few by the sound.

"Argh!" His roar confirmed the truth.

"Like you said, babe," Gianna breezed. "I intend to be the last owner of the ledger. If I'm killed, the knowledge of what it says goes with me—a fact St. John is quickly coming to. You won't get the name of your father's killer from that book." Gianna reached inside the drawer again and held up a single folded sheet of paper. "Because I have it written down right here.

"I'll give it to you if you kill Adeline."

My heart thumped loudly in my ears, drowning her out. It's the only explanation for how I misheard.

"What did you say?"

"You heard me," she replied, but she was looking at Saint. "Kill Adeline, and his killer is yours. You've waited almost twenty years. You became a killer to get this name, so do what you learned to do."

"Gianna, stop this!"

Slowly, Sinjin closed the ledger and passed it to Cash. "Why would I kill Adeline? Seems like all I have to do now is walk five feet, and take that piece of paper from you."

"Good point. How about I make your decision easier?" She put her fingers to her lips and blew sharply.

The door flew open, pouring out a stream of people, shouting, and guns.

"Back the fuck off!"

"Hands up!"

"Move!" Leah Tyler jammed her gun between my ribs.

Two scarred men grabbed me. A blow hit my knees, dropping me to the floor. I pushed up and looked in the barrel of his gun. In a blink, we were surrounded by them. Two aimed at Mercer's head—twitching the trigger if he breathed. I counted eight before I stopped.

"I never understood the point of bodyguards who clocked out in the evening," Gianna said. "You can kill a lot of people in that midnight window. I would know."

She patted my head. "That's why my new friends live with me, babe. You were never going to corner me alone."

Leah trained her gun on Saint as she moved to Gianna's side. A healing scar poked out of her shirt. "Good to see you again, St. John."

"You too, gorgeous."

She visibly flinched, and the reaction deepened her snarl. "You die first."

"No, Sinjin decides who dies first," Gianna said. "For his name. Yes, he. All these years and you finally have a gender. I'll tell you more. *He* is alive and well. He's spent these last decades enjoying every minute of it while you've been in hell. Paul Bellisario was your father, St. John. He died for you. Are you telling me you won't kill one girl for him?"

She broke away from his shadowed gaze.

"Or maybe Cash," she said. "Margot and Troy Hunt are gunrunners. Smugglers. There's no one to stop me throwing their asses in federal prison except for you."

"Gianna," I shouted. "What is wrong with you? Enough!"

"Brutal," she continued over me. "How long have you been looking for your sister, Bellona, and her baby?"

Baby?

"Wouldn't you like to know where to find the last of your family? Imagine how she's suffered over the years." Toxic, cloying miasma spread in her voice. "How does rescuing your blood compare to the girl you've been screwing for a few months?

"And Mercer. Mercer, Mercer, Mercer," she tsked. "You've been a very naughty boy, and I don't mean the kind that's handcuffed to the bed and whipped with a riding crop. You wouldn't want Adeline— Hell, you can't allow anyone to find out what I read under your name. I swear no one will. All you have to do—"

Gianna pulled a gun out of that damned drawer and slid it across the coffee table. Sinjin stopped it with his boot.

"—is shoot Adeline Redgrave."

I shot up and was thrown back. "What are you trying to prove, Gianna?"

"Isn't that obvious?" She finally dropped the smile. "I'm not the villain in this story, and neither are you. It's them. The four of them standing quiet and eyeballing that gun while the only one speaking up for your life is you. Or haven't you noticed that?"

The guys were not speaking. They weren't looking at me at all.

Cash, Mercer, and Brutal stared at Saint.

And Saint stared at the gun.

"One bullet for your freedom," she said. "Or a lifetime chained to the ledger and me."

"Saint?" I whispered.

Sinjin reached for the gun.

"Saint, listen to me. You don't—"

"I'm sorry, Bunny." He truly sounded it. "We tried it your way."

My silent guards cleared the path as Sinjin leveled the gun at my head.

"The better sister won."

Tears filled my eyes—warping that beatific grin that made my heart skip even now.

Saint drew on the trigger and twisted.

He aimed at Gianna, firing once, twice, three times.

Click.

Click.

Click.

Gianna laughed. "Oops. Did I give you the gun with the faulty firing pin?" She lifted another from the drawer. "I meant to give you this one. But it's better for me if we don't try that experiment twice."

"You are good, Cross." Saint dropped the useless weapon, slowly raising his hands above his head as Gianna's scarred men moved in on him. "Very good."

"I consider that a compliment coming from you." Gianna knelt in front of me. "Good news for you, babe. They truly do love you—choosing Adeline Redgrave over their families, freedom, and vendettas. But then it's hard not to." She stroked my cheek, collecting fallen tears. They glistened on her fingers as she took Leah's gun.

"The bad news is the truce is over."

"Gi—"

The butt cracked over my head.

I collapsed on the floor, darkness bleeding into my vision. The last thing I saw was her lips coming in for one last kiss goodbye.

Chapter Eleven

Buzzing filled my ear. Low, whining, and persistent. It flitted in and out, returning the instant I sunk back into sleep.

Something landed on my ear. It bit me.

Groaning, I tossed my head and a spike went through my brain.

I cried out.

"Adeline? Wake up."

"Are you okay?"

The voices pulled me back, drawing me further into consciousness. Another bite was the final shove.

"What happened?" I rasped. A heavy pit settled in my stomach, adding to the pounding head and gnawed ear.

"Cross."

One name and it all came back. The golden, purple, and blue fortress. The ledger. A disfigured army. And Gianna.

I peeled my eyes open. Slowly they adjusted to our situation.

"Holy hell," I breathed.

"Have I mentioned that I don't like your friend?" Mercer offered.

The heavy feeling in my stomach was gravity. Sinjin, Mercer, Killian, Brutal, and I hung suspended in the air.

It looked like we were in a disused factory. My bare feet dangled over a conveyor belt of dusty bottles. Meadows Dairy was stamped on broken-down boxes in the corner.

Despite the lump on my head, I sensed no other injuries. The same couldn't be said for my guys. There were varying degrees of bruises, lumps, and bloody streaks on their bodies.

The ropes looped around our waists, secured our hands, and were tied to a steel beam.

"How do we get down?" I croaked.

"With difficulty," Sinjin said.

"But quickly," Cash added. His right eye was swollen shut. "They took our phones and wherever the hell we are, it's not in the city. Can't hear a thing outside."

I listened. It was true. No honking traffic or the pulse of Cinco. *Where are we?*

"I have to get out of here and warn my parents," Killian said.

"Guys," I said, dropping my eyes. "Thanks for not... killing me."

Sinjin managed to shrug in ropes. "On principal, I don't do things people clearly want me to do. Can't have them getting ideas that I'm agreeable."

A smile tugged at my lips. "Of course not."

"Plus, you give wicked good head. It took me ten years to find the perfect girlfriend. I'd rather not kidnap another one."

"There was some sweetness tucked in there, so I'll just say I love you too."

"I kept my secrets to have you," Mercer said. "Killing you for them is counterproductive."

Killian gazed at me steadily—one eye and all. "I lost the last woman I loved to Kieran. I won't lose you to another one." He glanced up at the beam. "My parents either, for that matter. Save the rest for later and let's get the fuck out of here."

It took some doing and hours longer than we could afford. I was the last to be lowered down, dropping gently into Brutal's arms. My heart squeezed at the cuts and discolored bruises on his perfect face. Baris lost his first fight.

Because of me.

"I'm so sorry," I whispered. "Your sister— I should have known she'd—"

"Stop blaming yourself." Killian limped in front of us, leading the way out. "We walked onto her turf without numbers or weapons. She had the advantage."

"And we were set up," Mercer said. "Perez said she was ready for you and we already lost. Now we know what he meant. I'm betting the fifteen-odd mutilated escorts camping out in her penthouse didn't just slip his mind."

"She's going to come for you and your families. I know her. She doesn't bluff either."

"Should I have shot you in the head, then?"

I smacked Saint on the back.

"Ah. Good to see that pistol-whip didn't curb your violent streak," he said. "I will find my father's killer, Adeline. For years I didn't know where to look and now I do: Gianna Cross. You've gotten me close to her once, you'll do it again. I'll have my revenge and fuck her too."

Smiling, I said, "I'm not sure that analogy works, baby, but I'll take it."

Night blanketed our prison in darkness, casting long shadows over the gravel drive. The factory sat on a patch of land merging into the trees in three directions. The fourth was broken by the asphalt winding to the shining city in the distance.

"We're on the edge of Harlow," Killian said. "She dumped us in enemy territory. Nice touch."

"It'll take all night to get back to the city," Mercer added. "We need to steal a car."

"Follow this road..."

Their chatter faded.

"You can put me down," I said to Brutal. "You're hurt more than me."

He set me on my feet. I curled my fingers through his, syncing our steps.

"I know how the guys feel." Killian, Mercer, and Sinjin pulled ahead. "But I still owe you an apology. Choosing between someone you love and your family." I thought of my dad. "It's an impossible choice. I'm sorry you had to make it because of me."

Brutal pointed between us, closed his hand, and placed the fist over his chest. Again, he pointed at me, then him, and traced my lips. He pulled away grinning.

"I know it makes you happy to leave me confused."

He laughed.

"But as long as you're happy, we're okay?"

Baris nodded.

I buried my face in his arm—so relieved I could pass out. I didn't know what I'd do if the guys resented me for Gianna's twisted game of roulette. If they did, she would have succeeded in the true aim of her test. Destroying us.

"We'll find your sister, Baris. I'll help you."

He rested his hand on my head. Warm and solid.

"My sister got pregnant when she was sixteen years old, so my father called Kieran to get rid of her," he said. "The last time I saw Bellona, my father was dragging her kicking and screaming into the arms... of yours."

I stopped dead. Brutal turned to me, unbothered as the others left us behind.

"My father?"

Yes.

"He— He took your sister." I was saying it out loud and it didn't make sense. Baris and my father connected by this horrible event and circumstance brings me into his life years later. How did I not know?

"Baris, he—" My mind scrambled to put it together. "He didn't kill her, I swear. A pregnant sixteen-year-old girl? He was a fixer, not a monster. He would've taken her somewhere safe—far from your father. I will find out where that is."

Baris cupped my face, running his thumb over my lips.

"But... you already know," I said slowly. "You spoke to my dad. This is what you talked about." It wasn't a question. "Did he tell you what happened to her?"

I received a nod.

"Where is she?"

"Eighteen years." Baris grasped my hand, continuing after the others. "She may not be there."

"She'd be in her thirties," I calculated. "It's true. She could be anywhere. Are you searching for her?"

I am.

"We'll find her, Baris. Together," I said. "You haven't lost your chance. Gianna dangled old info over you. We've got a real lead."

He kissed my knuckles, warming me.

"Can I ask, why would your father do something like that? Your parents were Marshall and Bernice Alexander, right? Why couldn't he send her to an overseas boarding school, or invent a case of mono and quietly arrange to have the baby adopted? What would possess him to call in a man with Kieran's reputation to *fix* his kid?"

"My father expected perfection. Imperfect things were tossed away."

EIGHT HOURS LATER, Sinjin rolled our stolen car to a stop next to the hotel. I never thought I'd be so happy to see the place.

I trudged inside, heading straight for my room.

Shedding my jacket, I left it where it fell and went into the kitchenette. A cloth was run under cool water and then pressed to my aching head.

I shoved inside the bedroom.

"Oh." Raul munched on a granola bar I left on the nightstand before I took off for Fairfield. "You're not dead."

"Sorry to disappoint you." I gathered clothes and a towel. "We survived the ambush, but I can't say Gianna is going to go as easy on you."

He paused mid-chew. "What do you mean?"

"She wasn't pleased you gave her up so easily."

"Easily?!" He threw the blankets off his legs. "My career is over."

"No one told you to be so stubborn, Raul." I was far from sympathetic. "Next time, don't make me repeat the question."

"When am I getting out of here?"

"I'll uncuff you and you can walk out. How about that?"

His glare set my head on fire.

"No? Then, what's going to happen is I'm gonna hop in the shower, get dressed, truss you up, and deliver you to Gianna's with a message. We're past the point of truces, so now it's mutually assured destruction. I can't let her ruin the Hunts, or shield Paul Bellisario's killer to torture his son. If she makes her move, I make mine. I'll tell all of Cinco City she has the ledger. Won't matter that the info is filed in her head. They'll just make sure the torture doesn't kill her when they set to extracting it."

"I should have taken it from her the first chance I got. Neither one of you deserve it," he said. "You're both little girls in tiaras and poofy dresses, playing at being queens, except now your tantrums have consequences. Step aside, Addy. Crawl back into your kitchen, and let the real men run this city."

I rolled my eyes, making for the bathroom. "Damn, I just do not like you."

SINJIN CAUGHT ME HAULING Raul out the door.

"Grab that end."

He lifted by the legs and carried him into the stolen car. Raul had a lot to say about it, but bandaged and dressed in ratty clothes, he looked like an escapee from Cinco Psychiatric Institution and no one concerned themselves with us bringing him back.

"It hasn't been fun, Raul." I got him into the zip ties amid the thrashing and pinned a note to his chest. "I hope you have that chat with your parents, make amends, and all around become less of a human trash bag."

"Fuck you!"

"I'll miss you too, friend."

Sinjin squealed up to the curb. I threw open the door and kicked Raul out, sending him rolling down the pavement to smack to a stop at Fairfield's door. Sinjin sped off and found a spot to dump the stolen ride. Together we walked back to Mercer's car, ignoring the sirens in the distance.

"You've been so calm." I linked our arms, the two of us cutting through early morning pedestrian traffic, collecting bumps and brushes. "All through the night, you haven't said anything. You didn't rant or detail Gianna's excruciating death. Are you okay?"

Sinjin was silent for so long, I gave up on an answer and rested my head on his arm, soaking in his dominating scents of leather, bergamot, and something unique that was all him.

"My father used to say there are the choices you can live with, the ones you can't, and the ones made for you." Sinjin traced a half-moon from temple to chin, tipped my head, and captured my lips. "This is all three."

Funny enough, I understand what he means.

"Your father sounded like a wise man. Kind and patient. I wish I could've met him, but I do see him in you."

He raised a brow.

"I'm serious," I said, laughing. "The way you are with the children from the Catholic school. All these years and you still take care of Edie and the church. Your methods are unorthodox, but beggars can't be choosers, right?"

"Exactly. I used to get crap about it from this hot chef I'm banging. Glad you see things my way."

"Oooh. Tell me more about this hot chef."

We bypassed the scene unfolding outside the Fairfield. Police, security guards, an ambulance pulling up to the curb, and a man on his walkie-talkie likely calling the bosses who'd alert Gianna.

Gianna.

The name went through my mind and unearthed the pain that came with it.

"I'm not the villain in this story, and neither are you. It's them."

Two sentences and I understood. Gianna didn't blame herself or me for the trouble between us. She solidly laid the blame at the Merchants' feet.

Still, I have to wonder if there was any truth to Saint's speech. Deep down was there a part of Gianna that wanted to see me lose? Would we have a friendship left to save when this was over?

Mercer's car gleamed whole and untouched where we left it. Sinjin drove us away from the only person who might answer my question.

"Where are we going?" I asked, watching our turn grow small in the rearview.

"You'll find out."

"Ominous," I said. "Or intriguing. Guess I'll decide which when we get there."

Saint's chuckles filled the car.

We'd been driving for a while when I turned on the stereo and flicked through Mercer's music.

"Jazz, hip-hop, country, pop, and rock. The man has eclectic taste."

"I assume he keeps a wide selection for his dates."

My smile dimmed. Of course he did.

"Sometimes it seems like Mercer's played so many roles, he buried himself along the way. I understand why he doesn't go by a handle. His name is the one thing that's just him." I shifted in my seat. "How did you guys hook up with him? Brutal, too, now that I'm asking."

"It was just me and Killian," Saint said. "He was packing a ten-grand monthly debt, and we were both after Kieran. I suggested we make our money using our talents."

"Killing and stealing."

"Exactly," he replied. "Killian can't run with an idea though. He had to comb, rake, and examine the thing to death till he's worked out every angle. I give him stealing shit and fencing the goods, and he comes out with a gang."

"Naturally."

"We needed an enforcer. Heard about this guy—a loner roaming the circuit who wore gloves and beat a man into a coma for spitting in his face. It was like finding a soulmate."

I laughed. "Thus, Cash, Sinjin, and Brutal are born. When did Mercer come in?"

"Couple years later. Doing recon was tricky. Cash was the grifter among us and Kieran—La Roche—ordered him to stay straight."

"He couldn't be caught scoping out marks."

He nodded. "And while I have a natural charm and magnetism that people can't resist."

I'd roll my eyes but damn if it wasn't true.

"I'm not the one to simper and fluff egos to seduce a mark. Much simpler to kill them and take what we need. Pointing out this logic lost me the job."

I teased the blue hairs at the nape of his neck, enjoying just hearing him speak.

"We had a job retrieving corporate papers from a businessman visiting Cinco for a conference. Killian paid the bartender a handsome amount to spike the drinks of him and his date. That night, we broke into his hotel room and Mercer was sitting in an armchair drinking wine. He asked what took us so long."

"Wait, what?" I sat up straight. "Mercer knew you were coming?"

"He was the date, Bunny. Turns out the guy doesn't down drinks that have been out of his sight. He's had clients try to drug him before. When they went up and Biederman keeled over before the belts were off, it clued him in. He hung around to see who'd come through the door."

"The four leaders of the Merchants. Wow," I said. "It's almost as great a story as how you met the fifth." I waggled my eyebrows. "Funny, isn't it? How the right people end up finding each other. It's fate."

"I don't believe in fate." Sinjin reduced his breakneck speed. "Fate is accepting outside forces determine your life. I don't know if I was meant for you, Adeline, but I took you anyway." He hit the brakes. "In every version of our lives, Sinjin gets his Bunny."

"Hmm. What if I fell for another gang leader with natural charm and magnetism?"

"I did mention my talent for stealing and killing, didn't I?"

We kissed. "It's a good thing you stole me. He wasn't that good in bed."

Climbing out, Sinjin rounded the hood and met me on the curb.

"Where to next?"

"Right here."

He gestured to a bookshop. Stretching on top of it was a brick high-rise with decorated balconies and window boxes spilling bright flowers.

I held his arm, following him inside. I no longer had to ask if every strange place he took me to was my potential final resting place. Saint wanted me. He loved me more than he hated the person written on Gianna's paper. Deep in a place where I couldn't lie to myself, I once believed his love couldn't stretch that far. He proved me wrong.

"Killian said you have a place with the best view of the city." He opened a side door for me to go in. "I'm about to ruin it for good."

"Do you have to?" I asked, laughing.

"Yes. Once you see the actual best view of the city, second best won't do."

"It's the middle of the day. Should we come back at night?"

"You can't see it at night."

Saint and I stepped inside a stairwell. The scan pad locked us out of the first floor. A key card was in his hand before I opened my mouth.

The elevator called us from the other side of the hall.

"I love walking through hallways like these and listening to the sounds of life on the other side," I mused. "I try to imagine the couple in there watching *Doctor Who*. Are they cuddled on the couch sneaking in an episode while their little boy sleeps? Or the swing music pouring under the crack. Is there a grandpa dancing around the living room and mortifying his grandchildren?"

Sinjin pressed the up button. "You think about families."

I paused—that simple truth sinking in. "You're right, I do. These perfect snapshots of happy people." I peered at him. "Do you... think about families?"

"Are you asking me if I want kids?"

My face warmed. "Saint, for once can you not be you, with that blunt, straight-to-the-point, fuck-the-social-niceties self? Dance around the topic for me a little. I'm begging you."

"Alright," he said. "No, Redgrave. I don't walk down hallways imagining the people inside."

"Oh. Okay," I whispered.

"Because I don't have to imagine." He pointed to apartment 126. "In there, a devastatingly beautiful woman who knows one hundred and fifteen ways to bone a duck and a man, is cooking dinner with a reddish-blue-haired kid."

"What's Dad doing?"

"Polishing the cuffs he'll use on her that night."

"Saint," I cried. The elevator dinged to let us in.

"Don't stress. Their bedroom is soundproofed."

I shook my head. "Reddish blue is purple, Saint. I have a feeling Mom will forbid purple hair dye under the age of sixteen."

"Mom will make all the rules, and Dad remains the favorite."

Saint chose the twelfth floor, sending us up.

"What's this kid's name? Paul?"

His reply was immediate. "Sole."

"Sole," I tried. "Sun. It's beautiful."

The doors opened on another hallway. Saint stopped in front of 1259 and produced a key. A prod on the back sent me inside.

The apartment was stunning. An open-floor-plan loft laid the rustic kitchen, painting, art studio place, and the platform holding the leopard-print bed in one sweep.

"Saint, is this your apartment? Have you been keeping this place to yourself while your girlfriend and the family of rats living in her wall were stuck in that motel?"

"How dumped would I be if I said yes?" he asked, brushing past me for the balcony.

"Fifty percent."

"What's half a breakup?"

"Half the sex, half the home-cooked meals, double the talking about our feelings."

"Then, absolutely not. This isn't my apartment."

Saint threw open the double doors. A whoosh of city air rustled the pages on the drawing board. The breeze encircled me, transporting me into its playland.

The artist's touch escaped the confines of the apartment. Moving pallets were stacked in a corner and topped with cushions and blankets, transforming into a sectional couch. A hanging egg chair claimed the opposite corner, swaying beside a wall of leaves and vines shaking in the wind.

Candles dotted my path as I reached for Sinjin's hand. I curled into him, resting my head on his chest as we gazed at our city.

"It's pretty. I wouldn't say it's better than my spot though."

"Look again." Sinjin pointed in the distance. "Over there. That building is Prestige Apartments where I met the woman who will ultimately lead to my downfall." He swept the horizon. "Cinco Fairgrounds where an army of blonds kidnapped and inducted me into their circus."

"I'm sure that's how it went down, baby."

"Word for word." Again we moved, traveling distances. "Trapp Tower. Standing at the observation deck, my father told me the story of meeting and falling for my mother, Aelia."

I smiled up at him. "Well, damn. Now I have to say this view is best."

"Only because it's true."

"So, this is your place."

"No. We did a job for a guy who lived in this building. I used to break into his place. After he moved out, I've used this guy's. Nicer balcony."

"Are you kidding? What if he comes home?"

"He works two jobs to pay for this apartment he can't afford." Sinjin was breezier than the afternoon. "We're good, Bunny."

He dropped on the couch with that look saying he expected me to join him. I did so, giving into my fate. Despite Saint's feelings on the matter, I knew there were some things I could not control.

"It's beautiful, Saint. Thanks for bringing me up here."

"The view was the excuse, Adeline. It's not the reason I brought you up here."

"What do you mean?"

"Since this shit started with Cross, you've been asking after us. Can we trust you? Can we forgive you? Can we choose you over the ledger? Can we forgive that Cross forced us to make that choice?

"What about you?"

"What about me?" I laughed. "I'm fine."

"No." Sinjin stuck me with a hard, serious look. "I'm really asking, Adeline. How are you?"

"I—" I threw up my hands. "What do you want me to say? I am fine. This stuff with Gianna is hard, but it's not like my father didn't warn me about this. I've always said the ledger can't be shared."

"So, you were going to cut her out."

"No. Gianna wasn't included in that. It didn't occur to me she should be. Any more than I'd have worried my father would kill me and run off with the ledger. The very idea of that is insane. He's my family. Gianna—"

"—is your family."

"Yes," I stated. "She is. And she'll remember that."

"She's betrayed you twice."

"Yes."

"Attacked you. Had you tied up and left for dead—twice."

I clenched my teeth. "If she wanted me dead, I would be. I know Gianna."

"Does she know you?"

"Of course."

"Everything about who you are and what you want?"

"Absolutely."

He inclined his head. "Begs the question, why would she think you'd take the ledger and toss her aside?"

My response stalled on my lips.

"Doesn't she know you better than that?" Saint continued. "And if you know her, didn't you see through that flimsy excuse to what she was really after?"

"I—"

His penetrating gaze flayed me. "Didn't you, Adeline?"

"Yes," I whispered.

He stopped my chin as it dipped, raising me to meet his eyes. "Tell me."

Tears spilled down my cheeks. "It's always been me and her," I said. "Until it was me and you. And Cash. And Mercer. And Brutal. These are the first relationships I've been in that matter."

"It's not about cutting her out. It's about cutting us in."

I nodded. "She doesn't know you. She doesn't trust you. Involving the Merchants is a mistake that'll see us go the way of the original Kieran. That is how she sees it. There was never going to be a future where the six of us ran Cinco together. Gianna wouldn't allow it."

"That's why you pushed for us to accept serfdom. You were trying to head off the situation you're in right now—choosing between us."

"You see how well that turned out." I laughed—laughed and laughed. Loud, echoing guffaws bounced inside and carried out through the city. "Back-fucking-fired," I howled. "I tried to have Gianna and the Merchants, and wound up losing all of you. You guys don't trust me no matter how much you say you do. The ledger did exactly what it promised. Destroyed me."

My laughs got louder. Wracking my chest and stealing air before I breathed it in. I laughed as Sinjin blurred—warping in gushing tears. I fell against his chest, soaking the front of his shirt through.

Saint let me. He stroked my hair—calm and steadying.

"Adeline, I'm going to tell you something in standard blunt, straight-to-the-point, fuck-the-social-niceties form."

"Do you h-have to?"

"Yes," he replied. "I do trust you. If I didn't, you'd be lying on that pile of wood and ash along with the other blown-up garbage I don't care about." Saint drew his knife, flipping it on his palm. "I keep the things I need where they're safest.

"With me."

I quieted, reducing to soft sniffles. "Okay. You can tell me that."

He chuckled. "What happens now, Redgrave?"

I took a deep breath and released it slow. Settling in Sinjin's arms, I curled my feet under me, looking out over the city. "I haven't made my choice. Not the one that will break me from Gianna permanently, or rip me from the Merchants.

"She will force that choice, Saint. Whatever happens next, it's going to end the war. For good."

SINJIN AND I MADE USE of that poor man's apartment for hours. We made love once on the balcony and twice on the bed. Saint suggested we leave the sheets messed up to confuse the hell out of him. I reminded him the guy would change the locks if he found out Goldilocks was sleeping in his bed.

I approached a good mood when we returned to the motel. It was impossible to feel one hundred percent. Saint got to the heart of the problem with a nice view and a couple questions. I couldn't hide from myself or from the guys anymore.

I slipped my hand in his as we drove. *But I keep the things I need close too. I just have to believe we can face what's coming next.*

We returned to the motel to find the guys in Mercer's room.

"Cell phones," Cash said, handing me one.

"Did you call your parents?"

"I told them to go to ground."

"Can an entire circus of acrobats, stilt walkers, clowns, and an elephant go to ground?"

He cupped my neck—soft, soothing, and more loving than I deserved. "They've known for years this day might come, Adeline. They're prepared to do what they have to."

"They'll be on the run. What about your brothers and sisters? What about Kaylee?"

"Kaylee is going to be fine. My brother, Declan, and his wife, Jasmine, are taking care of her. They're Nova's parents and they have sleepovers every other night."

A knot of tension loosened. "Okay. How are you?"

"I'm fine."

I stroked his hand. "Don't be cold, hard Cash right now. You sacrificed your career and years of your life to prevent this happening. You can tell me that you're worried."

Cash kissed me till my toes curled. "It's me, Redgrave. I've been preparing for this since Kieran made that call. Fake passports, money, and a job I traded for a one-way flight out of the country. My parents aren't going to prison."

"I did forget who I was talking to for a minute," I said, smiling. "What's your exit strategy for the Merchants?"

"Die in a hail of bullets."

I whacked his arm.

"Or beaten to death by my girlfriend."

"Neither," I replied, wrapping him in a hug. "I've been thinking about the single thing more important than the ledger."

"What's that?"

"Family." As I said it, I saw that hallway full of doors, and for the first time, I was on the other side. "I want to leave a better city to Sole and Alfred Jr."

"I deeply regret telling you that name."

I poked him. "Listen, toy boy. You better start thinking of another outcome other than dying for the ledger because I have no intention of being another one of its casualties. Not me, the men I love, or my incredibly stubborn, volatile best friend. My original plan stands. Reign over Cinco with a firm, but guiding hand, and then retire with a boatload of money and four men who'll worship me for the rest of my days."

"I'm one of those men, right?"

Rising on my toes, I pecked his lips. "Do you want to be?"

"I could be persuaded." Killian tried to carry me out of the room.

"Wait." I skipped away from his grasping hands, coming up behind Mercer. "What about you? If Gianna launches her ammo, will you be okay?"

"She won't, love." He tilted his head to look at me. "We walked out of that factory alive. She still cares about you. Too much to pull the trigger."

"She does care about me, Mercer, but she doesn't care about you. I can't predict how far she'll go."

"I can," he said. "I know how far someone who loves you will go."

I buried my face in his hair. That was so close to saying he loved me, I couldn't breathe.

Cash picked me up. Tossing me over his shoulder, he carried me out of the room. I'd have to continue my discussion with Mercer some other time.

A KNOCK WOKE ME EARLY the next morning. I wrapped myself in a blanket, smooched Cash's scruffy cheek, and left him sleeping.

I flicked on the mini coffee maker, getting the hot water going for his morning roast and my tea. Weeks here and we'd begun to develop our routines. I was officially off cooking duty considering my kitchen blew up and our replacement was a poor substitute. We'd been picking up our meals at different restaurants and cafés. Ordering online and picking up in baggy clothes and sunglasses.

I opened the fridge, doing a little dance as I perused my ingredients. *Today, I'm mixing it up. I can do microwave eggs, honey yogurt parfaits, and blueberry muffins in a mug.*

They knocked again.

"Why are you being weird?" I called. "Just come in."

Knock. Knock.

My smile dimmed. "Who is it? Mr. Hall?"

No response came, heightening my wariness.

I backed into my room. If something was about to happen, it wouldn't go down while I was in a sheet.

Cash stirred as I tugged my jeans up. I pressed a finger to my lips.

"Someone's at the door," I said, barely audible. "They're not coming in or saying who they are."

Killian was up and out of bed before I buttoned my pants. He freed his gun from the holster.

"Stay here," he said.

"No, Killian, call the guys. One of them sticks their head out the door and we'll know what we're dealing with."

"Adeline, if we're *dealing with* something outside our door, what are the chances they are too?"

"They—"

"Ahh!"

A scream ripped through the second floor.

Cash and I tore out of the room. He flung the door open—gun at the ready.

Marcia from the room at the end streaked past, screaming her head off.

"Oh my goodness." I brought Cash's arm down. There was no need for a gun. He couldn't hurt us.

Slumped against the wall, Raul's unseeing eyes tracked my approach. I knelt before him and pressed my fingers to his neck.

"No pulse," I said.

"Whoever dumped him here is close by."

"The cops will be too. This place is burned." I moved to the letter pinned to his chest. "We have to get out of here."

I tugged it off. "Ugh!" Wincing, I clapped my hand over my mouth. A gaping hole oozed blood where Raul's heart should be.

"His girlfriend did this?"

Unfolding the note, I read it and carefully put it back—leaving the scene how the witness saw it.

"They broke up."

I brushed past him, beginning to pack the meager possessions I had left.

"What was in the note?"

Back to him, I stuffed my phone in my pocket.

"It said 'go ahead. I dare you.'"

BRUTAL

Mercer peeled off seconds ahead of the cops.

"That was grim," he said. "Gianna Cross knows how to send a message."

Adeline hugged me tighter.

"Where do we go?" Mercer asked.

Taking out my phone, I typed the gym's address in the GPS and handed it up. It wasn't a permanent solution. All the same, it was four walls, a roof, and an out-of-the-way property I owned under another name. No one would come looking for us there.

My gun dug in my back.

I had what I needed.

"One problem taken care of. Now for—"

Cash's phone went off.

"Yeah," he said. "Jasmine? Whoa, slow down."

Adeline raised her head.

"What? That's ridiculous. They can't— Shit!" Cash punched the dash. "Don't talk to anyone. No one speaks to the police. I'll be there as soon as I can."

Faint sobbing came through the speakers.

"It'll be okay," Cash said. "I'll find a lawyer. These charges are bullshit. They'll be dropped."

"What happened?" Saint demanded.

"Cross didn't go after my parents. The FBI received a tip that Kaylee Trevino was seen with Merriman Circus. Jasmine and Declan have been arrested for kidnapping."

Adeline shot up. "What? Kidnapping? How is that possible?"

"The broken-down, piece of shit who fathered her filed a missing persons." Cash gripped his phone hard enough to break. I heard the plastic and metal cracking. "It was to cover his tracks in case anyone ever asked the bastard where his fucking daughter is!"

"Are you s-saying Kaylee could be taken back to him?"

"Yes."

"Oh my— How could she— Not this," Adeline rasped. "How could she do this?!"

I held Adeline to my chest, her cries stirring a part of me I thought long dead.

I gave up everything to carry out the sole task I had left on this earth. I wasn't meant to meet Adeline. Circumstance wasn't supposed to put me in her father's path to give me a second charge—pull his daughters from the edge.

"She's not returning to her father," Saint said, "and Jasmine and Declan aren't going to prison. Timothy Trevino will be found dead in a crack den with the hotshot still in his arm, giving no doubt to the defense she ran away."

"They'll still face charges," Mercer said. "It's illegal to harbor a runaway."

"Their five-hundred-dollar-an-hour lawyer will have those charges dropped and paint them as heroes who rescued a survivor of sex trafficking." Saint clasped Killian's shoulder. "Go. We'll handle our end."

"Do not give him a quick death."

"I never do."

THUD! THUD! THUD, THUD, thud!

Mercer watched her over my shoulder.

"She's going to punch a hole in that bag."

She's entitled.

Cash's parents were refusing to run. Kaylee was in the hands of social services. The emergency stash meant to hide his folks was being spent on a lawyer. His brother and sister-in-law were sitting in prison, and the Merriman troupe were terrified. One sick boy, two desperate parents, and a man with a ledger. Years later, that was all it took to wreck dozens of lives.

"Lawyer fees add up," Mercer said. The three of us sat on the canvas drinking the beers I kept in the back. "Plus, your foster parents are still vulnerable. We need enough to get them through this and money for Mr. and Mrs. Hunt in case Cross isn't done yet."

We.

Four years and that's what we were. I wasn't certain when it happened. I didn't join the Merchants to solve their problems, protect their families, or enact their vendettas. I had enough of that on my own. These added obligations were unwanted.

I punched Saint's leg. He dropped his chin, seeing the three fingers I held up.

"Appreciate it."

There wouldn't be weeping, gushing praise and brokenhearted thanks from St. John Bellisario for my continuing the tournament and pledging the money to his foster parents.

Actually, that was the gushing praise. We were hard men in an unforgiving line of work. There wasn't room for sentimentality, second-guessing, or relationships that went above fuck buddies.

I glanced at Adeline.

So how did we end up here?

"Diego's tracking down Trevino," Sinjin said. "When he has him, we'll take him out. In the meantime, put this stuff to use." He walked off. "Win."

Saint disappeared into the back room. I kept a spare cot in there. In a few hours, I'd find him in the position he was likely in now—flipping his knife as he thought a dozen moves farther ahead than even Killian.

"I'm turning in too." Mercer got to his feet. Mats stacked in Jeffery's former office. They made a makeshift bed out of towels that Mercer probably invited Adeline to share. He stopped her assault to whisper in her ear. Shaking her head, she kissed him, then returned to punching.

It was just me and her.

I vaulted over the ropes, closing the distance.

"Baris, please." A sheen of sweat covered her body. "I don't need comforting, or kisses, or even sex. I just need to beat the shit out of this."

Without a word, I got behind, stabilizing the heavy bag.

She gazed at me—an emotion flickering in her eyes gone as quickly as it came. "Thank you."

Observing her stance and even jabs, it amazed I ever bought her act as an amateur. She boxed with single-minded precision like she'd taken on every issue in her life.

"I've been thinking about what you said," Adeline began. "Imperfect things were tossed away. I've been thinking about you period, Baris."

Jab. Jab.

"About what led you to joining the Merchants and all you've had to deal with alone." She spun, landing a kick that slid me back. "I know you're planning to continue on in the tournament. I say that like it's a choice. Jo has a target on her back. The Hunts need help. Kaylee was ripped away from another family. We're sleeping in a disused gym.

"You're doing this to keep us going when your fight isn't with us anymore," she said. "You should be out there looking for your sister and the last of your family. Eighteen years and the trail gets colder every day."

I frowned. Why was she repeating this?

"This is where you have to be, Baris, but... it's not where I have to be. You know where Gianna is. You know where to find her book of unreadable secrets." *Jab.* "I'll search for your sister."

I caught her wrist mid-punch. I didn't need to ask what the hell was she saying. It was written on my face.

"I'm not helping the situation by being here, Baris. Just the opposite, I'm making it worse. Gianna has something to prove to me and she's using you guys to do it." Adeline ripped off her gloves. "I was willing to fight her—the five of us were. But Kaylee wasn't.

"Family, Baris." She said that to me like it should mean something specific. "All this ledger has done since three foolish men created it is break apart families. Let me put one thing right. I'll look for Bellona and her child. When you've done what you need to do, you'll join me."

"No."

She blinked. "No?"

"No."

My throat was clear. No pressure on my chest. No shackle on my tongue. I said what I needed to in complete sentences.

"No."

"No, you don't want me to look for Bellona?"

"No, don't do"—I gestured to encompass all of her—"whatever this is."

"What is that supposed to mean?"

I walked off.

"Bar— Hey! Don't walk away from me." Heavy footfalls sounded behind me. "If you don't want me in your family's business, fine. But don't look at me like I said the stupidest thing you've ever heard. Hey!"

She grabbed my shoulder.

I twisted, snapping my arm up, and trapping her in a hold.

"Baris!" Adeline hooked around my neck. Using me, she heaved up, smothering my face between her thighs. A move not unlike the one we pulled in my bedroom—although this did not have the added benefit of eating her pussy.

Running at the bag, I smacked Adeline into it—dropping her flat on the mat. Her revenge was quick.

"Agh!"

The kick buckled my legs, and I fell on my ass. She was on me in an instant.

Pinning me down, Adeline clamped my neck. "You want a fight, baby? I'll give you a fight."

The pressure was there now. Adeline throttled the fuck out of me. Still, I could speak.

"No, Adeline. I want you to fight."

Surprise broke through her rage.

"You're the better sister."

Her round, full lips trembled. "There is no better or worse. No stronger, or tougher, or more sociopathic. There is just me, and Gianna, and the destruction we're leaving in our wake. Dammit, Baris." She flung away, rocking back on my lap. "I'm trying to be selfless for the first time in my life. Put you guys first. Can't you let me?"

Tears clung to her lashes. I brushed them away. "Not the first time," I said, "and no."

She laughed—a short, sharp noise that startled her. "Don't make me laugh," she said, wiping her cheeks. "I don't get to laugh, smile, or be happy while Declan and Jasmine are in jail for taking care of the little girl I dropped on their lap. Another example of my selfishness!"

"Mh-hmm." I pinched her hem, tugging the shirt over her head. Adeline was a post-workout mess. Wispy strands clung to her forehead. Sweat made her white shirt see-through. I had to give my girl a shower.

"I should've taken Kaylee in. She asked me to. She wanted to live with me, but I said no because of the ledger and the Kings. I couldn't put my revenge plots aside for one minute to look after a child who needed me."

I slipped her strap off her shoulder.

"And I don't get this either." She snapped it back in place. "No sex. No orgasms. I don't deserve them."

Laughing, I lifted her over my shoulder.

"Do not laugh at me, Baris Alexander. I am extremely serious."

I smacked her ass, making her yelp.

"And don't think that's going to get anything going either. I'm taking a vow of celibacy."

I know something about vows, sweetheart. This ain't one.

I carried her inside the gym shower. This was my place. Naturally the tile gleamed, the sinks were spotless, the mirrors smudge-free, and the water hot and scalding.

Adeline was set under the spray, her clothes peeled off under half-hearted protests.

"I will not enjoy any bit of this."

I stripped my clothes off slow.

"It's the Sahara between these legs, Alexander. My alter ego and I need to have a conversation about just how much of a soulless bitch I plan to be going forward. We're looking at a twenty percent decrease at least. But I can't figure all this out if you—"

Giving her my back, I bent at the waist. My pants pooled around my ankles with a wet snap.

"Fuck," she drew out. "That's cheating."

I gathered her in my arms, dropping kisses over her face. Soulless was out, but the woman was definitely stubborn. She bit hard to pen her smile and covered her laughing snorts with coughs.

Sighing, she tucked her head under my chin. "I haven't given up, love. I just don't see how to have you both anymore," she murmured. "I won't make that choice, Baris."

Shampoo sat atop the shower partition. I squeezed some on my palm, massaging it into her scalp. I pictured her eyes closing.

"Seems like the only way is to delay Gianna forcing that choice for as long as possible."

"It's not the only way," I replied, but it came harder that time. The load on my chest bore down. My small reprieve was ending.

"The next time I open my door, it won't be to find your body lying on the welcome mat with your heart carved out of your chest." She kissed me. "We've been three steps behind her since I missed hitting *end* on that phone call. Honestly, I don't know if we can catch up while she has the ledger."

She propped her chin on me, humming as my kneading hands moved lower. "But, she's not the first person to get her hands on the ledger and get high on the power—thinking it made her unstoppable. And a code? Smart for sure, but I know her too well. She hasn't got a photographic memory. Plus, she'll want to access the information quickly—not spend half a day decoding her own cipher.

"And you know what else?" she cried, voice rising. "I don't believe that book she tossed at us was the ledger, or even a copy of it."

I paused. *Now that's interesting.*

She must've seen the look on my face.

"Really, Baris, think about it. Over twenty years and countless owners, the ledger must be the size of a phonebook. Richard La Roche alone recorded a Harry Potter saga's worth of dirt on everyone who had the misfortune to meet the man. That book might be all she's finished up to now—which means she hasn't burned the ledger. She wants me to think she has so I'll ease up."

Adeline tossed her head, swinging her sudsy strands. "I want to. I fear we're heading for an escalation that's going to collide. Massive damage on both sides." Brown eyes hardened. "But Kaylee was too far."

I nodded. I made a promise to her father to intervene before that collision, but the answer wasn't for Adeline to slink off on a mission that's mine. I'd know the moment the tide turned, and despite what Cross did to Kaylee, this wasn't it. She wouldn't stop if Adeline disappeared because her gone isn't what she wants. Or it's only part of it.

The look on her face as we stood in Cross's penthouse and she owned her stage.

Cue the big reveal.

Raise the curtains on the hidden players.

Gasp for the twist.

Once an actress, always an actress. Gianna went from Adeline's partner to her adversary, and either way she has her full attention. What would she do if Adeline got rid of her audience?

Adeline smacked my ass. "Why does talking to you help so much?" She smiled in spite of her grand claims to never twitch her lips again. "Something about your calm, still sense of being."

I'm not calm.

"You know who you are."

I know what's been made of me.

"I feel safe when I'm with you, Baris. That's a big deal for me."

You are safe with me for as long as I have you.

"I love you."

I brushed a kiss over her forehead, holding her tighter.

"You're storing all your I love yous in there for me." She rested her cheek over my heart. "By my count, we're up to eight hundred and thirteen. You got the rest of your life to say them, baby, and I'll wait the rest of mine to hear them."

The band constricted—tightening, squeezing, forcing me down.

"It gives me no pleasure to do this."

Mom clawed at the grip on her throat.

"Baris must learn his failures have consequences." He tore his belt free. "A D in English for refusing to give his oral report. You gave me an idiot for a son. The boy can't even speak."

"Baris? Baris?" Soft lips brought me back. "Are you okay?"

I released her, reaching for the shampoo again. *Head, shoulders, back, arms. Scrub ten times, wash, repeat.*

The bottle slipped, splattering the tile.

"Argh!" I punched the wall.

"Whoa, love. It's okay." She held my face, rubbing her nose on mine. "Nothing's broken our routine. I'm right here."

"I will," I rasped.

"What?"

"I will break it, Adeline."

"What does that mean? Break what?"

The words sunk, sinking farther out of reach.

"Stop!"

"Make a fool of me! Cheat on me!"

I ran downstairs—skidding to a stop before his office, tripping, and hitting the floor.

"No, Baris. Get out of here!" Mom ducked.

The tumbler sailed over her head into the wall. Glass sprinkled her like rain, opening a cut on her arm.

I tried to speak. My chest contracted. Squeezing, choking, strangling. I couldn't breathe.

"I never loved you." Mom pushed herself on legs that shook. But she stood. "I'm leaving."

"Like hell you are!" Father's smack spun her.

"St— St—" I gasped.

She hit the bookshelf, rounded, and struck him back.

My eyes bugged as my father stumbled into the desk and dropped. Thumbing his jaw, the same shock beheld her.

"I'm leaving." Mom's shaky voice lined with steel. "And I'm taking my son with me. You've finally got what you wanted, Marshall." She grabbed the philanthropy award the city gifted him and smashed it at her feet. "To be alone with the shallow things you care about and the polite, empty-headed people who praise them."

I couldn't believe it. Mom had never spoken to my father this way. She was doing it. Finally, we were leaving.

Mom turned her back on him. "Let's go, Kainalu."

"Stop. You can't leave me. I said stop!"

She bent over me, gathering me in her arms to help me up. Over her shoulder, Father scrabbled at the desk drawers.

"Bernice!" He pulled out the gun.

"N—" I choked. My mouth opened in a scream that wouldn't come out.

I grabbed her, pushing her behind me.

Bang!

The shot rang through the mansion.

Mom slumped in my hold, head falling on my shoulder.

"No! No, Mom!" The stranglehold broke. "Mom, please."

I fell to my knees. Mom's face was beautiful and serene as if in sleep. I patted her cheeks, and stained them with blood.

"Wake up, please!"

"Shut up, boy!" Hands fisted my shirt, hauling me off her.

"What did you do?!"

"I did nothing." He threw me at the armchair. "You speak of this to no one. Do you understand me? She packed and ran off in the middle of the night. End of story."

Dad was flat and emotionless speaking of covering up his wife's murder while she lay bleeding on the floor.

The gun rested on the desk where he left it. Father reached for the phone, stopped, and straightened his tie.

A strange emotion overtook me—bleeding through my mind as I fixed on his pinched grip moving it into place. Even now, nothing else mattered.

I flew at him.

We struggled.

"You killed her!"

I blocked his punch. My elbow cut across his jaw, cutting his lip.

Dad snatched up the gun. Hand around my throat, he forced me onto the desk, lining his shot.

I kicked him off. Dad dropped it staggering over the coffee table. Righting himself, he sat up to me standing over him, gun in hand.

"Put that down, boy." Hatred burned his gaze. Why hadn't I seen it? How much he hated me. Hated all of us. "I'm your father."

"You killed her," I rasped. I could speak. Too late and of no use, the words flowed free.

"I did what had to be done. You never understood what it takes to be an Alexander. The standard we set. The sacrifices needed to uphold them."

"I understand."

"You do not! How could you? You're a weak, sniveling imitation of the son she should've given me. I should've gotten rid of you both years ago. That treacherous, lying bitch—"

Bang!

Bang, bang, bang!

The bullets tore through him—flopping his limbs, tearing his clothes, staining his shirt, ruining his tie.

He clutched his chest. "B-Baris..." The only thing in his eyes now was shock.

I knelt beside him.

"I do understand, Dad," I said. "I understand now what you've truly wanted and I promise— No." I laid a hand over his fist. "I vow to see it destroyed.

"I will destroy the Alexander business, ruin our reputation, and end our line."

Eyes bulging, blood gurgling from his lips as he tried to speak.

"In twenty years, no one will know the name Alexander, neither will they carry it on. A hundred-year legacy ends with me."

Water pelted us—washing away the kisses on my lips, cheeks, and jaw as fast as she left them.

"Baris, you have all the time you need. I'm not going anywhere."

Taking the memories and what came with it, I shut it away in my quiet place. All that was left behind was what I've always had. My anger.

"I will break us."

Adeline drew away.

"There's no future with me. You need to know that. I need to *say* it. You don't have the rest of your life," I said. "Not with me."

She studied me for a long time, her face unreadable.

"I don't believe that, Baris."

I dropped my head, frustration leaking out of me and running down the drain. My eyes on her were furious.

"You can get as mad at me as you want, but I know that's not true. Just as I know you love me and that I've changed you in all the ways you changed me. We may be apart for a time."

She thinks this is about Bellona. How do I make her understand?

"But you'll come back to me."

"No."

"Yes," she said, breaking her vow for the second time, and smiling. "I know you will."

Anguish squeezed the last desperate word out as the rest were locked away.

"How?"

"Because it's what you do, Baris.

"You fight."

She kissed me—a light, smiling kiss—and I broke.

Hoisting Adeline around the waist, I slammed her against the wall. She shoved my shoulders.

"No, Baris. This isn't about any vow of celibacy," she said over my growl. "We're not doing it this way tonight. Pounding me like an explosion of anger or fighting because you think you can't have anything good unless you bleed for it. Tonight, we go slow. Make love."

She pushed me down. "Slow."

My burning skin had nothing to do with the spray. It thrummed through my veins and Adeline was my outlet. I stood and was guided down again.

"Trust me. We're not out of firsts."

My tongue slipped between her slit.

"Yes," she hissed, running her fingers through my hair. "Just like that."

I buried myself between her legs, indulging her sweet well—head bobbing, tongue fucking.

She cried out. "Right idea, baby. Slower pace."

My fingers dug furrows in her skin. But I slowed, listening to her cries shift from feverish to soft, purring noises dripping from her lips.

I licked and teased her, hearing how the sounds changed and me collecting each breathy moan. My world wasn't silent. It wasn't the neat, orderly space I wanted. It was the world Adeline made her home in. Kicking through the front door and stretching out on the couch with her shoes on.

She had me, and no intention of moving out.

It would only make it harder when it all came crashing down.

"Baris." She shuddered. Tangling in my hair, she arched her back, making my favorite sound of all spilling her sweetness on my tongue.

Adeline sank to the floor, knocking the handle. The shower cut off.

"Come with me," she said in my ear.

She tiptoed through the water, fingers curled through mine.

We made it as far as the sink. I lifted her onto the porcelain and held her legs as my cock found home.

Adeline was all around me. Legs around my thighs. Hands running down my back. Body encasing me, and her in my ear telling me she loved me as I slowed my pumping—indulging the sensation of filling her to the hilt.

"Yes, Baris."

I nipped down her neck as the melody shifted, and I with it, moving faster to chase her over the edge.

Adeline's head fell back. She clung to my shoulders—body tight and wound on my ridge, and a second later I was gripping the sink, grunting as we came together. Hot, weakening bursts of cum filled her, and for a moment, the pressure lifted, and I could speak. I could say what she'd been waiting so long to hear.

She slumped against the mirror, a goofy smile playing on her lips.

"I told you." She kissed my fingertips. "There's only the future for us, ku'uipo."

I let the moment pass. It would be by far the cruelest thing I'd done to tell her I loved her.

There isn't.
"Fight for us."
I won't.

Chapter Twelve

deline

A boxing ring isn't a comfortable place to sleep. A fact I didn't expect to learn in my lifetime, but circumstances lead you to strange places.

On a mound of towels, Baris made love to me all night. I felt so connected to him—like his heart was hooked up to me and my steady pulse kept it going.

The next morning, my chirping bag dragged me out of his arms. I left him sleeping and ducked through the rings, padding naked to my phone.

A familiar number flashed on the screen, and it was about time. I'd been calling her since we fled the motel.

"Gianna."

"Hey, Addy. I'm watching the news now. Twin Lakes Motel is on every station. Luckily, your wanted poster isn't flashing beside the reporter's head."

"Definitely lucky for me," I replied. "Congrats on breaking up with Raul. I was starting to think you'd marry him and have his mini-model babies."

She laughed. "No. We were just never on that track, you know? Especially after I woke up to a gun in my face. He said I didn't deserve the ledger and demanded I hand it over."

I bobbed my head, wholly unsurprised. "He mentioned something like that. Get used to it, Gianna. You've surrounded yourself with paid-for loyalty. Doesn't stretch as far as you think."

"Don't worry about me," she said. "I don't trust any of these fuckers. The only person I trust is you."

Amazing how easily she said that.

"I control them with something a lot more effective than money."

"Fear," I said. "Is that how you hope to control me? You proved you were serious with Kaylee. How could you?" I hissed. "You knew what this would do to me, Gianna. It didn't have to be her!"

"I know, Addy, and I didn't want to. For weeks, I've hoped you wouldn't do what I knew you would and break the truce. Kaylee was cruel. Even so, it had to be her. She's the one in that circus you truly care about. What you're feeling right now, remember it. Remember that it could've been avoided, and you won't have to feel it again if we stop this right now."

I glanced at Brutal asleep in the ring. "How?"

"You know how."

"I will *not* kill them," I forced through clenched teeth. "And don't give me any shit about this'll all go away. Kaylee is still alone and terrified—ripped away from the family that loves her."

"That's just it, babe. I can make it go away. Kaylee and the Hunts are being brought back to Cinco. I can arrange for social services to *lose* her file. I'll get the case thrown out. What aren't you understanding, Addy? Every one of the slightest bit of importance or influence is in the ledger. No one says no to me."

"No," I said clearly. "I won't kill the men I love for what a good lawyer can do. Or a bad one. Bribes are as effective as blackmail."

"How about this? I take killing them off the table."

I frowned. "What?"

"Let them live if it means that much to you. Just come back." Something crept into her voice. "Move into Fairfield with me. Help me do what we've been planning. I've already started negotiations on the properties. One of them has a restaurant attached. And the Kings. Addy, there's enough in this book to topple their empire like a stack of blocks.

"This doesn't have to go farther than it has. Leave them. Walk away. They can't share what's ours, but at least they've proven they won't hurt you to get it."

I thought of that hallway and the lives shared behind its doors.

"I see my future, Gianna. I see the ledger. I see you. And I see the city we've wanted Cinco to be." Closing my eyes, I let out a long breath. "But I also see kids with purple hair, intelligent eyes, wicked grins, and clothes that have never met a stain. I'm thinking of my retirement, G, and it involves something I've always wanted: a family.

"Can you accept that I want to be your partner, and theirs?"

"No." Gianna didn't pause to consider it. Or even to breathe. "So, this is your answer."

"It's not my answer," I said. "Because I refuse to make the choice."

"No, Adeline. I want you to fight."

"Is that right?" Her voice was tight.

"Yes. I will not choose between the people I love. You think you have the right to make me because you don't believe it is love. You're convinced it's a delusion I need to be snapped out of. To be fair, I thought the same of Raul. But the Merchants aren't like him and I know I can make you see that, bestie. Just like I know one day you'll come around.

"So, no. I'm not moving in with you, Leah, and the Pips today. I'm also not taking your shit lying down. We can work out our stuff amongst ourselves, or you can lose the biggest advantage a Kieran has—masking their real identity. Pretend all you want that doesn't scare you, but I *know it does*," I sang.

"Hanging on to the ledger is a lifelong fight, and I'm prepared to take that fight into the open," she snapped. "I'll defend what's mine. And you, Adeline, are included. I will wake you up, boo. Those dicks aren't your family. I am."

"I still love you, Gianna."

"Remember this," she barked, voice rising. "Remember Kaylee and that I offered to stop this before it started. What happens next is on you."

"I understand. I'm prepared to defend what's mine too."

She hung up.

Dropping my phone in my bag, I climbed into the ring. Brutal was awake and watching me.

"Was I that difficult when you were trying to reason with me?"

Fuck yes.

How do you tell the difference between a "fuck yes" nod and a "yes" nod? With Brutal, you just can.

TWO WEEKS LATER, BRUTAL had another fight under his belt. Three down, two to go. An extra ten grand in his pocket.

The bulk of it went to the lawyer handling Kaylee's case. The rest got us out of the gym and into a North Quay loft Mercer rented through an alias. It wasn't well-located or packed with high-end finishes as the Leighbridge loft. Its charm came from three bedrooms, and the Korean restaurant downstairs with the delivery guy who delivered bulgogi without looking up from his phone.

"How are Declan and Jasmine?" I asked. "I talked to Kaylee. She said the family they placed her with is nice, but she's ready to go home. Mostly she's thankful she can't be sent back to her dad."

Of course she couldn't. Timothy Trevino was found dead in some crack hole as Saint predicted he would be.

"They're out on bail," he said. "Their lawyer is confident they won't receive jail time. Considering what Kaylee was rescued from, that she has no family, and apparently, she was assigned a caseworker. The woman missed six months' worth of home visits with Kaylee but has been marking them complete."

"Oh my goodness," I cried. "Saint said any alternative was better than Cinco foster care. Remind me never to doubt him."

"I will but don't tell him that. His ego's inflated enough."

I laughed. Why not? I was allowed now that I was confident the Hunts would be all right. "Will you be home soon?"

I glanced around the humble space. Lack of budget for furniture left us with what came with the loft. Wicker chairs, a plastic table, and dark blue shades on the lamps that made the room darker.

"What we have passing for a home, I mean."

"I board the plane in an hour. I'll have to meet you guys at the fight."

My smile dimmed. Brutal's fourth fight was that night. Lane texted the location two hours ago. It was another warehouse in Harlow. Unlucky for us, the tournament was providing the Kings all the money they needed to rebuild.

"They almost didn't let us in the last one. Something about me and an announcer with a dent in his head. The guards tried to get *forceful* about it, but it kicked off a fight with Brutal that Thiago Pais stopped. Something about damaging the merchandise." My lips pressed together thinking of the uneven grin and the wink he tossed me as he strode away, surrounded by an entourage almost as beautiful as him.

"I don't know what to make of this guy, Killian. Angelo was easy to figure out. Enzo Bianchi too. But the short-tempered pretty boy with barely two brain cells rattling around in his head is not the man I'm seeing."

"Thiago Pais has made a living being what people want him to be. It's anyone's guess who is behind the role," he replied. "I'd guess the man slashing up people is the closest representation of the real him."

His card burned a hole in my pocket. "Either way, he's not an enemy you want to have."

"You say that like he's not an enemy already."

"I don't know," I said softly—vision glazing out of focus. "I have this feeling he wants something else from us. He stopped his men laying a finger on Brutal. He stepped in between me and Desmond Lane. He went through the trouble of researching a supposed banger's girl.

"The man is sunshine and giggles until someone's no longer useful to him. Brutal's proven very useful. I think before this is over, we'll be offered the chance to be useful to him too. Or take a trip to the docks."

"There's a high probability that you're right."

"We have to be ready, Cash. When Brutal wins, and he will win, they're not going to let us walk out of there with half a million, singing bygones will be bygones."

"I have a plan."

"Odds of us all making it out alive?"

"Slim."

I dropped my head on the couch. "Same as usual, then."

BRUTAL WALKED AHEAD of us to the warehouse—straight-backed and impassively handsome like he'd been through the entire tournament.

I ran up behind him and jumped on his back, riding him piggyback-style.

He groaned. Staggering, Brutal bowed his knees like they were buckling under the weight.

"You know what, I will kill you after all."

Laughing, he twisted his neck and kissed my pouting mouth. Whatever came over him that night in the gym shower, it passed. In the last few weeks, I felt closer to him than ever. We spent the day teaching each other fighting moves, and curled up on his mattress at night, watching old comedies and munching on Korean candy from downstairs.

I told him of the future I saw with our own penthouse fortress, an army that dropped to their knees with a snap of my finger, and a miniature Brutal running between his feet.

Brutal told me nothing in return, but he did listen with a smile on his face, and only shut me up with a kiss when I started talking preschools.

We rounded the corner. A line of people waited outside the warehouse. The level of noise assured it was the right one.

"What's going on?" I asked. Sinjin walked in step with us. "Please, tell me they're not trying to pull something else."

"Look!" A woman pointed at us. "There he is. Brutal!"

She was the fire that lit the fuse.

"Brutal! Brutal, over here! Brutal, we love you!"

"What the hell?"

Brutal walked through the line and his fans rushed him. I noticed at the last match he was collecting more cheers and chants than the previous rounds. Half of the "kill, kill, kill" shouts were backing him up.

"You're a fucking machine," someone said. "You took out Axe in three minutes."

"They said tonight's going to be even better!"

"Brutal!" A young woman broke free of the masses. Long ringlets brushed the fabric of a strapless top. "Can I get your signature?" She held out a pen, and pushed her tube top all the way down, baring her breasts. She winked at him. "Please."

I grabbed her whole face and shoved, sending her shrieking into the crowd.

Brutal laughed his head off. I wasn't nearly so amused.

"I don't know what's worse." We got clear of them, stepping inside the familiar setup. "Death matches or death-match groupies. They don't have to enjoy it this much."

"I'd enjoy it too under different circumstances," said Saint, "and sponsors. Society's rules don't exist in this room, Bunny. This could be a beautiful thing. After we stomp out the Kings, let's keep the tournament going."

This is the man I want to father my children.

"Did I hear my name?" Lane appeared next to us. "I could've sworn I heard King. This city's and yours."

"Always a pleasure, Desmond," I said. "Tonight, can we skip the banter and get straight to your latest tactic to screw Brutal over? Last time, you put that chemically enhanced two hundred and fifty pounds of a man in the ring and he tossed sharpened metal jacks on the canvas. Funny that you added that new weapon out of nowhere. Even funnier Prophet stepped in wearing shoes."

Shrugging, he grinned. "What can I say? I really want your boy dead."

"No harm done," Saint said, matching his tone. "I'm actually liking the creativity, to be honest. See, everything you do to Brutal, I'm going to do to you. Come at you with a chainsaw. Stab your feet. Have some fun with an axe." Saint's grin made a passing guy give a wider berth. "You still live at 438 North Maple, don't you?"

Desmond's grin vanished. "Show up any fucking time. You're next, bitch."

Saint walked off.

"You're next!"

"Ahem," I broke in. I hopped off Brutal's back. "Something you wanted to tell us?"

"Tonight's the last match," he snapped. "Winner takes home the money and their stay of execution."

"What?"

"You heard me. This is the final match of the tournament unless both players make it through sudden death," he said. "No tricks. No spikes. No games."

My eyes narrowed. "What the hell is this? You're making boatloads of money from these fights as everyone keeps telling me. Why would you cut it short?"

"You're complaining? Damn." He smirked at Brutal. "Looks like your girl wants you dead too."

"Don't spread your shit to him, you sack of human waste. You're not fit to look in Brutal's direction. Let alone address him."

Lane got in my face. "You know." Hot, beer breath filled my nose. "I'm getting real tired—"

Brutal tossed him clear into the bleachers. He fell between the seats, screaming abuse at us.

"No one wants this tournament over more than me," I said.

Fans cheered us on in search of his changing room.

"Nothing smells right when it comes to that man. Cash said he was coming up with a plan against whatever they have in mind for the true end of this tournament, and he's not here."

He kissed my crown. *We'll be fine. No one is going to hurt you.*

I couldn't be sure that was what he was thinking. It was the reassurance I felt as he smiled at me, stepping inside the back room. I wasn't allowed in after the pre-match hand job I gave him last time made Brutal miss when they called out the fighters.

Someone has to keep his spirits up.

I turned, and bumped into Gianna.

I stared at her as if the mirage would vanish as quickly as she appeared. Blink and she's gone.

I blinked.

Gianna was still there.

"What are you doing here?"

"That's what you have to say after weeks of not seeing your best friend?"

She was glowing—no other word for it.

Her curly mane was half piled on her head. The rest fell around her shoulders—bare in a sleeveless peacock-print dress, tied at the waist in a bow. Matching blue Christian Louboutin wedges sparkled as she swallowed the distance, leaning in to smooch my cheek.

"How could I not be here? Everyone is talking about this match, Addy. It's the worst-kept secret in Cinco. I'm sure the Kings have paid off the cops to have their raid on the wrong night."

I was still staring at her.

"What did you do?"

She rolled her eyes, sighing. "I know we're in a fight right now, but you don't have to be suspicious of everything I do. I heard Brutal got himself locked in the tournament. I wanted to see a match for myself." Gianna inclined her head. "Okay. Maybe I have an ulterior motive. I also had to give it one more shot in person. I knew if Brutal was here. You'd be here."

"I won't—"

"Uh-uh." She put a finger over her lips. "Please, save the rejection for after I give my speech. For now, can we pretend none of this happened and just watch the match?"

She pointed. "My seats are over there. I bought out the front row. Sinjin, Cash, and Mercer can join us. I put Leah in the back. What do you say?"

What was there to say? Weeks of silence and suddenly she was here saying let's be buddies and talk it out when this is over.

I held out my hand.

Beaming, Gianna led me to her seats, sitting us down and holding my hand in her lap.

She was up to something as surely as my name was Adeline Redgrave. She wasn't even trying to hide it sitting there smiling at me with that grin she knew I saw through.

"Gianna, I'm not going to be disappointed in you, am I?"

"Don't know what you mean." She twisted around. "Wow. Look at this turnout. You wouldn't think so many people were this interested in watching guys beat each other to death— Hey, guys." She waved. "Saint. Killian, over here."

"That's Sinjin to you." He dropped next to me, tugging my hand free of her. "Everyone I want to kill calls me Sinjin."

"That's fair," Gianna said, hanging on to her smile. "I'm far from your favorite person right now. What if I told you I've figured out a way we can all get what we want?"

"I'd say that won't do, because the only acceptable outcome is you not getting a fucking thing you want."

I rubbed his leg, soothing him.

Killian didn't grant Gianna the dignity of a look.

"Hi, love." I leaned over to kiss him. "I'm sorry. She can't be the first person you want to see after the last few weeks, but something is up. The Kings have cut the tournament short."

His perfect face crumpled in a frown. "They what? Why would they do that? These crowds are getting bigger."

"I wish I knew. Can that plan of yours be moved up to tonight?"

"No, Adeline. It can't." Cash unstrapped his gun. "Be ready."

"Ooh, look," Gianna said. "We're about to start."

Two Kings unlocked the cage for Desmond Lane to climb inside. Looking past him, Pais locked eyes. He waved, tossing me a wink.

"Ladies and gentlemen." Lang echoed in the warehouse. "Are you ready for a match that will go down in tournament history?"

"Yeah!"

"I'm sorry to say this is the last match of this year's tournament."

The cheers turned to shouts and boos so fast, I wished he was out of the cage for the mob to get him easier.

"We're disappointed too," Lane said, "but these were the terms our warrior set to agree to the fight. Trust me, agreeing to those terms was worth every penny we stand to lose. Brutal has finally met his match!"

I gritted my teeth at the cheers. "Make up your fucking minds. First you want him to sign your boobs, then you're pissing yourself over another King trick."

"We're not wasting another fucking minute," Lane bellowed. "We've waited weeks to watch Brutal die! Let's bring him out here."

Brutal emerged bare-chested and barefoot. People chanted and heckled him alike. He didn't hear any of it. They sent him in the cage with Lane. His face remained blank as the man circled him.

"Looks cool, doesn't he?" Lane taunted. "Let's see his face as we bring out the baddest bitch in the East Coast! The terror of Tivoli! Dominator of the ropes, Mayhem!"

The front doors swept open, ushering a bunch of hooting, jumping half-naked guys running all over the place. Through the confusion, I saw the one who must be Mayhem. Dressed in a simple pair of baggy shorts and a tank, they revealed a hard, lean form. A fighter for sure, but I wasn't seeing the harbinger of the apocalypse that Lane was painting.

Turning away, I dismissed her. *Baris will have no trouble—*

I lurched to my feet. "Baris? What's wrong?"

Mouth hanging open, Brutal's serene mask was blown apart. He rushed the cage, throwing a club out of his way.

"Did I forget to mention?" Lane continued. "Mayhem is otherwise known as Bellona Alexander."

No...

"Brutal's older sister."

The audience went insane.

"Wow," said Gianna. "This is exciting."

BRUTAL

The noise clicked off. Vision narrowing on a single point, I was in a truly silent world, taking in no sensory information other than what my eyes told me.

Bellona.

Eighteen years later, and there was no doubt it was her. The heart-shaped face of our mother. The nose from our father. The sable eyes she got from neither one. The years had their effect in other ways. Lining her with muscle, lengthening her chin, and adding two inches in height.

For years I looked for a sign of her. I prepared to leave Cinco, Adeline, and the Merchants to find her. And here she was.

Bellona faced me under Lane's leering grin. The sound turned on.

"Hello, little brother."

Chest heaving, I said nothing. I wouldn't have been able to reply, my troubles with speech aside.

"The rules don't change for siblings, folks. We lock this cage and no one comes out till one of them is dead. What do you think? Will Brutal cut her head off with the same ruthless determination? Or will he surrender the fight, and his life, to his only sister? Cast your bets."

A flurry of activity. People rushing the bookies.

Noise. Noise. Noise.

From everyone but her.

Bellona stood as silent as me, waiting for the signal to kill each other.

ADELINE

"What did you do?!"

Gianna blinked slow in the face of my fury. "You're blaming me for this?"

"You're to blame."

She shrugged. "Yeah, I guess I am."

"How?" I croaked. "Dad didn't write down her location. Only the date and time Marshall Alexander hired him to kill his daughter."

"True. Daddy Red took precautions," she said. "What he didn't anticipate was her returning to Cinco and ending up in the ledger by her own misdeeds. She's had quite a life since Oscar spirited her overseas and placed her with distant relatives of her mother in England. Sometimes a girl has to do what she has to do."

Gianna stood, bearing down on me. "And when she does, she'll one day have to make a choice she can't ignore or wiggle out of. Follow orders and see her slate wiped clean, or tell me no. Like I said, people don't tell me no."

I grasped Saint's shoulder, stopping him from getting up.

"What do you want, Gianna? You win, okay? You fucking win! Just put a stop to this now."

"I haven't won yet." She smoothed out her dress and reclaimed her seat. "We're going to watch the match like friends, and depending on the outcome, I'll know if there's a conversation worth having."

"No," I hissed. "You worked out some kind of deal with the Kings. Undo it. Pull Bellona from the match now—"

"—and get her, Brutal, and Josephine Meza killed," she finished. "I'd say our life expectancy drops too. Look around you, Addy. The Kings are cleaning up. They're not letting anyone leave this warehouse, or that cage." She patted the seat next to her. "Sit."

I bolted. Running at Lane, I jumped him as he locked the cage.

"You can't do this!" I was wrestled to the floor. "Baris!"

Ding! Ding!

BRUTAL

"Baris!"

Ding! Ding!

Bellona crouched, taking her stance. Trained in the same gym I now owned, she didn't glance at the weapons decorating the cage.

"What are you waiting for, Baris? Your invitation just rang the bell."

I tried to take my stance. I bent my knees and straightened. Raised my fists and put them down. Over and over again, warring with instinct. She wasn't just another fighter and this just another fight.

What had the Kings done to get her in this cage? With who did they make their deals?

I flicked to Gianna Cross and the triumph leaking from her pores.

This was it. The moment she set her charges for total annihilation. And I was the trigger.

This is all wrong. Agitated, I backed away. *We weren't supposed to do it like this. See each other again as opposers!*

"Agh!" I yanked on the chains—roaring as they rattled and groaned, and held fast.

I had to talk to her. Tell the truth about our parents and what I did—

Pain reverberated through my back.

The kick smashed me into the bars, dropping me on the mat. The crowd hollered in near insanity—drunk on bloodlust.

"First rule," she said. "Never turn your back on your opponent. Didn't Theo teach you better than that?"

Theo. Our boxing coach after Jeffery.

He didn't tell me to use my anger as fuel. He said to win—at all costs.

I kicked out, sweeping her leg.

Bellona danced out of the way. "Come on!"

Pushing myself up, I took my stance. To the sound of our own bell, we flew at each other.

ADELINE

"Sit down!"

Lane forced me into the chair. Six guys wrestled with Cash and Sinjin, the blood seeping from their wounds telling of how hard they found the task.

"You won't get it easy, forcing us to throw you out. You'll watch every second of this match. The three of you! The piece of shit dies tonight, murdered by his own blood. Or he kills his sister, walks out of here, and shoots himself. Either way, Brutal doesn't leave that cage."

Tears soaked my cheeks. Lane was right. He had his victory no matter the outcome.

Gianna drew me to her, tucking my head under her chin. I hugged her tight, sobbing as she rubbed my back.

It was the tensest match of the tournament. Of any tournament.

The Alexander siblings traded blows, ignoring shouts to bash her with the crowbar or stab him with the spear. Baris received a bloody lip from her jab. Bellona cried out when a kick dropped her hard on her arm.

More than once, Brutal tried to back off—his jaw working like he was fighting to speak to her.

Bellona came at him too hard for him to let up. He dropped his arms and she punched him in the face. He broke stance, and Bellona put him on his ass.

Brutal was losing the match.

"Get off her!" Sinjin's growl preceded hands grabbing me. He broke me free of Gianna, shielding me between him and Cash.

Their match had not gone well either. They were banged up half as bad as the guards pointing guns at the three of us. We were staying in these chairs and watching each horrible minute.

Ding!

My head snapped up. Ten minutes? The round was over?

"Warriors, opposite sides of the cage," Lane confirmed. "Five-minute break."

Brutal staggered out. I went to him and didn't get farther than the blockade pinning us to our seats. Brutal wasn't getting to me either. They forced him at gunpoint into the back room.

"Gianna, please," I cried. "Do something."

She looked away. "I warned you, Addy. This time, you don't get to blame me."

I was a wreck in the second round. I took each hit worse than Brutal. He was in there with Bellona due to me. Choosing between his future and his family because I refused to.

"Adeline, don't cry." Cash wiped my face with his sleeve. "Watch. Seriously, watch. I've counted five openings where she could've gone for the kill shot. Six for Brutal. They're beating the shit out of each other, but they're not fighting to kill."

His words penetrated, slowing my tears.

"They're riding out the clock."

"L-Lane said if they end in a draw, the fighters are forced into a rematch and locked in until one of them is dead."

His eyes were hard. "That rematch won't be tonight. A lot of things can happen between then and now."

I didn't probe harder. Warm in his coat, I watched the match, holding on to hope that Cash was correct and they were running out the clock.

The second match ended, leading too quickly into the third.

Brutal bled from his lip and nose. Bruises were beginning to form on his chest.

Bellona had not seen her brother since he was ten years old and she was ripped away from him. How strong was the sway of Kieran that she'd spend their reunion like this?

Brutal blocked a kick to his abdomen. Seizing her ankle, he flipped her on her face.

"Kill! Kill! Kill!" The crowd was impatient and not shy about demanding what they wanted. If there was an ounce of feeling toward the brother and sister forced to fight, it didn't go further than the three of us.

Ding! Ding!

"Warriors, break."

Bellona and Baris went their separate ways. Bellona accepted water, a towel, and help to her room. Baris marched off alone.

"Now, now," Lane said, stepping in the cage. "No need for disappointment. Brutal and Mayhem fought hard and earned their place in the final match: sudden death!"

They howled and kicked up a fuss heard by everyone in Cinco City.

"Two warriors. Two swords. Ten minutes on the clock," he said. "This is the end of the road for Brutal."

"Trash, Lane," I called clear through the noise. "Always remember what you are."

His grin twitched, proving he heard me.

Gianna jerked her head to the side. She was calling me over. I pulled away from the guys and joined her beside the cage—under the watchful eyes of Lane's men.

"Finally ready to tell me what you want."

She dug in her purse and came away with a tissue. "It didn't have to be this way, Addy." She dabbed under my eyes. "It still doesn't. I heard what you said to Cash about a second match. There won't be one assuming you leave with me tonight."

The statement stirred no emotion. I expected this.

"If they both live, the Kings will want their rematch. They won't get it if I keep up my end of the deal, ripping out her page and sending her off with a new identity and a heavy bank account. She'll be blamed for running off. The tournament will be over. Brutal freed. And you'll be with me."

"What did Kieran have on her?"

"No, Adeline." She tucked the tissue in my hand. "You can't offer her a deal of your own. Sometimes there's only one way out, and this is it. Take it or leave it."

"The guys—"

"No."

"Brutal," I whispered.

"He won't have to kill his sister. I'm sure he'll accept that in lieu of a goodbye."

"Adeline," Saint called.

Gianna gave me her back. "Make your choice."

Bellona and Baris were brought out for the final "sudden death" match. I strangled Saint's and Cash's hands in my grip.

BRUTAL

Lane shoved a sword in my hand. No shield.

On the other side of the cage, Bellona accepted hers.

My blade skimmed the canvas, forming a groove.

Dull.

I assumed Bellona's blade did not have the same issue. Lane wants to see me finished. Why was he so certain Mayhem would do the job? Even I noted she missed countless opportunities to snap my neck.

Opportunities she shouldn't have had.

I was a mess. Unfocused. Dropping my hands. Pushing to speak and fighting physical reactions preventing me instead of fighting her.

"You haven't changed, Baris."

Bellona leveled her sword.

"You're still waiting for permission to fight."

Ding!

Our swords clanged over our heads.

I had zero experience fighting with this. Who the fuck did who wasn't a Las Vegas show pirate?

The metal was clumsy in my hand. The grip slipped between my gloves. Their reasoning for including them in the "sudden death" match became clear. Waving around these weapons like fumbling idiots, one of us was bound to kill the other by accident alone.

"Ah!"

Bellona's blade cleaved through the air. I brought my sword up, holding it lengthwise as a shield. Her force dug the edge into my palm, slicing through the leather and opening skin.

Fuck this.

I flung the sword away.

Swinging to the side, I caught her wrist like I'd done to Adeline countless times, and twisted. She dropped the weapon with a cry.

I tossed it out of the cage at Thiago Pais's feet. This wasn't a show for their entertainment. This was between me and my sister.

I spun and her foot slammed against the metal. *Never turn your back on your opponent.* I caught her calf and flipped her on her back.

Bellona grinned up at me. "You're learning."

"Pick up the swords!"

"Redo the match!"

"That's cheating!"

"I love you!" Adeline's voice was clear amid the chaos. "No matter what happens, I love you."

Nothing will happen. The Alexanders do not die tonight.

We grappled—neither one of us getting the edge on the other, and I offered no openings. I blocked her hooks, broke her holds, and glanced her jabs.

The final bell rang, ending the last match of the tournament.

"Rematch! Rematch! Rematch!"

The chant started up immediately.

"Folks, folks." Lane stood at the foot of the stairs, speaking into the mic. "You will get your rematch. In one week's time, we hold the final battle of the tournament and the final match of Alexander versus Alexander."

Lane's men jumped me coming out of the cage.

"Considering his opponent, we're going to shut down any thoughts of running and keep Brutal where we can see him. There will be a fight next week, followed by a funeral."

"Hey! Get your hands off me!" Bellona's crew turned on her, hauling her away.

And mine. Sinjin and Cash rushed Lane's men, bringing more down on us.

Through the swinging limbs and half a dozen men wrestling me down, I sought Adeline.

"Adeline?" Her name broke through. "Adeline!"

The shout alerted Sinjin and Cash.

"Adeline!" we shouted, shifting from fighting for me to fighting to get to her.

"Adeline!"

"Wait," Cash said. "Where's Cross?"

The woman in the peacock dress was nowhere to be seen.

Adeline! The shout was just as well unvoiced. She couldn't hear it.

Adeline was gone.

Six became eight men. They held me aloft, carrying me kicking and thrashing to the back room. I was tossed inside—door slammed shut and locked.

Chapter Thirteen

deline

A The pillow was soft and damp clinging to my cheek. Memory foam molded to my body, cradling me in the cool blankets. My bedroom was comfortable. I had that much going for me.

Gianna came inside with my breakfast.

"Morning, babe." Setting the tray on the nightstand, she climbed up and kissed my cheek. "Salty."

It would be. I bawled for half the night and twice this morning.

"Addy, I know breakups are hard, but this is for the best," she said, stroking my hair.

I shifted out of her reach and the chains rattled. My new home and room came with an ankle accessory.

"Give it time. You'll get over them. Until then I'm here for you."

She snuggled in with me despite my clear vibes to leave me alone. She draped over my waist and rested her cheek on my back.

"Tell me what to do to cheer you up."

"Give me space."

"No, come on. I mean it. Anything. I'll put on one of your favorite movies. I'll make caramel popcorn too. From scratch," she said. "It won't be as good as yours but it'll taste yummy."

I kicked, clanging the chains on the bedpost.

She sighed. "Yes, okay. I did say to find better ways of communicating other than imprisonment." Gianna left and returned with the key. "I'll let you out. Let me remind you of a few things first. St. John will be told the name of his father's killer in eighteen months. If you try to run, I tack another year on. If you try to steal the ledger, Mercer's secrets hit the airwaves. Agreed?"

My face slid up and down on a slick pillow, nodding. "Baris."

"I put the money in his sister's hand and wave off her flight to Southeast Asia tomorrow. Once they realize she's gone, Brutal will be released. Or maybe they'll make him fight someone else. He won't have trouble with them."

She unlocked my shackle and I curled tighter in a ball.

What were the guys thinking right now? This time I walked out on them for real. I left them to face the Kings alone.

Saint and Cash weren't men who forgave once—let alone twice.

They have to know I'm doing this for them. Baris searched for her for years.

It's not about the future I saw for us. It's about the one he sees for himself, and Bellona was in it. If I truly love him, it's enough for him to be happy. Even if he's not happy with me.

And Saint.

It's disgusting that he should wait another second for that name. I won't be the reason he does.

My Cash. His family were good people. They were the tight-knit closeness I wanted to have one day. They didn't deserve more misfortune.

Mercer.

His secrets were his to keep. I just wish he could've kept me too.

Look at that. Turns out I can be selfless.

"Do you hate being here with me that badly?"

"No, G. I've missed you," I admitted. "This used to be all I wanted. I just want something else now too."

"Someone else. Four someones."

"It's going to take time. Don't rush me. Don't tell me what I'm feeling isn't real."

She put her hands up. "I'm not cruel enough to kick you when you're down. Officially slipping into supportive and caring best-friend mode. Still want that popcorn?"

I was quiet for a while, studying her. Threats hanging over our heads and I couldn't shake that she meant it.

"Baking soda," I said. "That's the secret. Half a teaspoon."

"Got it." She popped a kiss on my forehead. "Rest up, babe. Everything will look better in a couple of days."

I dropped my smile as the lock clicked. Burying my face in the pillow, I cried.

BRUTAL

I bent in the chair. Hands cuffed behind my back, my head hung over my knees.

It was morning if the sunlight peeking under the crack was anything to go by. It had been hours since the tournament.

The door hadn't been rushed, so it was safe to say the guys had been stashed somewhere safe too.

Adeline wasn't here with her wicked grins or her hand sliding past my belt as she poured her dirty predictions in my ear. I didn't know what was safe to say about that. At least I didn't question why.

"You're probably wondering what happened to me after that night."

Slowly, I opened my eyes.

"Although, how I ended up in a cage beating the shit out of you is likely higher on your mind."

Lane's men had seen fit to cuff Bellona in the chair across from me. Straightening, I shook my head.

No.

"The guy that took me brought me to a nowhere town in the middle of a nowhere county in England," she said. "He warned me of the dangers of contacting anyone from my old life and took off. I never saw him again."

She scoffed. "My old life. Just like that, I was supposed to trade in parties, ballgowns, private schools, and ballet lessons for a farm, three goats, and a chicken. I begged him to take me home. Told him after I gave up the kid, I'd convince Father to take me back. Want to know what he said?"

I do.

"'Doesn't work that way, kid. I don't do returns.'" Her eyes—unique of all of us—bore into me. "I'm told his name is Kieran. Some kind of legendary kingpin, and the one holding my leash now. At least that's what the girl with half a face told me. Heard of him?"

I bobbed my head.

"Know where I can find him?"

No.

"Still doing that no-talking thing, are you?" She twisted her head side to side. "Look around you, Baris. There's no one to put on a show for. You can stop pretending to be Daddy's perfect little boy—seen and not heard, always by his side. Do you know where I can find Kieran?" she repeated forcefully.

Looking her in the eyes, I shook my head.

She blew out a breath. "It's true what they say. Little brothers never stop being annoying. Fine. We'll do this your way. I was twenty-six when I finally scraped up enough money to come home. I heard the news of Mom and Dad's death. Then, I returned and found all of it was gone. The company, the homes, the cars, the buildings with our name on it.

"The incompetent teenage CEO had driven it into the ground," she said. "Our assets were sold for nothing. Our collections and possessions practically *given away* at auction to cover our losses. The legacy Dad bypassed me to give to you, and you destroyed it."

My mind stuck on a single part of her speech. Bellona returned to Cinco City. She had been here, in the neighboring borough, while I searched for her.

"I realized there was nothing left for me in Cinco, so I moved to New York. Made a name for myself there and have been back a few times for work."

Been back a few times for work.

She cocked her head. "A lot's gone on since I've been away. You fell in with a bad crowd. The Merchants, right? I didn't believe it when she told me. Not Baris Alexander, golden boy, prodigal son."

One word broke through. "Baby."

"Ah, he does talk," she sang. "Why do you want to know about my kid? You going to introduce yourself?"

I waited.

"Nope. Don't pull that again. Tell me why and I'll answer you."

Closing my eyes, I resumed my position—bent over and sinking in my quiet place.

"You always were stubborn," she said under her breath. "Whatever. It's not a big deal. I had a girl. Gave her up for adoption. End of story. What was

I going to do with a kid? I never planned to raise her. I could've made Dad change his mind if not for Kieran."

"No."

"Excuse me?"

"No, you couldn't," I repeated—steady and clear. "Father called Kieran to kill you, Bellona. Cut off your fingertips, bash in your face, and dump you as unidentified trash under the overpass. You broke the rules. You brought imperfections into his rigidly perfect world. Daddy's little girl doesn't get knocked up by the mayor's son. Just think of the headlines. The stain on the glowing Alexander name.

"You know he never spoke your name after that night."

The lines around her mouth hardened.

"Not once," I said. It was easy to give this speech. I'd been holding on to it for a long time.

"All the photos of you were taken down. When people asked why and what happened, he said you ran away and it was too difficult to talk about. He didn't even give people the space to miss you. Not in his presence. He wouldn't have cared that you gave your daughter to another family and were ready to come home. He stopped caring about you when the bump couldn't be hidden anymore."

"Are you enjoying this, Baris?" she asked, head cocked. "Did you wait all these years to tell me I wasn't missed?"

No.

"No," I got out. "I'm saying this so that you understand how easily he made the decision to throw you away. It was as quick as his conclusion Mom had to die for leaving him."

Bellona's smirk vanished. "What?"

"He killed her. Shot her walking out the door," I rasped. "She died in my arms."

"No— No! That's not true. Joshua Hudson killed Mom and Dad. He shot them and raided the house, taking what he thought being Dad's gardener entitled him to. He confessed, Baris."

"Marshall killed Mom."

"No, he did not. This is what always got you in trouble. You couldn't stop telling lies."

"He killed her," I said, "and I killed him."

The denial halted on her tongue—mouth hanging open. "What did you say?"

"I took the gun he used on her and shot him four times. He died a gurgling, pleading mess on the floor, and my last words to him, a vow to destroy everything he cared about more than his wife, son, and daughter. You're welcome, Bellona."

She stared at me—mouth frozen.

"Father would not have taken you back. In truth, he would've gotten someone else to kill you—if he didn't do it himself. I saved you the indignity of begging for your life from a man who had no authority to judge or a right to take it."

I laughed. "The funny thing is the sniveling, whiny, Mommy's boy who was too stupid to speak, turned out to be the one most like Father. I made the decision to kill him in the straightening of his tie. In the last twelve years, I've searched for regret and found only one—that I didn't shoot him sooner.

"What do you think, Bellona? I spoke. Did I say what you wanted to hear?"

Bellona closed her mouth. It was her turn to be silent.

ADELINE

"That's enough."

Gianna blew in my room.

"Get up. You're done moping."

I sat up in bed, flipping through *Poor Fellow My Country*. I saw it on Baris's bookshelf enough times, and then here it appears on mine.

"I'm hardly moping." My eyes were dry. Throat clear. "I'm reading a book."

"You haven't left this room in a week."

"I've left this room multiple times, and Leah has gifted me with that shit-eating grin every time I do. If I see that look again, I'm going to kill her."

"Don't worry about Leah." The mattress dipped with her weight. "Her personality leaves a lot to be desired, but she's efficient. Gets the job done quick and without complaint. We'll need people like her when we move on to our bigger goals."

"I don't need her," I said simply.

"Leah isn't important right now. I've got a present for you." She hopped up on her knees, grinning ear to ear. "Remember the property with the restaurant attached? I bought it."

"Congratulations." I returned to my book.

Gianna plucked it from my hands and sent it sailing over her shoulder.

"I bought it for you, dummy." Her voice rose with excitement. "You were talking about turning that old sandwich shop into a little eatery and then I had it blown up. Sorry about that," she added.

"This place is ten times better. A kitchen to rival Raiden Spencer's. Prime Leighbridge real estate and the Leighbridge palates to go with it. Babe, you can open your own gourmet restaurant. From Ryan's bitch to the boss."

"Sous chef," I corrected automatically. "I don't know, G. It's a thoughtful gift, but I'm not up to it today."

"Because you're moping."

"I prefer mourning."

"I prefer my best friend taking charge of her dreams instead of slumping around, stuffing her face with ice cream, and moaning about the guys who knocked those dreams off track. This is not me belittling your feelings," she said. "This is me painting a picture of you for the last week."

"Grim picture," I mumbled.

Maybe she's right. I made my choice. Sitting around crying about it won't bring my boys back. Time to imagine a different family behind that door.

Behind this one, a voice said. *This is your home now.*

"Are we going now? It's getting late."

"So? We'll make a date of it. The restaurant has power. We'll pick up some food and you'll make your first meal in there."

I seized on a thought. "Let's pick up Dad too."

"No, Addy."

"Why not? I haven't seen him in a while and I know he'd like to spend time with both of us. Come on. Dinner for three."

"No. I let you talk to him three days ago."

Let me.

"I talked to him. You didn't. Why are you avoiding him, Gianna? Haven't we patched things up?"

"Yes," she gritted. "But I don't need a lecture from a man who isn't my father like I'm still fifteen years old. I appreciate everything Oscar's done for me, but it's time to get off the teat. You may consider doing the same."

"Is getting off the teat ignoring him and refusing his calls? If you continue trying to force him out of my life, we'll fall out again."

The air charged with headstrong personalities.

"No one is keeping you from him. You're free to see him whenever. But *I* do not want to. This dinner is just you and me, Adeline." She softened. "Come on. It'll be like old times."

"Fine," I said. "We'll stop by Organics and get a couple of steaks and a nice bottle of wine. You can afford it."

She laughed. "I can afford more than that. Splurge out for the Kobe beef and Maine lobsters."

"Deal."

I got up and dressed in a cropped top and distressed pair of jeans. Both cost more than my weekly salary at Salvatore's.

Gianna upgraded my room, my wardrobe, accessories, and even my restaurant. The strange thing was I knew this wasn't an attempt to buy me. She was simply setting out to do what we planned from the beginning.

Except now all I can think about is a run-down loft, threadbare mattress, and the smell of bulgogi.

I wound Sinjin's belt through the loops. It was the belt I hid his gift. The garrote. I wore it every day, taking pleasure from thoughts of him and of wiping that smile personally off Leah Tyler's face. I owed her a strangling.

Gianna's guards were watching television, playing cards, and messing around in the kitchen when we came out.

The fifteen of them didn't all live here, of course. Seven bedrooms and two were claimed by me and Gianna. The other five went to Leah, Caleb, Payton, Khalil, and Brooke. They were live-ins watching her twenty-four seven. The others were always on standby during the day to carry out her bidding, handle Kieran-related duties, and protect her the next time someone attempted an ambush.

They worked from nine in the morning to nine at night. The rest of the time, I dealt with Leah's smirking. Between them, I always felt watched.

"We're going out," Gianna announced. "You have the night off," she said as Leah rose from her seat.

"But, boss—"

"It's just me and Adeline on this one."

"How long will you be gone?"

"Till late." She hooked an arm through mine. "Don't wait up."

Downstairs, Gianna's new sports car shone in its designated spot. I slid onto leather seats, massive cupholders, a touchscreen display, and speakers to blow the windows out.

We blasted the music all through the streets, singing along at the top of our lungs.

Did I forgive her for Kaylee, Bellona, or forcing me to walk away from the boys? Not for a freaking second.

However, riding in that car singing with her, it was like old times. I was right. There was a friendship here to save. Eventually, sooner the better, my friend would see the Merchants were more than a fling. They were all the love I was going to get in this world. You don't toss that away lightly.

I will come back to you. When me in your life is a gift and not a death sentence. I'll come back.

I turned down the music. "Where are we going?" I asked. "There was an Organics on State Street."

"We're going to one closer to the restaurant."

"Tell me more about the place."

"There's original crown molding."

"Oooh, naughty."

"Big windows meant for your name in bold letters."

I moaned. "Tell me more about the windows."

"Think you're getting hot and bothered now? Just wait until you see the kitchen. I got you the centerfold stove with eleven burners."

"Oh no." I gripped the handle, shaking. "I think I just orgasmed— Yeah, I did."

Gianna howled. "You're so easy to please, Addy. A little cooking here, some city domination there, and you're good."

"I'm a simple girl, G. Always have been. Some people want the world, but I'll take Cinco." I squinted through the window. "Wait. You missed the exit for Leighbridge."

"I have to make a stop first. Won't take long."

I narrowed on her. "What stop?"

"You have trouble with surprises, don't you?"

"You know I do. Where are we going?"

"And you know I'm going to surprise you anyway. You can't get it out of me, Redgrave. I'm a fortress." Her tone was light and playful.

I eased up. I'd find out soon enough anyway.

Twenty minutes in, the landscape changed. We were skirting the edge of Harlow until Gianna turned on Dixie Avenue, leading into the warehouse district.

"Why are we going this way?" I asked. "Are we picking up those Maine lobsters?"

"Sure."

"Gianna," I hissed. "What's going on? The tournament is canceled, isn't it? Bellona took off to Thailand."

"Not quite." We drove past a growing clog of cars. "Our deal was that she brings the first match to a draw to get you free of the Merchants. The second match frees her from the ledger. Bellona Alexander has no intention of leaving Cinco. Leah got the impression her new life goal is tracking down and killing Kieran. Funny how that happens, isn't it?"

"You promised—!"

Gianna moved fast. She clamped the cuff on my wrist and quickly secured me to her, letting the car drift in the wrong lane. She jerked it back over a blaring passing car.

"Just in case," she said. "Can't have you running off with your boy toys."

I gaped at her. "What the fuck is wrong with you?! Why are you doing this?"

"I accept that you love them, Addy. Pulling the trigger yourself is impossible," she said. "So, I made it simple for you."

Gianna rolled to a stop before the warehouse, and the line of people queued to go in.

"The choice is out of your hands. Brutal is not going to kill his sister. He'll die tonight and this great love that's made you a pathetic mess will be one step closer to ending, and you returning to who you used to be."

She raised our cuffed hands to stroke my cheek. "This is for the best. Even so, you're my best friend. You had a right to know and to see him one last time. All without enduring Leah's smirking."

"You can't do this," I whispered. "Bellona won't do it. He's her brother."

Gianna shook her head, looking truly sorry for me. "You don't know that woman or the things she's done. Let's just say, she did not take her father's rejection well. She may love her brother, but not as much as she does her freedom. Half a mill and a new identity goes a long way to escaping her past.

"Leah said she agreed without a fight. Didn't even make a counteroffer."

BRUTAL

I stood in the entrance of the back room alone. Or alone as I could be with five silent sentinels riding their holsters in case I twitch.

Bellona was moved to the other room hours ago. The guys that helped imprison her were back to warm her up.

Sinjin and Cash were there too. Glaring at the gun pointed at them, I recalled Lane bursting in an hour before, crowing about the round-the-clock guard that caught each guy that came scoping out the defenses.

"They just gave up," he said. "None of them willing to risk their lives to break you out. This is how far the Merchant brotherhood goes."

No. It was more likely Cash thought up another plan with a higher survival rate. Forget brotherhood. They did me no good getting mowed down before they reached my door. They were my partners because they weren't fools.

I'd have liked to have told him that. But I couldn't speak in the place I was in.

Telling Bellona the truth made a gaping hole in my not-so-quiet place. It sucked me back in.

My mother's screams. The lash of Father's belt. Ringing gunshots. Repeated vows. The speeches I'd give to the right people when my tongue determined the time to say them.

Over and over again. Every day in a world so loud, I couldn't be heard within it. So why speak?

A flash of auburn bobbed in the crowd.

Adeline?

I came to life, following the bobbing head across the warehouse. They turned for the back-row floor seats and she broke through. It was her.

Adeline and Cross. Adeline cuffed to Cross.

My lips peeled back. Adeline hadn't left me. She was taken.

What will you do about it? A voice rose from that damnable, deafening place. *Kill your own sister to free her? You're not getting near her unless you get in and out of that cage unscathed.*

And maybe not even then. What does Lane and the guards that won't let us out of their sight have planned?

Sinjin and Cash brought the Merchants out in full force. Our numbers took up four rows.

Theirs took up the rest.

I kill Bellona and they kill me. Lane gets exactly what he wants? Isn't it better to die on my terms at Bellona's hands? Going to my grave with the death of one family member in my ledger? Not two.

I gazed at Adeline, beautiful and sad from across the room.

None of those were the question. The question is *was I done?* Did I do what I vowed to do?

Was today the day to die?

"We promised you they'd be back." Lane cut off the answers. I hadn't noticed him climb on his stage. "Brutal and Mayhem step into this cage and no one comes out until one of them is dead."

"Kill!" they roared.

"Who will it be? Mayhem's new on the scene, but scrappy. She kept Brutal on the ropes all four rounds. Let's hear it for her."

The audience stomped, clapped, and carried on.

"Brutal quickly became a favorite, mowing down our best warriors one after the other. What do you have for him?"

The cheers for me edged slightly higher.

I went rigid. Why the hell was I asking myself what the Kings would do to me if I won? It was so simple, it literally stared me in the face.

I wasn't leaving that cage.

I'd become the Kings' warrior—trotted out every year to entice the swelling crowd.

That may be their plan. I locked on Bellona as she came out. *But I would rather die than live in another cage.*

"Brutal versus Mayhem! Warriors, take your place."

Bellona and I faced each other on opposite ends of the bars. It was impossible to tell what she was thinking. She hadn't said a word to me since my confession.

We padded across the canvas, meeting in the middle.

Ding! Ding!

Bellona struck me across the face, snapping my head around.

"Murdering, psychotic, son of a bitch!"

"Nice shoes indeed. The best thing about leather is it laughs in the face of a little mud. Just washes right off."

"That's true," I said, perking up.

"Come on. I'll hose you down afterward and no one will know."

"Okay, thanks."

I went to step inside, and a foot hooked me around the ankle.

I fell face-first in the mud, coating my jacket, shirt, and pants.

Bellona howled.

"Ah! Ahhhh!"

I gazed at my mud-caked hands, screams climbing higher as Bellona laughed herself sick.

"You killed my father!"

She tackled me around the middle and lifted me off my feet. Bellona slammed me on the mat. Punches rained down.

"I knew from the start you were a worthless brat who'd ruin us!" My nose broke under her fist, spurting blood. "Father gave you everything and you never deserved it!"

"He's near enough to worthless! Your damaging influence will not be allowed to pervert my son!"

My nails pierced my forehead, hands covering my eyes. I tried to push it down. The pressure built—choking the air from me. I couldn't speak, but he had to stop. Stop or Mom would go away again.

A giggle drew my attention.

Bellona peeked around the wall, covering a laugh at Mother's beating. She told Father Mom was teaching me Hawaiian.

She told on us again.

Grabbing my neck, Bellona bashed my skull on the surface, jarring me out of the memory.

"He kept you and threw me away! Why?! He didn't love you. He didn't need you." She bounced my head again. "I made a better son than you ever could."

"Baris!" Adeline's sweet, smoky voice rose above the rest. "I love you!"

"You're going to die as he did." Bellona's bulging eyes were wild. Insane. Hatred etched in the hard lines of her twisted face. "Begging and gurgling on the floor."

She punched me. Pain resounded through my chest—stunning the air from my lungs.

"Then I'll undo the damage you've done. Alexander will be a name feared and respected once again." She tightened on my throat. "Die!"

"I will destroy the businesses, ruin our reputation, and end our line.

"In twenty years, no one will know the name Alexander, neither will they carry it on. A hundred-year legacy ends with me."

"N-no, Bellona," I rasped. I pried her grip off my neck. "Everything he touched must be destroyed. Including the monster he created."

Surprise flickered in her eyes.

"Thank you for coming to me. You saved me a trip."

Releasing her, I clapped my hands on her head, and wrenched.

Her neck snapped—the quick, painless death granted.

A hush overcame the audience.

Bellona fell on top of me.

Gently, I lifted my sister, cradling her. She looked almost peaceful as I placed her on the canvas—smoothing her hair down. Folding her arms.

I had hoped this wouldn't have to be done. That years away and removed from my father's influence, Bellona had become a better person. One look in those black eyes—barely concealing glee at another chance to hurt me—killed that hope.

She was a violent, sadistic sociopath and that she found another way to wind up in the ledger didn't surprise me in the least.

Lifting my gaze, I looked Gianna Cross right in those wide eyes. If she took Adeline from me with the promise I wouldn't be scarred for life killing my sister, I'd be taking her back now.

"W-winner," Lane said into the mic. Chains rattled, then he was in here with me. "Let's hear it for the newest winner of the tournament, Bru—"

I snatched the microphone and shoved him away.

"I have something to say." My voice rang louder than it had in decades. "I better do this while I still can." I pointed over the sea of heads. "See that woman? The woman sitting next to the most beautiful woman you've ever seen. Copper hair, pouty lips, and eyes like quicksand? The curly-haired one next to her... she has the ledger. Her name is Gianna Cross."

A deep, profound silence spread through the room.

"The ledger," I repeated. "Kieran's ledger."

The first guy moved, leaping over his chair and crashing on the people behind him.

The spell broke.

The crowd jumped, rushed, ran, and trampled each other converging on Gianna.

She and Adeline tipped their chairs racing for the door.

"Stop! Wait!" Sinjin and Cash's guards broke form under the pushing and shoving.

Lane jumped to his feet. "Stop them! Do something!" he shouted. "Get to her first!"

Who the fuck he was shouting at, I had no clue. I couldn't tell King from Outlaw from a mass of waving limbs.

Crossing the cage, my right arm banded across his chest, pinning his arms down.

"Noooooo—!"

I broke his spine over my knee, letting the dead man flop on the canvas. I picked up Bellona as the Merchants rushed in the cage, escaping the chaos.

"Now I see why we don't fucking let you talk!" Saint snapped.

"But it worked," said Cash. "I assume you started a stampede so we can get out of here?"

I nodded.

"Unfortunately, Adeline is at the front of it."

We needed to go. Now.

I pointed out the back door. "Let's get our girl."

ADELINE

"Faster!"

Gianna and I bolted to the car.

"Get them!"

"Stop!"

"Shoot her!"

My heart jumped in my throat.

Skidding around the corner, Gianna's car loomed at the end of the street. We held hands sprinting to escape as thunderous footfalls closed in.

We jumped in—bodies tangling with our linked hands.

"Close the door!" she screamed.

I got my foot in, shut the door, and smashed my hand on the lock in time for a man to fall against it, pounding the glass.

Gianna jerked my arm half out of my socket jamming the key in the ignition. Bodies leaped on the hood.

"Go!"

She stomped the gas.

We peeled from the curb, throwing our tailgaters off. The car jerked running over a human speed bump.

"What the fuck did he do?!" Gianna screamed. "They all know! I can't believe this!"

I let her have her meltdown in silence. Brutal had to snap his sister's neck because Gianna must have everything her own way. I tried that with them too and it didn't work out so well.

"They're following us!"

Our rearview window was blinded by headlights. I couldn't tell how many were after us. Five cars. Fifteen. Everyone.

"Calm down," I said. "You know how to lose a tail. They're about to set off a police car chase. Don't get caught in the middle."

A yellow convertible wasn't the most inconspicuous of getaway cars. After getting off the highway, she was forced to abandon it in an alley.

We ducked behind a club, breathing hard.

"Uncuff me."

She tossed me the key, peering around the corner.

"How far are we from the Fairfield?"

"Not far. Ten-minute walk that way. Once we get there, we're safe."

I threw the cuffs away. "Main streets. Lots of people. Lots of witnesses."

"Okay."

Together, we set out, joining the bustling flow of foot traffic. My heart pounded with every blaring horn and speeding car that went past.

It wasn't for us.

We stumbled into the lobby, still holding hands.

Stewart rose from his desk. "Is everything alright, Miss Cross?"

"No visitors," she said. "Ever. If anyone comes here asking for me, you say no one by that name lives here."

"Yes, ma'am," he replied, looking startled.

I took my first real breath in the elevator.

"This is a disaster." Gianna dropped her head on the metal. "He told half of Cinco my name. I'm guessing you approve."

"Don't snap at me," I said mildly. "I didn't do it. Look, what matters is we got away and no one knows you live here but the Merchants. We'll be safe here. In a few days, we'll know what to do."

"We?" Her lips twisted. "This mean you're sticking around?"

"I'm not going to abandon you in the middle of this, Gianna. Do I seriously have to remind you who's been racking up points in the 'bad friend' column? Hint: It's not me! You took me there to watch my boyfriend die!"

"He should've fucking died. Then we wouldn't be in this mess!"

The elevator spat us out.

"We're in this mess because of you," I hissed. "And because of me. Only children. We never learned how to share."

"Seems like you could've shared less with your boy toys."

"My goodness, you are incapable of taking responsibility."

"I'm incapable?!" A more outraged person than Gianna did not exist. "You're the one incapable of using your head now that your pussy is finally getting some dick."

She fumbled for the keys.

"Finally? What's with the finally?"

"You know what's with the finally? You couldn't find your way around an orgasm with a mega vibrator. Now that you're getting some, all you care about—"

Gianna threw open the door.

Leah and Thiago Pais froze in the middle of a heated kiss.

Everything stopped.

Sluggishly, my mind struggled to put the scene together.

The bodies of Caleb, Payton, Khalil, and Brooke bled on the couch, table, floor, and carpet—the surprise on their face immortalized in death. Leah and Thiago locked in an embrace, and hanging from Thiago's fingertips, a journal the size of a legal pad.

"Baby, that's her," Leah cried. "Get her!"

She whipped out her gun.

I threw Gianna down as the shot pierced the penthouse. It ricocheted off the metal door.

Thiago chased us into the hall. He jumped on Gianna steps from the elevator, tackling her to the carpet.

"Get off!" Fisting his hair, I socked him in the face.

"Argh!"

Movement out of the corner of my eye, then another bullet struck above my head.

Click. Click, click.

Leah shrieked and charged me. We ran into the elevator doors struggling.

Thiago hooked Gianna in a choke hold. "Tell me how to read the ledger!" He dragged her toward the penthouse.

"Gianna!"

Leah clamped my arms, forcing them down. She head-butted my nose.

Pain blew apart my senses. Head lolling, my blurred vision captured something on the wall.

Security button.

I brought my knees to my chest and kicked her off. Leah flew away from me.

I staggered to the button, pressing—

Agony erupted in my skull. My finger jabbed short of its destination as I tipped over.

Leah towered over me. "This has been a long time coming, bitch."

The gun hurtled at my face.

Darkness swallowed me.

"... THE CODE... NOW..."

"... baby... that will loosen... tongue..."

Voices dragged me from the dark.

Peeling my eyes open, blurred shapes illuminated in the moonlight.

What's going on?

"Fuck you!"

The jolt pulled me back. My vision cleared on the unseeing eyes of Brooke. Past her, claiming the raised platform that was her stage, Leah and Thiago held Gianna down.

"Tell me the code!"

Gianna spat in his face. The slap he gave her made me cringe.

"Do it, baby." Leah was practically humping his leg, getting off on Gianna's pain.

"Is that what it'll take?" Thiago drew his knife. It hovered dangerously close to Gianna's eye. "Should I carve up that pretty face?"

Leah laughed and my stomach heaved. The guy mutilated her. Left her for dead, and she'd been working for him the whole time. Thiago was here long before Brutal made his announcement.

"You think a few cuts on my face will make me give up the ledger?" Gianna laughed louder. "Please. Use your head for more than porking holes."

Screeching, Leah slapped her again.

I moved slow—inching toward my belt.

"If you wanted something more creative, all you had to do was ask," Pais said. "I'm in this business to please." He hauled her up. "Open it," he barked at Leah.

Tyler rushed to peel back the sliding glass door.

"Stop," Gianna screamed. "Get off."

They struggled. Gianna landed kicks, punches, and gave Leah as good a slap as she gave her. Two against one, they forced her closer to the rail.

"No," I croaked.

Grabbing her legs, Leah tossed them over the balcony. Gianna's scream echoed through the night, resounding to the thirty-story drop below. She clung to the metal. Pais's grip on her forearms anchored her.

"What's the code? You have three tries, then I let go."

"That's not the ledger, fool. It's a book of scribbles! Go ahead and kill me. You'll never find the real one."

"You're lying," Pais snarled. "Two! Tell me how to decipher the code."

"You're amazing, baby," Tyler said. "Kill her. You and I will rule Cinco together."

Gianna laughed. She wasn't the strongest woman I knew for nothing. "Rule together? He used you, Leah. You're next off this balcony after me."

Leah snatched a fistful of her hair. "Tell us the code, you—"

I jumped on her back. Dropping the garrote over her head, I pulled tight.

She choked. Hands flying to her throat, we fell back into the penthouse, Leah landing on top of me.

"Let her go, Adeline, or I do."

I yanked tighter still. "You drop her and the ledger goes with her! Who did you come here for, Pais? The book or your girlfriend?"

Leah desperately slapped my face and hands.

Thiago flicked between us. Snarling, he turned his back on Leah. "Tell me the code!"

Leah's hits grew weak. Her thrashing limbs slowed.

She went limp in my arms.

I tossed the dead body off me and crawled to the book resting innocently on the table.

"If you take that, I drop her and come after you." Thiago punched Gianna's fingers. "Leah said you're best friends. I bet you know—"

I ran at him, raised my hand, and threw. The ledger curved an arch over his head. Instinctively, he tried to catch it, releasing Gianna. The distraction was all I needed to crack him over the head with Leah's gun. He dropped, groaning.

"Adeline!"

I stepped on him, grabbing her as one hand slipped off the rail.

"Addy, help, please," she cried.

"I've got you. Don't let go."

I fastened her wrist in a death grip, heaving her up and over the side.

We collapsed on a heap on the tile, ragged breaths banging our chests together.

"Pais," she gasped. "He's gone."

"Course he is. He'll be running after the ledger."

"Oh, Addy." She buried her face in my neck. I hugged her as tight as she hugged me. "I can't believe you threw it off the balcony."

"I can't believe you burned the original. Tell me you didn't."

"I didn't. It was a decoy to flush out a traitor while also giving them incentive to keep me alive."

"Genius," I croaked. "But it worked too well."

Pain and the absurdity of our situation pulled laughs out of us.

"I'm sorry," she said. "You were right. I screwed everything up."

"Why, G?" We pushed ourselves up. "You know I wouldn't cut you out."

Tears glistened in her eyes. "You already were. You brought down the Castian with the Merchants. Killed Corbin. Conned La Roche. Got rid of Angelo. You were doing it all without me and I was relegated to the get-out-of-trouble card. For an angry, insane moment, I thought if you didn't need me, then I didn't need you. You refusing to kill the Merchants didn't help."

"I'm sorry, Gianna. I truly am. I never meant to cut you out. None of this makes sense if we're not doing it together." I held her hand. "It'll be the six of us. Equal partners. I swear."

Her smile grew uncomfortable. "Addy, no. I am sorry for stealing the ledger, letting Leah do what she did, and forcing you to watch your boyfriend die was a step too far. But Brutal just brought the whole of Cinco on my head. Sinjin's made it clear I'm on his hit list. And Cash imagines three hundred ways to kill me whenever he looks in my direction.

"They don't want anything to do with me. Or me with them. They're my enemies now, Addy. If we're partners, they're your enemies too. You can't play both sides."

"You have a point," I said, though it hurt me. My gaze dropped between us.

"What's it going to be?"

I shook my head. "I haven't given up on peace. I'll talk to the guys and work it out. In the meantime, you'll be safe with us. You can't stay here with Thiago Pais on the loose. He's proven this place isn't impenetrable."

"I'm not bunking in with you and the Merchants."

"Yes, you are."

"No—"

I hit her over the head with the pistol.

"Wow, this is coming in handy tonight."

I gathered my bestie in my arms and carried her downstairs where the guys were yelling at an increasingly terrified Stewart.

They rushed me. "Adeline."

Brutal reached me first. He kissed the crap out of me—broken nose and all.

"Are you okay?" Cash asked.

"I'm fine." I passed Gianna to Sinjin, who looked tempted to drop her. "Let's go home."

GIANNA WALKED THE ROOM, testing the limits of her chains.

"Nice place." A rosy bump decorated her forehead. Otherwise, she was her beautiful self.

I sensed the guys outside the door, listening for a whisper of trouble.

"We'll upgrade our digs once we get our hands on your stash," I said. "Six bedrooms and a new weapons dungeon. I'll load it up with sniper rifles."

She cocked a brow. "Bribing me?"

"Little bit. How's it going?"

"Not bad." Gianna got as far as the television. Her hand didn't reach the buttons. "How long do you plan to keep me here?"

"Until the five of you get along. The problem is you don't know each other. Along with interactions that have been... negative... you're racking up terrible first, second, and third impressions."

"Right," she replied. "Will you be satisfied we know each other by tonight?"

I smiled. "Unlikely."

Gianna whistled. "Might want to rethink that. If I'm not let out of here by seven o'clock, my failsafe goes into effect."

"Failsafe?"

"I told you the decoy flushed out traitors and encouraged them to keep me alive. I also needed incentive to get them to let me go. So, I have a program queued to send the secrets of everyone I've blackmailed so far to Channel Eight News. I've been a busy girl, so it's about twenty-eight people.

"If I don't log in and input the password in time, it goes out and there's nothing I can do to stop it."

"What's the password?" I asked. "I'll go to your place and do it for you."

She smiled. "I have to do it myself."

"Of course you do."

"Fine," she lofted. "Don't believe me."

"I'm not letting you out, Gianna, until everyone loves each other."

She laughed. "If I can't make you fall out of love, what makes you think you can do the opposite?"

"Because no one who knows them can help but love them."

She gagged. "Ugh. Never repeat that." Gianna tossed herself on the bed. "If I'm to be a captive, I expect the royal treatment I gave you. Movies and caramel popcorn, please. Now would be good."

I rolled my eyes—though it didn't hide how secretly pleased I was.

"Coming right up."

BRUTAL

"If I'm to be a captive, I expect the royal treatment I gave you. Movies and caramel popcorn, please. Now would be good."

I backed away from the door, satisfied. Adeline would be okay. She had her friend back, despite it being a rocky start to reconciliation. Cash, Sinjin, and Mercer were alive. The Merchants made it out of the warehouse unscathed. The night before, I made love to her till she fell asleep on my chest. She had everything she needed.

Time to go.

Picking up my coat and backpack, I left out the door, Sinjin and Cash none the wiser.

Anywhere in the city I was, I knew the direction to Global Consolidated—once Alexander Enterprises.

I knew the back door with the lock that gave way when you jiggled it. I knew there wasn't a code or guard blocking access to the roof.

Wind whipped and tugged at me as I stepped out on top of the building, bracing in the cool air. Finding a spot out of the gust, I laid out a sheet of plastic. I placed my bag on one corner. My gloves on the other, and a photograph of my mother facing me.

I took my seat in the last corner, holding my father's gun.

I traced a finger down the barrel. The night I killed him played in sharp clarity. It could've been yesterday.

It was right that I do it here atop the symbol of my vow.

I swore to erase everything Alexander in this world. All that my father touched taken apart. The monsters he created put down, including the worst of them.

Me.

I pressed the barrel to my temple.

Shutting my eyes, I pulled.

ADELINE

"Where's Brutal?"

I scooped broccoli pesto pasta in a bowl and handed it to Mercer.

"He went out," Cash replied.

"Do you know where? I've called a few times."

"Nope," Sinjin said. "The talking thing is a fluke so far."

Mercer set his bowl down. "No one's heard from him?"

"No," I said. "I'll try calling him again."

Mercer jogged upstairs to Brutal's room. "His pack isn't here."

I held the phone to my ear. It rang endlessly and didn't pick up.

"Anything?"

"No."

"Shit!"

"Is everything okay?"

"No, I— We need to find him now."

Cash and Sinjin rose from the table. "Why?" Cash asked. "What's going on?"

"Baris… I think he's going to kill himself."

The statement hung in the air.

What did he just say?

"Excuse me? Why would you say that?"

"It's just— just a feeling I've had for a while that something wasn't right with him." Thundering down the stairs, he brushed past me. "With his sister dead, there's nothing stopping him."

"Whoa, back up," Killian said. "It's terrible what he had to do, but he wasn't broken up about it."

"I've known he wasn't just any Alexander since the beginning," Mercer said. "I've also known he imploded his inheritance. Ran the business into the ground. Sold their properties for dollars. Practically tossed their possessions on the front lawn and set fire to them. You don't do stuff like that unless you're trying to punish someone."

Mercer was talking fast—half the reason I couldn't keep up. *Inheritance? Punish?*

"I assumed that someone was his father. Baris told us Marshall Alexander hired Kieran to get rid of his sister, and this search to bring her home was one last 'screw you' to him. But if he really killed her and didn't bat an eye over it, then it's not about living on in spite of his father. It's killing everything Alexander. And there's only one left."

"Hold on, I—" I grabbed my head. "Are you saying you knew all this and kept it to yourself?!"

"No, Adeline. I spoke to Brutal, asked him if there was something I could do, and told him I'd help him if he wanted it. He said nothing and walked off each time. It was just a feeling," he told me. "When he met you and started laughing and talking again, I decided I was paranoid, but now—"

"We need to find him right now." I snatched up my bag, racing to the door a step behind Cash and Sinjin.

"Wait," Mercer called. "I can tell you where he is."

That pulled the three of us up short. Mercer pushed through us, leading the way. "I put a tracker in his phone at the start of this tournament shit. In case the Kings decided he was too good to give up."

I loved him so much right then, I could cry.

I did cry. Hot, gushing tears as we piled in his car and sped to Global Consolidated.

Mercer screeched around the final corner, and the skyscraper loomed ahead.

"How are we supposed to find him in that?" I cried.

"Start with the roof," Cash said. "I'll check the basement."

I groaned, stomach heaving. I couldn't believe this was happening. Baris would never hurt himself. Mercer couldn't be right about this. I knew him. His heart was connected to mine. I'd have known if he was in such a dark place.

I will find him in that building whole and well. He'd chuckle at my fussing, smack my butt, and then carry me home.

Mercer slammed to a stop in front of the building. I was out before he shut off the car, racing inside.

"Ma'am. Ma'am, stop— Hey!"

I jumped the turnstile, not slowing down for the shouts and pounding footfalls behind me.

"This is a matter of life and death!" I threw at him. "Have an ambulance on standby."

The guard skidded to a halt. "Wha— Life and death?"

"Do it now!"

I hit the stairs, and he spun around, hoofing it toward reception. Job duties aside, announcing something like that got people's priorities in order.

At the end of the hallway, a smartly dressed couple stepped out of the elevator.

"Adeline!"

Saint's call didn't slow me. I plowed through the couple, knocking them aside like bowling pins.

The doors closed shut on me—too slow for my desperate finger jabbing the top floor.

He's okay. He's okay. He's okay. He wouldn't go without a goodbye.

I repeated it to myself the entire way up.

The elevator finally dinged on the top floor, opening up to a silent hall.

A row of empty offices greeted me as I sought out stairs to take me the rest of the way.

Baris is okay. He wouldn't do this. He wouldn't rob us of our future.

I burst onto the roof. "Baris? Baris! Are you up here?"

Cinco spread out in all directions, molding into the trees of Elmshire Woods. We were almost as high as you could get in this city. Global Consolidated was the third-largest building. There was a lot of ground to cover up here, but it didn't compare to the long way down.

"Baris!"

A crinkling sound pricked my ear.

I moved closer to the edge, scanning up and down for—

"Baris!"

There he was as if it was the place he was meant to be. Standing on a sheet of plastic, Baris gazed at the gun in his hand.

"Baris, no," I cried. I ran to him, snatched the weapon, and flung it as far as humanly possible.

"That's dangerous," he said mildly.

"Get away from the edge!"

I seized his collar and dragged him over the plastic. I slammed him against the wall, pinning him to the stucco.

"Don't you dare, Baris. Don't you even think about it."

Brutal smoothed my hair down. "Okay."

My heart raced a mile a minute. Panic laced my voice and made my fingertips tingle. "What are you doing up here? Why would you come up here without talking to me?" I shook him. "Was this what you meant when you said we had no future?"

He smiled under my manhandling. "Did I say that? For a guy who didn't speak, I still managed to spout bullshit."

I stared at him, breathing hard. *What did he say?*

"I'm sorry, Adeline." He brushed a tender kiss on my forehead.

"What are you doing up here?" I whispered.

"This is where I'm supposed to be today."

His words flowed freely. Jaw relaxed. Muscles unclenched.

"What does that mean?"

"It means twelve years ago, my father shot my mother in the back, and I couldn't speak to warn her. I killed him, and vowed as he was dying to lay waste to everything he cared about."

My mouth opened but nothing came out.

"My father was always a hard, cruel man," Baris said, "but what he wanted more than anything was a son. Those early years when I was a child who could do no wrong, he favored me. Took me to work with him and showed me this view—promising one day it'd all be mine.

"Bellona couldn't stand it. Passed over and ignored, she grew to hate me for Father's favor and my relationship with my mother. It started small at first. When the four of us took pictures, she'd pinch me behind their backs, making me cry or grimace until Father got fed up and sent me to Nanny.

"As I got older, she grew worse. She'd spill food on my clothes at events. Trip me in the mud or dirt. Destroy my homework. Make a mess in my room before Father did his inspections. Suddenly, I was a clumsy, messy slacker. I tried telling him Bellona was responsible. He refused to believe his sweet, well-behaved little girl would do such things. He'd say I was lying, and I'd argue back. Something people did not do with Marshall Alexander."

"Oh, Baris." I stroked his cheek, sending him waves of support.

"I wish he'd beaten me." The hoarse, ragged confession tore me to shreds. "Anything was better than what he did, Adeline. All his rage at his disrespectful, whiny embarrassment of a son, he directed at my mother. He hit her before, but I became the excuse he wanted to stop holding back. Smacking her, knocking her around, belting her. I was forced to watch."

I clapped my hand over my mouth.

"He said I had to see how my lies and disobedience hurt others. I'd scream for him to stop, and he'd extend the punishment. On and on it went until the lesson sunk in."

Be silent.

"But it was Bellona who refused to stop. Why should she when my father's blindness gave her license to kill his favoritism without consequences?"

"But your mother," I said. "Bellona was hurting both of you."

"She felt no attachment to my mother, and truthfully, I don't think Mom felt much toward her. Bellona was always too much like my father. It wasn't like that with us. I'd fall asleep in her bed, listening to stories of Hawaii and reciting the words she taught me. One day, Father decided the troubles I was beginning to have speaking was from bilingualism. He took that away too.

"It got so bad, my mother shut herself in her room for weeks at a time. For both our sake, she avoided me. And I did everything I could think of to bring her out again. I wouldn't utter a damn word for days at a time. No backtalk. No talking at all.

"I'd clean my room religiously—checking constantly to make sure Bellona hadn't struck and there was nothing out of place. Checking my clothes for stains. Hair neat. Snapping to attention when he called. I had to be perfect."

"You were perfect. You *are* perfect." I kissed just above his collarbone. "I'm sorry your father couldn't see that."

"He couldn't see past anything but the reflection of the Alexander legacy. I can't say when unwilling to talk became unable," he said, voice soft. "Eventually, I couldn't. Trying to speak would bring on attacks. It became a new reason to beat my mother. I was an idiot. Defective."

I squeezed my eyes shut. What I wouldn't give to go back in time and rescue my love from that man.

"After Bellona was taken, I shut myself away from my father too. Without her inciting trouble and me self-isolating, Mom was given some peace. She used it to venture into the garden to sit, read, water the plants. I'd see her out there through my window. We started miming messages to each other. Simple things since we couldn't sign."

He pointed to me and himself. "You and me."

Baris closed a fist. "Want."

He lifted his hand, spreading it out. "Freedom."

I sobbed—hot, flowing tears.

"The night my mother died, she took it, Adeline. She stood up to my father, said she was leaving him and taking me with her. We would finally be free."

Baris's gaze fixed unseeingly over my head. "My father killed her while I stood there struggling to say one word. One syllable. Gun."

Through my tears, a flicker of movement drew my attention. Saint peered around the corner, observed us, and stepped out of view.

"It was wrong to speak after that day. Wrong to even try. What right did I have to use my words for mundane, everyday conversations when I didn't have them to save my mother's life?"

"You can't put that weight on your shoulders, baby." I rested my palm on his thumping chest. "You weren't responsible for his cruelty or the final act committed by a monster."

"I-I am responsible." His chest shook. "Bernice Kalama was good and kind. The most beautiful person inside and out, and Alexanders destroyed her. Crushed her with their hundred-year legacy till the woman laughing on the beach with flowers in her hair became the stiff-lipped wife standing on my father's right. Bellona, my father, and me," he rasped. "We made her life hell."

"Baris." I reached for him and he stopped me short, grasping my wrists.

"She deserved better than us, and I couldn't be that even after she died." He tossed his head. "All those mornings in the garden with Joshua, they couldn't help themselves. They fell for each other. The two would spin dreams of setting off with me in the back seat, catching that plane to Hawaii."

Joshua Hudson. The man convicted of killing his parents.

"Joshua's wife was ill, and he couldn't take off and abandon her. After she passed, they made their plans to leave. Joshua said they should tell my father together, but Mom needed to do this on her own. The gunshots brought him running."

"How... did he end up in jail?"

Baris's hold on me tightened. "He told me to run. He would take care of everything—just get out and don't come back. A few days later, his arrest hit every station. Joshua confessed to the murders with the story of avenging his wife's death. I couldn't do anything, Adeline. I sat in that gym for days in a blank.

"Finally, I got in to see him and he told me to let him do this. He made my mother wait, enduring hell, and then, when she needed him, he wasn't there. To see her son locked away because I'd done what he should have, would've been the final betrayal. Joshua begged me to let him make this sacrifice, Adeline, and I d-did." His voice cracked, pain bleeding through. "I didn't speak up for her, and I didn't speak up for him. The man my mother loved. The only one in that house who gave her a shred of hope or happiness.

"He died in prison five years later."

"Baris..." I whispered. So much pain and loss he held on to for these years. In silence. "You've been punishing yourself all this time."

"Everything my father loved. Everything he created. It couldn't live on while she did not."

I brought his face down to me, kissing him fiercely. "You were not included in that! She loved you. She wanted you to be free. Bernice cut herself off from her child, suffering that untold pain so you wouldn't. That is not a woman who would want a sacrifice like this."

His thumb stroked the back of my hand—soft as his smile. "Now I have you to tell me that."

I hesitated. *What's he saying?*

"Whatever vow you made to a dying man, it doesn't come before the promises you made to your mother those days at the window—swearing you'd one day be happy."

"I believe I know that now."

"Then why did you come up here?" My tears began anew. "Why did I find you with a gun in your hand?"

"I— I—"

This was the first since the conversation started that he began to struggle.

"I h-had to," he forced. "I had to see it through to the end. Couldn't stop myself. The"—he crushed a fist to his chest—"was too strong."

I understood.

"I came up here to do what twelve years of planning, waiting, and self-destructing demanded I do," he said. "But..."

"But what?"

"But." He pointed at me and him. "You make me." Fist. "Want." Baris traced my lips. "To speak.

"You make me want." He put his hand on my heart. "To love."

Lips trembling, I watched him repeat the signs he made so many times before.

"You make me want."

Baris placed a fist over his chest.

"To live."

I sobbed and blubbered on his shirt—so small in the wake of his pain and love, I couldn't fathom how I turned the tide.

I saved him before I got on this roof. How had I for a second believed this love wasn't worth it?

"I stopped my finger on that trigger because I realized I wasn't up here to die. I was here to kill the man who couldn't speak or fight for you." He held our hands against his heart. "This man is yours in every way."

"This whole time you've been telling me you love me."

"No," he said. "Now I'm telling you, Adeline. I love you."

My wet, salty lips met his. Both perfect and messy. Heartbreaking and the happiest moment of my life.

"I love you too."

"There's only the future for us, ku'uipo."

BARIS AND I STAYED on the roof for a while, talking about his mother and his life after he lost her. We stayed until security's hunt for the person in danger made Cash alert us it was time to go.

I stuck to Baris like glue for the next week. He didn't seem to mind. Actually, I think he found my constant fussing and attention amusing.

A magical switch had not been flipped. Baris still felt his mother's loss and the deaths that followed keenly. There were still days it was hard to speak, but I felt the shift in him.

Our hearts were connected.

We sat around the living room, the perfect family scene.

Cash typed on his computer while watching the news, switching between screens.

Sinjin and Mercer talked new safe houses and where we'd set up our home. I curled up on Brutal's lap, content as he stroked my hair.

I hummed. "I'm thirsty but I'm loath to get up."

"Don't." Mercer got up, tickling my toes as he passed. "Tea?"

"Yes, please." I wriggled on Baris's lap, feeling his ridge thickening, and earning a smack on the backside for my trouble. I kissed him in apology. The kiss I received in return was not apologetic. I threw my arms around him, getting deep in our make-out session.

"Killian, turn that up," Sinjin said.

"What?"

"The news." Sinjin upped the volume himself.

"—today that they've confirmed the young man killed outside Opium four years ago has been identified as Mercer Santos."

I dropped my feet on the floor. *Santos?*

"Some may remember the headlines following this grisly murder. A man was stabbed and then the body disfigured to prevent identification. Since the nightclub concealed an underground casino, authorities had trouble discerning if his death was connected to the club or the illegal activities underneath. Now that Mr. Santos has been identified, we're hopeful the police can find new leads—"

Eeeeeee!

We spun around.

The teakettle screeched on the stove, trumpeting his readiness, and no one in the kitchen to respond.

The front door hung ajar—swinging as rapid footsteps faded down the hall.

Keep In Touch

Join Ruby's mailing list for news, teasers, and more: https://www.sub-scribepage.com/rubyvincentpage
Join Ruby's Facebook Reader Group:
https://bit.ly/3bNuCOq

ABOUT THE AUTHOR

Ruby Vincent is a published author with many novels under her belt, but after taking a fun foray into contemporary romance, she found her love of saucy heroines, bold alpha males, and weaving a tale where both get their happy ever after.